KU-466-341

THE
FRAUD

Barbara Ewing

Mixed Sources

FSC

Sphere
An imprint of
Little, Brown Book Group
100 Victoria Embankment
London EC4Y 0DY

An Hachette UK Company
www.hachette.co.uk

sphere

SPHERE

First published in Great Britain in 2009 by Sphere
This paperback published in 2009 by Sphere

Copyright © Barbara Ewing 2009

The moral right of the author has been asserted.

*All characters and events in this publication, other than those
clearly in the public domain, are fictitious and any resemblance
to real persons, living or dead, is purely coincidental.*

All rights reserved.
No part of this publication may be reproduced, stored in a
retrieval system, or transmitted, in any form or by any means, without
the prior permission in writing of the publisher, nor be otherwise circulated
in any form of binding or cover other than that in which it is published
and without a similar condition including this condition being
imposed on the subsequent purchaser.

A CIP catalogue record for this book
is available from the British Library.

ISBN 978-0-7515-4094-9

Typeset in Palatino by M Rules
Printed and bound in Great Britain by
Clays Ltd, St Ives plc

Papers used by Sphere are natural, renewable and
recyclable products sourced from well-managed forests and certified in
accordance with the rules of the Forest Stewardship Council.

MORAY COUNCIL LIBRARIES & INFO.SERVICES	
20 31 65 36	
Askews & Holts	
F	

For Henry and Matthew

I have perused with interest the Histories of Mr William Hogarth, Mr Thomas Gainsborough, and Sir Joshua Reynolds, those famous Portraitists of the Eighteenth Century. It is my belief that another History should be told also, and I present it here.

The Author

PART ONE

1735

ONE

Unfortunately that summer was cold in Wiltshire. There was a blizzard in June, and the Church blamed Sin.

The new bride, entering the huge old country house with her father (her groom already gone ahead of her and pouring himself a large glass of rum), was complaining in a not unquiet voice.

'Pray, Father, where are the Jewels and the fine China Plates? And why is it so dark? And look! The curtains are so faded and so old! Am I to live here now?'

'Ssshh, girl.'

'And I am so cold, and they have great slobbering dogs everywhere about the place! And his Mother looks as if she has swallowed a Pin-Cushion. Alas for me, you promised me there would be Jewels, Father, but I cannot see even one Pearl!'

'Sssh, girl.'

'You promised me, Father! I shan't stay, I swear I shall not! This is not what you promised me if I married him!'

Her father, the local Squire, carried his portly stomach before him like a pudding and shusssshed his foolish daughter. 'You are now inside a Stately Mansion as of right, Miss! You will be called "Lady Betty" by the servants and treated with all manner of civilities. It is an *Honour*. We are accepting an *Honour*.' And he and his over-ventilating wife urged the newly-conjoined bride forward. Portraits of older generations looked down in disapproval from dark walls: the disapproval had perhaps a slightly raffish air (or it may have been the peeling paint) and the big room grew colder and darker as the wedding day wore on and the bride looked in vain for jewels. A maiden aunt in a dark gown and a white cap, who was so self-effacing as to be almost invisible, finally closed the last shutters as the grey light faded. The candle-lit room was full of shadows now; the groom was greatly inebriated, as was his father, so their shadows weaved and stumbled; but the Squire beamed, infatuated by his own importance (he had managed a respectable dowry). He was *particularly* infatuated by his own importance today because of his triumph: this day his family was finally conjoined – he had hardly dared hope – with the Wiltshire Marshalls.

The Wiltshire Marshalls were an old, once slightly noble, foolish family of languishing landowners who had tried to inject new money into their ranks by being so utterly vulgar as to buy some of the first plantations in the West Indies. But there was something inherently reckless and wild about the Wiltshire Marshalls which seemed to pass down the generations: some darkness: something in their inheritance that was unable to stop the decline. Attractive, *louche*, beautiful dark eyes, irresponsible: their new money, like their old money, was frittered and gambled away.

Therefore the Wiltshire Marshalls had – reluctantly – supervised this day the marriage of their youngest, feckless, dark-eyed son Marmaduke to the local Squire's fair daughter, hoping that the young lady might at least bring new energy, new blood, to a fading family – not to mention a large purse of dowry-money to stave off immediate disaster.

The Squire's family departed – minus a daughter – still beaming.

Late in the night one of the maids finally, wearily, walking about the great, draughty house with a candle snuffer, put out the lights; her own shadow walked with her, fading as the candles were extinguished one by one. In the ancient baronial hall bones lay strewn, and dogs and humans snored. Upon one chair the maid passed the bridegroom, sprawled asleep with rum spilt upon his trousers. The groom's father had stumbled over a chamberpot so that the room stank more than usual. From the nuptial bedroom weeping emerged.

It was not an auspicious beginning to the marriage.

The Wiltshire Marshalls hoped that the pretty fair-haired bride would be economical with Marmaduke's small and fast-vanishing fortune. Unfortunately this young lady, Betty (who was to become the mother of Philip and Grace Marshall, whose history we are beginning) had only one attribute of note: she was extremely, eloquently, pretty. She was furious when she found she was not to be addressed as Lady Betty (or indeed anything regal at all: her father had been wrong) and she was not in the least interested in the domestic concerns of country life. Betty harboured Social Ambition: the innocuous old maiden aunt (who had been named so hopefully forty years ago, Joy) could supervise; Betty herself refused to dirty her hands in the household, tossed her pretty head. Betty yearned for cities and social niceties, but did not understand that Bath and its spas, not Bristol and its trading ships, was beginning to attract the gentry. Weak, good-looking, lazy Marmaduke had never thought of moving anywhere at all, he was quite happy misspending his time over gambling and imported rum. He played cards for money and the rest of the time indulged his one artistic hobby: he liked to draw or paint the high-stepping, beautiful horses that had been bred in his family's diminishing fields.

'*Painting?*' scoffed pretty, scornful Betty. 'What use is *painting* to raise us high in Society?' She kept nagging her husband that they must live in Bristol where this High Society, she was sure, reigned. Pretty and sulky and manipulative, Betty insisted on Bristol as the price for other favours.

So Marmaduke and his growing family (five pregnancies in four years, only two still-births: this was considered a good record) moved to a Bristol house in fashionable Queen's Square (unfortunately the less fashionable end). The house was ill-ventilated and narrow and high, hardly big enough for a gentleman and his children, not to mention servants and the maiden aunt and family heirlooms and the new mahogany furniture that Betty insisted upon. There was a tiny formal garden at the rear, containing one over-elaborate statue of a dubious Grecian goddess, to remind them of the nobler environment from whence the once illustrious

Wiltshire Marshalls had come. The neighbours, they soon found, were all vulgar tradesmen. Marmaduke continued his gambling. Betty, to comfort herself, acquired a white poodle and called it Beloved, and consumed much Madeira wine.

Children *would* keep being born, dead or alive: altogether five of the children lived, of whom Philip Marshall – a personage of whom we shall be hearing a great deal more – was the eldest. He was named after his paternal grandfather in the hope of largesse: alas none was forthcoming. He acquired two pretty, sulky sisters, Juno and Venus (named when Betty was briefly enamoured of Greek goddesses like the one in the garden) and later, two younger brothers, Ezekiel and Tobias (named when Betty was going through a brief religious phase).

To be the oldest of five children in a languishing family of extremely faded nobility was not an easy inheritance: always Philip Marshall had to look for the main chance. From a very early age he found that he had the kind of smile that made people look twice, notice him: *what a pretty boy* they said. He had learned to be charming before he knew the meaning of the word; by the time he was five he knew the meaning of the word and he was an expert in charm: roguish and cherubic simultaneously with dark hair and black smiling eyes: in short, Philip was delectably beautiful. He was the only child in the family to receive some sort of education: soon education was low in the priorities of this particular family.

Time passed, wealth diminished further. Over and over pleas were made to the Wiltshire Marshalls for financial assistance. In one spectacular row which used up more energy than the Wiltshire Marshalls had displayed for years, Marmaduke was cut off for ever from what remained of the family fortune and the almost invisible Aunt Joy understood she would never see the rolling Wiltshire hills again. She became a pale, grey ghost as she endeavoured to keep the Bristol household running, unnoticed by everyone unless something was needed: *Aunt Joy!* little children called imperiously then, *Aunt Joy!* Very occasionally, thwarted, the eldest child, Philip, he of the beautiful face and the dark eyes and the hint of education, erupted suddenly into terrible spectacular rages and screamed at Aunt Joy. Otherwise he continued to be immensely charming but had, as he grew older, no other obvious skills that could save the family.

Bristol was a filthy, flourishing port; trade and finance ruled everywhere: credit was easily obtained as coal and guns and cotton and nails were shipped out, sugar and silks and spices and rum were shipped in, and not too much attention paid to the other element of trade that gave the Bristolians their wealth: slaves. In the streets people hurried by: *money, money, money*: there for the making if you knew how. Stories abounded of fortunes made on foreign shores, of new continents and new wealth, of jewels and cruelty and sugar: Bristol became richer and richer as goods from across the seas poured in and occasionally black men in chains were auctioned on the docks. Naughty children were rebuked with threats of black Mohammetmen who would cut their throats and drain their blood. Occasionally a black man appeared in the town in footman's clothes and was stared at: bought at an auction on the docks, or brought back as a servant from the sugar plantations in Jamaica perhaps, or from the coast of Africa; nothing caused so much mirth and the pointing of fingers as a black man in a powdered white wig.

Betty (less pretty now) lived in Bristol almost entirely on credit and Madeira wine. But credit does not last for ever, even when you come from finer stock. Marmaduke placed larger and more dangerous bets. Betty bemoaned her fate upon the *chaise longue* with her poodle, Beloved, in her arms. She and Juno and Venus spoke more and more desperately of 'Nobility' and 'Marriage' and 'Fortune'. In the meantime the two wild, uneducated younger boys, Tobias and Ezekiel, having little else to entertain them, viciously stoned to death a piglet belonging to one of their tradesmen neighbours; they laughed and squealed (imitating the expiring small animal).

Into this household a last child, the sixth living child, had been, unexpectedly, born. Her mother called her, in her hearing, a 'trial'. (They named her Grace, as if that would help.)

Grace did not know the meaning of the word 'trial'.

'What is a Trial, that I am?' she asked her father, her three-year-old dark eyes wide with curiosity, but he hardly heard her: the smell of tobacco and rum and a half-smile from his *louche*, world-weary, alcohol-blurred eyes: that was all her answer.

Grace grew up a city girl, learning to avoid the drains and the pickpockets. Her mother half-heartedly tried to impose elegance and gloves but Grace was more likely to wave her hands about than put gloves upon them. To speak truthfully she generally ran wild about Bristol in a most unsuitable manner: as well as the Wiltshire Marshalls' dark hair and big dark eyes she had small strong chubby legs and seemingly infinite energy. Grace was tough, much nosier about matters than was acceptable, and avid for everything: as soon as she could walk she looked in cupboards, down drains, round corners, under her sisters' skirts until they slapped her.

'She waves her hands about her like a Foreigner and looks like her Father – does she imagine herself to be an *Italian*?' said her mother sourly (for she did not love Grace: Juno and Venus had inherited at least some of their mother's fair prettiness). But Grace could not help her inheritance or her enthusiasms: words and questions and observations poured from her, almost from the time she could speak.

And Grace had a kind of gladness about her: she enjoyed everything that went on around her, wide dark eyes full of laughter and questions. She had a most unacceptable habit of grabbing people by both their arms and talking loudly, to get their attention: utterly unladylike, and no one caring enough to do anything about it. If her eldest brother Philip Marshall had not been so bored, if he had been permitted by his loving, clinging mother to join His Majesty's Navy, then Grace Marshall would never ever have learned to read, would no doubt eventually have acquired the air of the un-literate Juno and Venus, her older sisters: petulance (which is what they thought of as sophistication). But because Grace was so curious and so bright, Philip, when she was only six years old, had a bet with his friends which he easily won: within six months he had taught Grace to read; within a year she stumblingly read aloud to anyone who would listen from the newspaper, the *Bristol Postboy*, including hard words like WEST INDIES and PROFIT. Philip taught her to write: the very first word she penned was GRACE, and by the time she was eight she had learned by heart a sonnet by a gentleman called Mr Shakespeare (for a few old volumes languished in dusty corners in the house in Bristol, a sign of Culture). The child had only a hazy understanding of that which she was emoting (the subject of Aging and Time not usually part of the experience of an eight-year-old), but she rattled out the words with gusto:

> *When I do count the clock that tells the Time*
> *And see the brave day sunk in hideous night;*
> *When I behold the Violet past prime,*
> *And sable curls, all silver'd o'er with white . . .*

and then she would forget a bit, look confused, and then she remembered some more words and would start again loudly with even more gusto and enthusiasm:

> *. . . Then of thy Beauty I do question make,*
> *That thou amongst the wastes of Time must go,*
> *Since sweets and beauties do themselves forsake*
> *And die as fast as they see others grow;*
> > *And nothing 'gainst Time's Scythe can make defence*
> > *Save breed, to brave him when he takes thee hence.*

'Breed!' cried Betty in outrage. '*Breed*? What rude Rubbish are you filling the Child's head with, darling boy? I shan't allow it! What does a Poet know? Let him come to Queen's Square whoever he is, and I shall educate him!' But Philip was going through a disconsolate phase and would not be criticised and Grace performed heroically if erratically when instructed, although in truth she would rather have been singing *Three Blind Mice, See how they Run*, a popular round that was all the rage; or playing in the back garden with Tobias and Ezekiel, who pinched their little sister's chubby arms for their own amusement. She squealed like the piglet as she pinched them back and yelled 'TimesScythe!' at them without any idea of its meaning, and then they all three played noisy hopscotch beside the fake Greek statue, hopping and cheating and laughing.

Betty (who may have despised painting but considered herself an expert on the Etiquettes of Society) insisted that, as with all noble families, it was absolutely imperative that they be memorialised for posterity: that is, a Family Portrait must be acquired as a record of the Wiltshire Marshalls in Bristol, which would be passed down from generation to generation, 'Until the World ends,' said Betty. 'That we shall always be remembered, and spoke of.'

What was required was a group portrait, known as a Conversation Piece, and nothing would satisfy Betty but that it was painted by a Frenchman she had heard of, 'For Foreign Painters are descended from the Old Masters themselves,' said Betty. (She had heard another lady say this, was not absolutely certain whom the Old Masters might be, but for once Marmaduke nodded sagely and co-operated.)

Somehow the Frenchman got the group of eight people posed (Aunt Joy was not included): Marmaduke and Betty were sitting upright and elegant on the remains of the Wiltshire Marshalls' old family furniture; Juno and Venus leaned languorously behind; Philip to the side, tall and handsome; and the three younger children sitting at their parents' feet in the foreground, with Beloved the poodle.

'This Painting,' said Marmaduke to his children, conscious for once of his heritage, 'will be seen by your Children, and your Children's Children, down through Time,' and Grace declared loudly: *And nothing 'gainst Time's Scythe can make defence, save breed, to brave him when he takes thee hence* and Marmaduke, smelling strongly of West Indian rum, nodded morosely. Unfortunately he then fell asleep; Beloved bit Ezekiel; Grace laughed at this (in an unladylike manner); Venus got pins and needles from leaning languorously. Only Philip remained completely still. All the Marshalls watched the Frenchman: how he looked at them and drew, looked at them and drew. Grace observed his eyes and his pencil and his portable easel that he had set up in the small drawing-room; she fidgeted with interest, wanting all the time to see what he had done.

After some hot hours had passed the Artist announced himself content with the first sitting; the Marshall family crowded the easel and then professed disappointment: who were those stick-people? Where were the colours? The Frenchman explained that this was a preliminary sketch only, and that more sittings would be required.

Painting a picture of eight members of this family would have tried the patience of a saint; the Frenchman persevered, finally delivered a rather odd and stiff assemblage of faces and bodies, and a dog: Marmaduke and Philip both immediately stated that they could have done better. This acquisition was hung upon the wall of the drawing-room above Betty's *chaise longue* and looked at with some confusion by various family members. 'Which is me?' said Ezekiel, and Venus pointed to the poodle: as she had never been known to make a joke in her life she may, indeed, have confused them. To be frank, it was a mediocre work.

It was when the fee was required (nine guineas) that difficulties began. The Artist sent several bills and then appeared in person requiring his money. Betty, with her best hauteur, replied it would be sent 'in due course'. He went away empty-handed that time, but not the next: he arrived in a fine French rage and wrenched the painting from the wall saying, 'It is fortuitous that I can scrape this ignoble Family off, and use the board again, *Madame*!' and he walked out into Queen's Square with the mediocre picture under his arm and nobody saw the Conversation Piece of the Bristol Marshalls ever again.

Time's Scythe scythed; days passed, and months, and years. Marmaduke gambled away what money remained; Juno and Venus sighed and sulked and talked of Nobility and dreamed of Love; Ezekiel and Tobias stole from neighbouring houses; Betty's cheeks became permanently Madeira-red.

Half-educated, bored with teaching a child, nowhere to use his energy, Philip would stroll the Bristol streets in a supercilious manner as the sons of gentlemen were wont to do, thinking of himself as a fashionable *flâneur* in the manner of the French (pretending his clothes were not becoming slightly shabby), and then suddenly, urgently, Grace would appear from nowhere, reminding him of a spinning top in her flurried hooped skirt, and then she would just as quickly settle to his pace and stroll beside him, chattering upwards.

'Why?' said Grace.

'What is that?' said Grace.

'Can we read?' said Grace.

'Look, look, there is a Clock: *When I do count the clock that tells the Time*,' said Grace.

Philip was aggravated by the girl's persistence, again and again sent her home, obviously no stylish *flâneur* recognised a young child as a companion: she should stay in the house in Queen's Square with her sisters and their mother. But over and over again, Grace spun out into the square in her little hooped gown, her bodice cut low – exactly like her mother's – and neatly laced over her embroidered stomacher: an exact replica of an adult, only small, and dragging her shawl behind her impatiently as if it slowed her down, as her lace cap bobbed above her dark, dark hair. Perhaps sometimes there was something endearing about a shadow, whose dark eyes were so large and bright, and some days Philip would point out the new houses on the Clifton hills, or the ships from far-off lands.

'Look, Grace, look!' he would say. 'Listen, Grace, listen to me! These ships,' and they would gaze at all the graceful, shabby vessels that came and went from another world, the tall masts like thin bare trees in lines along the quay-side, 'these ships travel the World, they carry Diamonds and Rubies and Rum – and real Gold,' and unexpectedly he smashed his swordstick violently against a wall in that raging way he sometimes had, 'Where is *my* Gold!' and Grace knew well to lag behind now, so that he would not take out his anger upon her. But she knew what gold was: she could picture the colour of gold in her head, her father's old crystal decanters contained liquid made of dark gold, the colour caught the candlelight in the dark family house, where nothing much else shone. While Philip brooded Grace stared, wrapt, fascinated, at the ships with their furled white sails, all the bustle and calling and unloading and loading; she smelled the tar and the filthy river port and, somewhere there – beside them, behind them – exotic spices on the air. She saw how the light changed as it fell across the water: observed an old sailor and a young one, their heads together as they talked. The grey Bristol light caught the bones of the old sailor so that his shadowed face looked to her like a skull, a skull that was smoking a pipe.

'Look, Philip, look!' she called, and she caught up with him again. 'Look at the sailors!' There was no breeze, the smoke from the pipe rose straight up, a cloud of blue mist rising above the heads of the two men, there beside the coils of rope and the big heavy boxes and a seagull, black and white, crying at the lowering sky, and Grace wondered if her father could paint such a picture instead of horses: the blue smoke and the grey sky and the bird and the eerie weather-beaten old face. The old sailor spat and somehow the seagull was looking the other way and the gob fell upon its folded wings, it squawked in outrage and shook its feathers and flew away screeching. And young Grace Marshall could be seen in her hooped skirt and her tight bodice and her shawl laughing uncontrollably at the bird's indignation along the wharfside in the city of Bristol; her dark eyes sparkled up at her beautiful brother who could not help laughing either, as much at his sister's merriment as at the affront of the bird from the sea.

Philip Marshall was so bored with life in general that once he even took his sister to the Bristol Library in King Street. There, up an old oak staircase, they found the librarian in a room full of books with a startling, wonderful picture on the wall: a picture of a fine, elegant gentleman in a beautiful coloured robe. The librarian however was neither elegant nor fine; he was a vicar in a somewhat shabby waistcoat: Grace and Philip observed he had red veins on his cheeks which gave him the look rather of a cross person but he was not cross at all, simply bored and rum-soaked. They understood at once that the rum was hidden behind the books – well, they were used to all that. Philip charmed the vicar as he charmed all others, and the vicar showed them, as requested, the library's copy of *Wm Shakespeare's Collected Works*.

'Not at all to today's Taste,' said the vicar, 'nobody has asked for this Volume for many a moon. You will see that a large number of the pages are stained, for our previous premises leaked badly. We thought not to keep this, as it is so damaged and hardly anybody ever asks for it, but my Father was fond of Mr Shakespeare.'

Philip leafed through the delicate pages, found part of *Henry the Fifth*, unstained, and suddenly cried out heroically, holding the volume aloft:

Cry 'God for Harry! England and St George!'

But although Grace and the vicar applauded appreciatively, the words quite took away Philip's good humour and he longed again to be fighting the French, to be serving in His Majesty's Navy in a bright blue uniform, not languishing around Bristol with an eight-year-old, and he dragged his little sister back out to King Street, marched into one of the new coffee houses where he would find other bored young men like himself, and Grace was brusquely sent home. It was dusk, pink clouds drifted there above the cobbled streets and the lines of masts. And unhappy Queen's Square with its dreams of fading glory. And a lone child, dragging a shawl.

It was her brother Tobias who first noticed how Grace instinctively copied the looks on other people's faces around her as she watched them.

'Be Venus, Gracie!' he would encourage her, 'Be Venus!' Venus was the most haughty of the Marshall family; she emitted little sighs of exasperation at the vulgarity that surrounded her even in her own home. Grace would sigh very softly in unison as she watched her sister, hardly knowing she did so, and then encouraged by her naughty brothers she would wrinkle her nose in a disdainful manner as Venus did, and her brothers Tobias and Ezekiel would snigger behind their hands as Venus, oblivious, suffered nobly from the vulgar trials of her Bristolian life.

Grace learned something important from Tobias. Ezekiel shouted and banged but Tobias could move without making a sound. Grace learned this skill from Tobias. He could be in a dim corner of a room and nobody would know, for nobody ever cared enough about him to say *Where is Tobias?* The family was too fractured to notice where small boys might be; he could be under a table, hidden by a long tablecloth, for hours, listening to the women talk of Nobility and Tribulation and Marriage. Why he should want to listen to such things was not known, but in broken families perhaps children try to belong when they can: often he would be there in the shadows. His mother was quite disconcerted if she suddenly understood he was near: 'It is like having a French spy in the Family!' she would cry, but Tobias had already disappeared.

Marmaduke's wilder and wilder card-playing became a real danger: money was owed, perilous shame loomed in the shadows of the dark, damp Bristol streets where honourable men paid on the nail (gold exchanged on the huge tables shaped like nails outside the Corn Exchange). It became urgently imperative for the older children to make successful marriages before disgrace destroyed them all: already there had been whispers about dishonest antecedents and financial difficulties.

Quickly, O Lord, quickly, whispered Betty to herself as she poured sweet wine, *Marriage, dear Lord, before we are entirely Doomed*, as she took very large and urgent gulps. But there was no dowry, their good name was long gone: who would have them? Finally through Betty's more and more desperate machinations Juno became betrothed to the short-statured son of an iron exporter, and Venus to a vintner: it was, alas, not what was hoped for but it was something at least. Betty then put all her energies into looking for a rich wife in Bristol society ('Such as it is,' she was heard to say bitterly, her expectations not having been reached) for her son and heir, the charming, dark-eyed Philip Marshall. *But Marriage, not the Navy*, she whispered to herself: he would be away too long, the Navy could not make him rich enough despite the rumoured prize money that some received. *He must be rich now: he must find a rich Wife now and support us all*. So Betty, a squire's daughter, was to be seen looking over the vulgar daughters of Bristolian ship-owners in a now panic-stricken manner – and what young Grace Marshall was doing now nobody knew or cared.

What Grace Marshall was doing now, aged eight, was following her father Marmaduke around Bristol, for she loved him and she thought to save him when he became too inebriated to play wisely at cards. By now Grace knew the streets of Bristol better than almost anyone. But following her father, sometimes a little behind him so that he would not order her home, was tinged with real danger: the Bristol gentlemen's clubs were now banned to him. The sort of card-room Marmaduke was allowed into these days was a dark den inside a tradesmen's club, or (the less salubrious and more violent ones) down dark Bristol alleys where small girls should never, ever go. But Grace had learned well from Tobias, she was scheming and clever as a cat, an ever-present nuisance in the hazy, smoke-filled rooms; no other little girl was ever seen in such places and when she somehow turned up in a dim corner or was half-glimpsed behind a chair it was never understood how she had obtained admission. As they seemed not able to shake her loose, as she seemed to be always, stoically, there, they finally ignored her.

Waiting in the gloom of dangerous rooms, always aware of her father, she became fascinated by something else: all the *faces*: the faces of the men as they watched their cards and watched each other. She saw on their shadowed, candle-lit faces the sly looks and the triumphant looks and the looks of fear – for they played for large sums of money: life almost, and death. Watching the gamblers she unknowingly copied their faces: a gambling man paused before making a wager, his face creased, he frowned, deciding, risking: the face of the eight-year-old girl creased up in anxiety also; he bit his lip in indecision, the girl bit her own lip over and over. And she saw also now the menacing looks that were cast often at the dishonourable Marmaduke, felt the danger in the air. When even his befuddled brain warned him that it would be politic to leave in the meantime, he would stumble home along to Queen's Square guided by his watchful youngest daughter.

And then, unwilling to confront his shrewish wife, he would often repair to a room at the bottom of the tall, narrow house. There, he stumbled and mumbled and sat in front of an old family easel and once more painted his elegant country horses on a piece of board. He had an old book of pictures of horses, Grace would see how he looked at them and then drew, first with charcoal. Looked and then drew. Looked and then drew, still mumbling incoherently to himself. Later he painted the colours: he took the paint from little packets of colour which he mixed with some kind of oil and then applied it to his horses with a long, thin brush.

The only time Grace was completely still was when she was watching her father in this small downstairs room. She stared – immobile, beguiled – as, smelling of rum like the vicar in the library, her father bent over the small packets and stirred and mixed the colours, his long white wig occasionally decorated with unlikely bright blue spots as he patted the paints on to the board with his brush, and sometimes with his thumb. And just sometimes he might even sing: some song from his past. *When I laid on Greenland's coast, and in my arms embraced my lass*, he would sing. And if some portion of a bottle of rum from the West Indies had found its way to the room at the bottom of the house, he would take a gulp and then his voice always rose to a crescendo when it reached the chorus, as if some memory of another time gave him strength.

> *And I would love you all the Day*
> *Ev'ry Night would kiss and play*
> *If with me you'd fondly stray –*
> *Over the hills and far away . . .*

Sometimes Tobias would appear from nowhere, and laugh slyly, and run away again. Philip might pass by, tossing a piece of charcoal himself and humming, as if he too might draw if he had the energy; he would observe his father for a while and then disappear again, humming still. Perhaps he drew other pictures in other rooms, perhaps Tobias did the same: who would know what anybody did in that disordered house?

Grace became so fascinated by her father's colours that she began 'painting' also, with anything she could find. Her father would not allow her to touch his colours so she found her own. She found she could draw with coal; she started with laborious, rather strange-shaped horses, trying to copy her father, had more success when she turned to drawing her father himself, caught something of him as he bent to his easel. Then she found she could make an orange colour by squashing marigold petals from the garden with her small fingers, so she gave him an orange waistcoat. She could make marks with clay; her mother's cheek-rouge gave her pretty pink; strong dregs of the new coffee from Africa gave her brown; even butter gave a hint of yellow before it melted – whatever she could lay her hands on: she was a menace and butter even got in her hair and her hands were slapped often. Her energy and her interests were most unladylike, her curiosity was insatiable – in short she was, quite simply, *unsuitable*.

'I do not understand where her tiresome energy comes from,' said her mother pettishly, 'for it is surely not from her Father; and I would not be so frantic for all the World.' But her thin, scrawny brother Tobias, ten years old, would sometimes follow her around: 'Gracie!' he would call, carrying a few green beans stolen from the kitchen, 'Here's a colour,' and once he came to her proudly with a large, juicy hyacinth he had stolen, so that she could mix blue.

One hot summer afternoon when the sky was clear and the children were particularly vexatious in the stuffy Bristol house, her father (the cards had gone well that week and Grace turned nine years old that sunny day) gave Grace the greatest present ever given: some paper, some coloured chalks and some charcoal.

'I beg you to draw me some pretty Flowers, Grace, and to be very quiet about it, like a good Girl.' He sat in the back garden, in his once elegant waistcoat, on a fading chair. In the shadow of the tall, narrow house he seemed to sleep, his wig hung over his chair:

17

his wife could hardly bear to look at him, so vulgar and troublesome did he now appear to her.

In the corner of the garden an ungainly pink delphinium drooped in the hot sunshine. Grace, trembling slightly with delight at the unexpected, wonderful gift, looked at the delphinium very carefully and then drew it exactly as she saw it, its pink, drooping despair. Most unusually, the family were all together in the garden, it being too hot to think of being anywhere else. (Except of course for Aunt Joy, who scraped together what she could in the stifling kitchen basement.) In the garden, escaping – frankly – the stink of the hot, un-aired house, the mouth-down-turned mother sat in an extremely large straw hat, clutching Beloved; Juno and Venus languished in tight corsets, dreaming of gentlemen and carrying parasols to shield them from the sun. Juno was to be married in the autumn to the short tradesman but the engagement of the vintner to Miss Venus Marshall had been most shamefully called off by the vintner's father. Venus's red-rimmed eyes told her rage and grief. Philip preened boredly by the marble statue; Tobias and Ezekiel fought angrily over a small cart they had no doubt stolen from somewhere. Grace's delphinium was shadowed, odd: not at all pretty like flowers should be.

'I shall be obliged to take all your chalks away', said her mother sharply, fanning herself with the large hat (which was decorated with wax strawberries) 'if you do not draw *pretty* Flowers.' Immediately Grace drew an immaculate, oddly-green daisy. 'But look, this is red!' said her father, observing from half-closed eyes, pointing to the flowers in the garden.

'There are green Daisies, Father,' said Grace. 'This is a green Daisy.'

'That Daisy', said Philip in a bored, patronising voice, 'is Insane.'

And although her mother and her father and Philip would have much preferred pretty peonies or sweet roses to the drooping, rather spiky delphinium or the perverse green daisy, with those they had to be content.

Grace kept drawing, absolutely concentrated. The small boys fought on, laughing viciously, the older sisters sighed viciously, Venus flirted sentimentally with suicide (*then* the vintner's cruel son would be sorry). Philip still leaned against the statue, watching idly: France was always there to be fought against if he joined the Navy, but he was prevented by his own lack of energy and by his adoring mother who gave him what coins she could while still she endeavoured to manoeuvre a financially-endowed young girl in his direction. So here he languished: no money, no prospects, no rich heiress, and life was passing him by.

Overcome then by a wild, angry burst of energy, Philip suddenly seized all nine-year-old Grace's drawing materials from her and – quick as lightning – drew her outraged face.

'My Heavens!' cried his mother with more spirit than she had shown for a month. 'Look at this! *Look at this!* Remember the dreadful Frenchman? My Boy has Talent!' Marmaduke opened his eyes just a little.

Philip drew his parents, his sisters, his brothers: easily, catching their look. 'I was good at Art at my School,' he announced airily. 'I draw in my room sometimes.'

'Neater, Philip,' said his parents, 'prettier perhaps?' Now everyone was alerted: all the siblings gathered round, the heat and the hot sunshine forgotten just for a moment.

Philip drew more neatly and more prettily with his sister's birthday present.

> *Three Blind Mice*, he sang as he drew.
> *See how they run.*

Grace grabbed some of the chalk back. 'I would have been good at Art also if I had gone to School!' she cried with great spirit. She drew her parents too, but there was something uneasy, or wrong, about her quick portraits: her mother had a look of discontent, her father looked dark, uneasy. There was no more interest in Grace's portraits than in her uncomfortable delphiniums.

'Girls do not draw *Persons*!' said her father. 'Girls draw Flowers. And if they do not draw pretty Flowers, they will not be given Chalks another time.'

Philip drew his mother again in quick, clever strokes, making her look young. *They all ran after the farmer's wife*, he sang, and Tobias and Ezekiel joined in gleefully and noisily, *He cut off their tails with a carving knife*, and the little girl suddenly grabbed hold of both Philip's arms to get his attention.

'These are *my* Chalks!' said Grace Marshall very loudly, today aged nine, but nobody took any notice.

For Philip Marshall had discovered his vocation.

The next day, however, young Tobias came to Grace with another flower. Tobias was so thin: sometimes Grace thought he looked like a black-eyed beanstalk, that is an eleven-year-old black-eyed beanstalk. He stood there with a red, red rose.

'I took it from a garden, Gracie,' he said gruffly, 'so you could make some red paint to paint red Daisies like they said,' and he had run off at once before she had thanked her brother, who had remembered their parents' complaints about her unlikely green daisy, and had sought to assist her, and neither Grace nor Tobias had any notion that red roses stood for love.

Philip Marshall began *earning* money, the first of the languishing Wiltshire Marshalls ever to do so: he could draw people's faces and he began to be paid for his portraits. But their father borrowed even more money for the card-table from the Jew money-lender at very high interest, in a kind of last defiance.

Then one afternoon the invisible Aunt Joy, in her dark gown and her white cap, expired. Had she not drawn her last breath in the dining-room it is unlikely her absence would have been noted. Betty complained bitterly about the expense of a funeral and Grace stared at the coffin as it lay in a hole in the churchyard and wondered if Aunt Joy, whom she had hardly noticed, lay in the box in the dark gown and the white cap, just as usual.

Aunt Joy was missed, however, after all; the household ran amok, it might be said, from the time of her demise: often now there was not food on the table, and voices shouted all over the house as it seemed to dis-integrate.

Slowly Philip's portraits started to be praised in the city: he began painting the newly-rich, those successful tradesmen who sold the iron and the black men. Rough paintings yet perhaps, but the tradesmen had never been painted by anyone at all before and paid him well; he painted a cloth-merchant, the cloth-merchant's wife, an alderman, a minister of the church, and – to his mother's delight – several daughters of real gentlemen.

'At last, my darling boy!' cried Betty, 'You will find a Wife worthy of your Ancestors, and we will all be saved!' But it was not the Bristolian gentry who would save Philip. The rough, hard-working

Bristol traders aimed to be real gentlemen themselves, or their sons at least, and their portraits already made them feel like gentlemen. They encouraged Philip's talent, were soon suggesting he travel to see the Great Old Masters, that he journey to Florence and Rome and Venice and Amsterdam with their own sons: add to his Artistic Education.

'I will come! I must come!' cried Grace, 'for **my** Artistic Education.' But nobody heard.

Philip for the first time in his life worked hard, experimented with colours, painted day and night: powerful businessmen and young ladies and gentlemen from the town. He too now talked of his Grand Tour but the financial and domestic situation of the family had become so embarrassing that, to his wild frustration, the money he was earning for his portraits had to be used simply to hold off the creditors, for Marmaduke had finally used the Queen's Square house as collateral in the gambling dens in the dark Bristol alleys.

And then the plague came.

It came particularly to Bristol: the ships perhaps, or the sewers, or the black men. The sun shone on, the pestilence flew over the land; whole families died in a city so crowded, so wedded to trade and ships (in the night rats ran from the ships, burrowed into the dark corners of the city). The plague was no respecter of class, made no special dispensation for the Marshall family, people were dying all over Bristol, whole families in some areas: hundreds and hundreds of people died. Juno, the oldest girl who nearly married the son of an iron exporter, succumbed early; at her funeral the mother wept loudly and sang 'How Great Thou Art' in a trembling soprano. Then Ezekiel died. Then Venus got her wish and died, to her own surprise, and the vintner's son did, after all, pay his respects. Finally the life ended of Betty, the fair-haired pretty young bride, who had wanted nobility and whose idea it had been to move to the filthy, stinking city that she thought had held such promise of fashion and of future.

Philip and Grace and Tobias huddled in disbelief with their father as hurried, smaller funerals were arranged and as more and more creditors called. Betty's mahogany furniture was taken away. Beloved the poodle disappeared and was never seen again. 'I hope somebody boiled it up for stew,' said Philip blankly, and Marmaduke almost smiled. But within a week Marmaduke stared listlessly at his paints and lay upon his bed: his lips took on the faint blue colour that was the sign, the sign that death was near. After only three more days Philip and Grace and Tobias were the only members of the Marshall family in Bristol still alive and they clung together, shocked, dis-oriented, as their father was taken away in a cart piled with bodies and Grace's tears fell upon her shabby skirt as she sat on the roadway, like any street child, long after the cart had disappeared.

Bristol's population was shockingly lessened. One of the newly-rich young men of the city, a trader's son, decided to leave Bristol at once: for Italy, for his Artistic Education, and would take Philip with him.

'What about the Children?' said the powerful Bristol business-men, pulling at their white powdered wigs and looking at the thin boy and the odd, dark-eyed girl. For they were responsible fellows and the elder brother had painted them handsomely. The Wiltshire Marshalls were unbending, did not reply to an urgent enquiry for assistance for the orphaned children of their scandalous son.

Solving Tobias was easy. 'The boy to the docks!' they cried. 'We will place him on one of our Ships!' And Tobias's scrawny face lit up: he would see the World, he would travel the high seas, he would fight Pirates, he would become a Pirate!

'I shall be a Pirate, Gracie!' he called.

'Indeed I do hope not,' murmured one of the kind businessmen.

'Goodbye, Gracie, I'll bring you Gold and Colours!' cried Tobias, and he waved to his brother Philip, and he was gone: a jaunty, thin thirteen-year-old boy with a small bundle on his shoulder (Grace had found him an old jacket and a bowl and one of their father's worn, once elegant, waistcoats). It was only when it was too late, the ship disappearing down the channel, that one kind business-man saw that his empty watch-chain flowed free from his waistcoat.

Grace stared wordlessly at the powerful Bristol men, refused to cry, clung to her beloved brother Philip, but he could not help her: the journey to Italy was his chance of survival and he must take it. Realistic tradesmen had realistic solutions: Grace should be put to a milliner. She would learn a trade after all, for was not this a city of traders? She would learn to make pretty hats that Bristol ladies wore (those straw hats with the rather large wax strawberries that Betty had worn, although Betty would have turned in her grave at the thought that her daughter might in any way be involved in their manufacture). In other circumstances Philip might have at least protested that Grace was a daughter of the gentry, but his own position – a son of the gentry but with no financial support of any kind – was too precarious: their father had owed money all over Bristol. By now not only the Wiltshire Marshalls but members of the Bristol nobility (such as they were) refused to have anything to do with this family, murmured of wildness and dishonesty.

But Philip made his sister a promise: 'I will come back for you,' he said.

The ship taking her brother Philip on his adventures sailed at first light; they forbad the girl to be there: she must begin her new life.

The premises of Mrs Falls, the milliner, to whence the responsible businessmen led Grace, were tucked into a small corner behind the old Christmas Steps on the hill: a tiny, narrow house with the hat-making workroom in the basement. Rickety wooden steps, lit by candles in holders that flickered dangerously, led upwards from narrow floor to narrow floor, to the attic where Grace was to sleep with four other assistants in the tiny room with the low ceiling. The floorboards of the staircase creaked loudly. On the first landing, in the candlelight, could be ascertained two prints hanging on the wall: *Gin Lane* she spelled out (all the people looking terrible, deathly: one woman so inebriated that her baby fell from her bosom – because Gin was Evil) and *Beer Street* (all the people looking happy and well-fed, and children smiling – because Beer was Good). And at the top of the house five mattresses in a row, so close that they touched, and one tiny window: Grace's new home. Grace was outraged beyond reason, stared out all night long at the noisy darkness from the small attic window while the other assistants slept: Philip was to go to study art in Rome, and she was to live in an attic and make horrible hats?

I will not stay here.

It was still dark when she drew her hooped petticoats about her with one hand and carried her small shoes in the other. She crept in her stockinged feet down and down the wooden staircase, past the dark candleholders, past the *Gin Lane* and *Beer Street* prints on the walls. Somewhere in the house somebody snored violently: she heard the sound gladly, hoping it would cover the sound of the stairboards creaking. The front door of the house of Mrs Falls locked with a long thin iron key; Grace had quickly observed that the key was then placed in a drawer of a narrow chest in the small hallway. She felt for the long key, put it into the keyhole softly, it rattled as it turned, she pulled the door gently behind her, it creaked as it closed. Most of the night couples who had come together in the dark on Christmas Steps had gone now although one gentleman was still engaged noisily near the ironmonger's house. Grace cared nothing for night couples and night noises, she had heard them all many times as she had followed her father, or led him home. Her flimsy shoes scuffed over the cobbles as the first light rose around her, she ran down and down the streets to the river. She would board the ship in the half-light: she would go with Philip.

The wind had picked up in the last hour and the captain, waiting on the deck, had felt it: the *Charity* was already in half-sail and pulling away from the dock as the small girl ran towards it.

'Philip!' she cried out in great desperation, 'Philip!' But the noise of the wind in the sails flapped and roared.

Philip Marshall looked back at Bristol to say farewell to his home, looked again, saw the small, indistinct figure beside the bargemen and the ship's clerk and the coiled ropes: knew it was Grace.

'I will come back for you!' he called but the wind whipped at his words. He raised his hand as a salute and a promise as the day lightened and brightened and his new life began and to Grace he seemed to cry, *'God for Harry! England and St George!'* and she was not included.

TWO

Grace Marshall, left on the quayside, was not quite eleven years old.

She haunted the Bristol docks for many months, like a small, hoop-skirted ghost. Grey stones of grief and abandonment and rage sat on the small thin shoulders, and colours gone, as she stared at the arriving and departing sailing ships, looking always for her brothers. If she was once a laughing girl who bowled through the Bristol streets like a spinning top, who cared for drawing, who made paint from golden marigolds or African coffee or from the red rose the boy had found – well, there was nobody else to remember.

Mrs Falls' assistants did not like Grace. She was smaller than they, and did not join in their whispers. They did not like the way she was so silent. At first they would trip her on the rickety wooden stairs but she scratched at them instantly, wildly, like an animal so they did not do that again, whispered about her instead, made her sleep on the end mattress, the smallest and the lumpiest. Mrs Falls' assistants fell asleep to the sound of cries and shouts and footsteps: boots and shoes coming down Christmas Steps and on to the steep cobbled path that led down to the Bristol port, lovers or street-girls huddling in the dark corners. But when the other apprentices were asleep Grace stared out: to the shape of the old chapel at the top of

Christmas Steps, to the same old cries and shadows in the streets in the night; or drunken voices would sing out everybody's song, singing as a round, joining in, losing the tune and the words and then picking them up again amid raucous laughter:

> *Three blind mice*
> *See how they run*
> *They all run after the farmer's wife*
> *She cut off their tails with a carving knife.*

and Grace thought if she had a carving knife she would plunge it into the nearest person, to assuage her anger and her loneliness and her pain.

Mrs Falls felt sorry for the girl, knew perfectly well the Bristol docks were no place for a wild young girl like Grace, but Mrs Falls had troubles of her own, what with her dropsy and her bunions and the water on her knee and her general protuberances. 'I cannot be expected', she would say, huffing and puffing to anyone who might be listening, 'to run after my Girls and lock them up so that they won't get In The Pits,' (her odd turn of phrase was understood) 'she looks for her Brothers, poor jade, as if they will ever return for her!'

There was, if truth be told, something vulgar about Mrs Falls' hats – the strawberries were a little hefty, the ribbons were a little bright, there were upon some of them many large, multi-coloured butterflies or even small feathered birds. Mrs Falls' hats were made for the Bristol ladies, wives of trade, who loved them and paid well, and Mrs Falls, nightly, bent over her financial affairs, often counting on her fat fingers as her girls worked late, late into the night, bending over their sewing in the candlelight.

Mrs Falls, however, was not an early riser, owing to her dropsy, and her gout, and her chest, and was never known to be ready before nine of the clock so her young ladies took their freedom when they could; at least one of them often nipped into the basement workroom in the mornings smelling of nights and flaunting money easily earned, but Mrs Falls never noticed. Grace would often let herself out of the old, snoring house before first light, that time when the ships sometimes left and the ships sometimes came home, and the girl waiting there beside the quays.

Just once she drew a face with some charcoal she had bought with her first earned pennies and a piece of card she had found. She drew the remembered face of Tobias: a thin face, she saw that the eyes she had drawn from inside her head were evasive, looked away slightly. Yet it looked like him. She took the piece of card with her down to the quays and sometimes she asked other sailors if they knew this sailor. But they shook their heads.

There were no letters, no messages from across the sea. As night followed night, Grace Marshall, milliner's assistant, staring out at the darkness from the attic window, or lying in bed hearing the night sounds and staring at the wooden beams of the ceiling, understood herself an orphan, alone in all the world. Tobias was surely a pirate by now – *I could have been a Pirate too!* – and Philip – *who stole my own coloured chalks and my charcoal* – was studying to be an artist in exciting foreign parts, and Grace making hats in Bristol. Sometimes that old voracious energy would be sighted, briefly, but then it was gone, a poor thing, as if the world had wrought too much damage upon it. However that was not exactly the situation: the energy had only gone underground, her chin only lifted just that little bit higher.

'*Goddam!*' she heard the sailors muttering, down on the wharfs as the ship-owners shouted.

'*Goddam!*' Grace Marshall muttered to herself.

She was lonely, but she was also *furious*, and her fury sustained her.

It went on then, this early morning haunting of the quays, month after month after year, though perhaps even Grace Marshall no longer really expected to find her brothers. She might have seemed to be a street girl but she was not exactly a street girl, except that she knew the streets. One of the other milliner's assistants who also haunted the streets, but for different reasons, found she was with child: she drank much gin and fell down the creaking stairs, blood everywhere. Mrs Falls discharged her immediately with no pay. Mrs Falls' contribution to her girls' welfare was to remind them of the prints on the first floor landing that a famous artist had made as a warning: Gin could only lead to destruction, it was Beer that would make them strong and hearty and she provided beer on Saturdays (water of course would kill them). Occasionally Grace too might be accosted by men down by the quays, or up by the Customs House, but the bargemen and the ship's clerks and the sailors and the tradesmen knew her, protected her in their indifferent way, for there was something about her resolute twelve-year-old stride, thirteen-year-old stride, fourteen-year-old stride: something about the determined little chin. She was part of the morning, always there and, besides, she looked as if she might bite.

The milliner girls were lucky: not only did someone care for their welfare and give them beer on Saturdays, they also had one half-day free a week. If Grace wasn't wandering down by the docks she sometimes would go to the Bristol Public Library and see the rum-drinking vicar with the red face. Her brother had taught her to read but he had never told her of one person who wrote a book except Mr Shakespeare, so (not knowing what else to look for) she would ask the red-veined but kindly gentleman if she might look again at the fragile, water-stained book. The library was so ill-used he was pleased to have a customer, even a rather untidy young girl. Some of the plays and sonnets, he thought, might be somewhat unsuitable. But he found for her the play of *Twelfth Night* thinking, with great breadth of mind for an inebriated vicar in Bristol, that it might interest her, as it was about young people, shipwrecks and love and there was much laughter also.

He sat and helped her with the more difficult words. The reading began auspiciously with the short first words: *If music be the food of love, play on,* and she thought of her father painting and singing, *If with me you'd fondly stray, over the hills and far away,* and she even smiled. It was more difficult when they came to the second scene.

VIOLA:	What country, friends, is this?
SEA CAPTAIN:	This is Illyria, lady.
VIOLA:	And what should I do in Illyria?
	My brother he is in Elysium.

Grace shed a small, angry tear which she brushed away rudely, and asked the vicar where Elysium was, and he had not the heart to speak of death, and just said 'far away'. Then they found that the next pages were so damaged by water stains that they were not to be read: the kind vicar told Grace the story of love and misunderstanding as best he could and assured her that the brother and the sister were re-united in the end. She bit her lip very hard, she never cried, she stared up at the picture of the fine gentleman with the beautiful clothes, on the wall.

'Who is that?' she asked crossly.

'That is a copy of a very great Painting,' said the vicar. 'The man in the picture is an Italian Duke, and he was painted by a great Venetian Artist called Mr Titian.'

She looked more carefully. 'How did Mr Titian paint those beautiful colours?'

'I expect he had beautiful paints, young lady.' She stared upwards, fascinated.

'What is Venetian, that Mr Titian is?' The kind vicar heaved down an old atlas, and showed her the world, and Venice, and she wondered if Philip and Tobias were sailing to such places and peered in astonishment at all the countries and all the sea.

'Show me Elysium?' she asked again, but the vicar (although he was one of God's servants) said he did not know, exactly, the whereabouts of Elysium.

She would come back to the library and look at the maps and the vicar would find a bit more un-water-stained Shakespeare and read to her, explaining words that she did not understand. She was always glad when he told her – the story cut short again by damaged pages – that nevertheless everybody lived happily ever after.

'Does everybody always live happily ever after?' she once asked him, and because he saw the longing in the small face he did not think of his own life.

'Yes,' he said gravely, and he added, although it was against every experience of his existence, 'Life always ends Happily Ever After,' and her smile lit up the cold library afternoon.

However they did graduate, after many months, to *Romeo and Juliet*, and Grace put her hand over her mouth in horror when the warring families went too far, thought of herself as Juliet, of course, but had no contender for Romeo. She perfectly understood that Mr Shakespeare was writing about the thing called *love* that the other apprentice girls sometimes giggled over in the night. She made up her own Romeo in her mind: a little like one of the bright-eyed laughing sailors she had noticed without perhaps exactly meaning to, down by the docks, and, perhaps, a little like the older, handsome brother who had deserted her. One afternoon, the vicar read:

> *Come, gentle night, come, loving black-brow'd night,*
> *Give me my Romeo; and, when he shall die,*
> *Take him and cut him out in little stars,*
> *And he will make the face of heaven so fine*
> *That all the world will be in love with night.*

'Have him Dead, and Cut him out?' she said in amazement, for that was not how the milliner girls talked. 'Is that what Love is?' and the vicar explained that Mr Shakespeare was making word-pictures.

'Do you mean that words can make a Picture, just like painting can?'

'Yes,' said the vicar.

She looked up at the colours of Mr Titian on the wall. 'I would much rather make a Picture with paint,' said Grace finally and firmly.

But that night the word-picture of Mr Shakespeare stayed inside her head and from the attic window she stared for a long time at the stars in the Bristol sky with an angry tenderness and a strange longing that she hardly understood.

Next morning, down by the docks, scanning the horizon as was now her ingrained habit, she saw the sailor of her Romeo imagination waving goodbye to a young girl with a baby as his ship set sail. Tears poured down the girl's cheeks; Grace was near enough to see that the tears fell on the baby's hair in the pale red dawn. She turned away from the docks with a tiny, inaudible sigh. She did not go straight back to the workrooms, walked further along the road, found herself beside a big Bristol church, the Church of St Mary's Redcliffe, that had big stained-glass windows. Usually the door was locked, but this morning it was wide open, like a black yawn. She stepped cautiously inside. It was summer and the early morning light soon began to insinuate through tall windows, and then – suddenly – caught the coloured glass spectacularly, making the blues and golds and red shine and glow in an unimaginable way. She stared up, like a hungry person.

She drifted further into the church. The daylight shone now on to a long curtain with a faded painting upon it, above the altar-place; dust caught in the shafts of sunlight, and an angel looked rather shabbily downwards from one of the high walls.

As the morning grew brighter, Grace became aware that the church was not after all empty. A small stocky gentleman sat there also, to the side, contemplating the altar with a fierce, concentrated expression: Grace thought that perhaps he was praying with his eyes open.

The open eyes had already taken in the girl: the huge, dark, curious, rather sad eyes, the delicate bones, the determined little chin. Feeling her eyes upon him now, the gentleman turned again to her.

'Good morning,' he said.

'Good morning,' answered Grace Marshall.

'See that Altar?'

'Yes.'

Their voices rose above them, echoing eerily in the empty building like disembodied bells, a deep sound and a high sound.

'Tell me, young Lady, what would you like to see hanging up there behind it? What Miracle would please you?'

'My Brothers,' she said at once. 'My Brothers returned for me from across the World.'

He did not seem in the least surprised by her answer, was staring again at the painted curtain above the altar.

'How would you have them look?'

'They would be shining,' said Grace. 'Like this light, like this light now – I mean the sun shining through that beautiful coloured glass, it would be shining all around them.' She saw now he had a crayon or a pencil, was writing something quickly. 'And my Brother who will be an Artist and I, who will also be an Artist, would have a painting Studio, like a Church –' he turned his head quickly, stared at her. 'The Light, I mean,' she said, thinking she may somehow have been blasphemous, 'I mean the way the Light shines in through these high windows so early in the morning and the way the Light from the candles moves and flickers and I would draw . . .' She thought for a moment, remembered the Frenchman and the Conversation Piece. '. . . I would draw my Father and my Mother and my sisters and my brothers.'

'Would they sit to you, your Family?'

'What does that mean?'

'It means: if you draw a person it is best if they are there, in front of you. Would they all sit quietly, for as long as it took you to draw them?'

'They are quiet. They are in my head.'

'What is it that you mean, that they are in your head?'

'They died with the Fever.'

His pencil stopped. 'All of them?'

'Except my two Brothers, who will come back for me. The other one is a Pirate.'

The pencil started again. 'Shining, as you described.' He was smiling slightly, perhaps he was laughing at her. She saw the way the light was changing: it was time for her to go back to Christmas Steps.

'They will be shining,' she said obstinately. And then she stood quickly.

'What is your name?' he asked, detaining her.

'Grace. I have to go to my Work.'

'How old are you, Grace?'

'Fourteen years.'

He stood also. To her surprise he was shorter than she. 'I hope you *will* draw in your Studio with your brother, Grace,' he said. Maybe he saw something bleak in her face. 'Let me tell you something. If I see a face I would like to paint and I cannot keep it in front of me, I sometimes make a quick sketch of it on my thumbnail.' Startled, she actually laughed in the empty church: the childish, uncertain laugh echoed upwards as she looked at her own very small nail and back at the short man. 'But of course you can also draw that which you remember, that can be a way of drawing too.' And he moved towards her with his hand outstretched, to give her a paper. 'I am going to make a very large Painting for this Altar, Grace. And there will, I promise you, be Shining.' And then the short man was gone to the front of the church where the small candles flickered and made shadows, and then he disappeared through the side door.

Grace stared after him in surprise, *is he an Artist? is that what real Artists look like? he seems rather short for an Artist, although I am sure it is allowable for short people to be Artists.* In the summer morning light, shining even more brightly now from the high windows, she looked down at his paper. A sudden gasp of surprise echoed. It was an *exact* drawing of herself as she looked up at the altar. She saw her own black eyes in her thin face. Her own chin. As if she looked in a mirror. Underneath, rather untidily, it said **Grace. Bristol. Fourteen years**. And underneath that the signature was clear: **Wm Hogarth**.

Hooped petticoats had never been a hindrance to the running of Grace Marshall. She ran along the cobbled paths and winding alleys, up the hill towards the milliner's house, she did not stop as she got to the bottom of Christmas Steps but ran up, holding her skirts before her, she burst into the house and ran up the stairs even as Mrs Falls' voice admonished her for her unusual tardiness, and on the stairs she looked again at **Gin Lane** and **Beer Street**.

There was the same signature underneath.

Wm Hogarth.

It was as if a magic key had been turned in her.

With the drawing he had made beside her, as a talisman perhaps, she began to draw her memories: she began to draw her life.

She acquired some proper paper, she acquired some more charcoal. In the attic room while the other girls slept she sat on her small lumpy mattress and heard mice scurrying and drew, by candlelight, the faces of all the people she had lost from her life, all the people who had gone. She drew them as she remembered them: her mother's petulance and disappointment; her father's rum-soaked eyes – she surprised herself as she caught a slightly shifty look in his face, the eyes slid away, did not look openly, just like Tobias. Her own lip turned down sulkily as she drew her two sisters, their petulance echoing their mother's; she drew her brother Philip's seductive smile: all that charm and good fellowship, the eyes that laughed and charmed, and laughed again. She drew her two younger brothers fighting: quick strokes. She saw at once that that drawing was bad – her brothers looked more like animals than little boys, she was unable to catch their bodies and their fierce, remembered battles, she rubbed at the charcoal marks and – suddenly – she was weeping. Big silent tears fell down her face, on and on, Tobias disappeared for ever and Ezekiel dead before he was twelve; once long ago, thin, dark Tobias, a black-eyed beanstalk, had carefully brought her the red rose he had acquired from somebody else's garden for her to make a colour. Tears fell upon the paper and she did not understand from whence they might have come, she had not properly cried for many years and she saw her Father, and the cart of bodies clattering away from her.

She rubbed away the tears, she rubbed away the charcoal, she found another paper, she started again at the boys' faces, caught something then in their expressions as they fought: vicious: half-fun, half-anger: Tobias and Ezekiel Marshall, her brothers. Long into the night she opened her heart and drew, and re-drew the remembered contents, and outside drunken voices laughed and sang:

> *Three blind mice*
> *See how they run*
> *They all ran after the farmer's wife*
> *Who cut off their tails with a carving knife.*

and she wished she had a carving knife herself: she would wear it at her waist – like a pirate.

Grace Marshall became herself again, and therefore infinitely more of a tribulation to Mrs Falls the milliner. With a charcoal or a chalk in her hand Grace remembered at last who she was. She drew half the night away. She used up all the paper she could find. She stole paper from shops. One day she found a marker in the sewing basement and tried surreptitiously to capture Mrs Falls' rather fat eyes on her own small thumbnail and began to laugh, biting her lip and looking demure when Mrs Falls looked at her rather severely. She then drew the face of Mrs Falls on the underneath of the table in the attic room and it was only because the walls of the attic sloped so sharply that she was not able to draw Mrs Falls there as well. She even, with a kind of unstoppable wild energy, began to draw faces of gamblers on the blank walls at the back of the milliner's house that adjoined a baker: she would ignore the nearby cesspit and smell the fresh bread and remember the faces as the sun rose, if the sun rose, and then she drew the vintner's son and Venus, smiling together. Mrs Falls at first expostulated but there was something unstoppable now about her assistant: she drew as if she was half-mad.

'That Scrape-grace!' Mrs Falls would say, laughing slightly at her own humour.

Grace drew on.

She stopped haunting the quays.

'I should prefer it if she drew Flowers,' said Mrs Falls, sniffing, but she left the girl alone, she was the best assistant she had, and what was it to her if charcoal faces lay upon the back wall of the house where nobody saw?

One early morning Grace drew someone she did not know: it seemed to be a girl of about her own age who just came into her head. The girl was quite clearly there, in charcoal, on the wall of the back of the house. It was still early: Grace sat beside the girl she had drawn as the early sun appeared between the tight buildings.

'Do you smell the bread from the Bakery?' said Grace, ignoring as usual the smell from the cesspit.

She half-thought she heard the girl drawn on the wall say *Yes*.

Next morning when Grace returned to the yard the girl was still there.

'I'm glad you are here,' said Grace and again, as the sun appeared at the corner of the building, the smell of fresh bread rose from the bakery and Grace sat beside the charcoal girl and felt content: a tiny oasis of real happiness. *I have a friend*.

'What is your name?' she asked on the third day.

Did the girl say *Mary-Ann*?

Grace hummed slightly as she sewed hats in the basement of the milliner that day: she had a friend, a friend called Mary-Ann.

On the fourth day it rained and rained and rained. Grace ducked out into the yard, tried to see through the rain if Mary-Ann was still there. She lay awake that night listening to the heavy water cascading. When next morning the rain had stopped she rushed out to the stinking, overflowing muddy yard. The girl who may have been called Mary-Ann was gone, black wet smudges of charcoal were all that was left. And no matter how hard Grace tried, how insistently she drew on the wall, Mary-Ann did not return to the yard by the bakery.

Grace slowly began to draw the children in the streets, the old sailors down by the quays and finally, quick sketches, the other assistants. Mr Wm Hogarth had indeed been correct: it was easier to have the face *there*. She would draw, and then rub out her charcoal and draw over again, trying to get faces right. The assistants stared over her shoulder in amazement as they saw themselves;

one of them gave Grace an apple. After some time Grace also began to draw the women who came to try on the elaborate fruit-decorated straw hats over their lace caps, and haggle at the prices. One day she even tried to draw Romeo and Juliet. Shakespeare made word-pictures, the vicar had said; *this is my word-picture, but I have drawn it.* Juliet looked perhaps a little like her imaginary friend Mary-Anne, but she could not draw a Romeo that she would cut out in stars in the sky: she could not see him properly. She thought of the sailor she had noticed and the girl on the quay weeping with the tears falling on the baby's hair; she drew them instead and one of the assistants said in awe, 'Is that the Holy Family?' Mrs Falls, despite her strangely decorated backyard walls, continued to find Grace a good worker, although possessed now (Mrs Falls sometimes thought) of some demon. Some kindness for the strange orphan girl meant she once or twice provided proper drawing paper, for this scribbling, surely, was better than the haunting of the docks and the ships as if Grace Marshall was a street-girl. The precious, precious drawings of her family Grace kept under her small mattress: her only treasures. She would take them out in the night and smooth the faces very carefully, very gently under her hands, as if they were gold.

And all the time, Grace Marshall drew and drew all the faces around her, trying to catch them, hold them, as if her very life depended on it, as perhaps indeed it did.

THREE

One early morning there was a loud, brisk knock at the door of Mrs Falls' premises, at the top of Christmas Steps.

Mrs Falls, huffing up from the basement, complained bitterly on every stair: customers only called in the afternoon. 'In faith, I suppose it will be one of those hopeless street-girls with no References, thinking she could make my Hats!'

Breathing heavily she opened the door.

'*Buongiorno, Signora.*'

There a foreign gentleman stood. She looked at him most suspiciously, but found herself somewhat overcome by the exquisite smile and the wonderful eyes of a man who wore a fashionable wig, had a long embroidered waistcoat of impeccable worth and the latest wide turn-back cuffs on his jacket. There was much expensive lace at his throat, and he kissed her fat hand, and made a deep and elegant bow.

'*Buongiorno, Signora,*' he said again.

The suspicions of Mrs Falls the milliner intensified when she heard his request: that he would like to see Miss Grace Marshall. Grace, now fifteen, was reluctantly called for from the workroom.

'*Goddam!*' she said, seeing the visitor, shocking both the visitor and Mrs Falls.

'*Buongiorno*, Signorina Marshall,' said the foreign gentleman.

Of course she recognised him at once but something in his eyes and his manner gave her absolute warning: *say nothing*. But why-ever was he talking in that manner and waving his arms about? She was so completely stunned that she did, indeed, remain silent. '*Signorina bella*, I am Filipo di Vecellio, *il amigo* – that is – a friend of your Brother, who 'as sadly – I am so sorry – passed away.' Grace Marshall looked at her brother standing there perfectly alive, in total incomprehension. Philip was wearing a wonderfully curled short wig that Bristol men were not yet seen in, and elegant clothes, and had shining buckles on his shoes. Under his arm, with impeccable, fashionable insouciance, he carried a fine, gorgeous hat.

'I have 'ere, *Signorina*' (she wanted to laugh aloud at his ridiculous manner of speaking) 'a letter from your Brother asking me to take you to London where, as you of course know, you 'ave a respectable Aunt to whom you shall become a Companion, *una compadre*. It was your late Brother's wish *assolutamente*.' As he brought forth papers with a flourish his sister stared on in astonishment.

Mrs Falls looked most indignant. She had never heard of a respectable aunt, indeed there was a complete lack of respectable aunts in the girl's family. 'She is indentured to me!' she said angrily. She did not want to lose her best hatter.

'Acquire your *bagalio* – that is your belongings, Senora Marshall – for we leave at once.' And while Grace scampered up to the attic the foreigner turned again to the milliner. '*Mi dispace, Senora*. The *signorina* was indentured for three years only, and you 'ave 'ad 'er for almost five! I 'ave 'er Brother's Signature, and your own. She is to come with me *pronto, multo pronto, assolutamente*.'

'There will be no payment for a broken Contract with no Notice!' Mrs Falls was frantic.

'I think there is no need of your Money, Signora Falls, and I think you 'ave 'ad a good Bargain.'

Grace, like the wind, passed **Gin Lane** and **Beer Street** for the last time, clutching all she had in her world which included her one treasure: her drawings of their family.

'Goodbye, Mrs Falls!'

'*Arrivederci*, Signora Falls!'

And the foreigner and the girl were gone.

*

There was a small closed chaise for their comfort and privacy; he had it waiting, attended by postboys, by the Olde Hatchet Inn beside Frog Lane: Grace could not believe her eyes when he handed her into it. Philip sat back, laughing – tears literally pouring down his face at the bewilderment of his sister. (And perhaps one tear was for the finding, after all, of his little sister Grace, for whom he had promised to return.)

'You look thin,' he said. 'I should like my sister to perhaps have more shape!' He was teasing her. 'But your face!' He wiped at the tears. 'Your disbelieving face! *Bella, bella,* I told you I would come back. You are to be my housekeeper. I have taken an address in London.' Still he kept up his incongruous, foreign, arm-waving manner, spoke in the ridiculous voice; still she stared, clutching her small bag. The chaise left Bristol, bounced over terrible rutted roads as it turned towards London. She had never been outside Bristol in her life: had heard of course of frightful danger, and pistols on journeys.

'Shall we encounter Highwaymen?' These were the first words she uttered to her long-lost brother.

But Philip showed no concern for any dangers. 'I have a Cudgel,' he said nonchalantly, and seeing her alarm, he added, 'One never travels anywhere without being armed, *cara mia,* and when darkness falls you will see that I have been prudent enough to choose the time of a full Moon for our travel.' He laughed again at her astounded confused face as the carriage rattled along the London road.

And then at last she found her tongue. 'Philip! Where were you?' she cried out to him, and she suddenly leaned across in the carriage and grabbed at both his arms, the way she used to do as a child. 'You left me too long!' Almost she punched him: she felt anger in her throat, like bile.

'I have come back for you,' he said reasonably, extricating himself firmly. 'Listen, *bella mia.* I could not come back. I was learning everything on that Tour, I went everywhere; I saw Venice, I saw the Frescoes of Rome, the magnificent Gallery in Florence. I have been to Amsterdam – I know everything! English Painters are nothing, we have nothing like Titian or Michelangelo or Rubens or Rembrandt.'

Venice. Titian: words she had heard. But she did not understand him. 'When did you return?' They had to speak all the time with raised voices, above the rattling and shaking of the chaise.

'Perhaps two years ago –' he saw her outraged face. 'Listen, *cara mia*, it was most necessary that I establish myself first. I have worked very, very hard – and I have become very, very successful, as you will soon understand. But I promised to come back for you and here I am. I need you, you are to become my housekeeper! You might smile, at the very least!'

She stared at him, her chin held very high. She was certainly not going to be a housekeeper. 'Why do you talk in that funny way?'

'Grace, listen. I have – this is the point *cara mia*, listen very, *very* carefully – I have transformed myself into an Italian Artist of noble blood.' She still could not understand him. 'When I left you I journeyed with my companion all around Europe: Bruges, Paris, Austria, the Netherlands, Switzerland. But the centre of Art is Italy. Ah – you should have seen me in Rome, wandering about among ancient ruins. Everywhere you turn in Rome, Grace, History is upon you, it is *meraviglioso*; *Roma meravigliosa!* I spent months – years – copying Old Masters, copying Michelangelo, learning of Classical Form. My companion returned to Bristol after a year – but not me, I did not want ever to see Bristol again! I determined to stay on in Italy but I ran out of money – so I drew the faces of people for my living, on the streets and *piazzas* of Rome!' His words tumbled out in a kind of glee. 'And my poverty was a Blessing, *cara mia*, a fortuitous Blessing for I found out how good I was at faces and I had my most important Education of all, the Education of a real Italian. My dark eyes, my dark hair: people thought I was Italian, of course they did. I stayed on there for over a year, copying, studying, listening, and there – like a wonderful, divine Message from the Lord above you might say – the idea came to me that I should change myself into Another! I look like an Italian, I speak Italian like a native they say. And all the Artistic Education in this country comes from Italy: from Rome itself, from the Vatican, from Florence, from the *Uffizi*,' (She had no idea what he was speaking about) 'Italy is the history of Art!'

So great was her confusion at his words that now she did not speak, not a word.

'And I made money and I charmed the ladies and I was invited to Italian *conversazziones* where cultivated ladies and gentlemen speak together of the World in a sophisticated manner that our noble family could never even dream of.' And she saw how proud of himself he was. 'I learned to converse in the manner of Italian gentlemen, just as I learned about Art! And then, when I was completely confident, I came back to London and presented myself up as an Italian Painter – Filipo di Vecellio – there are a few foreign Painters and Sculptors and Engravers in London, so it was easy! Nobody in London had ever heard of me, of course, so I could become anybody I wished. I said I was from Florence, always just hinting that my Father was a Florentine Nobleman about whom I did not wish to speak.'

Her dark, fifteen-year-old eyes were wider now, like saucers. But suddenly out of the blue she cried, 'Wait! Philip, stop!' And she leaned out of the coach and shouted, 'Stop!' with such loudness and authority that the driver did so.

'What is it?' Philip was astonished.

'We have forgot Tobias! He will come back to Bristol! He will not know where we have gone!'

'Has he ever returned?'

'No, but one day he will.'

Philip gave her an odd look. 'Drive on, man!' he shouted and the coach rattled off again. 'Tobias can look after himself, he is a man now with his own Life, he will not be running back to Bristol.'

'But we are all he has.'

'Nonsense. He is a thief and a ragamuffin and he has the World now. That is quite enough.' And then Philip went on talking as if he had not been interrupted, 'Grace you cannot imagine the money in London, London is *rich*! I paint Portraits and my Clients are *rich*! Rich in a way you cannot begin to imagine. I am making Money, Money, *Money*! You have to understand, *bella mia*, that London is now the centre of the World, it is flowing with money – and money, for an Artist, is in Portraits. I soon presented myself to the newly-rich tradespeople in London; they are just like the fellows I painted in Bristol.'

He hardly paused for breath, the words poured out of him now as if they had been dammed up, waiting for a chance to be told. 'These people want to look sophisticated, all these tradespeople, they want –' he was grabbing now for words, '– the Style and the Sensibilities that they are trying to cultivate in their lives to *show in their Portraits*. My Portraits create them as Cultured People. And most of all they are impressed that I am a Foreigner, whom, they assume, has some spiritual connection to the Old Masters, and who therefore will make them look wonderful!' On and on, the words tumbled out over the little sister he had found again. The little sister herself sat, stunned.

'First I took rooms in Brook Street with a woman I was told of, Miss Ann Ffoulks. I chose her carefully as my landlady because I knew she was acquainted with other Artists in London: she had a brother who was an Artist but he died. I suppose the other Artists kept up a Friendship with her out of pity. Miss Ffoulks is that sort of English lady who could never tell a Lie, so if she thought I was Italian others would believe I was an Italian because Miss Ffoulks said so! She knows nothing of my real past, of course (even though she is a vain old Personage who thinks she knows everything!), and she has been of much use to me. Through her I obtained my first introductions into the Art World, I met other Painters, English Painters and they accepted me for what Miss Ffoulks introduced me as – an Italian Painter from Florence, *Filipo di Vecellio!*' And he clapped his hands together in the coach suddenly and bowed to her, as if he had just performed a magic trick.

'So, I had already begun to find Clients but I required an Art Dealer to speak of me in the World, to get me more and more Commissions, and again it was Miss Ffoulks who introduced me. My Dealer is rich and powerful, James Burke, he knows nothing of my past either; they all believe I am Italian, and – listen to me, Grace – some of my sitters are now from further up the social scale. Noblemen begin to hear of my skills thanks to James Burke, my prices are rising, and now we have begun to receive *very large sums* for anything I paint. Indeed one day I hope to manage without a Dealer – for why should he obtain much of my money? I am become a Hero in London, *cara mia*, as you will soon see! They all want beautiful, flattering Portraits for their Birthdays, Portraits for their Weddings, even Portraits for their Funerals sometimes! They all yearn to be painted looking Cultured. The man Canaletto understood: he came from Venice and painted the Thames to look not like London but like Venice and they loved him! Most of the other Face-Painters are common men, and English – listen to me Grace, listen – the whole point is I am become one of the most successful

Portraitists in London! Mr Hogarth is furious, he calls me a "phizzmonger".'

'Mr Hogarth?'

Her brother lay back, gleeful, on the carriage seat. 'Phizzmonger! That is his dismissive word for Face-Painter. Let him be dismissive then! You will not have heard of him of course . . . *Dio Mio!* There will be much for you to learn if you are to join an Artist's Household, *bella mia*. And—'

'But Mr Hogarth—'

'William Hogarth is an English Painter, and he is well-known, certainly, but more for his caricatures than his Portraits: *A Rake's Progress* indeed! *Gin Lane*! You would not think we were painting in the same city, he and I! And his actual Portraits are bad: they are real in the *wrong* way, for there is a way of painting a Face and Mr Hogarth does not understand that. His skill is to paint an exact Likeness – anyone can do that, I say. It is to make people look *noble* that is the Art.'

'But Philip, Mr Hogarth—'

'He is a Painter falling and I am a Painter rising in the London Art World. All my sitters emerge from my Studio with a kind of nobility about them – even should they be merely an Apothecary. *That is why I earn so much Money.* Mr Hogarth is a fool: he paints an Apothecary to look like an Apothecary. And he is fractious to boot, and involves himself in Politics; he is forever suggesting a Society of Artists should be formed where all Artists are equal! Ha! I certainly do not want to be 'equal' to all the unsuccessful Artists of England, after all my strenuous activities! And who would want to be painted by the rancorous, argumentative Mr Hogarth when they can be painted by the accomplished nobleman from the European tradition, Filipo di Vecellio? I am already earning guineas beyond my wildest Dreams and I would never have received all the Commissions – believe me, Grace – if I came from Bristol.'

'You do come from Bristol.' The coach veered dangerously, a wheel caught in a rut. The brother and sister, falling sideways, hardly noticed.

'No, *bella mia*. I am Filipo di Vecellio from Florence and, I repeat, both the Nobility and the Apothecaries – for I do not discern, I will paint anybody who can afford me – think their Portraits are being painted by an elegant, talented, noble Italian soaked in the Classical

Tradition!' And Philip's eyes danced again with laughter and he sat back again in the coach, a satisfied man who had found his destiny – and incidentally his sister also. Grace felt dizzy: the rattling, swaying coach, or so much conversation, or so many emotions in half a day. 'But, Philip – you do come from Bristol,' she insistently repeated, for he was denying their past; she saw him in her head declaiming in the Bristol Public Library, and the words came out, right there in the coach, almost without her meaning them to: '*Cry God for Harry! England and St George!*'

He looked at her for a moment, and then his expression changed completely.

'Listen, Grace,' he said coldly, 'I see that you have no idea what I am talking of.' Quite suddenly his eyes were very hard, a new look that at once jolted her. 'I know a man who paints sky and clouds by the yard. He sits in his attic in London and that is what he does – day in, day out – and people buy his sky, by the yard, to place about their chimneys as Decoration. He is not a bad Painter but he comes from Newcastle. If it was known I came from Bristol I might be painting sky by the yard also. I understand what my Sitters want because *it is what I want*: to rise upwards. *That* is why I am so successful. And that is why you must realise how infinitely lucky you are.' The eyes were hard and the voice was hard. She stared at this stranger; it was as if her brother had disappeared and she sat before a stranger in a jolting, swaying carriage. She abruptly remembered his sudden, long-ago rages.

'Mr Joshua Reynolds, an Englishman, cannot command custom in the way I can; one day soon I expect to paint Royalty.'

She felt another question was expected. 'Who is Mr Joshua Reynolds?'

He shrugged dismissively. 'He is one of the Painters of the day to whom Miss Ffoulks introduced me. He returned to London from his Grand Tour long before I did, talking of nothing but Michelangelo! Ever since he painted a *shipwreck* in a Portrait he was spoken of – hah! – but I earn more money. He is not exactly a gentleman, there I have it over him.' Again she stared across the clattering coach at this new Philip. 'And he is a fool: forever speaking of the importance of Historical Art and Epic Art and Michelangelo. He speaks of painting Religious stories and Historical stories – Noble Visions, he calls them – but Noble Visions are not seen in Guineas. People want to look at *themselves* hanging on their walls, not an embodiment of Virtue, or Courage, or our Lord! And believe me, it is not always so simple to make them look cultured: I often have to paint common men who have hair in their noses and in their ears, and ladies who stink, with pimples on their faces! And horrible, ugly, spoilt little children. But I make them all look so fine – that is what I am paid for. As I say, be aware, Grace, how lucky you are.'

But she did not speak. She did not thank him. He leaned forward.

'Grace. This is not a game. You are not joining me in some jovial Prank. I will tell it to you plain just once more.' And here it was still, something sharp and cold and different. 'I have completely changed my Life and my Expectations. I am a very, very successful Artist in London, and I have come back for you, as I promised, and you too will have to change. You are to be my housekeeper and my hostess. I have just now taken a house in St Martin's Lane, a decent-sized house to set me above other Artists, larger than William Hogarth's house nearby and Joshua Reynolds' house nearby. I must have the most elegant Establishment – for the irony of my story is, as I told you, that I am now beginning to paint the real Nobility, as well as those who strive for Nobility, and I cannot ask the real Nobility to visit a Studio in the slums.

'And the other important matter is: I now wish to entertain, for a successful Artist must entertain. You will be charming to my guests. I want people sitting at my dinner table talking of the latest developments in Art and I am ready to pay for it. There are two people to whom I wish you to give particular Attention. One is the Dealer, James Burke, whom I have mentioned. The other is in his way even more important: Mr Hartley Pond. He is a very, very powerful Art Critic in London, steeped in Classical Knowledge and Old Masters, and he knows more about European Art than anybody else in this country. He supports me because he thinks I am Italian and I need his support absolutely. If he knew I was from Bristol he would cut me dead.'

Large, dark eyes stared at him across the coach.

And then: then it was as if he suddenly caught himself, heard his own tone. And his eyes softened at last, and he laughed again in his old charming way and again he sat back in the carriage, delighted with the world – and indeed with seeing his little sister after so long, for he remembered her fondly with her enquiring eyes and quickness to learn and her eternal questions! 'Oh London, London!' His enthusiasm burst forth once more and his own dark eyes that she remembered so well sparkled, no sign of hardness there now, and suddenly (reminding her of their father) he dropped his Italian accent completely for a moment and began to sing.

> *O London is a dainty place*
> *A great and gallant City,*
> *For all the streets are paved with Gold*
> *And all the folks are witty!*

'Are they?' said Grace in alarm, finding her voice again at last.

'But when we begin our entertaining *we* will be the witty ones: The fascinating Foreigners! London is ours! We shall have a wonderful life, Grace. We shall take a Golden Coach across London Bridge! People will clamour to dine with us. We shall be rich beyond our wildest Dreams!' And he laughed aloud, at life, at his own cleverness, at the world. 'Oh Grace, London is a place where, if you seize Life by the throat, there is Fame to be acquired and there are Fortunes to be made and I have already started to make mine. And now you are free to assist me, do you not realise?' And then at last Philip Marshall looked at his little sister very carefully, just for a moment, gave her his whole attention for the very first time: the thin face and body, the figure of a child not yet a woman, the shabby clothes. He had expected perhaps more immediate gratitude for his actions.

And Grace Marshall in that same exact moment looked at her brother carefully; many, many thoughts raced through her head as she teetered on the brink of her new life. Her beloved brother was alive; she could learn so much from him, he could teach her, as he taught her to read long ago. She clutched her bag that held her precious drawings as she stared at him in his modern wig and his wonderful waistcoat. She would talk of his ludicrous ideas about housekeepers and hostesses later – anyone could do that, but not just anyone could paint. There would be so much that she could learn: she was to join the world of the artist after all, her greatest, greatest dream. She saw herself and Mr Hogarth in the church, her talk of studios and Shining – and here was Philip, shining indeed. Her thoughts twirled and danced and then, at last, exploded.

'Oh Philip!' she cried, 'I am so, so glad to see you! I missed you so much, I was so lonely for so long, I thought you had forgotten to come back for me . . .' And she stopped, overcome for a moment, and he felt quite moved himself. And then she said again, oddly painful, 'I missed you very much.' In the first gesture of real intimacy she had made to any person since he had sailed away all those years ago, she put her hand to his face at last, felt the warmth. And at that moment, her hand at her brother's face, she felt an old, lost feeling: joy and laughter bubbling up somewhere inside her as it used to so easily, long ago.

'There is just one more matter,' said Philip, but he laid his hand tenderly upon her own, in a gesture of affection also.

'What more can there be than this?'

'Obviously you must become an Italian.'

She pulled her hand away: he saw her amazed face. 'But Philip, I cannot, I have not travelled like you, I know nothing of Italians or Italy!'

'But you have dark eyes like me, *bella!* You must learn – you cannot be my sister in public until you have grasped the essentials of Italian. You, of course, can be my shy Italian sister if you please—'

'I am not shy!'

'If you please, I said. But you *must* be Italian. And you must dress with –' he paused, not wanting to be unkind, '– more Style than you have at present.' (She put her scuffed shoes underneath her shabby skirt in embarrassment.) 'I have told all my Acquaintances that my very beautiful sister – you are a little thin but I am sure that will change – my very beautiful sister is arriving from Florence.' And again in the rattling coach he clapped his hands like a magician presenting magic: '*The Signorina Francesca di Vecellio!*'

'*Francesca*?' She said the name as if she was spitting and then she did laugh at last, at the ludicrousness of it all, at the excitement, and she laughed the way he remembered (startling him with a memory of a merry, urgent, spinning girl who had painted green daisies and been filled with mirth by the outrage of seagulls); her face suddenly became suffused with uncontrollable laughter and how should he know, so far away, how long it had been since she had laughed that way? 'This is all absolutely *unbelievable*!' she said, and her eyes were shining.

'How much can you earn as a milliner?'

Still laughing: 'I was receiving five guineas for a year, and my board.' She did not say she had spent almost all of it on paper, and chalk, and pencils.

'I already earn much, much more than that with one Portrait, *Francesca*! I earn more than the famous Mr Reynolds – he charges twelve guineas, but I charge thirteen.'

'*Thirteen guineas*?' She stared. 'For just one Portrait?

'Thirteen, and I am sure I earn more than the Purveyor-of-English-Art, Mr Hogarth! I tell you we shall be rich – rich just as our Mother required!' And at last they laughed together, like conspirators, there in the coach, although neither understood at all what the other was thinking.

Then his face became more serious. 'But I mean it: you must learn to copy how I speak in every way, Signorina Francesca di Vecellio. You are the sister of an Italian Gentleman and noble blood courses through our veins! You must listen to me, and copy me. And there is an Italian Chapel in London where you must go and observe. You must watch the people going into the Chapel. They are Italian. You are Italian.' He amended. 'Of course, it is not a good idea to go *inside* the Church very often. We do not want people to think we are Popish: we are a branch of Italians who gave up the Pope long ago.'

She looked so bewildered at this that he laughed again. 'There is much to learn, *Francesca mia*!'

'But I want still to be myself, Philip. Let me be Grace!' She spoke most stubbornly. 'My name is Grace. Grace Marshall.'

'No, I have told you.' He looked at her. She looked at him. 'Not Grace,' he said firmly, 'it is too solid and too English. You are Grace no longer. We hope that you will soon grow into a fine young woman from Italy: *Francesca. Signorina Francesca di Vecellio.*'

She tried the name again tentatively. '*Francesca.*' Despite herself she felt something like excitement in her chest. '*Signorina Francesca di Vecellio.*' And this time she rolled the words around her tongue.

'Copy me: *Buongiorno Signore*,' he said very carefully.

'*Buongiorno Signore*. What does it mean?'

'It is how you greet a Gentleman. It is really the only thing you must be certain of immediately. Oh, and "thank you": *Grazie*.'

'*Grazie*.'

'*Arrivederci*. That is goodbye. If anything gets too difficult, you merely just say *arrivederci* and curtsey and disappear. You will be charming.'

It was easy. '*Grazie, Signore. Arrivederci*.' Her eyes sparkled at him and then she suddenly clapped her hands together also and gave a little bow, as if she too was a magic person.

'Yes!' he said, pleased with her already, remembering again how quickly she could learn. 'Yes! We will manage. We will manage easily. And Grace, the whole thing is – *I have done it!*'

'Done what?'

'I am a famous Artist!' he crowed.

And I will be an Artist too, she thought, and her huge dark eyes gleamed like bright stars in the carriage evening.

They spent the night at a rollicking inn outside Swindon: the best rooms, and roasted duck, and a bottle of French wine which Grace sipped gingerly. She lay awake for most of the night; around and around her head spun all the things that had happened since the foreigner knocked on the door of Mrs Falls that morning, mixing in her head with the unaccustomed wine and the light from the full moon that he had promised shining directly in at her window. She got up finally from the tall wide bed in the large room, so unlike the room at the top of Christmas Steps; she unrolled her precious drawings in charcoal: their father, their mother, their brothers, their sisters – all dead but Tobias, but caught in memory, there with her in the moonlight. *But I will think how to leave a message in Bristol for Tobias, if Tobias comes back he must not be left alone*. And a painting of Philip himself, the handsome brother she thought she had lost, and something there of the devil in his eye that she had always remembered. But – there was something else there now. Something different. *A stone in his eyes*. She stared for a long time at her drawings, in the moonlight.

Underneath all her portraits was the drawing: **Grace. Fourteen years. Bristol.** And the extraordinary signature. **Wm Hogarth.**

She kept waiting, as they bowled next day towards the big city of London, for a moment to unroll the pictures again, now, in the carriage, but Philip spoke on and on, still like an unleashed dam. He explained again, over and over in delight: his adventures, his life, his success, his plans. By the time they reached the outskirts of the metropolis – the roads more crowded now, more carriages and coaches on their way into London – he was asleep: alone she saw the balloon of smoke that heralded the city. Then she saw the city itself emerge through the smoke from the seacoal: the houses, the churches, the palaces, the rubbish, the river, the people; at Tyburn, at dusk, she saw gallows and crowds: she could not speak, she clutched her small bag.

And her brother's song danced round her head.

> *O London is a dainty place*
> *A great and gallant City,*
> *For all the streets are paved with Gold*
> *And all the folks are witty!*

and she clasped her thin hands together and smiled at her sleeping brother and she hoped most fervently that she might get a little plumper as he desired, and learn to be witty also, as she became an Artist.

PART TWO

1760

FOUR

The Signorina Francesca di Vecellio (that is, Grace Marshall), so recently arrived in London, was absolutely terrified to open her mouth, in case someone shouted, 'Fraud! You come from Bristol!' and all her brother's careful artifice lost.

He took her at once to a Ladies' Outfitters in the busy, bustling, exciting Strand, where decorated shop-windows and colourful swinging shop-signs advertised their wares; She was to have three gowns: a grey working one for her duties as a housekeeper but the one for best was made of pale cream embroidered silk, and a beautiful silk fan to match. Side hoops were fashionable still but much smaller and more malleable now, so that petticoats rustled prettily beneath; still the embroidered stomacher and the tight, low-cut bodice, and the lace cap upon her long, coiled, hair.

'You will be in charge of the house and the servants,' said Philip. 'You will learn to buy the food—'

'But Philip, I do not know how!'

'I know how. I will teach you,' (she looked at this new Philip in amazement) 'and you and the cook will decide each day what to feed the guests I shall begin to invite here.' Her face showed bafflement and trepidation: surely he knew she was not a housekeeper? Nor had she any desire to learn that art. But everything was so new, so different, so strange; still stunned at the change suddenly to her life she was, for the moment, inarticulate.

He presented her to the house in St Martin's Lane, of which, he said, alarming her immensely, she was to be in charge: a pleasant house of four storeys, attic rooms at the back of the house for servants, and a room facing the Lane, also at the top of the house, just for her. There was a large dining-room, and a drawing-room. There was a kitchen in the basement. Philip employed a kitchen-maid, a housemaid, a manservant and a cook: in embarrassment the Italian sister spoke hardly a word, her eyes showed her panic: what had she ever learned of housekeeping in Bristol? The housemaid, Euphemia, was about her own age and the two young girls observed each other warily: Grace so thin and dark in her demure grey working-dress and her white lace lady's cap, the maid plump and fair with her mob cap on her unruly hair, and prone to giggling.

And then Grace entered a magical, enchanted fairyland: her brother's studio.

It took up almost the whole of one of the floors of the house. Her brother could not help but laugh at her, at the way her nose twitched almost like a terrier: smelling the paints, and the oils, and the Turpentine (for these were smells of memory to her: her father's little studio room downstairs in Queen's Square). Large and small portraits on all the walls, some by her brother she at once understood, but other paintings in different styles. Piles of canvases and bare boards were stacked in corners. There were colours in cabinets, wrapped in little parcels. There were large and smaller brushes on trays on a big bench, bottles of oil: walnut, linseed. There were rags and towels and pitchers of water and bottles of Turpentine. He showed her packets of something he named *size*, a kind of flour, that was mixed with water to paint over the new canvases so that paint would not leak through. And in the middle of the studio with its big windows facing the best light, there stood a large wooden easel. A canvas was stretched over a frame made of wood, 'That frame is a *stretcher*,' said Philip, and the stretched canvas on the frame stood on the easel. And there on the canvas was a half-finished portrait of a man who seemed to be – from his clothes, from the way he looked – a nobleman: an unfinished nobleman. Beside the easel lay a wooden plate of colours with a hole for his thumb – he showed her how he held it – the plate was called a *palette*. A palette and a small palette knife beside: many wondrous colours lay there like an exuberant rainbow, mixed, un-mixed, bright, dark: thrilling.

'It is the most beautiful place I have ever seen in my whole, whole life,' she whispered so that he may or may not have heard her; her fifteen-year-old face was suffused with wonder. For the first time she was seeing a real artist's studio: it was everything she had dreamed of. Her heart was beating so fast she could not say anything else. And a new thought came:

I must not, yet, tell him of my own Drawing.

I must learn more first.

She stared at the painting on the easel. *I know nothing about paint and colours. I seem to be able to draw a face but I have only used charcoal.* She looked about her brother's studio in awe. *I need to first understand how little I know. There is very, very much for me to learn.*

Not for one single moment however did she doubt her path and her calling: her hands tingled to hold one of the brushes. She looked around the studio, breathed the scents and the smells into her very soul, and knew: this was to be her life.

At night, from the window at the top of the house, she looked out on this new city, saw London flickering and dancing down St Martin's Lane. Swirling dark mists came down often, yet some nights stars shone like small lamps above her. Once she quietly took out her paper and her charcoal and in the light of her candle quickly drew the servants as she remembered them: the maid Euphemia's face was upturned and smiling. Every new night, with her precious small bag beside her, she lay in her new bed in her new room and heard the night-watchmen calling the hour as they made their slow way about the London streets: 'Three of the morning,' they would call, and, 'All's well.' And she thought to herself, *yes, yes all is well. I shall learn, I shall learn everything from my brother, and then, at last, I shall be an Artist, just as he is, the two of us, together, shining just as I said*, and new happiness almost overwhelmed her.

She curtseyed to the handsome gentleman her brother introduced her to, her cheeks flushed. '*Buongiorno*, Signore Burke,' she said, and he bent to her hand and smiled.

She must not make a mistake: she must sound right. This was the rich, important art dealer, her brother's art dealer, Mr James Burke: a tall handsome gentleman with a direct gaze and beautiful grey eyes. Mr James Burke did not wear a wig but wore his own hair tied back, in the fashion of sailors, so lightly powdered as to be almost its own colour. 'He may look like a Highwayman,' said her brother, 'but he is the most powerful person in my life! He arranges for me to meet all sorts of interesting and wealthy people – and he explains to them that I am the best Portrait Painter in the Town. He is one of the most important men in London and I do assure you that he makes more money than I do!'

'I am, after all, merely a Dealer in Art, *Signorina*,' said Mr Burke dryly. 'It is your Brother who is the Artist,' and he smiled at her again with the direct grey eyes.

Her brother laughed. 'I tell you he is powerful, *bella*! Dealers are the rich men, they are the Treasure Hunters – it is we, the Artists, who are the Workers.' Mr James Burke, although a little older perhaps than her brother, seemed young still to be the rich and powerful man her brother described. But she saw very quickly that the two were great friends: two charming, handsome men whose heads were often close together in business discussions, the short white fashionable wig and the soft, tied-back, dark hair. *I wonder if one day I could draw them, sitting together like that and talking?* She wondered if they knew how beautiful they looked. *I would name the Painting 'Friends'.* Mr Burke was continually at the house: looking at portraits, counting commissions and money as his grey eyes flashed, taking some of the paintings away, bringing new clients to the studio in St Martin's Lane.

But when James Burke had gone Philip said, 'In truth, he is the *second* most powerful person in my life. Soon you will meet Mr Hartley Pond, the Critic, of whom I have spoken. You will be silent, and curtsey to him, and listen to his Opinions, for he is a terrifyingly influential man indeed, and can make or break a Painter's career!'

On her third day in London an elegant young man addressed her in the hallway for some time, in only Italian; she blushed scarlet, managed *Arrivederci Signore*, curtseyed and smiled, blushed – and ran. The elegant young man was charmed and her brother made it known that his sister, newly-arrived in England, was most painfully reserved.

'I am not reserved, Philip, I am terrified!' she cried to her brother as soon as they were alone. 'They will *know*! How could they not know?'

'They are not Italian, *cara mia*,' he answered her patiently. 'He was not an Italian, he was showing off. I am careful to arrange that we do not mix socially with any Italians. And you must not be so loud, *bella*, Ladies are never loud.' Yet he could not help smiling at his earnest little sister. 'And you must refrain at all times from calling me Philip. Ever again. Remember that I am Signore Filipo di Vecellio, from Florence, Italy.'

She took his arms with both her hands. 'But I am not Italian! You know very well I have never been to Italy – I fear I will betray you.'

'Listen to me,' he commanded. 'Copy me! I speak Italian like a native – it is absolutely necessary to our plans that you speak very much as I do. And your English must be accented also, as mine is. I am relying on you.'

Immediately then she repeated after him Italian words and English words, over and over and over. Hour after hour she practised, following him about the house in St Martin's Lane, sitting in a corner of his studio, talking more and more, faster and faster, at last enjoying it, enjoying the music of the sounds. '*Buongiorno Signore*,' she cried when they were alone, waving her arms, dancing about him, '*doce vita, pardona*.' '*Buona notte, Filipo mio*.' '*Francesca di Vecellio. Si! Si, si!* I can do it! I can do it! *Si*. I am Grace Marshall from Bristol and I can even speak English like an Italian!'

He was pleased with her, for who would not be charmed by all that enthusiasm and anxiety and curiosity and laughter? But he also shook his head. 'As I have already informed you, Francesca *mia*,' he said, 'Ladies do not laugh loudly, or make as much noise as you! As you well know. I do not need to remind you of the teachings of your Mother.' She looked at him quickly, he never spoke of their mother, but he was turned away from her, pouring from a bottle of new Spanish sherry.

'Our Mother would indeed be proud of you!' said Grace, smiling at his back, and she knew they both remembered Betty then, that languorous petulance, and her frenetic, wife-chasing love for her

57

oldest, dearest boy. 'She would think all of her Dreams had come true and she would speak of you from morning till night, fanning herself upon the *chaise longue* in the drawing-room, and Tobias and Ezekiel running about and fighting!'

Still his back to her: the bottle motionless for a moment in his hand. Then he turned slowly.

'Francesca. I have put everything into this new Life and I will not see it lost. There are few Rules in my house but this is one of them: I do not want Bristol, or our Past, spoken of again, ever. You will anger me if you speak of those times.'

'But, Philip – Tobias might find us one day. He is our brother!'

'Once and for all: there is no room for Tobias in this new Life, Francesca. We are Italians from Florence.'

'But, Philip – you could not turn him away.'

'Yes, I could. You would have to choose. Between me and Tobias. And my name is Filipo.' And it was there again: the new, hard coldness.

Sometimes the grey mist over the city would not lift, smoke from the seacoal blotted out the sun and the light was so bad that Philip could not paint; her fashionable brother would then leave his studio and take his little sister, in one of her new gowns, to make observation of her new home: London Town.

Further down St Martin's Lane, a madwoman (Philip told Grace she was a madwoman) stood at her own special corner and sang. It was hard to know her age, or whether she had been pretty once, but she had the most beautiful high voice.

> *Where'er you walk*
> *Cool gales shall fan the glade*
> *Trees where you sit*
> *Shall crowd into a shade*

and there was a kind of yearning, pure sound that caught the breath: people dropped half-pennies or farthings into an old hat that lay in the mud, and as they walked on her voice drifted after them still, catching at their dreams.

First Grace and her brother would promenade in the fashionable St James's Park; she learned to rest her hand, most gracefully, upon his arm. Ladies with much more luxurious hairstyles and gowns than her own walked: some ladies had unlikely pale faces and rose cheeks (*What is upon their faces?* whispered Grace to her brother). The women swept into carriages or walked haughtily past as Grace looked about her, and it seemed to her that even the trees were elegant.

Philip then took her to the Sardinian Chapel in Lincoln's Inn Fields. Beggars congregated (not necessarily Italian it was clear), just beggars hoping for Christian charity, asking halfpence in the name of God. Philip ignored them.

'We will ourselves go inside just once, as I used to in Rome,' Philip said, looking about him to make sure they were not observed. 'But we must not be Italian Catholics: we do not wish to be thought of as Popish even though we are Italians, that is our only danger here. On Sundays if we are to attend any religiosity we will be seen entering Protestant Churches.'

She had no idea what he was talking about.

Inside the chapel, Italians knelt, some ordinary-looking people as well as the more noble, better-dressed communicants. A priest waved incense at the congregation continually: to Grace it seemed as if he wished to keep away the smell of his flock. There was an extremely long, scented and incomprehensible service which Philip whispered to her was in Latin; there was chanting and singing: he knew the responses, knelt, Grace followed him in some bewilderment. The priests continued to wave incense at them, the strange smell made her feel slightly ill.

'What is the point of *this*!' Grace whispered back. 'This is not Italian!'

'Ssssh. Do what I do. Look at the *people*. Watch the *people*.' She did watch the people through the long service, their dark servitude towards the priest and the altar. And she saw she and her brother *did* merge with the Italians: their dark eyes and dark hair.

Then from the chapel her brother took her straightway to Temple Bar at the entrance to the City of London. He told her to look up. There above her on top of the arches, on spikes, were two skulls.

'They are Catholics,' he said. 'We are Italians, but we are not Catholics.' The girl stared up in horror: afternoon light shone through holes where eyes had once been.

*

He took her to the Print Shops in St Pauls – to her surprise there were huge numbers of old paintings in piles, or hanging on walls in rows: one shilling each.

'These are either copies made from an engraving, or Painters who can get no other work paint hundreds of these – they are all very bad copies of what people call so reverently The Old Masters – paintings by Michelangelo and Leonardo da Vinci and Titian and Rubens and Rembrandt and Raphael.' He flicked through the prints dismissively. 'Look at this – *Annunciazione: The Annunciation by Leonardo da Vinci* indeed. I,' and she saw his shoulders roll back in pride, 'I have stood for many hours in front of the original in Florence, and copied it many times.' All about them were piles of copied pictures: Holy Families, Crucifixions, Self-Portraits, Portraits of Nobles, scenes of busy Cities, pictures telling stories from the Bible where men and women kneeled and looked up adoringly, or fell dramatically, stabbed with daggers, so that blood flowed.

'Oh look!' cried a young woman in a large hat near by to Grace, to her gentleman companion. 'Look at this dear little Holy Family, oh and this Venus – I am sure it is Venus, it is rather daring!' And she looked up saucily at the man who put a hand proprietorially and roguishly (Grace saw) upon her back. The Venus was rather undressed and draped with scarves: whatever would Betty have said of this Venus? 'It would decorate so tastefully,' said the woman, 'the same colours as my room!' and Philip stared at the prints and at the young woman, his sister saw, with a supercilious smile. But Grace understood she was seeing copies at least of these things she had only heard of: Old Masters. And then to her delight she came across *Gin Lane* that she had got to know so well at Mrs Falls' house, with the baby falling from the woman's bosom, because Gin was Evil.

'Look Filipo!' she cried (already now always using his Italian name). 'Mr Hogarth!' And then she stopped. She had not yet told him of Mr Hogarth. Philip gave the cheap copy of *Gin Lane* barely a glance and left the Print Shop.

Then he took her through Covent Garden. Here, all over the big square, the *piazza*, a noisy, bustling, dangerous screaming market was held every day selling, it seemed, all that anybody might require: animals, tin, fruit, vegetables, pies, nails, fish, gin, patent medicines, meat, flowers. Servants and street-girls and sailors and soldiers and gentlemen all pushed against and past one another. Small kiosks sold things Grace would never have guessed the use for without her Christmas Steps education, but she had learned very many things living on Christmas Steps: those pouches of sheep's guts with red ribbons were for gentlemen to wear upon their private parts when they met with the street-girls. There were emollients for certain dangerous sicknesses; she saw a long line of women queuing for something that was very brightly labelled DO NOT TAKE THIS MEDICINE IF WITH CHILD: WILL CAUSE LOSS and the women pushed and shoved to buy a bottle as if they could not wait.

Milkmaids carried pitchers of milk on their heads and shouted their wares: *Buy my fresh Milk! Buy my fresh Milk!* ('It is not fresh,' murmured Philip, 'they add water. Do not buy milk from the *piazza*.') Street patterers sang songs about the news of the day, each one its own story:

> HE THOUGHT SHE WAS A REAL PEARL
> IMAGINE THEN HIS PAIN
> THAT HIS REAL LIVE PEARL
> WAS A REAL STREET-GIRL:
> IN THEIR BED
> HE SMASHED HER HEAD:
> NOW SHE'LL NEVER WALK THE STREETS AGAIN

And Philip murmured to his young sister that a lesson from the poet Mr Shakespeare might be useful. Pickpockets loitered; black-faced chimney-sweeps ran with long brushes; filthy women actually lay in gutters and some of them looked as if they were dead, but nobody stopped. Dirty, scabby, thin children ran everywhere: street children who played in warm, fresh horses' dung and picked the pockets of those who did not notice. There was rubbish piled in every corner, in every doorway, gin bottles rolled across the cobbles, glass smashed. Footmen on the back of moving carriages leaned precariously and rudely pushed people out of the way of nobility as jingling, decorated horses threw up filth into the crowds, and everything so wild and loud.

All this was alarming enough in the middle of the day: once, they passed through just as a grey, whirling dusk fell and for the first time Grace held her brother's arm like a child (Grace, brave Grace, clinging to the arm of her brother like a faint-hearted maiden). Philip told her that some said there were ghosts to be found in the recesses of the dark alleys nearby: there were whispers, and cries, and the sound of footsteps as the dank fog swirled round them. A lady would not walk here alone; nor a gentleman either, be he prudent.

Suddenly a man ran through the narrow alley where they had found themselves, the man pushing past people, running, running: fleet, barefoot, they heard his fast, wild breathing as he passed them. In the half-light they saw he was a black man. Almost at once another man, an Englishman, appeared.

'Stop! Stop him!' The second man was sweating, unable to run further, his wig dis-arrayed. 'Stop him! He is my Property! Thief!'

'What's he stolen?' A voice echoed out from a shadowy doorway.

'He is mine! He is my nigger! I *bought* him from a trader. He is trying to run away, stop him!' He was mopping his face with a kerchief, the black man had disappeared. 'I will give him such a whipping when I catch him. Go after him. I will pay!'

A crowd had gathered around the perspiring gentleman.

'What are you waiting for, useless, useless drones!' he shouted in anger. 'Get after him!'

But nobody moved. A strange surliness came over the crowd, and as if in unison the flotsam and jetsam (for such they were) seemed to form a barrier, preventing further chase. Nobody spoke but the message was as clear to Grace as if they were shouting, *These are our streets.* Grace looked suddenly for her brother but Philip had turned away, moved on. The young girl followed her brother, glad to be away from the menacing crowd, but she could not help looking back, saw that the sweating gentleman was now making his way towards darker alleys by a different route. They heard his voice in the distance: 'Stop! Nigger! My Property!' one more cry in the raucous bawdy continual noise: fighting and shouting and music and the loud rumble and rattle of carriages and carts and dogs barking unceasingly, and somewhere babies crying unceasingly, and the knife-grinder grinding his knives unceasingly, and calling his trade. They pushed their way through the *piazza* again and crossed down towards the Strand. And there, along the

Strand only a few minutes from the *piazza*, they were in a different city where emporiums emitted perfumes of flowers and foreign lands. There were silks and Indian cottons and cardomom seeds and chocolate (much of it arrived through the port of Bristol, like the black man they had seen running) and everything so exciting, for this was the greatest city in the world: this was London.

And they heard the voice of the madwoman, still singing as they came back along St Martin's Lane, so high, so sweet, in the exciting strange night.

Her brother trained her to be his housekeeper.

One day, as she was going reluctantly down the stairs that led to the basement kitchen, a flash of memory came to Grace of her father's old Aunt Joy in her dark gown and her white cap who nobody noticed. She felt sudden, deep shock: *I shall never, never, never be like her*. Immediately she threw up her hands and said *Dio mio* loudly as she bustled about, as if she had been supervising Italian kitchens since she was a child, so that nobody could possibly confuse her with a retiring maiden aunt, and Euphemia the housemaid giggled and looked at her mistress from under her eyelashes.

Philip took her to the fishmongers and the bakers and the butchermen and the little vegetable shops round St Martin's Lane and Tower Street, as well as the stalls in the Covent Garden *piazza*. He showed her how to choose fresh produce, not old food: he taught her how to pick up and examine fruit and cabbages before she parted with his money; he took her to look carefully at the eyes of dead fish; he taught her to put meat to her nose. He taught her how to keep an account of her spending with a pencil and a notebook that he gave to her; regularly, at the end of each week, she was to explain to him every penny that she spent: if he considered she had paid too much for mutton he would show her where mutton might be bought cheaper. She tried to be stoic about the new, un-wished-for role she was somehow being pushed into: told herself that one day soon she would be her brother's colleague, not his housekeeper. But for now she did not demur, bided her time: because she had understood her own ignorance – *There is much, much for me to learn about painting, I know nothing, after all* – she saw the sense of it, she must be useful. It was hard for her to be so disciplined, it was not in her wild character to be disciplined, but she was strong also: she wrapped up her longings inside her heart and worked hard, she wanted to please Philip very much, she tried not to mind the tedium, tried not to long to be in a studio of her own for she knew that that would come, when she was worthy.

But: she was nevertheless still Grace Marshall of Bristol. Already she had her own plans. She told Philip she must be with him all the time, to hear his accent, to copy him (but Italian words came easy, being an Italian was easy – had not her young brothers always encouraged her, in that forbidden past, to imitate other people?). Perhaps he thought that was what she was really doing, there in the dark corners of his big studio, listening to his accent? But she was watching him (moved as she had moved so long ago in her father's betting-dens, down alleys, quiet, cunning, there but hardly noticed). Every day as soon as she had finished buying food she was in his studio, watching him work: watching carefully everything he did, drinking it in, learning every small thing – the preparing of the boards or the canvas; the mixing of the paints; the colours. He always removed his wig to work, wore a fashionable dark velvet cap as was the custom. He took out little bags of paint colours that had been already ground, little parcels wrapped inside pigs'-bladders: he would make a hole in the parcel with a tack, empty out colour on to his palette to mix with oil, and then put the tack back in the hole again to seal up the little parcel till next time.

Grace bloomed; early every morning now she set off alone at great speed in her respectable gown and bonnet with her basket over her arm: at great speed so that she could get the tedious business of purchasing food over, and insinuate herself quietly into a dark corner of her brother's studio. She realised very quickly that she was expected to arrange supplies of fish and beef and potatoes and bread and wine and beer and pies and fruit for anybody who might come for dinner: luckily the old cook was good at her job, finally took pity on Grace and told her what to buy, how to save something for the next day if it was not used. Down cheerful, busy St Martin's Lane, past houses and street-stalls and the madwoman singing, people hurried by, and carriages too, or a lady being run past by footmen in a sedan chair. Every early morning Grace stared in amazement – as she hurried from small shop to small shop, or to the stalls on the *piazza* – at the people, at the plentitude, at the filth, at the energy around her.

Occasionally if she had time, with her basket over her arm, she went back to the Sardinian Chapel in Lincoln's Inn Fields in the hope of seeing some Italians. Once she saw there two large women sitting under a tree, eating from a bread-loaf and talking Italian loudly; there were children with them, a boy with a bird-cage and two girls playing hopscotch on a path. Grace moved nearer casually, wanting to overhear everything (or perhaps what she really wanted was to join in the hopscotch, that she used to play with her brothers). The thin, dark boy was keen, she understood, to open the cage door so that the bird, *il uccello*, could fly round the fields. The women called out in Italian, *Fermi! No!* and then looked fiercely at Grace who was so near, as if it was all her fault, so she bobbed an apologetic curtsey, but she saw that the two girls played on so gracefully, almost as if they were dancing. Suddenly the small boy did open the cage and the bird flew out at once, straight up into the sky like a mad thing and the children screamed in Italian and the women screeched in Italian and Grace put her hand to her mouth in dismay. The children all ran about in vain with their arms reaching up, like demented trees, and then the little bird, it had yellow feathers, flew straight back again to the small boy and everybody laughed and included Grace in their laughter, and Grace laughed too, even as she hurried home with her basket, to continue her education.

One morning, her shopping finished, she was making her particular way – almost dancing herself, like the Italian hopscotch girls – back through the *piazza*, observing everything with great interest and curiosity but wanting to get back to her brother's studio, when she suddenly came upon a young woman being violently attacked by two older men with sword-sticks. Grace was surprised, horrified, nobody assisted the girl, everybody went about their rushing business, hurrying to make money. The girl herself did not make one single sound as she tried fiercely to fend them off, but the men were yelling at her in an incoherent manner and bringing their sticks down upon her head and shoulders. Grace was so incensed at such obvious bullying that, without any consideration, she quickly moved close enough to the *mêlée* to put out her foot sharply and unexpectedly: she felled one man who made a big noise, *splat*, as he fell in a pile of horse dung and then lay sprawled there. The attacked young woman then had a chance to kick the other man in a very particular place; she motioned Grace to run fast with her: they quickly ended up in a dark alley off the *piazza* before the two men had the chance to recover their advantage.

Both young women bent over to catch their breath, half-scared, half-laughing: apart from a kind of excited fear, Grace was breathless because she had had to run with such a heavy basket of shopping (a dead eye of a turbot stared coldly), and the young woman was breathless because she had been beaten quite badly by her attackers.

'Are you all right?' said Grace at last, peering back towards the *piazza* but there was no sign they were being followed. 'Whatever were they doing to you in such a terrible manner? Are you all right?'

'Goddam!' said the other girl, still trying to recover herself. 'Thanks, girl, yer came just at the right moment, so yer did, and the other girls are useless trolls. I don't usually work in the mornings.' Then she looked at Grace and at her basket carefully at last, as she rolled up a torn stocking. 'Why did yer help me?'

'They were hitting you!'

'It's dangerous getting involved like that.'

'They were hitting you,' repeated Grace obstinately. 'But why were they? Are you all right? There's blood on you.'

'I'm all right.'

'What is your work?' asked Grace. 'Whyever would they hit you?'

The girl looked at her again. 'Don't be silly,' she said, 'but thanks. Go back that way,' and she pointed to a street at the side of them, 'they won't find yer down there.' And she disappeared down a different alley and Grace realised at once, mortified: *of course, she is a street-girl.* She wondered why she hadn't realised from the beginning, but the girl was so pretty and so – *what is the word I am thinking?* – defiant.

Another day, hurrying home with her basket, she saw a whole garden of grapevines growing further up St Martin's Lane. An old lady was tending them.

'You must come and taste my wine one day,' said the old lady, 'I make it for my son, the Colourman.' And sure enough, just beside the grapevines which were such an unlikely vision in the city, she saw another vision – a small shop that advertised its wares thus: COLOURS FOR PAINTERS, and she laughed aloud for joy and at the changes that were coming to her life. Mr James Burke, the dealer with such piercing grey eyes, was walking down St Martin's Lane and came upon the laughing girl.

'Whåt is it that amuses you so, *Signorina*?' he asked but she only blushed and curtsied and hurried away, indicating the shopping under her arm. And then there she would be, somewhere in the corner of her brother's studio, watchful as a cat.

Philip saw how quickly she had taken on her new persona, perhaps remembered the days when he taught his little sister to read and she would say to his friends so proudly, *When I do count the clock that tells the Time* and Philip did not know how impassionedly she did indeed count the time now, and wait for her moment.

Several days a week now people came for dinner at three o'clock. The house filled with scents and smells: the arriving guests brought their own aromas and their own odours which mixed with the meat cooking and the fish cooking and the wine. The Nobility whom her brother sometimes painted were not present of course, that was not a Painter's social scale (or not *yet*, as Philip Marshall saw it) but Mr James Burke the dealer was often present; occasionally (though not as often as her brother would have liked) the feared critic Mr Hartley Pond.

'*Buongiorno*, Signore Pond,' said Grace Marshall, her head was bowed demurely but she watched him most carefully, this important person, the Art Critic. Mr Hartley Pond was a thin, scented, supercilious gentleman who took snuff from a beautiful enamelled snuff box decorated with an exquisite miniature painting, and who dominated the conversation with his very definite opinions. Grace, as instructed, listened carefully to every word. Mr Pond had what people described as a Roman nose but would have preferred it to be Greek: art began with the Greeks, he said – indeed *life* began with the Greeks as far as Mr Hartley Pond was concerned. Grace imagined he must spend all his spare time learning things from books so that he would know, always, better than anybody else.

An older man, a painter called John Palmer, was often there. Grace soon learned he was her brother's oldest friend, a wise and cynical man: a failed painter who lived in the wilds of Spitalfields where the French weavers had settled, although he was neither a weaver nor French. He was balding but often removed his long, unfashionable (and, if truth be told, rather grubby) wig; he would wipe his pate with his big kerchief and entertain them all with his stories of painting people less rich, and less salubrious, than Philip's clients, and of painting biblical scenes above fireplaces or in corners of poor, religious people's houses.

'I am a craftsman,' he would say wryly, 'not an Artist. I charge by the yard like the sky-men.' But Grace quickly understood that he believed that he *was* an artist, but one who had not had the luck of his Italian friend. 'I design also Epitaphs', he said another time, 'for poor families who bury their loved ones at Spitalfields Church.' He and Filipo di Vecellio had met in Italy, and the older man had befriended the younger. (Sometimes Grace wondered what exactly John Palmer knew of Philip: if he had any inkling of Philip's deception he never ever gave any sign, if he had been there when Philip was learning to present his Italian persona he never mentioned it.) The two of them would often, amid great roars of laughter, recall Roman stories to entertain the table – how they painted portraits in the streets and the squares to support themselves, how pretty ladies showed them much attention: 'Showed Filipo much attention,' amended John Palmer, 'for I was already stout!' But Grace, so used to looking at faces, saw that, for all his rumbustiousness, John Palmer's eyes were sad. He did not eat mountainously like some of the guests but once Grace saw him secreting a piece of bread in his pocket. She was so shocked, and so embarrassed, that she blushed bright red: she never knew if he had known he was observed or not.

Often too an older woman was present: Philip's first landlady who had unlocked so many doors for him when he first came to London, Miss Ann Ffoulks. She was a spinster lady of uncertain years and it was in her house in Brook Street that Philip had first lodged. Miss Ffoulks was proprietorial in his rise, and dogmatic in her opinions: she was used to moving in painterly circles and knew

Mr Joshua Reynolds, to whose dinners she also presented opinions on occasion. The large white cap on her head had flowing ribbons and the ribbons shook as Miss Ffoulks, who had rather a loud voice, imparted her views to the table not just about art but about the affairs of the day: the new colonies in America for instance, or the iniquities of the slave trade. But Miss Ffoulks knew very much about artistic matters also, and artists: she had travelled with her brother to Europe when he was alive and was one of a few Englishwomen who had seen the Pope's Sistine Chapel in Rome. She spoke of art auctions and of Michelangelo most knowledgeably but Mr Hartley Pond ignored her at all times, sniffing snuff up into his nose ostentatiously whenever she held forth, to which she paid no mind. Grace thought that, actually, Mr Pond and Miss Ffoulks were rather alike – sharp and knowledgeable and opinionated – but Mr Hartley Pond was the more rude. Grace also noticed that Mr James Burke often teased Miss Ffoulks, who would smile and blush and was obviously fond of him. Miss Ffoulks was conde-scending to the young sister from Florence, but also very kind: she would bring her small gifts of thimbles or pretty sewing-boxes (not, of course, knowing that Grace had hoped never to see a thim-ble again). Often Miss Ffoulks would rush off while the gentlemen were still twirling their glasses: she attended many meetings and acquired many pamphlets.

Sometimes Grace thought that her brother liked to have Miss Ffoulks and Mr Palmer there at dinner often, even though many of the other guests were much younger, because they somehow vali-dated him, were witness to how far and how quickly he had risen. (And she would again stare surreptitiously at the two of them, and wonder again if they knew the real extent of her brother's journey.)

Grace had never sat through such wonderful conversations in her life: they ate and they drank and they spoke of colour and line and painting and disputed warmly of Raphael and Tintoretto, and of Rembrandt's and Van Dyck's portraits, and of politics and poetry and war with France and casual stories of royalty – and then always again of paint and oils and canvases and Leonardo and Titian, and Grace thought, *I know of Mr Titian, there was a Picture in the Bristol Library by Mr Titian*. And always, always too there was talk of *money*: money in one way or another: Miss Ffoulks criti-cised the traders of slaves, described black people crowded and chained into dangerous ships and carried across the world for *money*; Mr Hartley Pond spoke of bringing foreign paintings to Britain and selling them for *money*; and Filipo di Vecellio spoke often of the money he could now earn for one portrait. *Money, money, money*: always it was there, at the edges of the conversations. And the welcoming table was arranged, and looked over, and the curtains and shutters drawn if it was cold, and the candles lit if the afternoon light faded, by Grace Marshall of Bristol disguised as the *signorina*.

And Grace had hardly been in London three months when the bad-tempered (so it was said) old German King of England died. Miss Ffoulks said briskly across the table that it would be hypocritical to mourn such a man, spoke of his brutish German manner. 'However: he did encourage the wonderful Mr Handel so that we should be privy to his glorious music,' she said. 'That is to the deceased man's good, but not much more.'

Signore Filipo di Vecellio was now so very well connected that he had managed something his mother would have swooned over: an invitation from one of his noble sitters (a somewhat raddled Duke) to Westminster Abbey, to the Coronation of the Grandson, of the new young King. To Filipo's surprise the invitation was firmly extended to the young sister also (the noble Duke having noticed the attractive girl several times, there in the shadows of the studio). There was quite a flurry over the dinner table in St Martin's Lane as guests like John Palmer (a declared anti-monarchist) nevertheless supported Miss Ffoulks (a fellow Republican) who suggested a further new silk gown for Francesca, and even Mr Hartley Pond (a great supporter of the Monarchy) showed interest in the invitation.

'I shall paint the solemn scene!' cried Filipo di Vecellio, waving his glass.

'I thought you despised Epic Painting!' shouted John Palmer, holding a bottle aloft.

'There would be money in *this* Epic Painting!' retorted his friend. 'Think of the number of prints!'

Mr Hartley Pond cried, 'An English-born King, another Monarch born in our own dear land at last!' and Miss Ffoulks raised her eyebrows in amusement and caught the young girl's eye and

Francesca di Vecellio's dark eyes sparked with delight and a hair-dresser attended the morning of the great day and wove flowers into her long dark hair.

The coronation of the young, earnest King George III of England, with his seventeen-year-old foreign bride of two weeks at his side, was a splendid event and certainly to be celebrated: the populace turned out in their thousands to join in such an auspicious occasion. Many people were in particular desirous of catching a glimpse of the new bride, Charlotte: it was rumoured she was *dowdy* – surely not – a glimpse must be obtained! They crowded the streets along the route and were then treated to the most splendid sight of complete chaos at one moment, as several coaches and carriages of the attending Nobility collided and teetered and crashed and fell in one glorious *mêlée* on the road to Westminster Abbey.

'God Save the King!' cried the less noble onlookers in delight as great bangs and collisions and screams filled the air. Bottles of best champagne from the crashed coaches rolled into open sewers where they were eagerly retrieved by the crowds; 'God Save the King!' they yelled again as the gowns of several ladies of the nobility unravelled in an unimaginable and most entertaining manner and dogs and horses went quite berserk.

Filipo di Vecellio and his sister Francesca had had the good sense to walk from St Martin's Lane, arriving on time but rather dusty and crowd-battered; on the way Philip had spoken yet again to his sister, very seriously, about how she must be pleasing to their noble host so that even more noble commissions would be forthcoming. The Duke, already ensconced, kissed the pretty sister's hand and plied them with champagne and cold chicken from a huge hamper he had had installed inside his box at the far end of the Abbey, whilst just outside the door a large chamberpot served duty for gentlemen (ladies of course did not need such vulgar appurtenances). There were a number of people in the Duke's small box and it was crowded and excited and already smelled rather hot: the Duke's elderly wife was unfortunately not able to attend but the young *signorina* was installed between him and another elderly noble gentleman in the front while her brother sat behind with various noble spinsters of uncertain age who waved champagne glasses pleasedly at his appearance. Grace glanced back to her brother in some alarm at the proximity of the

Duke, whose wrinkled hand was clamped almost at once upon her knee, but Filipo was smiling at the ladies, and searching the crowd for other noble faces. Many of the guests not directly in the eye of the waiting bishops had had the sense to arrange food and wine in the same manner as the Duke and a cheerful buzz of laughter and conversation filled the Abbey. People were soon calling in a most confident and somewhat inebriated manner to one another across the aisle; everyone was dressed in their finest clothes; much expensive lace was to be seen, gold lace even, and jewels sparkled and glittered and competed under the chandeliers. At one point the Duke indicated to Francesca a group of elegant, aging duchesses in a box nearby who maintained a silent, noble hauteur amid the loud sociability.

'They can do no other, m'dear,' boomed the Duke in a loud voice, 'they dare not speak or smile because their cheeks are full of little corks.'

'I beg your pardon?' said the young girl politely, thinking she must have misheard him as she tried heroically yet again to disengage her knee.

'Cork!' boomed the Duke. 'It fills out all the hollows where they have lost their teeth but if they smile or speak or eat, the corks will fall out!' On receiving this information the laughter of the girl rang out unchecked just for a moment around the Abbey: it ceased abruptly when she became aware of the Duke's old wrinkled hand now fumbling under her petticoats.

'Oh look! Look!' she cried extremely loudly (to her brother's mortification) as she stood quickly and pointed at where the Royal Couple, deposited at last, were making their way down the aisle.

'Huzzah for His Majesty!' the inebriated Nobles shouted: as their host stood to huzzah, Francesca took the opportunity to grab her brother's arms as she used to and, with some acrobatics in the small box, drag him into her own small seat and literally clamber backwards to sit behind him; the Duke and Filipo di Vecellio were both surprised when the nobleman felt again for a knee.

The organ blazed out and kettledrums rolled. A semblance of quietitude reigned briefly among the guests: the young King was red-robed and proud, the new young bride rather dumpy (it was true) and bewildered. There was comparative silence while the crowns were placed upon the heads of the new monarchs with much pomp and circumstance (with perhaps just a little to-ing and fro-ing to chamberpots and just a little tinkling of glasses to be heard, hopefully not by their new Majesties). However once the Archbishop of Canterbury climbed to the altar to begin his sonorous sermon, those whose position, like the Duke's, at the far end of the Abbey precluded any chance of hearing or seeing anything of the fine words, took the beginning as a sign for dinner to begin in earnest. A loud cacophony of knives and forks and mutton and fish and glasses and animated conversation ensued. It was noted at one moment that the Signorina Francesca di Vecellio had her face hidden behind her fan and that her body was shaking. Their host the Duke nodded approvingly into his claret, such emotion on such a day, by God he would like to take the little lady home with him, and his head fell gracefully on to his large glass as he became, for the moment, dead to the world, snoring slightly. Filipo took the opportunity to rebuke his sister quietly over his shoulder.

'You should not point and shout and I have told you it is so unfashionable to *laugh* like that!' he whispered, but then began to laugh himself when he saw the tears of glee in the girl's face as she surveyed the rumbustious scene in Westminster Abbey and the red-faced spinster ladies beside her screeching, and their snoring host. Indeed by the time the coronated couple appeared, crowned, walking slowly and solemnly back down the aisle, all pretence at decorum had disappeared and many chop bones and glasses were waved at them in a cheerful and well-wishing manner and the old Duke woke at once and shouted, 'Huzzah for the King!' and was only prevented from falling into the path of their Majesties by the dexterity of his guests.

Such exciting adventures in her exciting new life: but every day Grace was there, in a corner of her brother's studio, watching, waiting, learning from observing her brother some of the many things she would need to know, to be an artist.

Within a few more months Grace's new gowns were too small in all sorts of places and she needed unlacing and re-sewing: Miss Ffoulks' kind thimbles were put to use after all. And within a few months Grace, who had been too afraid of being found to be an ignorant Bristolian to actually speak at the dinner-table herself, became confident enough to join in the conversations: asked questions in quick, accented English, her dark eyes shining with curiosity and enjoyment, for Grace had a million words inside her. She laughed; she recounted the coronation, she waved her hands about, she asked everybody questions in an accent like her brother's: 'Such good English,' they all said. The guests enjoyed her: everyone loved to see the dark-eyed *signorina* laugh, nobody minded when she asked her inexperienced questions, *What is a fresco? Who was Van Dyck? What is lapis lazuli?*

Once she made the mistake of asking, in her enthusiastic Italian way, 'What is the Uffizi Gallery?' How was she to know that it was in Florence, her home, and one of the most famous art collections in the world?

'My sister was not educated,' Philip had said quickly, almost sarcastically. 'She languished in the drawing-room, thinking only of husbands!' and Grace was so mortified at this unjust description of her childhood that she blushed and the other guests laughed, charmed by the fifteen-year-old *signorina* who was blossoming into a beautiful woman in front of their eyes.

Other painters from the town banged the big iron knocker; a writer was sometimes to be found at the hospitable table, occasionally an actress: whoever became part of the artistic and social circle of Signore Filipo di Vecellio, portrait painter, half a dozen people or ten, it did not matter. The few women present did not interrupt the conversations to go into another room, the gentlemen availed themselves of chamberpots in the cupboard outside the door. A great deal of food and drink would be consumed before the gentlemen would go off to their clubs and coffee houses: on many a late afternoon voices would echo out into St Martin's Lane. The host's favourite song was a round that, he said, he had heard Englishmen singing, in Florence:

> *Three blind mice*
> *See how they run*
> *They all run after the farmer's wife*
> *She cut off their tails with a carving knife.*

Except that Mr Hartley Pond said that the words *he* had been taught were:

> *The farmer married an ugly wife*
> *And she cut her throat with a carving knife*
> *Did ever you see such a fool in your life?*
> *Three Blind Mice.*

FIVE

Signore Filipo di Vecellio's big appointment book got fuller and the money rolled in: people came by the hour. He did not care to spend money on such things as assistants but he talked now of employing them, to paint sky and sleeves and background. But Grace Marshall thought, *No! I have learned much already. I will be his assistant!* She had observed well from the corners; now she insinuated herself nearer, anticipated her brother's needs as he painted his sitters, handed him brushes. She began cleaning the brushes carefully with the Turpentine, fetching water when it was needed and clean rags. She watched and assisted as he mixed the colours with different kinds of oils: he despised watercolours he said, no matter that the great Michelangelo did not agree. It was oils he was interested in, oils were grand. Her eyes widened at his knowledge and his style and she thought oils grand also. More noble ladies came to the studio to be painted: beautiful ladies who smelled of potions and perspiration and food. Noble, florid gentlemen too were welcomed: they smelled of gin, or rum, and tobacco. Small children came, and exquisite actresses who smelled of flowers and paint: there were sometimes now several coaches at once outside her brother's house in St Martin's Lane, clients waiting, and the little sister assisting so carefully. And as the customers came to buy their likeness, preening themselves in a glass, she understood her brother was involved in trade now, of a kind. His studio was where he painted but his studio was also a showroom, and (how their mother would have fulminated) a shop.

All the time she studied his portraits carefully. She saw he often covered arms with sleeve or a drape of material (*He cannot draw arms and legs so well so he covers them*, her disloyal heart whispered, *I believe I draw as well as he*). For at the bottom of all her energy and activity and watchfulness and learning, something lay coiled, waiting: she waited for Philip to see her own drawings, she waited to tell him of her meeting with the Mr Hogarth he spoke of, waited to show him her treasured portraits of their family.

She smoothed these precious pictures in the night, observed them in the candlelight in St Martin's Lane, and she wrote her very first letter. She pondered on the words and on the writing for many hours.

> *Dear Mrs Falls,*
> *I have a fine life for London is a fine place.*
> *I saw the Coronation. My Aunt is Italian. So*
> *if my brother Tobias should ever ask for me*
> *I am Grace Marshall Care of Signorina*
> *Francesca di Vecellio, St Martin's Lane*
> *number 11, London,*
> *yours faithfully,*
> *Grace Marshall.*

And then Grace disgraced herself. She had completed her morning duties, whirling down St Martin's Lane as she had once whirled along the streets of Bristol. Now she had placed herself, as usual, quietly in the studio ready to help, watching everything; she was so quiet she was hardly noticed by either her brother or his sitter, that morning a noble lady of uncertain age and of portly demeanour.

For some reason that morning the noble lady insisted on viewing her portrait for which she had had several sittings.

'But *Signora bella*, Lady O'Reilly, it is not yet completed.'

'I nevertheless have been very patient, and I want just a *tiny* view my dear Signore di Vecellio.' She was proud of her Italian pronunciation for had she not travelled to Europe and seen real art?

She repeated his name, 'My dear Signore di Vecellio I must insist on one *tiny* peek.' And she stood from the chair upon which she had been sitting and approached his easel with girlish laughter. Filipo di Vecellio *always* flattered: nevertheless the laughter turned to a little flurried screech.

'No! But no!'

'As I said to you, *Signora*, it is not yet completed.'

'But no! That is not my face! That is not my hair!' Grace longed to look at the portrait but did not dare move from the corner of the room where she cleaned brushes so quietly. 'This is to be a Portrait of myself – and you were strongly recommended to me by the Duke, as you know – as a gift for my Husband. I do not care for the way that it shows my chin in quite that mode. I do not care for my hair to have that air of unreality. No, I do not care at all for the manner in which you are portraying me.'

Filipo di Vecellio was not known for his charm for nothing.

'Lady O'Reilly, *cara mia*. You do not, forgive me, understand the way I work. I first paint a shell on which I shall soon place your own,' he paused, 'your own tranquilly strong features.' Grace waited: *Tranquilly strong*. Was it enough?

Lady O'Reilly looked uncertainly at the painting.

'And your Eyes, *bella*, the deep depths of Wisdom in your Eyes has yet to be shown.' *Deep depths of Wisdom*: Grace peered forward. Lady O'Reilly was almost mollified.

'Until I have caught your Soul,' said the painter, and he actually took her hand for a moment, 'I have not caught your Likeness, and I view your Likeness with violent Admiration.' And he kissed the hand that he held in his, and a little florid sigh emitted from Lady O'Reilly.

There was also a sound from somewhere in the studio: it sounded like a snort, as Grace Marshall tried to control her laughter. Lady O'Reilly quickly withdrew her hand and her eyes were suddenly very small and tight.

'What is that?'

Grace's hand was over her mouth and her body was shaking: the more she understood that she must not on any account laugh, the more the laughter welled up.

The artist threw a look of great disdain to the recesses of the studio and spoke extremely quickly. 'My sister Francesca', he said, 'is suffering from a surfeit of emotion regarding her recent arrival from Florence. She is a foolish girl in some ways and I believe has not yet accustomed herself to your wonderful country, and sometimes she weeps. I believe she is weeping now. It is best, if you would be so gracious, *cara bella*, to ignore her.' Lady O'Reilly peered into the corner of the room suspiciously but said no more, for after all it was well known that foreigners behaved in a very un-English manner at times. Filipo di Vecellio ended the sitting at once by suggesting they have a small *aperitivo*, and they left the studio.

Afterwards he informed his sister most severely that the noble sitter was paying *fourteen guineas* for her portrait. 'That is more', he reminded her, 'than you could make in years as a milliner's assistant,' and she tried so hard to swallow her laughter, looked down at her hands demurely, he saw her pushing her nails into her palms. And then he laughed, and they both laughed, and he made her heart glow with happiness by, at last, handing her one of his brushes and a colour blue, asking her to see if she could paint the sky in the background after he himself removed several decades from the visage of Lady O'Reilly.

And Grace Marshall felt a brush in her hand and smelled the paint and the oil and the canvas, and her eyes shone as she meticulously put precious paint on the brush and applied it for the very first time to the canvas, and as she painted she sang.

> *And I would love you all the Day*
> *Ev'ry Night would kiss and play*
> *If with me you'd fondly stray –*
> *Over the hills and far away . . .*

and although Philip Marshall allowed no mention of his past, that day he joined in with the song that their father had sung in Queen's Square in Bristol when he mixed his little tubs of colour and painted his elegant horses.

> *If with me you'd fondly stray –*
> *Over the hills and far away . . .*

SIX

And then something happened between the brother and the sister.

It was not clear to the people who came to the house, who had so liked to see the beautiful, dark-eyed, laughing young girl, what it was that had happened: nothing was ever spoken of, but she was no longer seen in the painter's studio, not even in the dark, quiet corners. And when dinner was served she no longer laughed with her shining eyes.

Filipo di Vecellio suddenly hired two assistants, paying them (complaining at the cost) thirty-five guineas per year. Assistants now removed paint, cleaned brushes, were taught to paint the sky: the small things. They had to work hard, more work was coming in, they prepared Signore di Vecellio's portraits so that they could be varnished and dispatched, and new ones begun. The assistants slept on small beds in one of the far dark corners of the studio.

Occasionally one of the sitters, remembering the eyes, asked of the pretty, quiet girl. 'She is my housekeeper,' said Filipo di Vecellio, 'I teach her to buy fresh fish.' And they all laughed, knowing the skill required with some of the rascally fishmongers who tried to hide the dead, pale eyes of the less fresh fruits of the Thames.

And sometimes they caught glimpses of the girl with her basket,

and smiled, for she was a lovely girl, but she had become exceed-
ingly elusive and they wondered what had happened and several
smiled knowingly, presumed she had fallen in love.

The Italian sister still arranged the hospitable dinners, still lit
the candles, drew the curtains. But they saw, all the guests who had
found her so charming, that something had happened, something
had changed. Miss Ffoulks and Mr James Burke and Mr John
Palmer, there so often, understood perhaps more than the other
guests that something must have—

—no, no! not 'something changed' – that is not right.
Everything changed: everything.

He unbalanced our sky, my brother Philip, and created monsters, and monsters are disguised, they wear embroidered
waistcoats or their petticoats rustle as they pass by.

only –
only –
– oh I cannot do words well, I wish I could *paint* it: *the joy
before*, before it changed, before everything – our Lives – changed
forever, Philip and me. I wish I could paint the happiness, working
for my brother in his Studio, learning learning learning – here at
last was *my* Artistic Education, a hungry fifteen-year-old-girl, I
was destined (I really really did think in big fancy words like
Destiny then but of course I did not say them to my brother who
would have laughed, who had not yet seen my Drawings), I was
destined, it seemed to me, to be an Artist just as my brother was;
but as I blossomed, like Flowers do, as I went from painting the
sky that first time of laughing in the corner at poor Lady O'Reilly
(who smelled not just of perspiration and perfume as all the ladies
did, but of Madeira Wine like our Mother) – as Philip allowed me
to paint what he called 'the boring appendages,' (he only cared to
paint faces): as I painted the ground on the canvas, and then a cloud
in the blue sky, and then at last – like a gift – the sleeve of a
Doctor's wife, the fall of the sleeve of a gown, the way the light
fell to make the fold and the shadow (I looked at my own sleeve,
I could see the shadow there) – oh then how my head expanded, no
I mean my mind expanded, and in my dreams I saw candlelight
catching the falling green silk and it was beautiful.

And that light falling on the sleeve in that way made me look,

look at everything around me even more than I was used to – Miss Ffoulks had pale skin, it was like old paper and fine, and grey hair and wise eyes and the large bonnets that she favoured with the coloured ribbons that shook as she spoke *can I paint that?* her stiff kindness and her knowledge with the white skin like old paper; and in the early mornings there were birds low in the sky like a shadow, a chattering shadow of black small birds flying low across St Martin's Lane from Leicester Fields – *can I paint that?* – and I noticed carefully that first morning light, the brightness before the fog so often came down – my eyes then, which had before been intuitive, began to be educated also – these were joyous days and I hugged to me the big words like Destiny because I knew this was to be my Life – and sometimes when we were quite alone we did sing the song of our Father, *if with me you'd fondly stray over the hills and far away*, holding on to a small piece of our past so that we might know, just for a short time, who we really were.

I watched and I copied and I learned – Philip outlined what he wanted to do with a lead pencil or with charcoal and then when he started actually painting I saw that to obtain the effect he wanted he used layer after layer of paint, sometimes using different brushes, sometimes putting paint on the board or the canvas with his palette knife, sometimes placing different colours one on top of the other (and I saw again that although he sometimes painted more than just the face, part of the body too – they were called *half-lengths* and *full-lengths*, which cost more – he very often covered an arm or a hand in drapes, for his skill was for faces, not so much, as I had observed before, for other parts of the Anatomy) –And I felt the firmness of a wooden board for painting on, or the way a stretched canvas still had some movement, like a little bounce; and he talked all the time about *light*, about the importance of the Studio getting as much natural light as possible, how he must rise early to catch the most light in the day, how in winter Painters had to stop painting when clouds and fog loured down, like the day he took me to the Covent Garden *piazza* and the black man ran away. —And I learned that when a painting was finished it must be varnished over, to complete it.

And the *colours.* —I looked longingly at his beautiful palette of many colours like – like, I suppose, my Father looked at a bottle of rum – more than anything I wanted my own palette of colours –

and the most beautiful blue colour of all that the Artists used was also the most expensive, it was called ultramarine and it came from the pounding of a precious stone called *lapis lazuli* that only came from a country called Afghanistan, Philip kept a little of it, quite separately, on his palette, his beautiful palette that he held with his thumb, all the beautiful enchanting colours – there was lead white, there were yellows and yellows – cheap ones and more expensive ones like Naples yellow that lasted longer, that shone; there were different reds – lakes, vermillions, I learned the different names – some of the colours were vegetable, some of the colours were mineral, some of the colours were synthetic, some of the colours lasted, some of the colours faded and I saw also how he had learned so carefully to *mix* colours in his own way – they all did it, all the painters, and most of all I began to learn that they hold their Secrets one from the other.

My beloved brother had come back for me, I was working with him in his Studio. —It was a grand, grand time and words are not my skill but the old inebriated Vicar in Bristol said Shakespeare painted word-pictures and these are my word-pictures, as best I can.

My Sixteenth Birthday came and I remembered my Ninth Birthday in the Bristol garden, when my father gave me Colours, those days that were gone, and the day of my Sixteenth Birthday I gently, carefully, unwrapped my Drawings that had been waiting so patiently for my beloved brother to see them, and validate my Future and my Destiny (I know I know, but I *did* think like that): my Portraits of our Family.

And that day I brought my precious, precious parcel to him in his Studio, the Portraits all drawn from my memory and my loneliness in the attic on Christmas Steps (for some reason I left Mr Hogarth's picture in my room, I thought he might despise it I suppose), and although I was shy I was also proud, and there in his Artist's Studio, just like the one I was determined soon to have, I unwrapped our Life, I unwrapped my own Work at last.

'Look Philip,' I said to my brother, and I looked up at his dear face.

He was totally, totally shocked.

It was as if he had completely forgotten that *I had drawn too,* that summer stinking afternoon in our garden in Bristol but how could he forget? because it was that day, with my chalks, that set him off on his own Future.

I saw his face.

He stared unbelieving, I had to look away for a moment, so naked was the expression there: it was as if he *burned* me with the expression on his face: I heard the paper as he lifted one Portrait after another – I knew he saw Juno and Venus thinking of husbands, and Ezekiel and Tobias fighting and our dissatisfied Mother and our dissolute Father and my drawing of Philip himself, all his gaiety and charm and beauty, for he was beautiful, my brother Philip and I had caught his beauty.

I made myself look back at his face now.

I knew he saw his Past. I knew he saw himself.

But it was not that at all.

I stared at his face, he tried to compose what showed there – and then suddenly, violently – even as I threw myself at him and flailed wildly with my arms to stop him – he began to tear the papers that I had treasured so carefully: in half, then again – even as he violently pushed me away, still ripping at the paper and he kept shouting, 'That time is over!' tearing and ripping – and then again: 'That time is *completely* over!'

But it was not that at all.

And then:

'You are the *housekeeper*, that is why you are here, that is why I came back for you! You are the *housekeeper!*'

He ripped our Family into tiny pieces and pushed me away from him again so wildly as I tried to stop him that I fell hard against the bench where all the brushes lay drying and an open bottle of Turpentine was knocked and the liquid fell downwards into my hair and onto my clothes where I fell and at the last all the Drawings lay like scraps, upon the floor beside me.

The draught as he opened the door caught the paper, drifted the torn pieces all over the room, I heard his footsteps running down the stairs then I heard the loud bang of the front door echoing in the hallway as he went out into St Martin's Lane and then the echo faded away and the house was silent.

I knew faces so well and I had seen at once: it was not Memory, not the Past that undid him.

It was my Drawings.

I understood in an instant, so naked was his expression, a child would have understood and I sat myself up slowly and then still on the floor I picked up the remains of my treasured, precious work: a scrap of Juno's curls; an eye; a torn smile.

My brother was Jealous.

That is what happened, that day.

Late that night as I sat, still so shaken, in my room with the smell of Turpentine everywhere, remembering Philip's occasional violence in Bristol, remembering it always passed and he became himself again, I heard the downstairs door again, the servants' voices: Philip returning – then I heard his footsteps – they were coming upwards towards my room, and I stood up and my heart beat with anxiety but with anticipation too, it would be resolved, my beloved brother had returned to say that I was an Artist too, how could he not? – again I explained it to myself, it was with *my* chalks, which had been given to me for *my* enthusiasm, that he had found his own calling – and most important of all I *knew: I knew my Drawings were true.*

He swayed in the dark doorway to my room with his candle, his shadow swayed and the candleflame flickered and I saw he was not recovered, I caught that look in his eyes that I had seen in the coach to London, that I saw just sometimes in the house in St Martin's Lane before he flicked it away: that hard, cold expression of a completely different man and he talked to me and his voice was thick with drink.

'Listen, little sister. I will only tell you this once more and then we will never speak of it again. *I am an Artist.* I have fought for this – for everything I have achieved – with all my energy and determination and I will become the most famous Painter in London, because I am a *Foreigner.* And I brought you here as my housekeeper because I promised I would come back for you. I need not have come back for you but I did. But never, in a thousand years, imagine that you too could ever be an Artist! I cannot believe that is what you have been thinking! You are an ignorant, ignorant girl and of Art you know nothing at all.' And I thought *it is true – but it is not true* and I felt wild, hysterical laughter welling up inside me and I could not control it: my brother had torn my Drawings and now told me in a dramatic voice that he was a Foreigner – but I was the one person in the world who knew perfectly well that he was Philip Marshall and I was Grace Marshall and we came from Bristol – I pushed the laughter down as it tried to get out of my mouth and then my voice came bursting out instead, not full of laughter but full of rage.

'You destroyed my Portraits, my precious, precious Work, they were good Drawings – you know that! I want to paint like you! – you always knew I wanted to paint!' And out of the depths of me the words erupted: '*I have to paint!*'

His voice was so much quieter than mine had become, and the words so slurred and indistinct, and now – for he moved the candle – the face so shadowed. 'Listen to me, Grace. I do not intend, ever, to have two Painters in this house. You are an uneducated girl, not a Painter, you know nothing. You are not trained. You have no Knowledge. Women do not paint Portraits. *I am the Painter.* I have studied and trained for years and years and your Pretensions anger me immensely – how could they not? You stupid, stupid, ignorant girl.' He spat the words at me and his voice rose and rose again, 'You know nothing in the world about Art – I lived in Rome and studied the greatest Masters in the World, what have you done? You have sewn strawberries on to hats! And you have the temerity to compare yourself to me and to speak of *being a Painter*! Do you not understand how ludicrous you sound? I have suffered for months and months your careless way of talking across the table, to real Artists, to men of infinite Education and Knowledge like Mr Hartley Pond, men who have studied Art for many, many years. You are *not* my equal or their equal. Women do not paint Portraits. You are an embarrassment, and if you stay that must stop. You are no longer nine years old, saying the first thing that comes into your head, you are a Woman and I see you have not yet matured as women should.

'Well, make your Decision, and make it quickly. I came back for you: I kept my part of the bargain and I have offered you my home. But you may leave it at any time and make your own way – I will, of course, not stop you, you are not a prisoner, this is not some tedious Melodrama from the Theatre.' The candle flickered in his hand, for his hand shook.

'But, if you do not live with me here in this house as my housekeeper, you will be on the streets, little sister. Have a look at the women on the streets, you cannot miss them! I have spent time with one of them in St James's Park this very night and they are disgusting,' (he could not see the look – was it shock? – on my face in the shadows). 'Remember there is nobody – *nobody* in this ferocious city who will help you – and *then* understand the magnitude of my Triumph! In Bristol, we had the veneer at least of Nobility still, we were still related to the Wiltshire Marshalls, we knew people, they liked my Paintings, they helped us, they found you a position as a milliner because whatever disgrace our Father had brought they knew of the Wiltshire Marshalls, and I was of use to them, and portrayed their pretensions as nobody else could. But here in this big city nobody has heard of the Wiltshire Marshalls! There is no-one to find you a safe position somewhere, you do not even have references from Mrs Falls the milliner. You have nothing of your own at all!'

'*But I only want to paint!* All I want to do in the whole world is paint – why can you not help me and teach me? Why will you not?' (I knew why he would not: why did I not say it?)

His voice shouted out at me (as if indeed we were part of some Theatrical Performance), 'Do not presume too much because I am your brother! I tell you one final time: you are here as my housekeeper, and painting has *nothing* to do with you. You are welcome to stay, or leave, for I no longer care. But make your Decision quickly. If you leave I will not, I assure you – *I promise you* – lift a finger to help you when you fall – as you most surely will, alone in a city like London.' He turned away, and then he turned back. 'I will however – for after all I am not some Villain! – arrange a coachfare back to Bristol, if you so desire.' And then he left with his shaking, flickering candle and I heard his footsteps as he stumbled to his own room below.

—I did not sleep, of course I did not, I could only grieve for my Dreams and my torn, destroyed pictures of the people of my Memory and it felt as if I could not see them now, that he had destroyed them all; all I could see in my head were colours, the colours on the beautiful palette in Philip's Studio, at dawn I went downstairs because I did not understand what else I should do: I had no plan as I went out of the door of my brother's house, still the smell of Turpentine in my hair with my straw bonnet that I had made myself and my basket over my arm as the housekeeper sister was supposed; further up St Martin's Lane, the old lady with the grape-vines, the Colourman's mother, was there – although the sun had not yet properly risen she was out there, looking carefully at her city grapes in the dawn light – I nodded to her somehow as usual, hurrying past in case I would have to speak – but this morning she stopped me.

'I know you're a Foreigner, dear,' she said to me, 'but you've got a lonely look in your eye, I can see it from here. I've got some of my St Martin's Lane wine ready, come in and try it dear, you look as if you could do with a cheery glass.' —Candles were still lit in her kitchen this early morning and there were flagstones on her kitchen floor, I remember, grey and soothing against the anger and the colours that seemed to dance in my head, and if the Colourman's mother was perhaps a little mad and if it was strange to have wine at dawn, nothing was strange to me that day and she poured the wine and then she blew out the candles so we sat in half-darkness still, for the windows of her kitchen were small – the wine was a little sour, but I drank it quickly in the strange dawn light to blur the rage inside of me and I literally could not speak.

'You'll be missing your Home, dear,' she said, and I tried to think where my Home might be and she poured more wine into our glasses. 'And your Family, your Mother and your Father, but Lord love you, there will be compensations, a pretty girl like you and those big eyes.' —Slowly as we drank, the first proper rays of morning sun rose up across the city and through the small window, and then almost at once disappeared again, as grey London fog came down – I gulped the wine in big, angry gulps, and I laughed, and I said, speaking at last (in my fake Italian accent), *Signora, I do thank you for this delicious English wine!* and I felt giddy and numb and foreign and angry and gay, she talked on and on, I only had to nod a little, and try to smile – she recalled for me St Martin's Lane as it had used to be, trees just like the countryside, she said, and chickens and pigs and sheep and we kept drinking and then the Colourman appeared, rubbing at his eyes, doing up his jacket, he seemed not at all put out that his mother was drinking wine at that hour with a strange young lady, grabbed a glassful himself as he went past to open his paint shop; by the time it was truly morning the

Colourman's mother and I had finished off a very large bottle of St Martin's Lane wine.

Finally I stumbled to my feet, I immediately felt dizzy and hot, I collected myself and curtsied to the kind old lady and thanked her for her hospitality and said I must buy food for my brother's table.

'You are welcome, dear girl,' she said so kindly, apparently not at all inebriated, and I suddenly wanted to weep, for hearing the kindness, I could feel tears at the back of my eyes and I *never* cried, I had never cried once since that night I drew Tobias and Ezekiel and the tears had come out of my eyes without me expecting them, and I pulled the gate at the end of her garden (quite missing it the first time) and then the latch clicked and I waved goodbye and further up the lane I vomited into the gutter – I was ashamed but not one person seemed to notice or say anything, people were always vomiting in open sewers in this city – I wiped my mouth with part of my gown then automatically I went to the butcherman, to the baker as usual; then I bought a penny glass of ginger beer from a woman with a jug in Monmouth-street with my brother's money that I would have to account for, and I gulped it down trying to wash away the taste of the St Martin's Lane wine, and the taste of pain; London spun about me and the basket of food was heavy on my arm, the glass eye of a dead rabbit stared out – I tore at a piece of bread and stuffed it into my mouth, I walked quickly, hardly knowing where I was going, yet going there all the same because somehow I did know exactly where I was going – I had seen hats in milliners' Emporiums in the Strand that even the elaborate Mrs Falls would have been surprised by – I walked under a small swinging sign of one of them, and pushed at the glass door – there were hats everywhere: hundreds and hundreds of hats it seemed: some most elegant, some with strawberries even bigger than those of Mrs Falls, no sign of any milliners but I saw a shadow of a girl run down some stairs at the back into the basement below.

A woman appeared, looked me up and down, taking in the basket and the rabbit. 'Yes?'

I did not know how one was meant to begin, 'I wish to make Hats for you,' I said, abruptly.

She had a hard, ugly face. 'I have plenty of hat-makers,' she said, 'they are two a penny in the Strand.'

'I am experienced,' I said, 'and my Hats were admired.'

She looked at me again, looked at the eye of the rabbit. 'I do not employ Foreigners here,' she said, and turned away.

'But I am good at it!' I cried, 'I have made Hats and Bonnets for years, for many years, much better than your Hats.' I tore my own off my head, 'Look! Look at this stitching!' but she kept her back to me. —Four more milliners shops I visited, more and more desperate, and I suppose dishevelled – not one would answer me, assistants did not just walk in off the Strand and I had nothing, no paper to prove that I had once been so accomplished, for Philip had whisked me away and I never thought to care about hats ever again, up and down the Strand and everybody saying no (and afterwards, when I recovered myself, I laughed at that: that I should walk inebriated down the Strand with my dead rabbit staring upwards and, likely, still Turpentine-scented hair – and demand a position in a millinery establishment!) but now I walked towards Covent Garden, the street-girls plying their trade even in the early morning with smiling, wheedling, desperate faces and in St Martin's Lane the madwoman sang on her corner, a very mad song it sounded to me.

> *If all the World were paper*
> *And all the sea were ink*
> *If all the trees were bread and cheese*
> *How should we do for drink?*

the high true voice, and in desperation, wanting to see the faces of my Family, and colours flashing inside my head as if I was the madwoman, not she who sang so sweetly, I thought *what shall I do?*

'*Seenyoureena*, where was you!' cried Euphemia, opening the door as if she had been looking for me, and then looking at me properly in some surprise, the wine I suppose or my despair. 'The Master says that that Painter is coming, that Joshua Reynolds! He says it must be Special and the cook says what is she to do Special with when you ain't come back with it?'

For on that same grey, dizzy day, along with perhaps half a dozen other guests, Mr Joshua Reynolds, my brother's Colleague and Rival, was to come to dinner and my brother Philip who had destroyed my precious Drawings in the night seemed to be dancing on hot coals with nervousness at the visit and drank several large glasses of wine and certainly gave no indication that anything had happened between us, as if I had dreamed it all so I threw water on my face and as the guests arrived I smiled and smiled as if I had suddenly turned into a frozen, smiling doll; but I was there, after all, I smiled, after all – I made sure the food was ready and lit the tall candles but I, for the first time I uttered scarcely a word: I could not speak, I was the housekeeper.

I was surprised on that – unforgettable – day to see that the acclaimed Mr Joshua Reynolds was nearly as short as Mr Hogarth and Philip towered over him (and enjoyed that he could do so) – a fool could see that my brother and Mr Reynolds were extremely wary of each other, competitors for Trade, and at first they talked carefully with the other guests of other things: of Mr Goldsmith's plays, of Dr Samuel Johnson's new English dictionary – but the critic Mr Hartley Pond was present and soon talk of Art was in full flow.

'It was the ancient Greeks who elevated the figure of Man to that of a God,' said Mr Hartley Pond. 'That is the beginning of Art as we know it: nobody can speak of Art until they have studied the sublimity of the Grecian human form as crafted by the Master Sculptors,' and as he spoke I felt my cheeks redden: what my brother had said was true – I knew nothing, I had never even *seen* a Greek statue, apart from the fake one in the Bristol garden.

Then Mr Reynolds began: he praised the Religious and History Paintings of the Old Masters – this was Sublime Art indeed, with Moral Purpose – but before he had got much further my brother poured more wine and laughed. 'I think you know very well, Sir, that such is the Vanity and Self-love of this Age that a person would rather have a Portrait of himself on his wall than a moral portrayal of the Death of Judas!'

'You sound like that untalented fellow, Romney,' said Mr Reynolds somewhat impolitely. 'But I insist that Morality is the Artist's role – and, after all, engravings can be made of History Paintings, and there is much money to be made from Prints.'

'But surely then, it is the Engraver that takes most of the money!' answered my brother (who had failed miserably with his projected Epic Painting of the Coronation, all the Nobles looked like sticks). 'Nothing is as profitable as Portrait painting when you are at the top of the Field, as we are!' and Mr Reynolds regarded Philip with a look that was indecipherable, and drank more wine also, nodding to me without actually looking at me as I filled his glass, and then the conversation turned back to canvas and paint and colour, and I could see Philip's beautiful palette inside my head, all the bright colours flashing with my rage.

Someone spoke of Plagiarism (Miss Ffoulks, seeing my puzzled face, explained to me quietly it meant copying someone else's work); they told of how one artist of their acquaintance had copied Botticelli.

Mr Reynolds sat back in his chair, holding the glass I had refilled; I looked at his face – it was bluff and red rather than fine; amiable certainly – but there was something cold, there in the face, as Philip had and suddenly I thought – yet I did not know where the thought came from that night for I was exactly sixteen years old and ignorant – *Perhaps, to succeed, great Artists must lose some other part of themselves.*

'I believe', said Mr Reynolds, 'that there is no such thing as Plagiarism. We must find, I think, that by being conversant with the Intentions of others, we learn to invent ourselves. The mind is a barren soil which will produce no crop, or only one, unless it be continually fertilised and enriched with Foreign matter.'

I looked at my charming, hospitable brother: the man who had thrown me against the bench and torn up my Drawings: Foreign matter.

'I agree absolutely,' said Mr Hartley Pond. 'Artists can learn only from those greater than themselves, and that means old Artists from Europe,' and he held a wine-glass delicately to his thin lips, and Miss Ffoulks nodded also and one long pink ribbon from her bonnet caught on the wig of Mr Hartley Pond, and seemed to suit him.

John Palmer had kept his old wig on as long as possible, in honour I suppose of Mr Reynolds' visit, but now he took it off as usual and it hung on the back of his chair; he polished his bald head with his big kerchief and addressed Joshua Reynolds. 'You say, Sir, that the mind must be enriched with Foreign matter. Of course.' His kerchief still polished. 'But what of "home-grown" matter?' he added mischievously. 'What, Sir, of the views of that fine English painter, Mr Hogarth?'

Mr James Burke laughed, and finally Mr Reynolds joined in. 'You know very well, I think, yes, there should be an *English* Academy of Art, John Palmer,' he said. 'But Hogarth wants to have an Academy to help Artists survive. I think an Academy is to dictate taste. Hogarth is a fool to think that British Art can grow here with nothing to fertilise it. Without the example of the great Old Masters of European painting, without the example of Michelangelo, we are nothing,' and they spoke then again of this mysterious thing they often spoke of, the Sistine Chapel in the Vatican in Rome: Michelangelo's masterpiece, its scenes of the Old Testament, its wonderful figures, its beautiful colours.

'It needs a great *clean*,' said John Palmer suddenly into the praise and glory. 'The smoke from all the candles in that Chapel over hundreds of years has dulled the ceiling, dulled the colours – it would be interesting to see if it could be cleaned. I would like to get up there on a scaffolding also, just like Michelangelo, only with a scrubbing brush!' and everybody laughed for John Palmer was rather rotund, and who would attack such glories with a scrubbing brush? but Mr Hartley Pond nodded in agreement with him for once, took extra snuff. 'I too wonder what Beauties might be excavated,' he said in his thin, pompous way.

Mr James Burke spoke of paintings of Rembrandt and Rubens that had found their way to London, there was much talk of prices and bargains and True Art. And Money. Money.

They talked and argued all afternoon till the light had almost gone and more candles were needed. —I listened, I saw them all, and yet I saw them differently: Mr Reynolds' rather bullish head, that handsome James Burke with his hair tied back like a sailor, Mr Hartley Pond's elegant, supercilious white curls, Miss Ffoulks' floating, insistent ribbons, John Palmer's sad, intelligent eyes, my brother's easy charm – and rage at my brother colouring everything I saw.

But then suddenly – as they talked on and on – with a great shock (so tremendous was my shock that I actually stood up wildly) I had if it does not sound preposterous a Revelation, a flashing wild Revelation.

They stared at me for my chair had fallen: I managed somehow to curtsey and retrieved the chair with the courteous help of John Palmer, I did not look at my brother, I went to find the candles, they went on talking – but I had seen what I had seen: my brother would not teach me, I could never study at any Academy, I could never go on a Grand Tour of Europe and see this Sistine Chapel – but of course *this dinner table* had already been my Academy and my Grand Tour – I was sixteen years old and I was a pupil here, I was privy to the thoughts and ideas of well known, influential Artists and Critics in a way that could teach me: did they not speak of Drawing and Painting all the time, *all the time*? – day after day here they talked of their own work and of the work of Old Masters, of the great Venetian artist Titian, of Michelangelo again and again – they talked of Rembrandt's self-portraits that they had seen and studied and copied – they talked of Raphael and Miss Ffoulks said it was well known that Raphael and Michelangelo had worked together and fought with each other – and my brother and his guests fought also, they disagreed with each other, they were jealous of each other, sometimes they knocked over the wine or even threw bread at one another, but they *never* stopped talking – they talked of egg tempera: of the exact mixing of egg-yoke with colour and water and secret ingredients; they spoke of the best oils to mix with colours; or they talked of the Religious Paintings all over Italy, Madonnas, Jesus after Jesus. —Everything they said I knew I could learn from, I could take everything inside me and take it back to my attic room to consider, think about – if I listened carefully I could surely, *surely* learn even if I was the housekeeper, and the word mocked me – *housekeeper* – and then someone in my family *did* come into my head ... *I saw a silent spinster in the dark dress, her hair pulled back under her white cap: the housekeeper who nobody noticed. I saw Aunt Joy* – and as the wine flowed freely and the laughter and the voices got louder and louder I understood what I might do to survive: I could be like Aunt Joy and *nobody would notice that I was learning.* —But then – but then – how would I paint? physically paint? for I could not just learn and not practise what I was learning – I would have to obtain paint, and brushes, and charcoal – very well, very well: I could work in my brother's Studio in the night, steal from the dark corners where the discarded, damaged canvases and boards lay, use the old brushes (he was always discarding brushes) steal his paints, he had so many paints – all around me the Artists spoke of their work and the new, wild ideas poured into my head.

And then dinner was over and Miss Ffoulks went off to one of her many Educational Meetings and my brother and Mr Joshua Reynolds and the others, still arguing loudly, all left the house together to go to one of the coffee houses to talk further of Art, and Euphemia cleared the table and I sat in the empty dining room as if I had been turned to stone, and no-one would have known what ideas exploded: *I could listen to them all in the day time and I could work in my brother's Studio in the night – for nobody ever noticed Aunt Joy.*

Later, I heard my brother return: he went straight to his own room, crashing against the walls.

All the next day I walked and walked around London, faster and faster, making my plans, planning my life, everything so intense in my thoughts, I was fuelled with such an angry energy that should anyone have attacked me or stole from me I believe I might have pulled their wigs off and kicked them; I walked towards the *piazza*, I slipped on fish-heads and shit, picked myself up again, everyone slipped in the London streets, and I could smell the filthy stinking gutters and rubbish heaps and then, just round a corner, down towards the Strand, I was assailed by a woman's perfume that was so overpowering, a kind of metallic rosewater and lamp-oil and onions and lavender and sweat, that I was no longer sure which was worse, the gutters or the woman, and that made me laugh, and I passed two small boys with pink eyes and no eyelashes and white hair who played flutes really badly and I kept walking; I passed men pissing in corners, one man lay on his side on the ground and pissed a fountain that he watched proudly, and women in rags squatted and shit poured in gutters, past all the stalls with their medicines and sweetmeats and cabbages, and coaches rattling through it all; all the wild noise, and all the shouting and laughing and screaming and singing of the crowds and me part of it all, and everywhere the brash, dirty street-girls – the girls with nothing: their youth and their age and their brave laughter (so it seemed to me) and the swellings on their faces that they tried to cover with paint – here was my other future Philip said, in the dim alleys – and if I closed my eyes for even a moment I saw it again: the look on his face as he stared at my Drawings, and then the way he pushed me away and tore the Drawings into tiny pieces *he destroyed my Pictures but he can never, **never** destroy me*, and I kept on walking, I kept on walking and in my rage I fell almost upon a cock-fight across an alley in Broad-street, I did not know then that it was a notorious and dangerous place: screeching, squawking fighting birds, blood and feathers and birdshit and the sweating wild cries of the gambling men in the shadows like the gambling men in Bristol, their cruel, wily faces, throwing their money down, calling their Bets and the screaming birds and I thought, *I will call mine, my Bets against my brother: I have the Gambling Blood.*

And at three o'clock there I was lighting the candles and the dinner was served as usual.

They were talking of a Titian painting that had been auctioned lately, talked of its worth. 'Absolutely remarkable,' said Mr Hartley Pond, 'the most glorious Colours, a velvet, gorgeous Painting. I should have died right there as I studied it in the Auction Room, it went finally for almost fifty guineas!' and there was a gasp about the table and I kept my gambling head down demurely and made not a sound and thought again of the beautiful print on the wall of the Bristol library, the first Old Master I ever saw.

They were talking of this new place: America. 'Full of Revolutionaries and Republicans, mark my words,' said Mr Hartley Pond, 'good Riddance to them,' leaning back with his wine-glass and smiling with his thin lips and I thought, *one day, when I have learned, I will do anything I like! I could go to America!*

They were talking of madmen and the lunatic asylum of Bedlam where you could go and watch the Lunatics. 'They say you may see them without Clothes,' said Mr Hartley Pond, 'but I doubt we would see such Figures as those of the Greeks.' And again the thin smile and I thought, *I will never, never be mad and seen without my Clothes.*

And then they went back again to Painting.

Miss Ffoulks made an excuse to stay a little longer after dinner that grey, gambling afternoon when the gentlemen left for their Clubs – she did not ask me any difficult questions but that day we sat together in the drawing room of the empty house, and – bending her head over some embroidery she always carried with her, 'I cannot bear to waste time, my dear,' Miss Ffoulks just began talking, talking about Art: she spoke as if the Old Masters were Artists of her acquaintance, not born hundreds of years ago – that afternoon she spoke of her visit with her brother to Rome and all the wonderful old Statues on every corner and I listened like a starving person, and then she told me about going to the Pope's palace, the Vatican, and about Michelangelo painting the ceiling of that Sistine Chapel there, lying on his back.

'Think of him!' she exclaimed, 'Painting the frescoes while lying upon a Contrivance made to hold him up there, all the colours falling into his hair perhaps as he painted each piece of damp plaster!' and she made me see him: the dark-haired young man Michelangelo (I had no idea if he was dark-haired but was he not Italian?) lying on his back and painting his pictures, piece by piece.

'I have heard, my dear,' said Miss Ffoulks, 'that Michelangelo quarrelled with the Pope who had commissioned the Ceiling. And that very Pope climbed right up, in his robes, and – right up there on the scaffolding that had been erected – His Holiness and Michelangelo punched each other about the ears!' and she looked at me slyly as I laughed as if to say, *I've made you laugh at last, as you usually do.* —Miss Ffoulks never once asked me what had happened between my brother and myself but I understood, that day, that this was her proud, spinsterish, kind way of comforting me because she saw I was in some way distressed.

'What happened to your Brother, Miss Ffoulks?'

She said very briskly, 'You are lucky to have a Brother, my dear. My own Brother died of the Fever,' and of course I wanted to say, *like our family in Bristol* – but all I could do was put my hand for just a moment on her arm and she nodded, as if to say thank you – and then we spoke again about Mr Titian and Michelangelo and later that night in my own room I went over everything that had happened and I vowed: *I made my own bet at the cock-fight and I will win against my brother*, and I thought about kind Miss Ffoulks, who had lost her brother but had looked after my own: Miss Ffoulks had no money it was clear, she let rooms and her gown was patched, and her gloves, but Miss Ffoulks had something, some fortitude inside herself so that people like Mr Hartley Pond could not make her feel slighted – some strength of intellect inside – but – *of course*: like the gentlemen, Miss Ffoulks had Learning – and had I not observed often how the gentlemen did tease her, sometimes kindly and sometimes not, for this Accomplishment? and I understood at last: *Miss Ffoulks was the first woman with Education that I had ever met.*

That is what I had to acquire – I not only knew almost nothing about Art, I knew nothing about anything, no wonder my brother thought me impudent – I was lucky that I could read and write, and that was only because of him – I had never read a proper book, all I knew from books was two pieces of Poems by that man Mr Shakespeare: *When I do count the clock that tells the Time . . . take him and cut him out in little stars . . .* and what use were those to me? that was hardly Education – the Father of Miss Ffoulks had been a curate she had told me, and had made sure that his daughter was educated by books, as well as his son, and then she had been on the Grand Tour with her brother, and so Miss Ffoulks had that inner thing that I hardly knew how to put into words inside my head, that confidence that came from Knowledge, and I was sixteen years old and I had no Knowledge at all and I understood clearly: *I will not succeed if I do not acquire Learning,* but I knew I could acquire real Learning at my brother's dinner-table, and then I could paint my learning in his Studio in the night, while he was out in the Town talking of Art.

I had decided to take my Gamble.

I planned coldly. My brother took five years to become a Painter: that was as long as I had spent on Christmas Steps.

Very well.

I could bear that.

Five years.

And then I would leave him.

'Filipo,' I said to my brother next morning.

'I have been waiting for your answer,' said Philip coldly: he saw me with my shopping basket. 'Pack up your belongings today if it is your decision to leave, for I shall require another housekeeper to take your place.'

'Thank you, Filipo,' I said, my head bowed. '*Grazie, mille grazie.* You have been very kind, I have thought of everything you said to me and I will do my best to please you. As your housekeeper.'

There was a small silence. I kept my head bowed so that he could not see my eyes.

'Well.' Another silence. 'Good. That is settled then,' said my brother, Philip. 'You have the makings of a good housekeeper, as long as you keep to your part of the house and your duties, and then we shall manage perfectly. And all shall be well – as we know it can – and our life shall be gay, Francesca, as I promised you: I will take you to the Theatre, you will see the very fashionable ladies. But,' my head was still lowered but I heard his change of tone, 'I forbid you to enter my Studio again. I will not have it, under any circumstances.' And then suddenly he laughed most charmingly – as if all between us was as it had been, and he was pleased.

'*Sorridere*, Francesca *bella!*' said my brother to me that morning. Smile.

And so.

And so I lifted my head, and I smiled at my brother.

Everywhere I walked in London I saw faces, they crowded into my head over and over, but now I thought, *I will learn, and I will paint them* – I looked at the rich men and the tough market women and the angry thin children whose faces would suddenly break into a smile as they went sliding through piles of horse dung, *I will paint them*, and the dark, chattering Italians in Lincoln's Inn Fields. I called out *Buongiorno* as I passed and a group of young men by the chapel called back *Buongiorno Signorina bella* and I wanted to paint all the faces I saw, capture them forever, I would learn how; I walked and walked and I heard a girl singing as she washed clothes in an open basement and I walked along the River with its masts and its coal-barges and London smoke drifted in the wind and I saw a body of a woman being hauled to the bank nearby with a hook on a long pole *not me, never me! they will never haul me out of the Thames!* and I walked to the Parliament where the laws were made and I walked to the Abbey of Westminster where all the Nobles had drunk and waved chicken bones at the Coronation, and I saw religious-men in long black cassocks buffeting together down Whitehall in a wild wind, and one afternoon as I returned to St Martin's Lane the madwoman sang:

> As I was walking one morning in Spring
> I heard a maid in Bedlam, so sweee-i-ly she sing
> Her chains she rattled with her hands, and this she sigh
>   and sing
> I love my love because I know he first love me

and I put one of Philip's precious pennies in her bowl, glad that she was not chained even if she was mad, and she smiled at me as she went on singing and her voice so high and sweet – *I know he first love me* – and I understood then what had happened to me – oh – oh what I am trying to say, but I do not have Mr Shakespeare's word-pictures, what I am trying to explain is that *London saved me.*

I mean that I believe to this day that I became firm about my Decision and about my Future and calmed my wild raging thoughts by walking the streets of London. —I fell in love with London you understand, all the bits of London: the wild streets and the old lady with her grapevines and the extravagant noise and energy and the Italians by the Chapel and the sumptuous shops on the Strand with their swinging signs and the river and the mad-woman whose voice haunted St Martin's Lane and the cock-fighting men and the pink-eyed flute-players and the street-girls in the shadows: I fell in love with London, for my love – and I had loved my brother so much – had to go somewhere.

London saved me.

And my brother? I was sixteen years old. I hated my brother.

—and then

and then, having made my bold plan, I had to be strong enough to carry it out.

Oh – at first it was slow and it was painful (it was so painful not to be *me*) to be what I was not – *five years* I whispered fiercely to keep my spirits up, *only five years, only the time I made hats, and then I will be free* but I was sixteen and ebullient and of course I could not *really* be like our Aunt Joy but how I tried, how I tried to learn to be the quiet sister, the Signorina Francesca di Vecellio, from Florence, Italy; the unobtrusive housekeeper, the indispensable woman in the background – like those ones who are running households all over London – me, Grace, become the lady in the dull gown and the white cap who lit candles as the grey evenings came down. —I learned the art of listening, I bit my tongue, stopping myself when a question seemed almost to pop out of my mouth, looking down as I listened, so that nobody could see the flashing and questioning and planning in my eyes *only five years*, Grace Marshall of Bristol: that wild, cunning girl . . .

. . . for my time was the night-time – my time had always been the night-time – had I not done my best drawing in the attic on Christmas Steps when the other hat-girls were asleep? —My brother was always out and about now in the evenings with his fashionable friends and the new assistants had to finish eventually, they slept in the Studio but they required Entertainment and food, I would hear them finish up, go out (one was a young man, a boy almost, he had a bright open expression and a cheeky smile, looking for life; the other was much older, already a disappointed artist, you could see the look in his eye, of failure and anger, mixed) – they very often came in late, laughing and unsteady. —So at night, when I heard the assistants leave, I lit two large bright candles and I slipped back to the empty forbidden Studio and began studying the colours, the oils – now I learned properly to name the colours absolutely: the different yellows and reds and greens and blues – and in the light of my candle I stared at the thickness of the paint on my brother's unfinished Portraits, touching it, feeling the textures with my fingers, guessing his paint mixtures from all that I had learned when I had been privy to his Secrets.

Mr Hartley Pond and Philip and Joshua Reynolds and John Palmer and all the painters who ever visited talked always of the importance of *copying*; well then, now that I was teaching myself, I set myself to copy my brother's Paintings in the night, in his empty Studio, by candlelight, with his own materials. —At first I used only charcoal – I copied the faces night after night, but it was easy, I copied the faces easily, I *had* to start to use paint, I had to begin to properly steal. I worked sparingly using *his* paints and *his* brushes and *his* boards (for it was harder to use his canvas and leave no trace): everything I always cleaned meticulously afterwards: he would never notice smeared paint on the old, discarded boards – and the disappearance of the paint? if it was noticed, I told myself, he could blame the assistants, and so quite soon working every single night as soon as the assistants left, I could easily paint exactly as my brother but was greatly dissatisfied with such work – but I did not understand what next I should be doing to learn my craft, so I kept on copying, especially trying to mix the exact colours that he had mixed. —But then one night I found myself looking at his Paintings in another way for the first time – and I saw that they were clever, but that in my heart I had not ever really liked them – I somehow, instinctively, felt they were – even the men – *too pretty.* I had never, out of loyalty, allowed myself to articulate criticism of my brother: now I said it, aloud in his Studio, *They are too pretty.*

One night I thought there was somebody there in the dark, closed Studio and I felt that horrible jumping feeling in my heart; I lifted a candle so nervously the candle-flame shook, I saw it – and then I laughed aloud: Philip had acquired a Greek statue! I lifted the candle higher and saw that the statue was naked and I felt quite strange: I had never seen a naked body before, it was a man so every now and then as I was working I would throw him a glance and then I got quite used to him and then I started to converse with him sometimes as I was copying, I called him George, after the King of England.

And then one night I thought of something different I could do.

I was copying Philip's Paintings, but because of the candlelight (for it was always dark by the time I could slip into his Studio) I realised that in reality I saw his Paintings *differently* and after some time I began to *copy* his Paintings differently: not trying to copy them as they were, but using more light and shade than he used, actually trying to paint how the light from my candle caught the faces … something … something … I liked these copies better but, but … something was hovering in my thoughts – oh how I longed to put my questions about light and shade at the dinner-table, how I bit my cheek and my lips to stop myself blurting out my words for I had quickly come a long way and I simply did not know how to proceed.

Then, one morning in an Auction room I used to pass, always staring at the Pictures for Sale, I found a small Painting by a Painter called Mr Joseph Wright of Derby – Mr Wright had his characters lit by candlelight but the candlelight was *inside his Painting.* —I felt a thrill of recognition, carved his name on my heart: Mr Joseph Wright of Derby – from that moment I understood then that there was a *different way of painting*, nothing like the way my brother the Portrait-Painter worked, and because of my own experiments with candlelight I understood, and I was elated. —I asked the Auction-man but he knew nothing of the Artist, 'Just a young man starting is all I know,' said the Auction-man, 'you can have it for a guinea,' but he may as well have asked for a hundred guineas but on the way home I found an old hopscotch square drawn in an alley and I jumped and hopped with joy round and round by myself with my housekeeper's basket because I had found Mr Joseph Wright of Derby and now at night I would copy one of Philip's paintings but with the light coming from *inside* the painting: I painted a candle placed on a table *inside* the painting that would catch only one side of the face, something like the way Mr Joseph Wright of Derby painted (and I remembered with glee what Mr Joshua Reynolds had said, *There is no such thing as plagirism*) and I said *look at this, George* to the naked statue and I even signed my first new kind of painting with a flourish, MISS GRACE MARSHALL OF LONDON – I wiped everything clean at once of course, tidied up the Studio so that it looked as if nobody had been.

Slowly I understood what it was I had discovered – the light could come from inside the painting, or it could come from outside the painting but it was as if . . . as if the light and the shadows would – could – add some mood, some *feeling* to the painting *that would otherwise not be there* – it was like a miracle because I had worked it out for myself.

And then:

One night one of the assistants found me there, in my brother's Studio – the older assistant, the one with the angry look as if life had already cheated him – he caught me red-handed: there with my brother's paints and my brother's board – I had been so concentrated I had lost, for a moment, my cunning, and stayed too long.

'Well *Seeengoreeena.*' He just looked at me, expressions crossing his face one after another, 'I thought you was a thief,' he said, with much meaning in his tone and I could not hide, I could not pretend, I could only stand there with the brush still in my hand and then he looked at my Painting, he came closer, I could hear his breathing and I could smell him: dirt and despair, and I heard his surprised intake of breath as he looked at what I had done.

'I see,' was all he said. But he *knew*: I understood that he knew: that I was not playing with paints.

'I was a Painter once,' he said. And still he stood there too close to me, I could smell sweat and onions and beer and dirt and Turpentine – I did not move, and he did not move, there very close together by my brother's portrait of a Duke and my own smaller, differently-lit copy – I could hear both of us, breathing, and the two candles I had placed by the easel flickered, almost went out but I saw his stained hands, his black, filthy nails.

'He said you ain't allowed in here,' said the assistant. 'He said no-one from the house,' and then he touched my neck and I flinched and looked at him in horror, and then, he watching me all the time, I moved away quickly, washed the brushes quickly, put the colours away quickly; quickly I wiped the old boards with Turpentine, I could hear my heart beating – the assistant watched me all the while, never speaking, and then as I put the last cleaned brush back where it had been he moved quickly: *pphhht ppphhht*, he blew out both the candles, and he lunged at me in the darkness, so near, that smell so close, and he took my shoulders and then one of his hands with the black nails squeezed my breast so that I cried out and then he pulled at my petticoats and pressed against me I could feel the thing, the milliner girls said *the thing*, pressing into me and I screamed so loud that he got a fright and then I punched his head and slipped underneath his arm and ran from my brother's Studio and into my own room where I locked my door and still I could smell onions and sweat and dirt, it was disgusting, and I heard footsteps and then Euphemia's voice called, 'Are you all right *Seeegnorina*? What's happened?' and I called back 'Nothing, go away!' and finally the house went quiet again and only my breathing as I leaned out of the window trying to breathe in air that was cleaner, and much later my brother returned.

And then, the very next day, the younger assistant, the one with the cheeky smile, was dismissed – he was sent from the house without warning that morning – for stealing my brother's paints, my brother was shouting, 'Very much of my paint has gone!' and I heard the boy so loudly protesting his innocence, and I saw his very small bundle of belongings on his back as he left, and I saw him wipe his nose with his hand, as if he did not care for any person; he was even younger than me, he had had that bright hopeful face, and

I saw that now he was frightened even though he tried to hide under an air of nonchalance, and I felt ashamed, and then I saw the face of the older assistant: he did not care about the boy, perhaps he even got the boy dismissed, and he stared at me – he remained silent as the protesting boy was shut out, stared at me coolly and I saw him sizing me up and I felt a kind of panic arising inside me – as he passed me in the big hallway he said very quietly and he was smiling, *I will see you there, just you and me now*, and I could smell him again and I felt physically sick – if my brother knew what I had been doing he would turn me out of the house also and all my plans finished: it was as if the assistant held me in his hands.

But what else could I do, for paints? for boards? for brushes? for a place to work? —I had no money, the older assistant would not let himself be fired – and he was expecting a reward, for his silence – I was desperate and wild and ashamed for the jaunty, dismissed boy sent out into the London morning, and I had no idea what to do and I sat at the dinner table that afternoon and my hands were like ice as I lit the candles and went for more wine and that night the man came to my room – how did he know which was my room? assistants did not come to the top, that was not their part of the house – luckily I had locked the door but he knew my brother was not in the house and he knew I was inside.

'Open the door, my Fancy.' The voice was low but I heard every word and wondered who else might hear – where was Euphemia? – where was the cook?

'Open the door, open it now or I will tell your Brother.'

My voice was low also. 'Why should I care? He will not mind.'

'I think he will mind.'

'I do not care!'

'Why did you let the boy take the blame then?'

I was silent and again saw the boy who was younger than me, his small bundle and his stricken face as he was turned out into Pall Mall without references, or money.

'Open the door!' His voice was louder, and now he rattled at the handle.

'I will tell my brother that you have been bothering me, he will dismiss you at once.'

'No, he will not.' His voice came muffled through the door. 'He needs me, he cannot afford to lose two assistants at once when there is so much work, I will be working there every night now, he has had to give me more wages! So we will be meeting – you need me too, my Fancy.' I could hear his heavy breathing, 'Let us come to some Arrangement then or I will tell him who is the real Thief!' My silence agitated him, again he rattled the door-handle. '*Open the door!*' and it seemed an Eternity before he went away: perhaps he heard the servants, perhaps he got tired but he kicked the door as he left and called one more thing through the door, as if he did not care if all the servants in the house heard him.

'I think your Fate depends on me, *Seeengoreeena*.' And I wished I could kill him.

All my plans, all my ideas for teaching myself in my brother's Studio – I who never cried wept in the night out of frustration, in the day I hurried past my brother's Studio as if it no longer interested me – I often made Euphemia accompany me up to the top floor, I saw him waiting, still as a cat in the shadows, ready to pounce. Euphemia said to me, 'Why do you not tell your Brother he is bothering you?'

'Never mind!' I said to her angrily. 'It is not your business.'

My brother's Studio with all the treasures it held: the paints the colours the charcoal the boards the canvases the brushes, was closed to me, *I have to find money to buy what I need and I will paint in my bed-room* – Philip still went over the accounts with me each week, protested that I had spent too much, that there were cheaper stalls, that his hospitality meant I must shop more carefully, even one penny glass of ginger beer made him tighten his lips; he counted out the money carefully as I closed his Notebook until next time.

'It is my hard-earned money you are spending on pennies given to the mad singer,' he said when he left me. 'Never forget that.'

I became desperate – everything: *everything* depended on stabbing the assistant to Death (I dreamed that I did) or getting some money of my own – I would do without canvases, I would do with the oldest boards and the cheapest brushes, but I *had* to have charcoal and paint – even a black-lead pencil was sixpence. —I thought of asking help of the two people I liked the most and had known the longest, Miss Ffoulks or John Palmer – but obviously they had so little themselves, both of them, Miss Ffoulks had re-sewn her gown, and I remembered John Palmer hiding a piece of bread from our table in his pocket, and how, anyway, could I speak to them without betraying my brother? and all the time the assistant lurked, biding his time, I could smell him I could smell him in my sleep and the house seemed now to trap me and I kept thinking *I cannot stop now I have to paint **I have to paint**...*

... well then.

Well then. I was sixteen years old and had perhaps once been respectable but I knew more than might be expected – had I not haunted the docks for years? – I had lived for years on Christmas Steps where the cries in the night echoed up in to the attic room while I drew my Family from inside my heart, I had heard the laughter, and the groans, and the clink of money, and the fights; I had seen the odd shapes, jerking up and down in the shadows, I knew more than might be expected. —I worked it all out, finally, quite coldly, in my head – if I went to the assistant I could keep using my brother's materials perhaps but every night I would have to, as usual, destroy my Work. As well as destroy my heart.

I may as well get money for it then.

So, finally, knowing exactly what I was doing, I went where I guessed I could earn money for certain – was I not one of the wild, dishonest Wiltshire Marshalls? – what did it matter? – what did I care?

At first I watched them from further off; with my basket and my respectable bonnet I watched them, the street-girls: I knew girls worked in St James's Park down behind the trees – was not that where my brother told me he had been with a street-girl, that night? – I walked there, sometimes the red jacket of a soldier flashed against the green; sometimes it was a young boy who disappeared with a soldier, and re-appeared again, clutching some pennies; it was all just like Bristol in the end, but if my brother chose that place I would keep away from St James's Park: I started haunting the *piazza* at Covent Garden. —They worked even in early mornings, took their customers down those dark alleys off the *piazza*, down there where daylight did not come, where I had clung to my brother's arm, where ghosts very likely walked, where the girl that was being beaten had taken me – so I began to follow them down the alleys; in dark doorways the girls lifted their skirts, the men unbuttoned. —Soldiers and sailors and crooks came, but gentlemen too, and a vicar – every sort of man, crowding into the *piazza*, looking over the goods, sometimes it was over in a few moments – the men just emptied themselves almost as if they were pissing, only with a bit more jerking and groaning. —I watched and saw that the more experienced girls asked for their money *first*: a shilling, sixpence – despairingly sometimes a few pennies; they had to be really desperate, or old, or ugly, to lift their skirts before they clutched the coin and I wondered if my brother ever came here also as well as St James's Park? – and the young ones, the pretty ones, the ones who therefore got the most customers, insisted on the pouches of sheep's gut with the red ribbon that the men wore; if the men refused they flounced off: they could afford to be more choosy – yes, I knew how important the red-ribboned pouches were, the men used them to keep clean and the girls used them so as not to get a child, the pouches were made of sheep-gut and the men had to draw them up upon themselves. —I had seen them, discarded, on Christmas Steps – *O God what am I thinking of?* but then I heard the assistant *Open the door, my Fancy,* and his foul heavy breathing and his black nails and I saw again the young boy who did not steal the paints with his small bundle, and the gesture of courage as he wiped his hand across his face and I did not want to think that that boy was braver than me and most of all *I must go on painting.*

If I earned a shilling I could buy three parcels of colour; if I worked at the *piazza* for a whole evening I could even buy my own brush perhaps; if I had a brush and three parcels of colour I could just steal charcoal, paper and perhaps one other colour, if I worked for two nights I could perhaps buy my own charcoal and some paper as well – that's how my thoughts ran around my head – and slowly I tried to converse with some of the girls as I went about my morning shopping: they spat at me and swore at me and told me to get out of their area, I did not seem like them, this was their place. —I always had my shopping on my arm, they stole bread from me, one of them took my lady's glove and threw it in the gutter with the shit, and then retrieved it and hid it in her clothes; I became more and more desperate: *I do not know how to proceed by myself, they have to let me join them*: but, day after day – as they took my shopping, and pulled at my hair – they would not, and in the evenings I could smell the assistant as he hung about the staircases: again I quite seriously considered how I might kill him.

And then one morning a voice spoke right behind me as I tried once again to get someone among the street girls to talk to me with my basket full of food and a big fish-eye staring out: 'Why don't yer get a rich gentleman, girl?' said the voice, "Stead of hangin' around us?' I turned round quickly: it was the girl I had helped when she was being beaten with the sword-sticks. 'They told me someone was bothering them, I couldn't think it was you, girl! We don't want yer here, sorry, yore not one of us but if yore so desperate yer could get a rich man to set yer up, yer've got the look, yer've got the manner, leave us alone.' Some of the other street-girls crowded around but now they did not say very much, just listened and watched.

'I cannot,' I said. *'Please, please help me!'* I was desperate, I saw this one girl would be my only chance even for a proper conversation, I was so anxious that my Italian accent was completely gone: I was me, Grace Marshall. 'What else can I do but work here? I *have* to.'

She looked at me suspiciously. 'Why?'

'I have to work, I have to get some money but I can only work in the early evenings,' *when Philip is at the clubs or the coffee houses,* and perhaps there was something in my face, or perhaps she remembered that, once, I had helped her.

'Yer wont like it, and yer can't play at it, it's not a game, this.'

'I wont play at it, I have to get some money.'

'Are yer sure?'

'I am sure.'

'Well.' She looked me up and down. 'Yore pretty I spose.' Still she looked at me quite coldly, as if I was a horse perhaps, tweaked at my petticoats to see I had two legs and two feet. 'Well then,' she said slowly at last, shrugging, 'well, at least I know you can run fast!' Still she looked me over. 'I tell you what, I'll show yer and see if yore any good.' She shrugged again. 'You can try with me, I'll see, yer look as if yore a bit of a lady, and fine, they'll like that, we might get a better class of gentleman, but if yer try any tricks I'll ruin yore face and that's a promise. All right, get off,' she said to the other girls and some of them murmured and one of them laughed and then they began to disperse. 'I use a flower name,' she said to me, 'since we're round the Garden, everyone who works with me has to be a flower. I'm Poppy.'

Quick as a flash I answered her, 'I'm Daisy,' and she laughed, genuine laughter, 'You sound like yer been before!' but I shook my head.

'I gotta good place,' she told me. 'I'll show yer now, only hurry up, I gotta get back to work, I'm needing extra customers today.' She took me eastwards through even darker alleys, expertly pushing me out of the way of a chamberpot being emptied above us, past open sewers and stinking gutters – suddenly we came upon a dark, disused churchyard; it took us only a few moments but here a fog or a mist seemed to lay like a garment. 'Not used now,' she said with satisfaction, 'not for prayers anyrate, but where they buried the bodies is an arch, and a walkway, look, here.'

'Oh,' I said.

'Are you scared?' she said, seeing my face, mocking me. 'Course there's ghosts – but they ain't got money,' and she laughed and I managed a smile. 'Here, look here, see this wall, you can sit on it to lift your skirt and it's easier, and I know little hidden paths – there, see, and there – where you can run if there's trouble, they won't know the paths, and the fog keeps us safe and sometimes yer can feel in their clothes at the back while they're at it and if you ain't greedy you can take a bit more and they'll never be aware.' And she showed me the winding way back towards the *piazza*. 'But yer can hardly bring your basket, or your bonnet! Yer'll have to let down your hair.'

'Very well,' I said, as if I did not care.

'*Very well*,' said Poppy, imitating me but she was smiling. 'Just at eventide is the best of all,' she said, 'before they go for their sociality and spend all their gold,' and I thought *yes, that time, just at eventide* and I clutched my loaves and my onions and my milk and the heavy, cold fish.

So that I would not have time to fear I said to Poppy, 'Will you meet me this evening?' She laughed again and nodded – somehow I liked her laugh, I would have liked to paint her laugh, it was too hard for a young girl, but it was real.

That afternoon I could hardly listen to Mr Hartley Pond as he looked down his nose and pronounced his pronouncements about the Sublime Male Body. —As the day drew down I shivered as I lit the candles and then I quite simply left the room and did not return: everybody was talking, everybody was inebriated and loud and speaking of Art. —I told Euphemia to make sure everybody's glass was filled and to clear afterwards: they would hardly notice it was not me, I took my cloak but not my bonnet and slipped out into St Martin's Lane and the high sweet voice of the madwoman echoed into the evening, *If all the world was paper and all the seas were ink* . . .

'I was just going to start without yer,' said Poppy into the dusk. 'Undo yer hair.'

My dark hair fell over my shoulders, and my heart beat so loud I thought it to be heard all over the *piazza*. She looked at me as if she did hear it. 'Ain't yer ever done it before?' I shook my head and I saw her regarding me in the half-dark.

'I know everything,' I said. Still she stared at me. 'I have to have the money,' I said quite desperately: she could not leave me now.

'Then you shall have it, Daisy!' she said, and she offered me a bottle. 'Here. Gin helps it to pass better,' and we both took large gulps and it burned my throat, so fast did I gulp it. 'But just for trust – what's yer real name?'

I answered her straight off and I think she saw I was telling her the truth. 'My real name is Grace,' I said to her and she did a strange thing: leaned over and briefly kissed my cheek as if we'd made some kind of bargain.

'We'll be Partners then,' she said and then she lowered her voice, 'we each charge two shillins a go, because we're classy, and you pay me sixpence of that every time, all right?' I must have looked dumb-founded, *nearly two pods of paint I had to pay her every time I had a customer?* 'Yer can't think I wouldn't charge yer! This is a business, same as any other and I'm teachin' yer,' and I nodded, of course she was right. 'But if yer steal, yer can keep that, but you take the risk, right?' and I nodded again. 'Well you've got a bonny face, only cheer up for God's sake! and follow me,' and I heard her laughter echoing across the *piazza* as we walked away from most of the other girls, towards one end where there was half-light from nearby windows, we were shadowy but clear.

'We're pretty, we can still afford to be seen in the light!' she said and her experienced little face looked about. 'They often come in twos,' she said, 'to protect theirselves! And that'll suit us too!'

And soon, sure enough, two gentlemen sauntered – their clothes were fine enough and their voices were fine enough, they spoke together in the dusk and laughed; they rejected several advances, obviously looking over the goods.

'Hello my dears,' said Poppy, stepping forward and pulling me with her. They stopped.

'Well, well,' said one, 'well God bless us, here's a pretty thing or two.'

'And we stay pretty,' said Poppy cheekily, 'by making sure you cover your weapon, me and Daisy here, so don't come near us else.'

'O come, come, not so much fun,' he said it like an old refrain but Poppy was having none of it.

'Then walk on gentlemen,' she said, and she turned away and me with her, even as my heart sank. 'We're not going with anyone who doesn't cover their poxy piece, that's for sure,' she whispered. 'But they'll be returning or I ain't a judge!' And sure enough they stopped and turned, and from their pockets showed us the red ribbons dangling.

'Two shillings each,' said Poppy and this time they were affronted.

'Two shillings *and* a cover? By Jingo, you should be in Mayfair child, not Covent Garden.'

It was then that Poppy pushed me forward.

And I stood in front of the gentlemen and I thought of the two shillings minus sixpence and what I could buy and I smiled and something made me say, as cheeky as Grace Marshall used to be, 'I'm Daisy, you'll be lucky with me gentlemen, don't you see it?' and I saw them smile at my brazenry in the half-night and take in my face and my long dark hair and had I not been told often enough of my dark beauty now that I had grown?

One of them pushed forward. 'This is mine,' he said and the other gentleman took Poppy's arm, but she brushed him free.

'We know a fine, private place,' she said, 'you must follow us,' and I saw them exchange a glance as if to say *Will this be safe?* but we were so young, and so pretty, they could manage us and more besides, but one of them had his hand on his sword-stick as he walked. 'You ain't scared of us now?' said Poppy and they laughed, for her confidence had a kind of charm and she was young and she was pretty and they were lustful and we all walked back through the alleys she had shown me in the morning, Poppy was sure-footed and fearless and the clock struck six and I thought of the safety of the dining-room in Pall Mall and it got darker and colder and we were soon by the deserted church and the arches and the swirling mist that seemed to live there and I was never so frightened in my life.

'Now come by here,' said Poppy, 'for two shillings you are safer than anywhere, no-one to disturb our little delights, so give us the money and put on your armour.' And with some little grumbling the money was given over but they kept their hands upon us quite roughly so that we could not run away and I saw they looked about them, in case we had accomplices, then Poppy jumped upon the wall and pulled her gentleman, who was already unbuttoning, towards her.

The other man could now hardly see me, nor I him, there was not even half-light like back there, at the *piazza*. 'Now what can you offer me that is worth two shillings, little Daisy?' he said to me as he, too, urgently unbuttoned and put the sheep-gut upon himself, muttering, and then pressed himself against me.

'This is her first time,' called Poppy from her place further along the wall as her gentleman thrust at her. 'You are a lucky fellow.'

'I do not expect that that is the truth!' he said as he fumbled at my skirt and my petticoats, pushing them upwards, I could feel the cold air on my skin and his sweating body with its extrusion as he felt me *paints* I said to myself wildly, *paints* as he pushed to enter and I half-sat half-lay on the low wall *four parcels of paints*.

I do not know what I expected as he clasped at me and pushed into me except that I did not expect it to be so painful; I cried out and there must have been something in my cry, or in my body, that made him know it was indeed the first time as he tried to enter me, because he got more and more excited, again and again he pushed, sweating and sweating and his breath became wild, on and on as he understood, on and on pushing but now the stone wall bit into my body as he plunged me back and back, I was aware of other sounds from further along the wall *four parcels of paint*, I kept almost crying, *four parcels of paint* perhaps I cried aloud and as I cried something made me remember Poppy's instructions and I felt round him into a pocket and felt many coins, I took only three in my hand and left the rest as I cried out and at last my gentleman called out *God God God* in the churchyard as if it was appropriate and fell upon me, and at last was still.

I serviced four gentlemen that night. The third complained that I was pretty but that I was bleeding. The fourth complained that I was crying.

I told myself I'd seen it fifty times at least on Christmas Steps, so what was it to me? It was nothing.

I gave Poppy four sixpences: two shillings.

'See yer tomorrow,' said Poppy.

'See you tomorrow,' I said.

Next morning, my basket on my arm, my back and all inside my body hurting and ripped and bruised, I was the first customer at the Colourman's shop in St Martin's Lane – as well as my one shilling and sixpence multiplied by four I had extracted three guineas from the first gentleman's pocket as he called to God above me, and a half-guinea had fallen from another's cloak as he left. —I had a *fortune.*

I bought some charcoal, two sixpenny pencils, three brushes, two boards, sheets and sheets of paper, and twelve little parcels of paint, *twelve* – all these things were mine – and I was to be seen lighting the candles, making sure all was well, at three in the afternoon, as usual.

As if nothing had happened.

But: I could not, I *could not* go back. *I could not face the idea of doing that again.*

From that night, I was driven in a different way: you might almost say that from now on demons drove me as I began to turn myself into a proper Painter – and in my bed-room, I secreted the things I had obtained: I had no palette to hold my colours, I did not have an easel, I sat on my bed and laid out my brushes and oil on the chair and smoothed out the paper on the table as my candles flickered and danced – and I had Miss Ffoulks' little sewing boxes that she had given me, hidden side by side in the drawer in my mahogany wardrobe, and these sewing boxes held my treasures: my colours, and I wished that I could tell her so – and right at the back, a smaller box still, with the remains of the money that had changed my life.

My small bed-room in St Martin's Lane was my very first Studio.

The assistant, frustrated that I had truly abandoned my brother's Studio, nor given him any answer, grabbed my arm from the shadows on the staircase one night – I had almost forgotten him, I did not fear him now, I punched his ear, he was so surprised he cried out, 'What did you do that for?'

'You keep away from me,' I shouted, not caring who heard, 'or I'll get you dismissed!' and I added 'I was only playing, all those weeks ago, I'm not interested in such tedious matters as painting Pictures any longer!' and I laughed to myself, my new laugh, when he disappeared back into the Studio. 'Tell him what you like!' I called after him, 'I'm never going back there, I do not care and you should take care to say nothing for the maid saw you by my room, and will speak for me!'

And so I began, tentatively, painting in my own space. —Every night I drew, and then painted (with my heart beating oddly at how far I had now travelled) people I had seen in the streets outside, but *differently*, painting the light and the dark. —Sometimes I made the faces turn away from the source of light in my mind so that shadows fell; I never, ever went near my brother's Studio, unless I was certain the house was empty, I only stole now discarded boards and torn canvases from dark corners if I absolutely had to and with my money, my own money, I bought more paper and more charcoal and more brushes and more tubs of colour and some linseed oil and another board. —My Paintings were darker than anything I had seen, or perhaps more weird, anyway, less distinct – perhaps this new way I had found was insane, but it was my own way – I was not sure where the new darkness came from: it was not just Mr Wright of Derby, it seemed to come from inside me. —The assistant lurked still, confused, I could smell him along the passageway but I took no notice, he had no power now; I worked and worked and worked, night after night after night – yet over and over again I saw it was not right, I could not remember the faces I had seen clearly enough, if only I could have a model, my own model, a real face before me as I worked – but I persevered and sometimes in the night when I was painting with such concentration, the girl I had painted on the wall in Bristol, my pretend friend Mary-Ann, seemed to come into the room, or at least into my head, and I talked to her quite naturally, told her what I was doing; I tried to draw her face but could not get her exactly, as I had that morning in Bristol when the baker was making his bread, because, although she was the only friend I had ever had, I could never, now, exactly draw her sweet face – but it was so wonderful to be able to speak to someone even if – I was quite sane and knew I was talking to myself – she was not a real person. —I told Mary-Ann how painting by candlelight had made me paint differently – I did not tell her about Covent Garden and yet she seemed to say to me, *You never went back. You never even thanked her. Poppy looked after you. You should have told her you were not coming back*, but I could not go back.

I avoided the *piazza*.

Once in the night when I was painting with such concentration, I painted the young, knowing face of Poppy, but when I finished it I was so shocked that I destroyed it: a face that was knowing and pretty and hard and cold.

Because I saw there was much in that face, of me.

Because I had become so cunning with all my Secrets now I realised there was one more very cunning thing I had to do; my brother must not know what I was doing, he must not, not till I was ready to be free, I knew that he did not want me to paint, *that he was nervous that what I had might be a Talent* – so I hit then upon my plan, to make him think I had forgotten such foolishness.

I knew that because of the long hours I was now working in my room it would not be possible to completely hide the fact that I dabbled in painting in this house; that assistant already knew, eventually someone would see, or guess; it was not possible that someone would not walk into my room one day; it was not possible that I would never have paint on my fingers – but I lived in the house of a Painter, after all. —They said Mr Joshua Reynolds' sister dabbled, an *amateur* – it would be natural, would it not, that the sister of an Artist might dabble, might paint flowers say: an *amateur* Lady Painter?

Very well. I would add yet another layer to my pretence, I would pretend to be a rather untalented Lady Painter, who occasionally painted flowers in her room – that is what people had to think – so one evening I painted, in crude oil paint (I did not mean to laugh when I painted it but I could not help myself: of course I had learned perfectly well to mix the oils and the colours but I did not want Philip to know that) a bunch of Lilies: stiff, white Lilies, as far away from anything in the world that I was interested in as the stars in the sky – although actually I am interested in the stars in the sky *take him and cut him out in little stars and he will make the face of heaven so fine that all the world will be in love with night* as I learned from Mr Shakespeare, they are part of my firmament and my learning, the stars – and in London I often watched how the clouds and the smoke of that dark night-city moved across the stars sometimes, like drifts of pale silk, how beautiful it can be, and sometimes how unsettling, the stars.

The Lilies, then, were not my style, but it was to be the one painting you would clearly have seen should you have felt called upon for some reason to enter my room – the Lilies were there, on the wall, my secret and my defence.

And I painted something else with the white Lilies: a green Daisy – like the one I had painted that day of my Ninth Birthday in the garden of the house in Queen's Square, and where was Tobias now to bring me a red Rose? – a green, spiky Daisy – *My name is Daisy*, I had said on the *piazza* – as a tiny warning to my brother, Philip Marshall of Bristol: a green and dangerous Daisy.

And my Masterstroke was to show it to him while the assistant was present: I actually took my Painting to the Studio. '*I fiori, Filipo, caro mio,*' I said to him in my now rather fine Italian accent, 'I am painting, as Mr Reynolds' sister is painting – here are my own Flowers,' showing him the finished Picture – and I caught it, *I saw it I saw it I saw it*: the look of – *relief* – upon his face – he did not even notice the green, menacing Daisy – *Insane Daisy* as he had called it so long ago, *fool* – for it seemed clear to him from the clumsy Painting that I was to be, after all, no threat at all to my illustrious brother, Filipo di Vecellio; he did not even ask where I had got the board, the oils (I was prepared: I was going to say that I had met Mr Reynolds' sister, Fanny, and she had given them to me, he would never have been interested enough to question her) but he asked me nothing: he no doubt explained to himself that I had given up my childish fancies of painting faces – *fool* – if I wanted to paint bad Flowers in my own room in my own time what was that to him, why would he care where I got my rather badly-mixed colours from? —And it was always said that Mr Reynolds' sister Fanny painted rather badly, it was what Artists' sisters obviously did, in the shadow of their Famous Brothers, and I saw the assistant looking also from a corner of the Studio and I know that I flashed him a look of Triumph – he was just lucky, that horrible man, that I was not a Farmer's Wife, and did not have a carving knife.

'I shall now buy old Art from Europe,' Philip announced casually at dinner one day. 'I am rich enough to buy such Paintings now – even one day an Old Master perhaps,' and the others nodded approvingly but my heart did a somersault: *an Old Master that I could properly study! a real Old Master living here in St Martin's Lane!* and he did indeed begin to invest in old Art: some Paintings from the Netherlands, from Italy, always asking Mr Hartley Pond to verify that he was not being defrauded (for it was known there were many fake paintings that had made their way into London from across the water) and finally he put a painting of Venice, believed to be an early Canaletto, just at the bottom of the stairs and people commented at its Form and Beauty – I could have wished for more faces, but this was better than nothing. —I would spend hours in front of it at night when the house was empty, studying close up by candlelight old paint, old skills, old colours, how he painted water; trying to discern secrets, always in the night, always by candlelight. —To copy it from where it hung so publicly would have been impossible: one night I lifted it – it was quite large and heavy – and took it to my bed-room, copying this was a much harder task than copying Philip's Portraits, and I stared at the wonderful colours and the light, the way the light glowed on the water and the small boats and the figures and the great buildings – I tried to guess the Recipes for colours, experimented with my own colours secretly as small candles flickered, hated taking the Painting back to the hallway.

And every week I counted my supply of money: it grew smaller and smaller: I closed my thoughts to what I would do next but soon it would start all over again: no money, no paint – one of the little parcels I had bought, a vermilion, seemed to have been mixed with something else to give it bulk, I had heard at the dinner-table of this practice, I saw when I used it that it had been meddled with and was not pure paint, I had been cheated and I wept with rage.

I was staring at a good, honest portrait of an old lady in the window of Mr Valiant's auction house in Poland-street, DUTCH SCHOOL it said, when I felt the pull on my arm, sharp, fingers in my arm.

'Well, Miss Grace?'

It was Poppy – I was so shocked and so ashamed I felt my face burning: shocked at her accosting me in public but much worse – shame that I had not at least gone back to talk to her.

'Please do not be angry with me Poppy,' I said at once. 'I could not.'

'You could not what? Speak to me? Have the decency to speak to me after all I done for yer? The other girls said I was a fool and I was. Ungrateful cow you are when I shared my Secrets, and rude as well – look at yer – looking up and down the Street now, in case yer seen with me. And why are yer talking funny?'

How did I know who I was, there outside the auction house with Poppy: Grace or the *signorina*? 'Poppy please, it is my fault but I could not.'

'An' if I feel like that? That I "could not"? No choice, me!' She was almost spitting, her pretty face hard. 'Too High and Mighty to even tell me you ain't returning, and me your Friend – I waited for you.'

'Poppy, I beg of you, do not be so angry, for I was so grateful to you – but I cannot do it.'

'Too late. You done it, Miss. He come back looking for yer, he wanted you again even though yer took his money. He said you was worth it.' She did not even bother to lower her voice.

I was so ashamed and so angry and so embarrassed that I took her shoulders and shook her, Grace Marshall from Bristol. 'Poppy, listen to me, I was grateful, I needed you, I needed the money and I promise, one day, I will repay you for your kindness!'

'*Kindness*!' she said and she laughed her laugh and tossed her head but I saw I had hurt her, for she thought she had found a good partner and she had taken a risk and trusted me and shared some of her secrets. 'Bugger off, Miss Goddam Grace,' she said. 'Little

Madonna,' she said, and she said it like an insult. 'But don't forget I know yore Secret, Grace, whoever you are, and I'll always know yore Secret, you're a street-girl, you, just like us!' and she turned away.

I watched her in silence: shame, embarrassment, anxiety. —I thought of the small, diminishing pile of money left. 'Poppy!' I called to her retreating back, I thought she would not heed but she slowed a little and I ran to her, took her arm.

'Let me come tonight,' I said.

She looked at me in silence for such a long time. 'You'll have to pay me ninepence a time,' she said at last.

So: I replenished my store of money regularly – what did I care? What did it matter? – as long as I got paint and paper and charcoal; and the more I achieved the more I wanted, most of all, I needed an easel, like my brother, and one day I would have a real palette for colours, and I wanted canvas of my own, to become very familiar with the difference between painting on board and painting on canvas and that meant I somehow had to make stretchers in the small bed-room, to nail the canvas upon, I would have to make the stretchers myself, I could never afford the services of a frame-maker like my brother so I would have to become a carpenter: I needed a hammer and nails – all these things cost money. *I needed all these things for my work*, what did I care how I paid for them? —I always carried the small notebook and a pencil, to write down what money of Philip's I spent and sometimes I would see a person in the street who took my attention: I would, surreptitiously, quickly sketch what I saw into the back of the accounts notebook, taking care to remove it so he would not see – I still remembered Mr Hogarth's advice but my thumbnail was so small. —Then using every precious second when I was not being my brother's housekeeper or a street-girl, I went on painting, late into the night, in my bed-room my own Studio; trying to make the quick drawing turn into something more: failing often, succeeding sometimes, but I could not draw arms and legs, the fall of a shoulder – would I have to be stuck with just a face for ever and ever? night after night I puzzled over my painting—

—and in the evenings in the dark alleys afterwards, Poppy and me as I paid her, ninepence a time, and we jingled our money, we used to talk sometimes (we would thrust away any thoughts of what we had just been doing, we did not speak of the things we had to do, to earn our money: the rakes and the soldiers and the businessmen and the sad men and the vicars and the drunk men and the bad men who tried to cheat us), we would swallow some gin and talk of ourselves: Poppy told me bits and pieces about her life on the streets – growing up in the Rookeries, 'I tried to better meself but I never found one place where I wasn't treated bad.' Learning the street-girls' trade was easy though she ended up in Newgate Prison once when she was caught in her thieving. 'I seen things there made me sure I ain't goin' to get caught again, they whip women in Newgate, Grace, and I heard the cries of men being pressed!'

'What do you mean, *pressed*?'

'*Pressed*! They said he was a spy so they pressed him, to make him talk. Between slabs. They turned a handle and splattered him.' I looked at her in horror. 'I ain't goin' back. I'll kill myself before I go back there again.' She told me she lived in warm rooms if gentlemen took to her – for weeks and weeks sometimes; getting rid of babies with pieces of copper stuck up her, and – still – she was only seventeen years. —I did not have such adventures to relate but one night I told Poppy the truth: that I needed the money to buy paints, that I was a Painter.

'A *Painter*?' She could not believe me.

'More than anything in the world I want to paint.'

She looked at me as if I had said something that was completely insane. 'What d'you paint?'

'Faces. I paint faces.'

'You're doing all this because you want to *paint faces*? You're mad! Where d'you live?'

I told her. I told her I lived with my brother until I could become a Painter.

'Why don't yore brother give you money?'

'He does not wish me to be a Painter, I am his housekeeper.' I am not sure if she ever quite believed me but she knew brothers were trouble, she had plenty of her own, tolerated me now if I appeared with my hair tumbling down my shoulders as long as I paid her; she knew I would not come often, but every week I would come – because I had to. **I had to paint**: that was all.

And from the time I painted my ugly Lilies my poor, clever,

foolish brother felt safe, but he should have taken note of the dangerous green Daisy, he should have remembered his little sister Grace Marshall better than that.

'Your Brother is a funny Fellow,' said Poppy one night.

Everything fell: I could feel my heart, falling – this had been the risk, this would put an end to everything, all my plans, all my Work.

'I had so hoped he would not – oh, this will – have you seen him?'

'I have. I seen him last night. He looks something like you.' She said nothing more, watched my face.

'*Goddam Poppy!*'

'Don't be silly, course I never said nothing, stupid girl! Because he had the look of you I just asked him casually after, if he had any sisters.'

'What did he say? Was he surprised you said it?'

'Nah, I was just making conversation while we walked back after, I talk to them, just sometimes. Oh well, we are obliged only to lift our skirts for the money but they're only lads some of them, they want someone to talk to, you can tell – he said he had a sister called Grace, that's only how I knew for sure he was your Brother and he looked quite sad, said he's lost you. That's not what you told me is it, Miss?'

I stood like a stone – *Tobias* – and then I whirled and held both her arms, 'Where is he? Where is he?'

'I dunno!' She shrugged. Poppy had lots of brothers and sisters and she never saw any of them. 'He's a sailor ain't he? And you told me lies, you said he lived in St Martin's Lane—'

'I've got *two* brothers!' I actually shook her.

'—all right then, all right, anyway he said he was going back to the Indies, but I tell you what, I didn't trust him quite – excuse *me*, Grace!' and she disengaged herself from my arms for I still had hold of her, 'I knew to hold on to my money, you know, how you do. I talked to him a bit, but I left him quite soon.'

Tobias. Tobias in London.

And I thought how it would be if Tobias found us, looking like Philip and me; I tried to see him at the table with Mr Reynolds and Mr Hartley Pond, sounding as if he came from Bristol and even stealing their watches and then, like Poppy, I shrugged. I had to choose, Philip had said.

I told you: he unbalanced our sky, and created monsters.

And then one evening at dusk, Poppy was not there at the side of the *piazza*. I waited and waited, but she did not come as the dusk drew down. —I asked the other girls: they shrugged.

'A man came,' one of them said. But whether to destroy her or to save her I did not know, for they could not tell me, and I understood at that instant as I stood there on the *piazza* how much I needed her, how I had come to rely on her, how much I needed the money; I had wanted more than anything an Easel to put my paintings on; I was still saving up, for an Easel.

It was now very dark. A gentleman approached me – suddenly, without Poppy, I was frightened, I made myself concentrate on an *Easel*, I saw the Easel in my mind as I smiled. 'You'll have a good time with me,' I said, as we always said. 'I'm Daisy.'

He showed me his red ribbon.

I took him down an alley, and while he was about his business and all in a state and crying to God like they did, I took seven gold coins from his pocket – I must have been insane to do that – I was gone in a moment, back to the safety of St Martin's Lane, before he could properly recover and ascertain his large loss – I knew I had been too greedy – how could I ever go back to the *piazza* again? they would be looking for me, girls were often taken away by the King's Men for stealing, I'd seen it, and hadn't Poppy herself once been taken away? I would be whipped in Newgate Prison she said, or pressed with slabs and wheels; I would have to make that stolen money last and last for I could never go back for months and months.

I got my Easel.

That is how I got my precious Easel.

After that night I walked every day as usual with my basket and my very respectable grey dress and cap but nowhere, *nowhere* near the *piazza*. —I did not buy food there, I told my brother there had been a Murder – what would he know or care? there were always Murders, the street-patterers sang about Murders every day – HIS REAL LIVE PEARL WAS A REAL STREET-GIRL, IN

THEIR BED HE SMASHED HER HEAD – and whenever I saw the King's Men trotting by I quickly looked away, turned a corner with my heart beating in such a horrible way: for many months I was trepidatious because of my stupidity and my greed, always I thought someone might shout, the gentleman himself might shout, *There she is! The thieving street-girl!* I made the money stretch and stretch, I would not think what I would do when it was gone.

One night Philip insisted we go to the Theatre in his new carriage and the horses took us past Covent Garden, past alleys I had walked, and I sat back in the safe shadows of the coach in my demure gown and I smiled at my brother in my new way – in fact I laughed – and I watched everything at the Theatre, my first visit to the Theatre: the audience was more interesting to me than the play which seemed tedious (and badly-spoken Philip told me). —But the *audience*: the excitement, the smiling eyes, the money, the shadows thrown by the hundreds of candle-lamps – I watched everything with my cold damaged heart – I saw the way ladies leant forward from the red and gold boxes knowing they showed themselves at their most alluring, the exquisite fans and the plumped up lead-white bosoms and the deadly nightshade making eyes sparkle and the lips that trembled with rashness, I heard whispered Assignations in the box beside us where candle-lamps flickered and cast such shadows of desire, and I thought, *it is about transactions, like the dark alleys: it is all the same, in the end* – I watched everything, and then in my bed-room I tried to paint the faces of the women in the audience, and the dark girls outside loitering for a shilling or sixpence or tuppence and over and over I found I thought of Poppy and her rough kindness – had she found another way also? what had happened to her? what would I do when my money was spent? and when I painted the street-girls almost always they had the face of Poppy – that is, often, the face of me. —Oh, what I am trying to say is that my Paintings were better and better – and they were also cold and clever and angry, because that is what I had become in the loneliness of my sewing-room with all my Deceptions: angry, ambitious, very cold, and very clever. And watching everything was my Painting of the Lilies, and my insane green Daisy.

One day I took a long mirror from a downstairs room. I, after all, was responsible for such things as mirrors: I was the housekeeper.

I looked carefully, deliberately, into the glass.

I was the same, yet different.

I was a very young version of Aunt Joy, but different, and, like Poppy, I laughed my new, cold, harsh laugh in my room, and staring at myself I remembered the thought that had flown into my mind as I had watched the charming cold eyes of my brother Philip and the jovial, cold face of Mr Reynolds, *Perhaps, to succeed, great Artists must lose some other part of themselves*, and I knew: I was not yet an Artist. But I had lost some part of myself already.

I took off all my clothes; I was shaking slightly and I told myself not to be so foolish and I looked into the mirror, at my naked Body, never in my Life had I looked at it in a mirror before and I could hardly bear to look at it now for the dirt and shame of what it had seen and what it had done – but it had arms and legs like the statue in Philip's Studio, and it was the Body of a Woman.

I took a deep breath, I picked up a piece of charcoal, and I began drawing myself.

That: that is what happened between my brother and me.

PART THREE

SEVEN

It was imperative that the successful portraitist Signore Filipo di Vecellio of Florence (that is to say Philip Marshall of Bristol) make every effort to move up the English social scale. He understood that it was imperative. A good marriage was part of his plan: for his daring masquerade to succeed even further he needed to marry a woman of quality, he understood that and was looking as carefully as his mother Betty had used to do. But, in truth, he should have known better. He should have known that even his Wiltshire Marshall antecedents would never have got him far, socially, in London; he was foolish to think that a Painter (who after all was a man of trade even if he was also an Italian Nobleman) would ever be part of *le beau monde*. He could aspire to be *fashionable*, but he could never be noble. His matrimonial ambitions received several rebuffs.

Sometimes his old, perhaps more disreputable (certainly less successful) friend John Palmer looked at him speculatively across the dinner-table.

Among the sitters who flocked to the charming, successful, young foreign painter, finally there came 'the most beautiful woman in London', a young lady recently arrived in the Metropolis (there was some confusion as from where).

Later the romantic story was often told: how the famous Italian Portrait Painter fell in love, how he sat all night, unbelieving, gazing at what he had created – his Portrait; how he would not release the painting from his studio until he had captured the original. The young and fiery lord who had originally brought the beautiful young lady to be painted by the fashionable artist challenged the usurper of his lady to a duel: luckily (for the Italian) the noble lord was accused at this very time of some sort of underhand behaviour at the card-table and was bundled out of the country hurriedly by his noble father. So Filipo di Vecellio won the beauty *and* the portrait – and then had to make further decisions.

Perhaps it took a fraud to recognise a fraud. Perhaps he married her because he understood they would keep each other's secrets – secrets he would never have been able to share with a woman of quality, should one of them have fallen under his dark-eyed charm. Perhaps the only instinctive thing Philip Marshall ever did in his new life was to fall in love with Angelica, who had the name of an angel but who had secrets also.

Whatever the reason, the well-known portrait painter and the beautiful young woman were married and lived happily ever after: she became Angelica, Signora di Vecellio, and it is likely he married her because he could not live without her.

If they were not exactly respectable, or noble, they were, indeed, truly, madly fashionable – and after all what better *entrée* into London society now, than fashion? Her exquisite beauty and his flattering skill and charm and wealth made them a success in the wild, bustling, dangerous, scheming London world; they became part of the fashion because he painted the fashion: indeed they *were* the fashion. They were seen at the theatre and at opera houses and regattas. They were seen promenading in St James's Park, walking through the candle-lit trees in Vauxhall Gardens, or laughing beside the Rotunda at Ranelagh Gardens. After their marriage, when Filipo di Vecellio was at the height of his fame, he moved to one of the most expensive addresses in London: to a huge house in Pall Mall, not far from where Royalty sometimes resided, indeed the gardens at the back of the houses backed on to the wall of the King's Garden, and windows looked out across the garden and over St James's Park, and the sister, the housekeeper, had a room at the top of the house and was heard to say how very, very glad she was to have a sewing-room attached, how very, very useful it was, for a housekeeper.

And upon the turn of the stairs in the elegant house in Pall Mall hung, always, that first wonderful portrait of Angelica: the powdered hair, the extraordinary pale oval face, and the large dark eyes. The most beautiful woman in London.

The much-talked-of marriage (and perhaps their air of mystery) had made them celebrities. Angelica's eyes sparkled brightly, made even larger by the definition of black (so carefully applied), and colour-shading the eyelids emphasised the eyes' dark depths. The fashionable white, white skin, leading down to the white, white bosom, seemed to gleam; the cheeks held a delicate blush of beauty, matching the colour (so very carefully, so very tastefully applied) of the perfectly shaped, slightly-smiling mouth. She wore gorgeous gowns of beautiful colours, with tight waists and low-cut bodices, and her shoes were made of embroidered silk and her silk and satin petticoats rustled seductively as she passed by, trailing a drifting hint of musk, or jasmine. Other painters clamoured to paint her: beautiful portraits certainly, yet none, somehow, caught her as Filipo di Vecellio, just once, had caught her.

The house in Pall Mall was always full of people: sitters for portraits, and dealers and framers and assistants, and hairdressers and dressmakers and visitors to Angelica's dressing-room, and tradesmen bringing canvases and boards and paint, and extra new servants. And there, in the large house, Filipo and Angelica presided over the same hospitable afternoon dinners, where Art was always the main subject of discussion, where the painter's quiet and retiring – but indispensable – sister, Francesca, was always in the background in her grey gown and the white cap on her dark hair, to make sure all was as required. This quiet, retiring sister very seldom joined in the artistic conversation; almost you might not notice her as she sat there: who would notice that she was listening and watching so carefully? She observed how light from the window, or from one of the candles, caught the smooth white cheek of her beautiful sister-in-law, or the charming face of her famous brother, or the papery skin of the indomitable Miss Ffoulks. Once she watched the fading light from the late afternoon, how it crept along the table, slowly shadowing the china plates, the wine-glasses, the old hand of Miss Ffoulks as it lay there upon the fine linen tablecloth, up towards John Palmer's wig, hanging on the back of his chair. It was summer, late summer, almost time to light the candles but for a moment she did not move, watched the long shadows, thought she heard in the distance the evening starlings calling as they made their way home to St James's Park. 'Leonardo, Michelangelo, Rembrandt,' cried Mr Hartley Pond, and the face of Mr Burke almost in complete shadow now except for his listening grey eyes; that night in her sewing-room at the top of the house she tried to paint the fading light and the dining-table and the colour of the wine in the glasses and the beautiful, shadowed face of James Burke.

Such agreeable and rumbustious afternoons in Pall Mall: good conversation and good food at one of the fashionable London addresses. And Filipo di Vecellio addressed his guests and said, *I like to live in an Avenue named from my own Country*, and then took great delight in informing his listeners that *palla a maglio*, a kind of Italian croquet, had been the favourite game of King Charles II. John Palmer listened inscrutably, staring into his wine-glass; and Miss Ann Ffoulks smiled with pleasure at the success of her *protégé*; and James Burke the dealer continued to wander freely in the house night and day as if he were one of the family, collecting finished canvases, bringing sitters, arranging commissions. Mr Hartley Pond found Angelica charming and brought her small tokens in the manner of a courtier; and painters sat back in their chairs with their wine and talked of the art of portrait painting and sometimes of women and occasionally the subjects came together: *But of course Women must copy Countryside Views and Flowers if they must paint, for it is not becoming for Women to paint Portraits, it is not seemly that a Woman should stare so openly at another person in that way.*

In Pall Mall Filipo di Vecellio had a huge studio, and such was the number of his commissions now that he fired that older assistant of St Martin's Lane days (he may have been very good at his work but in truth he made the studio smell), and nobody noticed how the quiet sister's eyes shone at this news. Four new, young assistants were employed to paint the drapery and the background, as the portraits were churned out and the money poured in. (The assistants were now charged with washing themselves daily, for they mixed more and more with nobility.) Filipo also acquired a white parrot named Roberto for he had heard that Mr Joshua Reynolds, making such a name for himself also, had an eagle. Roberto would not leave Angelica's side, he cried bitterly each day when she went out. Sometimes Roberto was allowed to sit on her shoulder after dinner: perched there with his head on one side, his bright eye observing the guests.

And now, in the evenings, in the house in Pall Mall a new kind of gathering was also held, Angelica's *soirees*, and a new kind of visitor came – younger sons of the nobility perhaps, and ladies with the new high hairstyles and fashions from France. At Angelica's evening *soirees* the talk was of the theatre, of the *affaires* of fashionable society; small tales of royal connections and corruptions wafted, and perhaps new liaisons wafted also, amid much laughter, as Roberto, close to his mistress again, observed. Occasionally he gave a short, sharp squawk as if he disapproved (as indeed well he might, for the more libation that was consumed, the more disreputable some of the conversations became, behind the fashionable laughter and the flickering fans). Sometimes the evening was musical: they acquired a harpsichord and invited musicians; sometimes a man would play upon a violin and the guests would sit in little rows. Once Angelica asked a black musician who was all the rage to play his own music on the harpsichord; the quiet sister observed not only the black man, but the fascinated faces of all the ladies as they stared from behind their fans, for the musician was dressed as any gentleman. He was wearing a white curled wig, and he was beautiful – but he was *black*. He bowed to the assembled company when he had finished playing and the ladies twittered like birds, and sighed, and some of them wrote in letters or in their journals of seeing such a strange, unsettling sight.

Sometimes, now that the house and the company were so fashionable, Lydia, the wife of James Burke, who of course never attended the noisy dinners in the afternoons, came to these *soirees*. She was elegant, her clothes always of the latest fashion: a fair-skinned, knowing woman with coiffeured hair and jewellery at her throat and stories from the Palace. She was extremely elegant but she was not beautiful as Angelica was beautiful. (Francesca di Vecellio observed the faces of all the women: Angelica herself was hospitable and kind as well as beautiful, but many of the visitors

133

laughed and looked about them and speculated behind their fans as they watched each other with hard eyes, and smiling.)

Angelica's beauty was always added to. One might almost say she had a studio of her own where artfulness was applied to nature: her dressing-room. Roberto the parrot presided over the *toilette* of his mistress: talking, chattering, indeed screeching if he did not approve of something. Angelica often had visitors at her *toilette*, mostly gentlemen: it was an accepted social norm that fashionable gentlemen should take morning chocolate in a lady's dressing-room. Noble gentlemen visited, young men about town; the dealer James Burke was there occasionally, even the critic Mr Hartley Pond was so seduced by Angelica's charms that he sometimes attended. And Filipo di Vecellio went on painting his fashionable portraits and for those few years at the height of his fame he could charge thirty guineas for a head, the amount some families in London lived on for a year.

They were, indeed, wealthy.

Filipo and Angelica were invited everywhere: young and beautiful and above all fashionable. They were very fond: *cara mia*, he would call: all had heard the way Angelica sparkled up at her husband in answer and sometimes she would say 'Lud, *Signore*,' and everybody would laugh at the odd juxtaposition of languages. Occasionally Angelica absolutely insisted that the painter's sister accompany them: Francesca was already nineteen years old and unmarried and must see (and be seen admiring) the fashionable sights of London like any young unmarried girl.

'You have made yourself old too soon, and you do not show the correct interest, my dear,' Angelica said often to Francesca, of whom she had grown fond, although she found her a little quiet, spending too much time in her attic room, not enough attending Angelica's fashionable evenings. 'And you must smile with your eyes, behind your fan – you do, if I might tell you, dearest Francesca, not smile enough, and when something so very occasionally makes you laugh, you laugh with your whole face and it is most unbecoming! Laughter like that is a little vulgar and there is much for you to learn if we are to find you a husband!' And Francesca could not help but smile back at her extraordinary sister-in-law for who would not smile at Angelica? Angelica from the wrong side of the Thames, who had the name of an angel and who looked so beautiful, and who meant so well.

They all took a boat one summer evening from Whitehall Stairs to cross the Thames, and London in the dusk looked strange and thrilling: all the crowded, anchored boats and barges and the Cathedral etched against the skyline and a fading rose light as the sun set over the smoky city and Francesca sat quietly on a little cushion provided and carefully observed everything. Angelica seemed not to notice the dye-factories that, perhaps, had once been part of her life. With extra hair added to her own under a spectacular bonnet, she was wearing the latest fashion: a *sacque*-dress that opened in the front to show a skirt of gay brocade gathered over the hooped petticoats. She looked wonderful; dye-factories were nothing to her; all the little boats arriving at the landing pushing and fighting to disgorge their passengers meant nothing to her; she merely smiled behind her fan, and people smiled back, at such beauty. Arriving to the crowds at fashionable Vauxhall Gardens they saw a small orchestra playing Mr Handel's music as people wandered in the summer evening (past a statue of the late composer himself, holding a lyre). Filipo and his bride bowed and smiled in fashionable promenade, laughing together as they saw several well-known raddled old dukes, and the dubious old quack everybody knew, Dr Graham, who painted silver on his hair. In the Pavilion artists had decorated the supper boxes with all sorts of scenes: kings and battles and heroics. Ladies in gorgeous hats leant back now against painted horses, and laughter echoed.

'I do not care for these little Epics,' said Filipo dismissively, looking around the painted walls.

'But at least it is somewhere for Artists to display their work,' said his sister mildly, for there were not many such places in London.

Filipo laughed. 'Let us hope they do not mind to display their work in the remains of a *bagnino* then, for this is where Ladies of the Night – or indeed the day – plied their trade for many years gone by – just there!' and he pointed to the fashionable gardens with their long straight walks and their neat trees and the twinkling lights.

'I think, my dear,' said Angelica sweetly, 'that the Walks are put to much the same purpose now!' and they laughed again, these fashionable, worldly creatures, and whispered together, while the quiet sister observed figures appearing and disappearing in the enchanting, flickering lantern-light.

They went to exhibitions at the Foundling Hospital in Coram Fields where the artist William Hogarth had arranged for many English painters' work to be shown, including his own. Again Society promenaded, they were after all supporting the poor deserted little children by their very presence (heard stories of small bundles left at the gates): sometimes the visitors even graciously allowed their names to be given to the little children at the christenings. Francesca looked everywhere in hope of catching a glimpse of the famous painter, was entranced by his portrait of the sea captain who had had the idea of the Foundling hospital, but Filipo disagreed.

'He makes the man *look* like a Sea Captain!' he said sourly. 'What is the point of that?' and Francesca did not answer, and Angelica smiled and nodded at the passing people behind her fan.

And then Mr Hogarth himself did appear in the distance, with his wife on his arm. Francesca di Vecellio felt her heart beating fast: how very much she wanted to meet again the man who had drawn her in the church in Bristol, who had somehow unlocked her heart and inspired her to draw again.

'He is a scurrilous little fellow, and ill they say, but we will make ourselves known nevertheless,' said Filipo di Vecellio, 'for he of course knows my work and may like to arrange to hang it here. But he is not a real Painter.' He spoke with disdain. 'His *Gin Lane* and *Beer Street* and *Harlot's Progress* – they are nothing but Caricatures – and he hates Foreigners!'

His sister stood stock still. She was older – surely she was much changed? But he was a man who drew faces, he would remember faces. She remembered his face: she saw him coming towards them. As Philip waited in his path and William Hogarth approached so that the meeting was inevitable, Francesca di Vecellio knew she must not betray her brother: wistfully, but honourably, she turned and moved away towards the other side of the gallery of pictures, heard her brother's pleasantries and her sister-in-law's pretty laugh.

Mr Hogarth, she could hear, hurrumphed to see her brother, but at least bowed politely before walking on. The sister, from where she now stood, could not help looking back over her shoulder to catch another glimpse of the short man who had given her hope. *Thank you, dear Mr Hogarth,* she thought, and, just for a moment, the painter stopped and looked back, puzzled, almost as if something whispered in the air.

Only a short time later Mr Hogarth died and the populace who had his prints on their walls mourned him – he had drawn and painted his pictures for them – but the newspapers said he had become rancorous and angry and sad about the lack of support for English Artists, for an English Academy.

'He had become a Bore,' said Mr Hartley Pond. 'And his Painting was vulgar.'

'I liked him,' said the artist's quiet sister suddenly from across the table, 'I am so very sorry to hear of his Death.'

'Did you know him, my dear?' asked Miss Ffoulks, surprised, for the girl wanted to hear so much of Art, and yet had never mentioned Mr Hogarth.

'I met him once, and he was very kind,' answered Francesca di Vecellio and her brother commented, laughing, that *kind* was not a word that could be used about that vain, disputatious Caricaturist, now – so sadly of course – taken from them.

In the middle of all the innumerable conversations about Art, Miss Ffoulks sometimes talked forthrightly about quite different subjects like the Slave Trade and its iniquities: 'People chained and crowded in foul conditions and then sold as goods! How can one Human treat another in such a way!' she would cry indignantly and Mr Hartley Pond looked exasperated at her interruptions, as usual, and took snuff ostentatiously. But Miss Ffoulks was not to be deflected.

'We are a Brotherhood of Men!' she cried one day, causing Mr Hartley Pond to snigger now, but again she took no heed. 'We are a Fraternity of Human Persons and we have a Moral Responsibility to care for our Fellows.' And the ribbons on her bonnet shook in indignation.

'What a shame', said Mr Hartley Pond in his most supercilious manner, 'that those black persons upon the sea', (his voice so full of distaste) 'do not know – and indeed probably will never know! – what a Champion they have in Miss Ffoulks.'

It was the only time they saw Miss Ffoulks, so controlled, so clever, become really angry: her ribbons swirled as she turned upon Mr Pond. 'As I say, Sir, I believe that we are a Brotherhood, that we owe it to our World to care about the Human Beings who inhabit it.'

'Including illiterate black men?'

'Including black men and women who are transported and sold like Cattle, and including, Mr Pond, the people in this great City whose lives are blighted by lack of money and lack of the light, bright air of Kindness.'

'Tell me, Filipo,' said Mr Pond, 'have you visited the new Colour Shop at the far end of the Strand?' but Mr John Palmer leaned across and patted Miss Ffoulks' arm; she bit her lip but said no more. Dusk was falling and the artist's sister moved quietly to light the candles and gently touched the shoulder of Miss Ffoulks as she passed.

They went sometimes to the theatre: the Haymarket or Drury Lane; they saw the most famous actor in England, Mr Garrick, reviving an interest in William Shakespeare, playing Macbeth. Hundreds of candles in chandeliers lit the stage. Sometimes Mr James Burke the grey-eyed art dealer and his most elegant wife, Lydia, would join them; the men spoke of money and prices, the women spoke of fashion and gossip. Francesca di Vecellio watched all the faces: the life and the gaiety and the colours and the energy of London – and part of her longed to go home at once to her room at the top of the house in Pall Mall: the attached sewing-room may once have seen embroidery, but was now her very own studio. She had to remember the fashionable faces in her head, of course she could not make sketches on these occasions, so she watched intently: the women in their glorious gowns promenading in Vauxhall Gardens and laughing behind their fans, the elegant men with white wigs and crimson cheeks in St James's Park, the street-girls in the shadows in the Haymarket plying for trade, and the grey eyes of Mr Burke. And Mr Garrick himself, crying to the heavens where the chandeliers hung, in a beautiful voice.

It was outside the Haymarket, there, that a voice called one night.

'Dottie! It's you, Dottie!'

Francesca di Vecellio saw: only Angelica could have done it: in a crowd of fashionable people Angelica stopped. She saw the street-woman who had called to her.

'Essie!' she said. And then as if it was the most natural thing in the world Angelica drew the street-woman away from the fashionable people. She spoke to Essie for several moments and then from her cloak she took a coin which she pressed into the woman's hand. And then she stepped towards the waiting carriage, and smiled at her husband and her friends.

The wonderful Angelica di Vecellio was now one of the most sought-after guests in London for she was so beautiful, and she was now respectably, and very publicly, married. Sometimes now Duchesses would invite her to do good works: to go again to the Foundling Hospital and look at the dear little lost children; to go to Bedlam where the mad people were incarcerated and see how factory-girls and maids thought themselves Duchesses. Angelica did not like going to Bedlam and avoided it when she could, for the wild cries from that place echoed out into her head long after the fashionable ladies, chattering like birds at what they had seen, had waved goodbye to the Director and entered the carriage home.

'They are like lost souls,' she said to her husband and he saw that she shivered and he put aside his brushes and paints for a moment, and put his arm about her small waist, and told her she was beautiful, and made her smile. And later Miss Ffoulks informed her that the Government was thinking of passing a bill so that visitors may not observe the patients at Bedlam in that cruel way, and Angelica was glad.

And it was Angelica who insisted one late, dark afternoon at the end of dinner that a great party of them put on their cloaks and walk to Drury Lane to see *The Beggar's Opera*.

'You too, Francesca. It is an old thing that is all the rage again, I insist you come, it will entertain you!' And after more wine they finally, with much laughter and gaiety, crossed the *piazza* of Covent Garden to Drury Lane: a chill autumn evening where they could see their breath before them and small street-children cried for pennies, warming their feet in horse dung from the carriages. There was the smell of chestnuts by the small kiosk that sold the purses of sheep's guts with red ribbons for the use of fornicating gentlemen, and the emollients for certain dangerous street-sicknesses, and the special bottles which were labelled DO NOT TAKE THIS MEDI-CINE IF WITH CHILD, IT WILL CAUSE LOSS. And the street-girls everywhere and the painter's sister glanced into dark corners as they passed, and held her cloak about her.

They sat in red boxes in Drury Lane and the ladies in their bright gay gowns whispered behind their fluttering fans and observed the crowds lit by the myriad of candle-lamps as the music began. Suddenly the Italian portrait painter stiffened and his sister at once felt the hair at the back of her neck shiver, as though a ghost walked. *When I laid on Greenland's coast, and in my arms embraced my lass*, sang the hero and Angelica leaned forward and smiled with pleasure and did not see how Filipo di Vecellio stared unseeing at the stage and did not look in the direction of his sister as the song went on.

> *And I would love you all the Day*
> *Ev'ry Night would kiss and play*
> *If with me you'd fondly stray –*
> *Over the hills and far away.*

and all the way home Angelica sang again in her sweet voice with some of her gentlemen friends and in the darkness nobody observed the stone face of Signore di Vecellio, or the pale, dark face of the *signorina* who held her cloak about her, and everybody singing:

> *If with me you'd fondly stray –*
> *Over the hills and far away*

EIGHT

'Come and see my Rembrandt,' boomed Mr Joshua Reynolds one day and Francesca di Vecellio had her bonnet on long before the others were ready, so fearful was she that she would not be included. Filipo would not arrive at Mr Joshua Reynolds' house by foot; insisted on the fashionable carriage being driven to where the painter now lived, in Leicester Fields. Almost the first thing they saw – having been introduced to (Angelica almost fainted with delight) Mr David Garrick, the actor, who was visiting – was Mr Reynolds' eagle. It soared above them, in Mr Reynolds' garden, but Angelica was not convinced.

'He does not have Roberto's Nobility of Character,' she whispered to Francesca (meaning of course the eagle, not Mr Garrick) while the gentlemen were discussing what had been paid for the Rembrandt painting.

'Sixteen pounds and five shillings and sixpence when I bought it some years ago!' said Mr Reynolds proudly as he led them into his studio. 'A Bargain.'

Perhaps they might have shown his own work in progress more notice, but all eyes were drawn to the picture on the wall.

It was a picture of a woman. She was bathing in dark water, she held up her gown in perhaps a slightly shocking manner and stared at the dark water, which reflected the gold and red colour of a gown on the rocks behind her. She was not a fashionable woman, not one of Filipo di Vecellio's women, she wore nothing on her head, and her light shift was simple, a nightgown even it perhaps could have been. And an ineffable sweetness about her face, about the way she gazed down at the water, and light caught the side of her face and her body and one side of the gown. She was not beautiful but there was an extraordinary beauty about her face and her expression and the whole painting.

'Hmmm. *Multo bene*,' said Filipo after some time. 'Very good. I should like to own a Rembrandt also.'

'The *light*,' said the usually quiet Francesca di Vecellio in a loud, breathless voice. 'Look at the *light*, look at the Reflections on the water, and look at the way the light and the shadows are so different!'

'Different from what?' If she was aware of her brother or Mr Reynolds staring at her she gave no sign.

'From – from the way many things are painted.' She stared as if transfixed, seemed hardly able to breathe at all.

'I do not admire his Nudes,' said Joshua Reynolds to Filipo di Vecellio over her head, as if perhaps the word 'Nude' was to be discussed only by men. 'And Rembrandt has many Faults: he does not follow the Classical Style. Beauty does not consist in taking what immediately lies before you.'

'It is so beautiful,' said Francesca doggedly and Mr Reynolds smiled at last.

'It is indeed beautiful, Signorina di Vecellio,' he said, 'and well worth the money I paid for it. It is of course worth very, very much more, even now, for Rembrandt is slowly coming back into Fashion, mark my words.' Nobody noticed that the *signorina* turned back as they left the studio, as if drawn back by an invisible thread, she stood right up close as if to touch, almost, the light and the shadows and the strokes of the paintbrush and the thickness of the paint. Mr Reynolds' sister Fanny finally had to call the *signorina* in to tea with the most famous actor in London.

Mr Garrick told them he wished to reform the theatre so that people would *listen*. 'I no longer want to have young rakes sitting on the Stage and poking at the Actresses, it is not respectful! We have our own English Playwright of great stature of whom people know so little, William Shakespeare – I have re-written and fore-shortened him where necessary – and I expect people to *listen* to him.' And it was clear that Mr Garrick meant he expected them to listen, also, to himself.

And as he spoke Mr Garrick was also smiling at Angelica as if he would expire from the delight of her beauty. 'Signore di Vecellio,' he said, 'we must present to you our thanks for marrying such an Angel, a truly beautiful Woman, and bringing her into our Orbit. We owe you, dear sir, a debt of Gratitude.' He was of course a man of much charm – he was an actor, after all – but Filipo di Vecellio and his wife smiled, knowing the world was theirs.

—and the greatest, hugest, gigantic debt of Gratitude *I* owed to Angelica was this: although she was the Mistress of the house in Pall Mall she was not interested in its Organisation in any way whatsoever – she expected me to be in charge – and she would no more have thought of going over the Accounts with me than telling her true age – and that meant that I was, for ever, free of the *piazza* and the dark alleys full of ghosts and men and shame and pain and the discarded sheep-guts with red, red ribbons lying there in the mud and the shit and the fish-heads: that was Angelica's gift to me. —I was now in charge of the money that was needed for running the house in Pall Mall, well then, a few parcels of paint, sticks of charcoal, brushes, paper – they were as nothing at last, and Angelica could never, never know how much I owed her.

Angelica. We had our Deceptions, she had hers, so we under-stood one another – her Beauty and her Charm and her Determination had taken her to so many places she had only dreamed of across the Thames when she was growing up by the dye-factories; one day she told me she grew up in a room of ten people.

'How did you learn to speak like a Lady?' I asked her, for she did not sound like someone from across the river, and Angelica smiled her charming smile, told me one thing one day, and one thing another, sometimes stories half-told – Dukes, unwanted pregnancies dealt with, bad times, better times – I understood that as she rose in the firmament of the Courtesans she was taken up by one of the older ones, and taught many things, including how to speak in accents unlike those of her birthplace – just indeed as we had learned – and she enjoyed our Italian Deception, she even, as the years passed, very slightly, perhaps unconsciously, adapted her way of speaking to ours as she became so well known as *the beautiful Signora Angelica.*

Angelica. She freed me – and then wailed at me.

'You are nineteen years old, Francesca!' she would cry at first. 'It is not yet Old Age, you cannot always go to your room in the evenings, you have not lived! You must dress and dance and dine, just as I do,' and I could not tell her of my Plan, that I would be gone so soon, and it was hard at first to refuse Angelica, she was so artful and yet also so artless, she wanted to find me a Husband more than anything else, for she thought I was not fulfilled – so although I literally *ached* to be in my attic sewing-room I at first had indeed sometimes found myself doing all the things a young unmarried girl of Fashion should do: the Theatre, the Opera, Balls, Vauxhall Gardens – until one night Angelica persuaded me to attend another of her *soirees,* for a lady singer was to sing songs of Mr Handel and she thought I should hear. —She had me sit beside her as the guests sat in little rows on little chairs in the drawing-room in Pall Mall and a rather shy plain girl with a beautiful voice, although not as beautiful as that of the madwoman in St Martin's Lane, sang

> *Where'er you walk*
> *Cool gales shall fan the glade*
> *Trees where you sit*
> *Shall crowd into a shade*

and I felt a very peculiar feeling as if someone was watching me, finally I turned slightly – oh – never was I more glad of my spinster's cap and my dark gown as that night, for I saw one of Angelica's Gentlemen friends staring at me – I gave him a polite nod and he turned away and the girl went on singing

> *Trees where you sit shall crowd*
> *Into-oo a shade*

and my heart kept jumping and beating against my breast even as I turned and smiled at Angelica, who wanted everybody to be so happy – and I did not excuse myself at once, I did not run away, I allowed myself to listen for a long time to an old rich lady of Angelica's acquaintance who spoke to me, lovingly, of her small dog, which sat there upon her knee. 'He is called Jupiter,' she kept saying to me, 'Jupiter, little Darling,' and she cuddled the dog to her breast – I could not have been more respectable as my legs literally trembled to hold me there; I think the Gentleman must have told himself he had made a mistake, for how *could* the famous Artist's quiet sister in her dark clothes and spinster's cap be the girl he had first seen in the shadows of the *piazza* whose Virtue he had so manfully undone? It was, literally, unthinkable.

But after that I did not want to attend further *soirees* – what if the Gentleman came from whom I stole so much money, what if he too was a friend of Angelica? Slowly, although her face fell, I persuaded her that I was truly content in my other role as the housekeeper, slowly I stopped the jaunty trips to Vauxhall or yet another Ball – I did not want to take more risks like that, certainly, but most of all I needed to be in my Studio: *I wanted to paint* – and now (smiling at Angelica so that she could see I was not unhappy, she always wanted everybody to be happy) I would sometimes paint almost all night, then hurry out to buy the food and then hurry back to my room and I began to understand very well that my portraits of the people I saw over London – the market-men, the painted women, the wild children – were better and better, my use of the colours and the oil and the way I had begun to paint real shadow and light were sometimes beautiful – but that sometimes in the faces I painted from my memory the eyes were still cold. Cold eyes.

One day I found myself at Mr Valiant's Auction rooms in Poland-street: there was to be an Auction, some Old Masters (a Raphael someone whispered), crowds were inspecting (I heard an English Painter muttering, *When will they crowd like this about English painting?*) and I found a small portrait by Rembrandt van Rijn – it sounds ridiculous but again I had the feeling that I could not breathe, as when I had seen Mr Reynolds' painting by Rembrandt because I recognised the light and the shadows – this one was simply titled, *Portrait of a Young Woman.*

The woman sat, not looking at the Painter but at one small, pink flower in her hand, in light and in shadows; she wore a simple but rich-looking gown with wonderfully-painted sleeves – this Painting was not as beautiful – or so it seemed to me – as the bathing woman, and it was clearly not the same woman, but it had the same – I tried to find the word in my mind – the same *soul* as the one owned by Mr Reynolds – and most importantly to me in my learning he used *the same dark light* as in the other picture: with Rembrandt van Rijn I had found someone who painted the light and the shadows in a way I had begun to really understand. —I stayed by the Painting in the Auction rooms of Mr Valiant in Poland-street for a long time; I went away and then I came back again – I sat beside my easel that night trying to capture that Painting in case I never saw it again – all night I saw the face in my head, she was not exactly smiling but she was *thinking*, it felt as if she was thinking something over, and light shone across the painting, it was alive, the face was *alive*, I could not sleep, I went back early the next morning, terrified that someone would have bought it before it was auctioned, taken it away.

'How much is it?' I asked Mr Valiant who knew me of course and presumed I was enquiring for my brother.

'Rembrandt van Rijn is not so fashionable as Titian, say, but interest in him is growing and Prices are rising fast; these days I expect thirty-five Guineas at least in Auction,' he said, watching my face.

I told Mr Valiant that it would be bought that very morning, begged him to take it down for an hour, out of the Auction, and I ran: I took the short-cut along Broad Street, past Orange Street, past the statue at Charing Cross and along Pall Mall, it was raining that day I remember and the bottom of my gown was splattered with more mud than usual but what did I care about rain? – my hair was falling down as I barged into my brother's forbidden Studio and begged him, *begged* him to come with me, to buy this Painting to add to his collection. 'You said you wanted a Rembrandt,' I said, trying to catch my breath.

He looked at me oddly.

'Why are you so interested?' he said and something flashed between us then; almost four years had passed but it flashed between us, the memory of what had damaged us so but of course he could not guess – *fool* – but I knew I had to risk all this: I could not let that Painting go. —The dull light that day was preventing his own work, he came with me back to Poland-street in his elegant carriage, the horses blocked the street as we alighted and the rain poured down, he stood for a long time, in front of the Painting.

'It is very small,' he said, 'it is smaller than the picture of Mr Reynolds. And who knows if it is a Fake? And Rembrandt – he is not really the fashion, whatever Reynolds thinks – thirty-five guineas is far too much money for a Rembrandt, Reynolds paid less than twenty.' —Yet I saw that he too was caught by the simplicity of the expression and the beauty, the colour of the gown, the folds of lightness and darkness in the sleeve – he could not find Mr Hartley Pond to ask his valued opinion but by great good fortune James Burke came upon our carriage and enquired for us and Mr Burke nodded, staring at the Painting – finally Mr Valiant was somehow persuaded not to wait for the Auction, finally Philip was somehow persuaded to pay to Mr Valiant the thirty-five guineas (although grumbling very much) and he took the Painting home that very day, under his arm, in the carriage, as the grey day drew down and I heard the horses' hooves on the cobbles and the rain on the carriage roof and my heart sang.

I prayed he would hang it upon the stairs next to his beautiful painting of Angelica and the Canaletto – but he finally hung *Portrait of a Young Woman* in his Studio, although this day we all crowded about it in the dining-room: Mr Hartley Pond when he came looked at it for a very long time.

'It is very, very lovely,' he said. 'Look at that gown. No-one can paint the richness the way he does.' And after another long time, 'The face. Yes. The shadow and the light. Yes. I am sure. It is genuine.'

I heard my brother, often, boasting to colleagues and guests, of his Acquisition. 'I have a Rembrandt,' he would say. 'Like Mr Reynolds,' and my heart sang *I have a Rembrandt, like Mr Reynolds.*

It meant I still must haunt my brother's Studio after all but I was safe now in the night-time, my time the night-time: he had long been dismissed, the dangerous assistant, and it was a long time since I had had to look in dark corners with my heart beating. —My brother and Angelica were always out and when I heard the assistants go out also, their boots clattering on the wooden staircase, I went and gazed at that Rembrandt picture to my heart's content, saying hello to George the Greek statue in passing; in the light of my candle I copied it over and over, over and over, never bored, trying to understand how the light in his painting refracted and reflected, trying to understand the thickness of paint in some parts – *impasto* they called it – almost as if he put it on with his fingers not with a brush, or so it seemed to me; night after night after night I copied the painting, breathed the Rembrandt picture inside myself; I was never, never satisfied, never getting it right at all, not understanding then that the great painter Rembrandt van Rijn had painted not just with paint, but with love.

Angelica, be-gowned and beautified and ready, wanted to sit with me: Angelica, ready for the dinner guests, fashionably prepared for them, time suspended until the next entertainment happened. Occasionally then she asked me about Bristol; very occasionally spoke to me of her own past across the river: after her mother died her father had made her, Angelica, pregnant, she was not much more than fourteen, had left that side of the river, come to London City, she had come on her own.

'Did you – have a child?'

'It had not quickened, there was no problem to lose it, copper wire is best, I have used it many times,' and I remembered that is what Poppy had said.

'Was it dangerous?'

She shrugged. 'No more than any other thing in this world – my Sister died of the copper wire it is true when she left it too late, but my Mother died of the plague. So it is all the same, when they die.' And I saw that she quickly pulled herself up out of her dark place. 'When they cure the plague they will cure the copper wire I expect,' and I saw that she meant it, that she hoped it would be so – and then we would hear the knocker and her face would shine bright.

And I found Angelica's workroom almost as fascinating as that of my brother – for were they not both painting, in their own Styles? —Sometimes out of curiosity I used to go in when they were out about the Town, my languishing older sisters had had nothing of this: the big table by the window where Angelica worked, covered with the most extraordinary array of receptacles and glass bottles and little pots; the candle-lamps to give her extra light, and the mirrors, and the false hair — I loved the way shadows fell and light shone upon her wooden workspace and the glass of the bottles, I loved the different colours of the bottles with their blue or green or golden contents of oils and essences from France and Turkey, and the Ivory Combs, and the soft white rabbits' feet she used, to put the colours and powders on her face, and grey pumice stones, and red cerises and vermilions from the Indies, and the many pots and jars of the white Venetian Ceruse that she smoothed over her face and down to her bosom, to make her skin so white. —One night in Pall Mall I *joined* the arts of my brother and Angelica: the connection in what they were doing delighted me in some odd way and I couldn't help my old laughter as I took a little pot of the vermilion rouge from Angelica's table and I went into my brother's empty studio in the night, I found there drying a Portrait of a particular Duke whom I disliked (he had brushed past me in my white cap almost knocking me down with his sword-stick as I welcomed him to my brother's house), I saw that the vermilion from Angelica's pot would blend into his cheeks, that it would actually make the Portrait more like the sitter, like his red-veined cheeks that my brother had slightly disguised – I held my candle close to the Face and very carefully and with great glee, with my thumb, I blended a little of Angelica's rouge into the cheeks of the Duke knowing it would remain there now under the varnish the apprentices would soon be applying to the painting.

And the fragrance of Angelica's workroom: the scent of perfumes and potions and unguents and ointments: Jasmine drifting, and Musk: who could forget that? and sometimes there was an echo of the scent of Cloves, and I knew she had been putting small Cloves into the flame of a candle then marking her eyebrows to make the shape required; oh – the scents here were so different from the rest of the house where, everywhere, food-cooking and London and people brought all their own smells; sometimes, alone in Angelica's room, I breathed in the Fragrances on the air and dreamed of other, bright cities where Tobias might be; I dreamed of the sea where Jasmine grew and where pumice lay upon the sand: the places Philip had travelled to on his Grand Tour, where he had seen the Old Masters, Old

Masters like the small Rembrandt that hung quietly now in his Studio.

I stole the money and bought the paints and haunted my brother's Studio and studied the Rembrandt painting in the night and copied it, and painted and painted in my sewing-room in the house in Pall Mall and I avoided Angelica's *soirees* and one night as I was painting I found that I was singing my Father's song, *If with me you'd fondly stray – over the hills and far away . . .*

Yet the only thing I, still, could not do was paint my Family: their faces slipped away from me no matter how I tried to recall them – then I stared in frustration at my empty, second-hand boards and canvases. (Once I woke in the dark with tears pouring down my face and I could not understand, then I caught at it as it disappeared, my dream: the Bristol quays and a spinning girl – only it was the dark shadowed alleys off the *piazza*.)

Angelica had saved me without knowing she did so and I painted her in my sewing-room, smiling in a gay hat that I had made for her, and my own real laughter came back as I painted her so beautiful and enchanting and I wished Angelica could see what I had done, how beautiful she looked, and sometimes at the table I laughed at something they said, I quite forgot I was Aunt Joy and I laughed, like myself.

I would so soon now be ready, if only I could go *now*, I wanted to leave *now* but still I had nothing, not one penny, I had to ask my brother if I required shoes; I could steal enough money from the weekly housekeeping allowance for paints and paper and brushes but he did not give me enough to do more, I could not make a little fund of my own ready – oh – I knew I could do without so many things in my new life I was planning, but I had to live somewhere and paint somewhere. —So I had, first, *to sell a Painting for Money* – yet I kept up my own spirits by myself because I believed implicitly that my work was getting better, that one day it would be good enough to sell, that if I worked all the time, every moment of my time – *only one more year*, I informed George the Greek statue one night, in another year I believed I could show a small body of work to someone – not Mr Burke of course, not my brother's own Dealer, but someone like him, I would find someone like him, who might obtain for me real Patrons (for the street-people who were mostly my subjects could not pay for paintings!) and I would have, for better or for worse, my own life at last. —Now that it was so near, *only one more year*, I imagined myself living differently: I allowed myself to plan my Dream – I looked up at the big windows of houses in Compton-street, Meard-street, Leicester-lane, at tall windows where the best north light shone – my white-painted room would be large and light; there would be a cabinet for paints, there would be a bed in the corner, a small chair and table, a stove for the winter and for boiling water; I would buy wood for the stove from the *piazza*; I saw a hat stand in a corner for my clothes and my hats, for perhaps on dull days I would make a gay hat for myself also – paintings hung on all the walls – and in the middle of the room stood an easel and beside the easel lay a beautiful palette, holding all the colours in the world.

NINE

There were strange purveyors of Astrological Fortune to be found in the basements off the Covent Garden *piazza*: they would take people's days of birth and cast their horoscopes by reading the stars. Angelica consulted the Astrologers, to know of her future; she was chided for visiting such charlatans but she would not be dissuaded. She said she did not know the exact day of her birth but what did it matter? She would visit the tellers of fortune and future and give them one birth date, or another, and ask them if she would always be beautiful and the fortune tellers looked at the stars and looked at Angelica and said, *You will always be beautiful.*

And there it was still, upon the turn on the stairs in the elegant house in Pall Mall, that first wonderful portrait: the powdered hair, the extraordinary pale oval face, and the large dark eyes. Angelica: the most beautiful woman in London.

Roberto the parrot disappeared one day over St James's Park but in the evening he found his way back, battered and bleeding; after that he was more timid, and more demanding of his family. It was Angelica he adored but she had other commitments. The painter's sister, Francesca, learned to calm Roberto, stroked his feathers, but Roberto looked always for Angelica.

These were the painter's golden years, when the carriages

queued outside the door, bringing their noble ladies and gentle-men, and sometimes noble children, for their sittings with the Italian Portraitist. Filipo di Vecellio worked hard, there was nothing left of the strolling, bored Bristol boy: sometimes he was working on four or five different Portraits in one day and his boards and canvases lay all about his Studio. His assistants were occasionally busy till midnight with sleeves and folds of a gown and blue sky. They slept in the studio, their dreams full of the smell of paint, sometimes now the only time they saw the real sky was in their dreams.

And at the hospitable dinners Art was discussed, day after day after day. Inebriated painters would thump the table so that glasses tinkled against each other; some said Portrait Painting was the only real way to paint the human condition; others shouted that the real subjects for paintings were not insignificant human beings but Moral Questions: that Epic paintings were the only paintings that would live on; one particularly drunken young man, who nobody quite knew, kept insisting that the death of Caesar as a subject was more important than somebody's wife.

'We are the Arbiters of the Age!' he cried, thumping the table again and tinkling the glasses.

'Ah, but who will *buy* the Death of Julius Caesar?' shouted the host. 'They would many times rather spend such money on their own Portrait!'

'There can be Moral Force even in a Portrait!' cried John Palmer and the glasses and bottles clinked and the voices shouted and fought and laughed and the quiet sister listened to everything they said.

And always, as darkness fell, John Palmer would place his old wig back on his head and put on his shabby cloak and light his small lantern to walk back to Spitalfields. Sometimes James Burke the art dealer left at the same time and would walk with him. Once when the Signorina Francesca di Vecellio saw them to the door she stayed and watched them go, caught by their unlikely shadow: the tall Mr James Burke and the rotund Mr John Palmer, disappearing into the night.

These then were the special years of Filipo di Vecellio's greatest success and his greatest wealth, the years before Mr Joshua Reynolds and Mr Thomas Gainsborough became so very much more sought after than he. He was immensely rich and happily married. He had acquired Old Masters, was known to own an exquisite small painting by Rembrandt. And success and happiness attended the great house in Pall Mall.

The golden years.

But life was not quite that simple, there in rich and wild and squalid London: it was a world of false appearances and none so false as the occupants of the house in Pall Mall. **Money, money:** *that was the commodity that separated success and happiness and fashion and promenades in the Park from the rest of London; that is from shame and terror and starvation and death and scabbed knowing children; from women spewing gin into open filthy sewers and from apothecaries with their potions and men with knives; and from sheep's guts with red ribbons lying there in dark disgusting alleys. Success and happiness hung there with death and betrayal and pain: balanced, swaying, teetering as the great wild city of trade and business expanded its grasping, avid tentacles and the artist's sister painted alone, night after night after night, in her sewing-room.*

Twins were born – *Lucky*, people said, *twins are good luck*, people said. A boy and a girl, to complete the happiness of the golden years.

TEN

'—so here are the babies, Francesca,' Angelica said to me from her bed and she handed both the small squalling bundles to me. I stared down in real horror – *she could not mean that I was to look after them.*

'No,' I said.

'The boy shall be called Claudio,' said my brother firmly.

'No,' I said. *No!*

'What is wrong with Claudio, *cara mia*?' asked my brother, smiling his charming smile at his bewildered sister as I stood there (perhaps he thought I wanted to call his son Marmaduke or Tobias or Ezekiel, or his daughter Betty).

'**No!**' I cried and the babies placed into my arms cried also (as well they might).

'And Isabella,' said my brother.

'You will manage them better than I,' said Angelica weakly, 'you are so calm and efficient,' and already she looked to her mirrors and her paints, as I stood there looking in disbelief at what I held and thinking of my own paints, of my Studio, of my precious hours, of my Plan, my Plan for the rest of my Life – there was a wet-nurse, and the maids of course, but the moment they were born Claudio and Isabella were given over to me as if it was the most natural thing in the world that they were my personal Responsibility: that I should look after them and be accountable for their welfare, for my brother and his wife were busier and busier with Life and all I had to do was run the house.

I had never dealt with any baby in my life – I *was* the baby – but much, much more than this, I was so very nearly ready: six months more I needed, I had just stopped using my precious boards over and over, for the first time I had kept two Paintings, one was Angelica in her gay hat, I thought to have six paintings and then show what it was that I could do but Angelica left the small bundles in my arms, *in my arms*, and turned away even as I cried, 'I cannot do this!' and I stood there holding two babies and my plan for my Future was torn to pieces, as my Drawings had been torn to pieces years before.

Claudio looked like our brother, Tobias.

I stood in shock and disbelief with the small bundles – they were not even crying now, just small fists clenching and unclenching – with all my heart and soul I wanted to leave them: I wanted to *leave them right there*, put them down somewhere, anywhere, on the dining-room table, and seize up my two Paintings and run even with no money with no paints with no lodgings with no Poppy, *I am not a cruel bad person but I do not want them I do not want them*, I had to get out of here this prison to run to get away get out of here – but Claudio and Isabella were here, and I was holding them, and my brother and his wife already moving away, moving on—

—*money, money: that was the commodity that separated success and happiness and fashion and promenades in the Park from the rest of London; that is from shame and terror and starvation and death and scabbed knowing children; from women spewing gin into open filthy sewers and from apothecaries with their potions and men with knives; and from sheep's guts with red ribbons lying there in dark disgusting alleys—*

and over my head I felt it: a dark trapdoor smashing closed upon me and the echo went on and on and on.

ELEVEN

Miss Ann Ffoulks was very fond of Filipo di Vecellio and his beautiful wife, Angelica, but wondered that they did not have nurses and governesses for their two small children rather than leave them almost entirely in the care of Francesca, who became so pale and strained and distracted. Miss Ffoulks of course would no more have dreamed of commenting on this situation than flying with angel's wings (not that Miss Ffoulks believed in such things as angels, she was thinking metaphorically).

The children lived upstairs in a room by their aunt (the cook whose room it had been was sent to sleep in a room off the kitchen), so that the rest of the busy house in Pall Mall would not be in any way disturbed by this addition to the household. And more and more visitors came to the hospitable, somewhat hurly-burlyed dinners over which the beautiful Angelica presided like a bright, shining angel, Roberto the parrot perched on her shoulder or very near, and the artistic and social life in the house went on quite unchanged. Very occasionally the growing children were allowed into the magic place that was their mother's dressing-room. There they were presented to the most beautiful woman in London, who was their mother, and they felt as bereft as Roberto the parrot when they were left again. Scents and perfumes assailed them; they saw mirrors and draped gowns and shawls; their mother smiled and held out her hands. They must not touch her high, pomaded, powdered hair that was becoming more and more fashionable, or the pots of white paste that made her skin so white (the famous Venetian Ceruse), or the blocks of crimson, or the brushes and the black tablets of kohl. Their small, round eyes took in the unguents and the toilet waters; when they had learned to read and write, tutored by their aunt, they spelled out a special large bottle always there in front of their mother: it said, SOLIMAN'S WATER. FOR A PERFECT SKIN. When they were called into the room, the grey-white hair already sat perfected on their mother's head, always; Roberto perched nearby, preening. And, always, her perfume caught them – musk or jasmine, they could not name it – the perfume enfolded them. Then gently, so as not to disarray, they were embraced by their beautiful mother.

They were very seldom invited into their father's studio either, for people of fashion came there all day to sit to him. But just occasionally they sidled in and again the special scents caught them: the sharp pungent smells of oil and colour and pictures on the walls and boards and canvases leaning there; always they remembered the smells of mixtures and pigments and Turpentine and rags and easels. Sometimes they caught a portrait, half-finished, waiting to unfold; once they heard that a half-finished portrait was the Queen of England.

And then at last: King George III agreed to give his formal patronage to the forming of a first Royal Academy of Art. There was very much drinking and shouting and waving of goblets in Pall Mall that night as they waited to learn who would be members, who would not: who amongst the Artists of England would be elected as Royal Academicians.

'What does it actually mean, a Royal Academy!' shouted John Palmer. 'It will only be an Exhibition Hall after all!'

'Do not complain of Exhibition Halls!' said James Burke, laughing and raising his glass. 'There is nothing wrong with Exhibition Halls, they will add greatly to Business!'

Mr Hartley Pond sighed. 'It is all very well, this talk of a *British* Academy but nothing changes the facts: it is the Old Masters that can be learned from, and none of *them* are British!' And Roberto squawked very loudly at Angelica's side and Filipo di Vecellio's heart was in his mouth, he could hardly speak: he had had one commission from Queen Charlotte at last but what if foreigners were not to be eligible?

The house in Pall Mall breathed again: Filipo di Vecellio was elected as an Academician (several foreigners were deemed acceptable). His old friend John Palmer congratulated his old friend Filipo di Vecellio on his elevation – John Palmer would never be a Royal Academician of course.

But: it was Joshua Reynolds who became president of the Royal Academy, it was Joshua Reynolds who was knighted. *Sir Joshua Reynolds*, said all the newspapers. There was also very much talk of a new wonderful Portraitist who had been elected even though he did not live in London: Thomas Gainsborough. The years had been passing and Filipo di Vecellio felt the first cold draught, a feeling in the air, of change, of fashion: the carriages outside the house in Pall Mall were not so numerous as once they had been. (And his sister Francesca di Vecellio felt it, as clearly as if he spoke to her, her brother's keen, keen disappointment: he who had tricked them all with his charm and his brilliance now saw the first public signs that his own star that once shone so very brightly, had begun to fade. Joshua Reynolds had gone ahead of him.)

John Palmer spoke yet again of the Old Masters they had seen in Italy, perhaps hoping to cheer his old friend, but Philip was tiring of such talk.

'You are becoming boring, Sir!' he would shout. 'Do you not understand what has happened now? We are the Masters now!' And John Palmer, until more wine or Angelica's charm loosened his tongue again, would fall silent or he would take himself off, with a gruff 'good evening' as dusk fell, to walk back to his life in Spitalfields, of which no-one knew anything. Or Miss Ffoulks, seeing old John Palmer hurt, would change the subject completely again, bring her distant cousin James Cook into the conversation – a master sailor who had set off to explore the world – and the talk might turn briefly to the Pacific Ocean and lost continents and the Transit of Venus and other stars.

And then all talk would turn back again to the main topic of conversation: Art and—

—and I was trapped of course—
The children were so small and they needed me and I felt them

eating me, *eating me*, eating my Painting and my Plans and it was not their fault, *Zia Francesca! Aunt Fran! Where are you?* and I felt their small, warm arms reach up, and I cared about them and resented them and was trapped by them and wanted to dump them in the Foundling Hospital for Unwanted Children. —Isabella had dark eyes and smiled but Claudio was thin and scrawny and watchful, so like Tobias, and I looked at him and I remembered that Tobias had always seemed to me to be a beanstalk, a thin, black-eyed beanstalk; Claudio had a way too of trying to get a person's whole attention – I had grabbed people by the arms when I was a child, he, rather, threw his arms about a person – that is, about me – demanding and absolute – all day long they took my time, I had no moment to think, to plan, until everybody was asleep and then I would take up my paintbrush once again and some nights now I was so tired I fell asleep with my brush in my hand: I actually had to destroy one of my gowns and tell Philip I had burned it, 'I was too close to the fire in the basement kitchen, Filipo *mio*,' for red, bright paint had seeped all down the front of my skirt as I slept and I could not remove it.

I had been so near.

My time had gone: the children were my responsibility for weeks, months, years: exhausted always now I believed that although I still tried to work my Portraits were hardly ever successful; when they talked at the dinner-table about classes at the new Royal Academy I listened in a kind of trapped rage: I felt I would have *killed* to get to those classes, I would have taken the Knife, of the famous Farmer's Wife, and cut off their tails, or their heads – *whose heads? the children's? the Artists'?* – to attend classes in Form and Construction and Technique – but of course the classes were not for women, *o God if I could sell one Painting, even one, I would run away from here so quickly*; and Claudio and Isabella grew, soon they learned to get into my sewing-room (that is, my precious Studio), they banged at the boards, they found pods of paint and jumped on them making colours jump out over themselves and over my Paintings so that all was Pandemonium, they hit each other with brushes or bits of old board – for God's sake they hardly ever left my side, *Zia Francesca!* (their Father wanted them to speak Italian) *Aunt Fran!* – sometimes they would fall asleep there in my room and I would seize up my pencil and try at least to catch their faces and their tumbling dark hair and the small legs and arms that were still at last, believing I still must lack Form and Construction and Technique – I had had no proper lessons in those formal, technical skills although I had drawn the form and construction of my own naked body for many hours and I could paint an arm or the fall of a shoulder – and then I would carry the children into their own beds and try and take my brush and begin again and I occasionally, still, slipped through the house in the night to study the Rembrandt portrait, stared at that way he used light and shade itself to catch a mood, as I tried to do (not at all with his success, I speak of this dis-interestedly, I do not mean I was successful), but just sometimes I *did* catch the light in that way, and I believed I sometimes had caught an expression on a face (my own face?) in the way that he painted – I wasn't sure of course, if I was doing the same thing as an Old Master, for there was no-one to guide me and my confidence seemed gone and then voices would call again, *Aunt Fran! Aunt Fran! Zia Francesca!* and sometimes like an echo I heard again my own, long-gone voice, or Venus or Tobias or Ezekiel, *Aunt Joy! Aunt Joy!* and one day at the dinner-table I heard the name of Mr Joseph Wright of Derby mentioned – he had become well-known – and I hugged my knowledge to my heart, *I chose him before he was famous!* and always I would hurry (with my bonnet and my shopping basket) past the chop houses and the taverns and past Old Slaughter's Coffee-house just near where we had lived in St Martin's Lane, and I could not help stopping there, I knew it was where Artists congregated, I looked in through the smoky glass and saw all the young ones: shouting, waving their arms about, holes in their jackets; they showed each other – *I could see it* – their own paintings, right there in the smoky room, heads together, looking, talking, disputing – the shadows and the light and their bright hats and their own hair tied back instead of white wigs and the jaunty girl in the corner pouring drinks, and then I hurried home again to the children – and the madwoman's voice, still there on the corner of St Martin's Lane, echoed in my head long after I dropped a penny into her dirty hat, *London Bridge is falling down.*

And all the time, all those years as the children grew and I was trapped, I understood: *I am a Coward – I should have joined*

Poppy as soon as I met her and taken my chances, I was getting older and older, I had lost my chance, I had lost my Art, my dream of a Studio was hazy now, only an easel and a hat-stand in an empty room – I had, truly, become Aunt Joy – what was the point any more of the boards in my sewing-room all turned to face the wall?

One early morning I caught sight of my unsuspecting mouth in the mirror – dour, turned down, disappointed (something, I saw, like John Palmer's mouth: someone who knew they had failed) – so in some wild frustrated explosion I seized the mirror and I smashed it in the garden at the back where we burned rubbish and old canvases, and the children called *Aunt Fran! Zia Francesca!* ten now, eleven years old, running out through the house in the early morning and jumping on the glass and Claudio cut his arm, blood everywhere, and I was sure I heard a rooster crowing in Pall Mall (and indeed I had: Mr Thomas Gainsborough had moved to Town) and Claudio yelled at the sight of blood and Isabella wept at the sight of blood and I caught some glass in my finger and Philip called from his Studio for quiet – and so it all went on: their Lives, my Life.

One day I found that I was thirty years old and lost words echoed: *When I do count the clock that tells the Time . . .*

I was a middle-aged woman.

TWELVE

The golden years had, indeed, waned.

Despite the success and the fame and the grand house and the hospitality, something was changing in the world of Art. There were some who now called Filipo di Vecellio's portraits facile, some said his sitters all had the same privileged look: people much preferred Joshua Reynolds and Thomas Gainsborough who painted (it was said) the soul (and sometimes the soul of ladies of less certain breeding, even actresses). Sir Joshua Reynolds, President, began to lay down laws regarding the Royal Academy:

> 'The wish of the genuine Painter must be more extensive: instead of endeavouring to amuse Mankind with the minute neatness of his imitations, he must endeavour to improve them by the Grandeur of his Ideas.'

Sir Joshua Reynolds had become even more famous. Mr Thomas Gainsborough who had lived far away, in Bath, had come to London; people clamoured to be painted by him. And the appointment books of Filipo di Vecellio became less and less full.

Mr James Burke, his friend and dealer, was abrupt and honest.

'I am doing my best. But you have gone out of fashion, Filipo. It happens to everyone. It may be time for you to find another, younger dealer.'

Filipo begged James Burke not to think of this. Angelica begged James Burke not to think of this, and nobody could resist the charm and the beauty of Angelica.

Filipo di Vecellio was devastated by the change in his fortunes. But had some things with which to console himself. He was rich: he would never now want for money: it was not money that was lost.

And whatever happened to the fashion, Filipo di Vecellio had what Reynolds and Gainsborough did not have: *he had a son*. When he was old enough Filipo would take Claudio on the Grand Tour to Paris and Rome and Florence and Venice and Amsterdam. Claudio would experience the Old Masters and then he would paint Grand Epics, History Paintings: he would paint in the Heroic Style that the Royal Academy so cherished.

Filipo thought not at all of the once-noble name of the Wiltshire Marshalls.

It was the name of di Vecellio that he vowed would never die.

The young di Vecellio children did not walk the streets of London freely, their father did not want them to become common, but just occasionally he insisted their Aunt accompany them somewhere educational. One very particular evening he arranged for them to see a play by Mr Shakespeare called *The Tempest*: he said that, because tonight was special, their Parents would be waiting for them at home to hear what they had learned. Isabella and Claudio were excited at first – the crowds, the night, the red and gold theatre boxes, the gorgeous clothes, the stage, all the bright candles and the storms – but they quickly became bored with all the words and started kicking at the seats. Luckily (or unluckily) the actor playing Prospero set fire to his beard with a candle, to the children's delight: there were shouts and screams and the last third of the performance had to be cancelled and the children came out of Drury Lane greatly excited again. The aunt walked them past Covent Garden and the *piazza*, their eyes widened at all the wild life there, and she showed them the house she and their father had lived in years ago. And there on the corner of St Martin's Lane the madwoman, older now, still sang and the children too stopped for a moment, caught by the sweet sadness of the voice.

> *Amazing Grace, how sweet the sound*
> *That saved a wretch like me!*
> *I once was lost, but now am found,*
> *Was blind, but now I see*

and their aunt told them, as Miss Ffoulks had told her, that the song had been written by the owner of a slave ship, who had repented his ways. But the children did not know of slaves and lost interest, yet the beautiful voice drifted down the lane in the distance and they listened still, without knowing that they did so.

And in the house in Pall Mall, most unusually, their Parents were, indeed, waiting.

'You will be leaving this house tomorrow,' said the father to the children.

Filipo di Vecellio had decided that his children were to be sent away to be educated: Claudio to a Private School for a proper education with particular emphasis on the Theory of Art, Isabella to a Finishing School for Young Ladies with much emphasis on Manners and Gloves and Deportment. The visit to the Theatre had been their last London adventure.

And so in the house in Pall Mall, without any warning for either the children or the aunt, there was silence.

—yes.
The Silence.
And the Time.
The ticking of clocks in empty hallways as loud as voices or so it seemed to me at first, but my word-pictures are useless.

That first day I slowly turned the old boards back to face the little sewing-room and looked at my Pictures. —Most had been destroyed over the years either by me or the children, only a few remained: one of Poppy, other street-girls in shadow; women at the theatre leaning from their boxes; John Palmer without his wig; Angelica in her gay hat; myself; myself—

—I picked up my brush and like some ghost of the past I began, at once, to paint – unstoppable again – that first day I actually sent word to Euphemia that I was ill and I stood at my easel and as if in a trance – in all the silence of the upstairs room I painted for hours and hours, nobody called *Zia Francesca! Aunt Fran!* the door did not burst open I did not eat I did not sleep I painted a girl, my long-ago imaginary friend Mary-Ann whose face suddenly appeared on the board, she was laughing at something: the shoulder of another woman just showed, half a fan, and Mary-Ann laughed, she was there again, caught, on my easel.

Next morning I was back on the streets of my city – my streets, my dear London streets – buying turbot and pies and potatoes; in Pall Mall lighting the candles as the afternoon drew down and the light faded: back there: the housekeeper: partly listening (I had thought, later, to catch a different likeness of Claudio for I saw always the connection to my brother Tobias); and they talked of Mr Thomas Gainsborough who had moved to Pall Mall and brought animals with him, they talked of Titian and of Michelangelo; and Miss Ffoulks had her own, other, enthusiasms: the on-going adventures of her distant but dear cousin, Captain James Cook.

'Not content with discovering the New World,' she exclaimed, 'the dear Captain is now looking for the South-West Passage!' Captain James Cook was always in all the newspapers now: thrilling journeys, new continents for Britain, beautiful wild birds and exquisite flowers and friendly natives and fish that could fly up into the air from the ocean.

'Where will it end?' cried Angelica. 'Will the world grow more huge yet, before our eyes, in our Lifetime?'

'I should have liked to have been on the *Endeavour* myself,' mused John Palmer, 'or the *Resolution*. I should have liked to be the Official Artist of such Discoveries.'

'Why, the *Endeavour* had two Artists, Mr Palmer!' cried Miss Ffoulks. 'Although one suffered from fits and unfortunately died. Two Artists, and all the crew, and Mr Joseph Banks, in his own cabin of course, to collect specimens of exotic plants and flowers – and the ship no more than one hundred feet long! Oh – that I could have travelled like that, and seen the things that my dear Cousin has seen and done the things that he has done!' and for just a moment I saw all the pent-up longing of the constraints of her

Life: I – of course – was not the only one. 'And they have found so many new continents and islands and claimed them all for King George!' —The world was bigger and brighter than we could imagine and Miss Ffoulks glowed at the enchantment she had often brought to our table by her consanguinity with such a Hero, and then the gentlemen left for their Clubs and Miss Ffoulks hurried to a Meeting about Slavery and Angelica prepared for the Opera and I went back up the stairs almost in a trance and Mary-Ann still sat there on the easel, laughing. —I placed her on my wall; now I would try Claudio, there was something about Claudio's eyes when I tried to paint them – a shifty, uneasy look – but did not Tobias have shifty eyes too when he fought with his brother Ezekiel so wildly and they had no-one to warm them and watch over them? —I thought of the face of Claudio, or of Tobias, and I knew: we were a shifty family, the remnants of the Wiltshire Marshalls, all those years ago, and when the small, mysterious tap came on the door – this was long before Angelica found her way there in despair – for a moment it seemed to be the children, they had not gone away at all, they would come and jump on my painting and then I pulled myself together and closed the door of my sewing-room, occasionally the housemaid, Euphemia, grown older as I had grown older, knocked for something concerning the house: otherwise nobody ever came there, and if Euphemia knew more than anyone else she never spoke.

At the door stood James Burke, my brother's friend and dealer. 'I have been watching you for many years,' he said without any preamble at all. 'You have paint on your hand again. I have seen it there often but tonight you were distracted and it occurs to me that perhaps it is the children gone, perhaps you are a Lady *amateur* – but just perhaps you are not. Let me see what you have done.'

Afterwards – after he had seen my paintings: Angelica in that gay hat, Poppy, Mary-Ann laughing; afterwards when that unforgettable look of total shock came to his face (his face, that I quickly began to read so well, always betrayed him, always, he could not hide it) – afterwards when he had turned towards me in the way that he did as if he literally *could not help himself* – afterwards then, he told me he had been watching me for a long time; he had seen years ago, he said, that there was something, something unspoken, between my brother and myself; he said I had a way of looking at my brother when he was talking about his painting that betrayed me; he often saw paint on my hand or on my gown – perhaps a little too often for a lady *amateur*, although he had thought perhaps, lately, that I no longer painted, but tonight there was paint on my hand again, and a strand of my hair drifting out from under my cap, he said, was blue.

He stared at my Paintings that night without speaking and when he turned to me he said slowly in utter, utter astonishment, 'These are beautiful, Francesca. Quite beautiful. You are a much, much better Painter than your Brother,' and his arms reached out towards me as if he was a man in a Dream, who did not know what he did.

I loved James Burke, as the poets say, with my heart: with my whole, damaged heart.

How could I not? he saw that I could paint, and he affirmed me, my Talent, it could be said – anyway, my fierce, fierce passion for capturing, in my way, what I see. It was his shocked, amazed face that made me love him, *the first Affirmation of my Work I had ever, ever had*, and I was now over thirty years old, how then – seeing that he understood – how could I not give him myself? my heart, my soul, my body – and my painting. I was like an over-flowing stream – no – I was like an over-flowing ocean: if the sea should ever flow over its shores and race upon the land *that* might describe the passion in me.

All my thoughts, all my ideas about painting, all I had tried to teach myself from watching and listening to my brother and his colleagues without seeming to over all the years: listening to Joshua Reynolds and Hartley Pond and John Palmer, Miss Ffoulks' stories of Rome and Florence, haunting Print shops and Art Auctions, seeing the painting by Mr Joseph Wright of Derby, copying the Rembrandt over and over – all these things poured out of me – all the pent-up emotion of those years since the pestilence destroyed our family in Bristol and put me to hat-making and then my hope when Philip came for me, and his denial of my work, my imaginary friend Mary-Ann – out it poured into the hands of James Burke, art-dealer. – I gave him every single part of me, including my paintings. And he saw that my paintings were different: full of strange light and shade because I had always painted at night: my paintings were full of night and shadows and colours and secrets, and James saw and *understood* what I was doing, that is what James Burke gave to me.

And James Burke made me know that perhaps I did not have to be a solitary person: that I could be part of someone else, that someone else could be a part of me. I learned from James Burke how one could have another person as part of one's heart; how one's heart could actually race at the sound of a beloved voice; how one could share, at last, *at last* one's innermost thoughts, and have no Secrets – oh to have no Secrets at last! – I who had had so many; when I met James Burke I had never ever opened my mind to another person and showed what lay there; I had had no real friend, or *confidante* – except my imaginary Mary-Ann who came to me sometimes when I could not carry my own loneliness; and I told him who I was: Grace Marshall, from Bristol. And, in return, James Burke loved me.

And so I understood at last something of how the Artists like Rembrandt van Rijn had painted: I had thought it was only matters like Form and Technique that I was lacking. —In Bristol on Christmas Steps how often had I seen couples in dark stinking corners? we heard the cries from our attic rooms – the other hat-girls whispered shocking words to each other, and sometimes we spoke the word: *love*: and then I had been there myself in the dark alleys behind Covent Garden and it was nothing in the world to do with *love*.

(When, later, I met a man who painted with words instead of with paints he said to me, *You were not the only person in the world who put your love in a place or a thing: look about you.* And I have seen them now: they who lay their very passion that all of us have upon books, or caged birds, or money, or a small animal, or a glass of something that comforts them, as I did upon London, because another human being is not there.)

It was James Burke who affirmed my painting, and it was James Burke who made me understand about love.

I cannot say I knew nothing of a wife, of course I knew Lydia Burke, Lydia of the speculative eyes and the gently-moving fan; it was the only subject of which he would not speak: *Please Grace*, he said, *do not speak of her* so I did not.

—I showed him the drawing of me by Mr Hogarth and he looked at it in amazement. 'You might sell this for a sum,' he said, shocking me, 'for his prices have gone up since he died.' And he held me, and he listened to my story of meeting Mr Hogarth in the church in Bristol and why I could never sell my drawing, and he held me, and he told me what Mr Hogarth had said, *It seems to be universally admitted that there is such a thing as Beauty, and that the highest degree of it is Grace.* 'Amazing Grace,' James Burke said to me, and he held me.

Poor James, I might say! poor James, what he unleashed by that unbelieving look when he stared at my paintings, when he turned to me then and took me into his arms as if he could not help himself – and I believe he could not: when he took off my disguise, my spinster's cap, and let down my long dark hidden hair with the streak of blue he did not know what he was doing, I had not been held in anybody's arms since the days of my childhood and not even then that I can remember – perhaps Aunt Joy had held me as part of her duties – I was like a starving person who had never had food – so one might say, perhaps, poor James – and later, when I met the man who painted with words, as I painted with paints, he said to me, *Love is about the self, as much as it is about the person whom one loves,* but I did not yet know such philosophies.

I hid nothing from James Burke. I, my real self, Grace Marshall, told him how I had disguised myself in the middle of the shifting, twisting, malicious world of London that went on around me: the quiet Italian sister, the housekeeper, the keeper of the two young children, whose Paintings in her sewing-room were turned to the wall. And finally I told him how I had first earned my own money to buy paints and brushes.

He listened to me, in disbelief almost, but because he saw my Paintings he understood that I spoke truthfully. And he held me.

That night then, that unbelievable night: *take him and cut him out in little stars, and he will make the face of heaven so fine that all the world will be in love with night* – then I understood, *then* I understood.

And that night James Burke, when he finally left me, almost at dawn before the servants rose, left my room and my paintings and my heart and my body – my newly-born body – when he left as the stars went out he took the small painting of Mary-Ann laughing and gave me six guineas.

'It is a painting of you, of course,' he said.

It is impossible to describe how – how – unbelievable that was to me – I who had sold my own body and stolen pennies and guineas for more years than I cared to remember, had at last *sold a painting* – at last it was true as I had dreamed all the years; somebody else had validated me: somebody had cared for one of my paintings enough to pay money for it.

At last then: *at last* it was really true.

I was an Artist.

When James made me understand that it was true, I could hardly bear to leave my Studio; I worked furiously, all night if necessary, to paint what I saw in my head; day after day James looked at my work, praised me, made suggestions, *Grace*, he would say (my real name at last, over and over), *Grace*. —He made me find another mirror to watch carefully still the turn of a neck, the way a hand lay, to paint them still, over and over; he took me to auction rooms if Old Masters were to be auctioned, he took me to shops that had books and books of beautiful Paintings; he told me of the artists of Venice and Rome and Amsterdam and Paris, he told me that one day, one day – as I had, it seemed, been mystically born in Florence – he would take me to Florence and to the Uffizi Palace where great Art was shown, and we would stand on the old bridge, the *Ponte Vecchio*, and see the sun set across the city and across the water, I saw it, I saw it in my head and in my heart, the old bridge in Florence and the dusk. 'They have *cafés* with roofs made of lemon trees entwining,' he said. 'You will smell the lemons on the warm night air.'

He took me to the houses of noble people to whom he sold paintings, who had many Old Masters on their walls – showed me, showed me, showed me, taught me, taught me. —He took me to Gerrard Street, to the art shop of Mr Newman: there I saw the fine, expensive, wonderful hog-hair brushes, I had never owned one, and the best black-lead pencils, and the colours I knew so well and some that I did not, no adulterated paint here: the small bags of prepared colour that I loved so much, all ground, tied up in pig's bladders and he bought them: brown ochre, Naples yellow, Prussian blue, vermilions, lakes – all the small bags of beautiful colours that I wanted to *eat* I wanted them so much, all ready to be mixed with oil. —Green had always been difficult he said, made from copper: he told me to use the new, synthetic greens that did not fade, or to mix my own greens from other colours; he showed me the best oil, the best boards and canvases, he pointed to the more exotic colours also which I had never dreamed to buy, and he purchased for me my very first tiny bag of the exquisite ultramarine from the beautiful blue stone, from the *lapis lazuli* of Afghanistan: I felt as if I would swoon in delight, I wanted to clasp my purchases to me and spin back to my sewing-room and pick up my new brushes and dip them into my new paint and we passed the corner of St Martin's Lane and the madwoman with the beautiful voice sang:

As I was walking one morning in Spring
I heard a maid in Bedlam, how sweetily she sing

and I was there, always, quietly in the dining-room, lighting the candles as James Burke sat there as he had sat for so many years; it was the same but not the same, for there I was in my disguise – *but now somebody at the dining-table knew* – the dull spinster's gown, the small cap, the keys – only now someone *knew;* and now also I had some other, wonderful energy as I listened, and learned, and painted – as if something had been released inside me and slowly my paintings became the same but different, a new warmth, a subtlety that had not been there before – I saw it, he saw it. —The paintings were still dark and shadowy but they were different because I was different: there was light in the eyes, and James, so free and easy in our house, spent more and more time in the upstairs room, looking at what I had done, encouraging me, holding me in the night, I had had no idea that one's body could lift and lunge and *love*, I did not know that the skin and the smell and the soul of another person was what the poets and painters and Rembrandt *knew.* I changed: my face changed, my body changed.

But because I had never caused notice to myself, who, as I quietly lit the candles, would notice anything different now?

We made many plans, James and I: he was to sell my work at once but under the name of a man, 'It would be too hard to sell your work under the name of a woman; the two Women Royal Academicians—'

'*Two Women Royal Academicians?*'

'Yes, there are two – but they have important Patrons, that is quite, quite different. I will sell your Paintings under the name of Michel Grace,' – I began laughing – 'No, it is slightly Foreign, which will make them more saleable still,' but he was laughing also, and holding me; he was so sure of selling my work that he had paid me more money *in Advance.*

He had one word of warning about my work. 'All of the Women you paint are yourself, Grace, in some way, however small. If I am to sell them under another name at first, then you must learn to paint a Girl or a Woman who does not look like you at all or Sir Joshua Reynolds may pass by and recognise you! Indeed Miss Ffoulks would recognise you immediately!' We laughed, and I thought how much I would like that. 'Indeed, your Brother himself would recognise you! I am serious, Grace, you must learn to clearly paint someone else.'

'But what do you suggest I do?' I cried to him in frustration then. 'You know I cannot paint freely until I leave here! When I see the women from the Theatre or the streets and I want to paint them I have to carry a face *in my mind,* not like the real painters who have people in front of them – of course my paintings have something of my face because mine is the only face I have been able to study properly.'

'You have often painted your brother and Angelica and the children without them sitting to you. Look at that beautiful picture of Angelica: the wonderful hat, and the gaiety!'

'But I know them so well! I have seen them every day for years.'

'You told me you painted your Family from memory.'

'Yes but now I cannot! Since he destroyed them. It is as if I cannot paint them now!'

'Until you can have people sit to you, you must memorise faces, other faces.'

'It is so *hard*!'

'It is a hard life you have chosen, Grace, for a Woman,' and his arms encircled me again.

Day after day after day I studied people in the street, tried to bring the memory of them home again: I truly now longed to see

Poppy again – how would she look, now, so many years later? would she still have her bright eye and her infectious laugh? and I painted James when he was away from me: the very direct grey eyes, the beloved face, half in shadow, half in light (and I remembered the night I had painted him in the late afternoon shadows, years before); I destroyed these paintings, these I did not show him, they were not good enough: how hard to paint Truth, how hard to paint *love*; how Rembrandt must have loved the woman he painted in the water, I thought, even as she was there before him, to make her, in the shadows and the light, so exact and so real; and the other Rembrandt woman in Philip's study, I felt as if I knew them: both paintings were so – so accessible to me all these years later and to thousands of people like me, so recognisable and so real.

One night in my room, in my small bed, James fell asleep – I crept out of the bed, I found my charcoal, I did not dare disturb the covers more but I drew him – it was the first real naked body of a man I had ever seen, it was the same and yet so different from George the Greek statue, of course I drew James, me naked with my charcoal and my paper, how could I help drawing him? I drew the long limbs and the way his hip turned and one thigh was uncovered, his beautiful thigh, his shoulder, was turned away, I drew the way his hair fell on his shoulder such a different shoulder than my own, and his long beautiful back, I drew so quickly I was shy as if I was spying but I saw only beauty, when he stirred and moved I thrust the paper and the charcoal away into a dark corner, and jumped into bed like a child – it was the only thing I did in all that time that I did not tell him, later I tried to paint what I had drawn but it was never right, never.

And always I made it clear, crystal clear: I would sell my Paintings, through James, under a false name, a man's name, only until I could make enough money at last to leave Pall Mall and find my Studio in Compton-street or Meard-street or Leicester-lane and set up on my own at last, and be myself.

'Are you sure, Grace? It will not be easy, no matter how much I can help you, I am not a Patron as Women Artists must have.'

'I do not care that it will not be easy! Nothing that I have done has been easy! I have been waiting for this moment since I was a child!' My paintings – the paintings by Michel Grace – would sell, I would have money of my own for the first time in my life and finally I would have a proper Artist's Studio like my brother at last, and at last – this portentous word, I know, still sounds naive but it is how I felt – fulfil my *Destiny* – I may have been over thirty then but there was still time, still time to become the thing I wanted more than anything, more than love itself: to paint freely and openly, to be a Painter, to capture all I see – it mattered to me then not one jot if my work must first be sold under the name of a man: I was sure enough now to believe that one day I could be Grace Marshall again, Grace Marshall of London.

Over the months I saw – he saw – my painting got better and better. Happiness filled me.

Within the shortest space of time imaginable I not only understood what the Poets and the Painters and Rembrandt van Rijn knew about love – the meaning and the magic of love and how it could permeate a painting – I was also pregnant with James Burke's child. And mine.

For the first weeks I could not believe it. *A child*. It was not possible. I had had validation of myself for the first time in my life and I was by then a middle-aged woman. —About a *child* I simply had no thoughts at all – but it was there, just under my hand: the child of our love, growing I supposed, beneath my hand.

And I could not bear it *not again my heart cried not again* the children had not been gone six months.

I told James as soon as I was certain, one evening as we lay there; from my room you could see the stars over the city, *take him and cut him out in little stars and he will make the face of heaven so fine*, of *course* I understood those words now, James had told me a telescope was invented to look at stars, but we did not need a telescope, it was autumn, a clear bright night, the shutters open and the stars shining so bright, and our breath made small patterns in the candlelight and his arms were warm about me and I thought: *now. I must tell him now. He will know what to do.*

I sat up and lit another candle beside the bed before I spoke – I am glad I did for I saw his face, his face betrayed him yet again, man of the World though he was.

'Grace!' he said.

I could not believe it. *He was pleased*. James Burke, rich art

Dealer, married to a beautiful woman, Man-about-Town, would be immersed in a huge *scandale* if this was known, and he was *pleased*?

'Are you glad, Grace?' he said to me.

I stared at him.

He took my hand in his warm, dry one and laid both hands upon me, where the child lay; and as his hand lay there, because I was so used to speaking to and acting towards this man with complete honesty (I – who had become so adept at dissembling – had not, with him, a prevaricating cell in my body except not telling him I had tried to paint him), I said, 'James, James, you must help me at once!'

'Of course – of course I will help you!' He was smiling and smiling and smiling. 'Did you think I would run away and leave you? It is our child. I have longed all my life to have a child, of course I will help you. You must go away very soon, far away from London, and have the child quietly somewhere, you must live somewhere else with the child. We will make plans.' They were such strange, unexpected words that at first I could not understand that he did not understand: *another child: another Life. He did not know but **I knew**, I knew what that meant: I saw the two bundles placed in my arms and my brother and Angelica already turned away, not again **not again** – and gone from my beloved city so that there would be no scandal? gone from my city? gone from London?*

'James, you must help me to – to,' – it was very hard to say the words but there was no question of anything else, '– lose it at once, you must help me, I cannot have a child, I am a Painter, I cannot have a child.' Suddenly I was weeping great heaving gasps from somewhere deep inside me that I did not even understand. 'I must paint, James, please *please* understand, I must be free to paint at last, after all these years of hiding in a sewing-room, all my life here I have been looking after people, I have had, you could say, two children already and they have just left, *just left* – I cannot have a child – I do not want a child – I cannot wait any longer, I am a Painter.' I heard my own voice rising in the room. 'I do not want another child!'

It was as if he had been stung, or stabbed. He sat up at once, he stared at me then with a look of disbelief as if I was talking heresy.

'You cannot mean that. I will look after you, I will send you away, somewhere far away.'

'No,' I said. I had not prepared anything of what I said then but it was my words that came tumbling out with the weeping, 'I do not want to be sent far away, London is where I work! I have to be here, in London, my portraits are here!' all my pent-up feelings were bursting their banks and somewhere Poppy's words, Angelica's words, *it is all right if it has not quickened*, 'tomorrow! I want it over tomorrow, if I have a child I will never, never, never fulfil my Dream and I have waited for my Dream, I have given up everything – freedom, innocence, time, years, self-respect, for years and years until it is *almost too late*,' and all the despair of all my life flooded into my words to the one person in the whole World who knew what I could do, I wept and wept as if I wept out my life; it was a long time before I could stop the deep, dark weeping.

There was a long, long silence.

The house in Pall Mall was completely silent.

I believe I heard the beating of both our hearts.

Finally James got up, slowly put his clothes upon him, buttoning slowly. I waited. 'Very well. There is a woman in Meard-street, off Covent Garden. Tomorrow,' – he was thrusting now at his clothes, putting on his coat – 'tomorrow I will arrange it and you will go there. I will send a message.' And then he was gone.

Of course I thought he would be there. Of course I thought he would come with me. But James did not come with me, he had paid money to the woman in Meard-street – twenty pounds I believe it was, so much money, more than a milliner could earn in years, more than Mr Reynolds paid for his Rembrandt painting; there were basements all over London for this sort of thing for a pound: everybody knew it: Angelica, Poppy, all women knew, it was part of the city – but the woman in the basement in Meard-street (*Meard-street where I had thought to have my Studio*) that woman, I came to understand, was the person the Nobility used: she was very Expensive and very successful, she knew she could command her Fee; he did not come to me, he sent me a message, where to go, he left me to deal with my decision alone – money, nothing else. I went to the door of the house as he instructed me in his note and in Meard-street, in the large basement with thick drawn satin curtains and a four-poster bed and two maids and – she may have been for the Nobility but it was the same process used all over London as I knew from Angelica and Poppy – and there was a thin copper stick that was thrust into me over and over, then I was served tea by one of the maids, then I was sent home in a small covered carriage, part of the twenty-pound service, I alighted at the corner of the Strand.

It was after I walked back then to the house in Pall Mall with tell-tale blood still dripping (somehow I got to my room and sent word downstairs that I was, that day, unwell) that colours suddenly began to *flash* inside my head and I could not stop them: it was as if my head had turned mad and had fireworks exploding inside of it, great explosions of bright green and red and yellow inside my head, and nothing I could do to stop them – it was more terrifying than anything that had ever happened to me, all night over and over in my head churned the details of my life, my Work and my Love, they became muddled, the colours in my head were the colours of the body of James and arms and blood and canvas and shadows and James again and a child, the children, and always somewhere underneath it all Philip tearing my Drawings: the record of our Past that had been lost.

The next morning I somehow, somehow, cleaned myself tidied myself and went downstairs – I had changed my life, yet I had only missed, as it were, a day.

Philip was walking around the dining-room in a fury, could not speak for anger; Angelica was full of gossip and explained.

In that one day that I had missed, in that day I had gone to the basement in Meard-street, Mr James Burke had sent my brother a brief note concluding their Partnership – and Mr James Burke, Art Dealer, and his wife Lydia, had suddenly left London for Europe.

'It will be because of Lydia!' exclaimed Angelica.

I stood very still. 'Because of Lydia.'

'Oh Francesca, my dear, you know nothing of the world! The wife of Mr Burke is known to have lost a great deal of money at the gambling tables, and he has been hard-pressed to pay her debts. She is too close to the Duchess of Devonshire – and everybody knows of her gambling. No doubt he has taken her away on a long Grand Tour.'

During which time, I supposed, they visited the Uffizi and the old bridge called the *Ponte Vecchio* in our home town: in Florence, where the sun sets over the river and catches the Florentine spires that reach up into the night, and the scent of lemons.

I had made my Decision; he had helped me to carry out that Decision; and he had gone.

Frantically I tried to keep painting: wild slashes of bright colour appeared on my canvases as if they had not been painted by me but of course they had been painted by me: they were the colours screaming inside my head *what have I done what have I done?* my body ached with loss: of James? of a child? of the chance to be Michel Grace? who is to say: I literally could not stand the pain, *I cannot stand the pain cut off their tails with a carving knife and nothing 'gainst Time's scythe can make defence save breed, to brave him when he takes thee hence save breed save breed save breed,* I only know I could not stand such pain after giving my heart and my body and my mind so completely; I thought I was in Bristol, I saw myself whirling along the streets with my brother, I saw myself on the quays waiting for the sailing ships to bring their treasures from far-off lands and my brothers; when I tried to carry out my usual duties with my shopping basket over my arm I stood in horror as the madwoman's voice echoed and followed me down St Martin's Lane, *her chains she rattled with her hands and this she sigh and sing* ...

Next morning I threw the coffee pot at my brother – he gave me one of those odd looks we very occasionally shared, wiped at his jacket and left the room without saying anything – Euphemia was on her knees picking up the pieces, she looked at me from under her eyelashes, and as it was the only unsober thing I had ever, ever, done in all my time as housekeeper and *confidante* of Angelica, Angelica was at once puzzled, worried by my uncharacteristic behaviour for I was so *reliable,* and later I heard them say, Philip and Angelica, that I was missing the children, *she is missing the children,* the voices said.

But it was when I walked in the night through the huge sleeping, creaking house of lies and slashed Philip's painting of the Duke of Norfolk, *cut off their tails with a carving knife,* wild screaming slashing with a kitchen knife so they said, I remember but do not remember – that I was taken away; perhaps I was mad, but perhaps I was not: *before* I slashed my brother's painting I had removed every sign from my sewing-room that I had ever *ever* harboured a desire to be an Artist like my brother – I had burned all, all my precious Paintings and the old canvases and the boards and the brushes and the paint – all in the garden at the back of the house, I told the gardener it was rubbish from my brother's Studio and he helped me.

On the wall I left the painting of the Lilies and the green Daisy: that was all that was left of my work of all the years.

I knew what I was doing.

Madness is clever, and chooses its moments.

My attack of madness when I slashed the Duke of Norfolk was so sudden and so violent there was no time to enquire of more suitable places – I was taken at once to Bedlam – Bedlam bedlam bedlam bedlam **BEDLAM** – just to write the name now – *Bedlam* – I cannot even . . . *I cannot* . . .

bedlam

. . . the screams and the manacles and the smells and the wild, drab, loud fornication that even somebody in a tiny padded cell (a private padded cell at least: my brother insisted) could not pretend was not happening – I supposed it was padded in case I threw myself upon it – Bedlam was the most terrifying place I was ever in, in the world, so whatever I write will not describe what I know, and the sound of the shouting and the screaming and the pain . . .

. . . at first I too screamed, one of the tortured Souls in that place, or so it seemed, I screamed out, for the first time in my life, trying to scream out all my anger and despair and pain and loss, yet I *knew* I was screaming: it is almost unexplainable, this wild abandon of screaming aloud for the first time in my life, over and over, something about *time's scythe and the mad farmer's wife cutting off their tails*, words and colours and pictures that made no sense, yet made sense to me at that moment, there, in Bedlam.

The pain of it.

And yet. And yet . . .

Also, the relief of it.

I was *Grace Marshall* (not Francesca di Vecellio from Florence – a place I had never even seen), Grace Marshall wildly, passionately screaming, on and on and on not in an Italian accent either, but wild, untrammelled sound.

They put me in the Strait-Waistcoat then, the canvas and wood tightening over my chest so that I could hardly breathe, my arms in the sleeves and then tied behind me and they forced purgatives down my throat, to purge the madness they said and I fouled the mattress but still my wild, perhaps elated, screaming somehow poured out of me – part of the madness they said, and gave me laudanum, huge amounts of laudanum; when I slept I dreamed of my Father and his card games down the dark alleys and my first Chalks and my sisters with their new hooped petticoats and the disappointed face of my Mother and my brother Tobias with the red rose – I saw their faces clearly, as I had not seen them for years, and all the colours – I dreamed I think for days, doctors stood about me and several times Philip, always without Angelica, and somewhere in my mind I remembered Angelica saying of this place to which she was brought to visit for her Entertainment, *they are like lost souls,* and over and over I wondered: can I paint Pain? can I draw Love?

Finally I could see Philip's tight, closed face in the small stinking padded cell. 'Can I be alone with her, *Dottore?*' The doctor bowed, and talked again, before he left, of *Hysteria.*

Philip and I were, then, quite alone.

Perhaps, if he had called me Grace then, just once.

I think, if he had said something *even then*: something to show that he understood even a small portion of what had happened over the years and years, if he had – oh I do not know what I am trying to say: if he had – validated our realness? the Past? my destroyed Drawings that had been my Treasure? – perhaps I could have forgiven him, perhaps even then, in a house of the mad – while I was mad – who knows? with nobody to hear us but ourselves. Philip leaned over the bed.

'Francesca,' he said. 'You must pull yourself together, Francesca, and as soon as you have done so we will find a more suitable private Sanatorium. We will find a private place. Can you hear me, *cara*? Francesca?'

I closed my eyes then, and began screaming again and Philip went away.

After some time I stopped.

And then I heard the noise.

The wild, riotous, forlorn, madhouse noise, a screaming crying hell: the sound of human beings who were as animals, all of us, animals not humans, crawling and stinking and yelling with irredeemable desperate pain and I was one of them, mad.

After more purgatives and cold rice or something pushed down me and more bed-fouling I stood up for the first time – you could walk in a Strait-Waistcoat – there were things crawling on me, on my head something was crawling: a flea? a cockroach? *what was crawling over me?* I had no hands to scratch or hit but as I was wildly shaking my head and my hair I at once saw there was an old long tear in one of the canvas sleeves of the Strait-Waistcoat, it had been sewn up. —I could reach the shoulder stitches with my teeth and I bit at it for hours and then I tore the hole bigger by getting myself under the bed and catching the sleeve with the leg of the bed, I managed to tear it enough so that I could see my elbow inside and the elbow could push and tear with the bed-leg and – my triumph – finally I could move one of my arms and poke it through the hole, I could push and pull it in and out, nobody seemed to notice or care, the sleeves were still tied together at the back but my arm could come out, it meant I had one hand to scratch or hit or eat if you could stand the gruel or use in the outside privy, I was filthy and stinking but I had one arm and the wood and the canvas flapped and rattled as I walked about inside the cloud of noise, the violent shouting and the desperate cries and the clanking of the chains that chained people to walls.

... who were we? We were everybody and we were nobody, people, human beings locked up, people who had killed somebody else, living and re-living the moment, was that the madness? or people who had slack jaws and crossed-eyes, was that the madness? or because they wanted too much to paint? or stole a jewel, or a heart, or money, how much of it was about money? or just lost people, all calling and crying and laughing until a half-quiet hour, two or three in the morning when sometimes there was a noisy silence of snores and sighs – and then somebody would scream as if they were in Poppy's press being flattened and perhaps they were, in their heads – most patients lay on stinking straw, I was privileged I had a bed with a fouled mattress, but there were fleas, or something, inside the straw and the mattresses, and Strait-Waistcoats were nothing to fleas – I was covered in terrible, itching red weals, everybody was: it was *torture*, the great bites on everyone's body were a torment, almost a Biblical Torment as if from Hell, as if to pay us for our Madness, which was our Sin. –The smell of urine and shit filled the building, patients drew on the walls with their own faeces as I had once drawn on the walls of Mrs Falls' with charcoal, the markings were obscene and grotesque, and the most grotesque thing of all was the occasional Visits by Ladies – it was this social Activity that had given Angelica her knowledge of Bedlam – and if a law had been passed forbidding such visits as Miss Ffoulks had promised the fashionable ladies nevertheless still came to look at us, came to see the mad people. –They stood in the elegant hallway and stared at us, whispering behind their fans – and to the ladies' delight there was a man who held out his open arms to them and said *I am Christ Jesus* (from whom they shrank, screeching and laughing and putting their noses behind their fans) and there was a fat, dirty woman who wept right in front of them and said *Call me Your Ladyship!* and then they were suddenly ushered away screeching loudly again as a mad manacled murderer roared and crashed from where he was chained as if he would pull the walls upon all of our heads – maybe the Director was a bad person letting the Ladies stare when perhaps it was now forbidden, I do not know, he spoke to my well-known brother the Portrait Painter in a low concerned (it seemed) voice, but to me, myself, he never spoke or asked, and the visitors still came – and so many of the Staff were evil people, more evil than the lost people on the *piazza* – the *piazza* was wild too, but different, the *piazza* had a different kind of energy and noise and freedom, here we had no privacy and no protection at all from the whims and desires of the people who were purported to be our Guardians – they really did call them *Guardians* and some of the Guardians were actually old Patients – they could do anything, to anyone, young girls (and young boys) were in the worst situation, they were stripped, sat astride, lain upon, shared; one of the Guardians hated Foreigners and pulled at me as if I was a tied-up cow and lifted my shift and laughed at me when I kicked out at him as best I could in the Strait-Waistcoat but I hid my arm, he must not see my arm, I needed my arm, I could only kick and he spat upon my face, his foul-smelling saliva dripped down my chin and always the red torturing bites of the fleas or roaches or whatever the small animals were, and no protection for anyone, anywhere.

—one day I saw that same Guardian coming back and I ran out of the door of my cell rattling and flapping in the canvas and wood of my Strait-Waistcoat and I lost myself in the sad wild pieces of humanity in the common spaces, part of the abandoned jetsam of the world of London who had not been strong enough, who thought themselves Barons or our Lord or murdered their mother, all kicking and crying all like human beasts and scratching at their flesh, as I did, the red and itching bites bleeding and as big as pennies – I tripped in my hurry to get away from that Guardian, I fell and landed in a shadowy corner in my shift and the Strait-Waistcoat, next to an old man who was chained to the wall with all the other chained men. —I had not even noticed at first in all the shadows and darkness that he was completely black, and he smelled – we all smelled but he smelled differently – and I saw that he was crying silently, not screaming like the others, tears pouring out of his eyes and down his face in stillness and silence and if he was bitten by insects or vermin as we all were, he took no heed in all the noise and wildness. I stared at the black man. I had never been so near to a black person in my life, not even to Angelica's musician in his splendid jacket, I thought of the black servants in the white wigs that we all laughed at in Bristol, and the man calling for 'my nigger!' when the slave ran away in the *piazza* in Covent Garden – he took no notice of me, just silent pain in all the noise, his manacled hands and the tears pouring down his face, his skin was very dark, I found myself thinking it would be hard to find a paint quite the colour for there was a blueness there almost, in the twilight that came in from the tall high windows, and his hair was grizzled and grey.

'Why are you crying?' I said it without thinking, glad that the Guardian had not seen me, I could slip back in a moment to my cell and the black man probably did not hear me in the noise, but then he turned for a moment towards me.

That look, in the shadows and the filth and the screaming.

His terrible look seemed to tell me that there were not words to tell how he, from some other different Land with some other different Life was somehow chained inside the house of the mad, in London. —And something inside me instead of turning away went towards him, and in a silence inside the raucous noise all around us I thought I heard the wafting and whispering of perhaps his story as Miss Ffoulks had so often told: the sun on a Foreign place of singing and laughter, the holds of the sailing ships crushed with black bodies, the sea and the night and the betrayals. —And then he turned the weeping face away from me, such a *black* man among all the white ones, and weeping with no sound in all the noise and wildness and I wanted to move, go away from more pain. And I did not. I put out my one hand with its weals and its filth, and the Strait-Waistcoat rattled as I put my hand into his completely black manacled one, his hand felt cold and clammy like Death.

I had learned something after all.

I had watched and studied the faces of people for so long, and I had learned that eyes were not always cold, that there were good people, and I had learned from Miss Ffoulks about humanity in the World, a Fraternity she called it, and because of James Burke my humanity was informed by love, and in that way at least the terrible pain of the old black man weeping so silently in all the chaos was to be noticed and I wanted to turn away and I did not.

I had no knowledge or understanding how to help him, some instinct made me stay sitting close and I stroked his black arm with my one hand, stroking it over and over, and all the time in that hell-place the rattling flapping haunting sound of my torn Strait-Waistcoat as I stroked him: another human being with no other idea of help, or love, than this – but the tears ran on down his face unheeded and I thought, his suffering is so much it is as if he is dead but he is not dead, for he weeps still – I understood very well that he did not even know that I was there but still something made me go on stroking his arm: *his pain is from another world that I do not know and have not suffered and* – it was like some blinding white light instead of all the colours – *in the world that I know, whatever has happened to me, I am one of the lucky ones.* For a long, long time, sometimes scratching at the bites that so tormented me as dark night enveloped that place through the long windows, I sat in the noise and the filth with the man from Africa and stroked his arm, my arm got tired but I kept on stroking his, just to be another person there, he never acknowledged me, or knew me, and at last as that odd, breathing, night half-silence came in Bedlam I stumbled up and went away in my Strait-Waistcoat and as I stumbled in the darkness I sounded like bones, rattling. I never saw him again.

That night the Colours stopped flashing in my head. That night I dreamed of my love, of James Burke, and I understood then what I had done when I went to Meard-street, *that was the cost* – I understood that my fierce, wild desire to paint had cost me very many things. —And I remembered again what I thought one day in my brother's house, watching the somehow closed-off face of the sociable Joshua Reynolds: *perhaps, to succeed, great Artists must lose some other part of themselves.* There was a huge price to be paid for my choice, but I had paid it – that would be my private pain *but I was nevertheless one of the lucky ones*, my pain was not the same as the haunted murderers or the ranting street-women who thought they were duchesses or the black man who had lost his hope, and I lay awake in my private, padded room and heard the confused calling out of dreams and the sad sounds of lost humanity in the Bedlam night and then from somewhere in the distance a broken cry of such loss, *where are you Rosie?* and I understood that James had gone from me for what I had chosen to do, but before he had gone he had made me know the truth: I *had* found a way to paint over the long years, and I was an Artist.

From that night I began to get better.

I asked the Doctors if a message might be sent to my brother.

Philip kept saying he wanted to send me to one of the small private hospitals for the mad that had recently opened, 'Until you are recovered,' he said, 'I know you are missing the children,' he said, but I assured him I was recovered already and asked him – begged him – to let me come back to the house in Pall Mall, and as I begged I forced, *forced* myself not to tear at the tormenting red lumps all over me. The Director shrugged indifferently: it was up to Philip of course. —And as they looked me over, the quiet and gentle and acquiescing woman who no longer screamed, I understood again: once again everything, *everything* in my life depended on the word of my brother.

'*Per favore*, Filipo,' I made myself say. *Please.*

THIRTEEN

Although Philip and Angelica needed me in the house, just as long ago in Bristol we had needed Aunt Joy, they were at first anxious about having me back in Pall Mall (they watched me nervously, looking for the first sign of portrait-slashing or coffee-throwing) but my calmness, my efficiency, and I believe my general good humour, won them over at last. —I washed and washed my body – the terrible tormenting red weals went away at last, the last remnant of the nightmare – and all the time I held on to my mantra: *I am one of the lucky ones*, and soon I was lighting the candles in the dining-room as the afternoons drew down, and although I saw shadows again sometimes in this comfortable, hospitable room, I remembered the desolate look of utter despair and the death of hope and understood again: *I am one of the lucky ones*, and Angelica hugged me to her, the most beautiful woman in London, and I smiled at her and held her tightly.

And when, finally, weeks later, in the privacy of my sewing-room, my Studio, I was able to look at last into a mirror and stare at my face, I saw that I had changed. Something older, but something knowledgeable. There was an expression, a wry look that seemed to say: *I made a decision and it has caused me much pain, that is my Secret, but let us see what will happen for I have*

seen real pain now; that pain is about the death of the Heart
and the death of Hope and my Heart is still kicking and fighting inside of me and I have Hope, I am not beaten, I am one of
the lucky ones.

Once more I walked every day, with my basket, I walked slowly
and carefully about my city, along my London streets; I watched
people differently: I knew even more about faces now, what they
could hold, what they told. The madwoman – if indeed she was
mad and I thought now she was not – sang near St Martin's Lane:

> London Bridge is falling down
> My fair lady . . .

At first I could not paint: that was not possible for me yet, and
in truth I had nothing in the world to paint with, I had spent all the
money James had paid me on wonderful hog hair brushes and new
canvases and paints and I had burned everything. I had nothing at all
left of my Artist's secret life, only the painting of the Lilies on the
wall. And the small green Daisy.

My sewing-room actually became my sewing-room and I
worked quietly at a brightly-coloured quilt, all my pain and distress I put into my quilt, but bright colours, not dark – I found
bright colours in the most unlikely places, gay pieces of stuff
from old gowns and shawls, all the small pieces sewn together
with small, small stitches, all the colours, all the shapes. —I had
never seen such a thing as I was making, I just made it up, and
whereas my painting had been shadows and light, my quilt was
very bright, all the colours of the world I put there, to be gay and
bright and into the quilt I put away all my pain.

One cold, sunny day I walked in St James's Park, right down to
the less fashionable part, Rosamund's Pond, where it was said that
sad Ladies killed themselves: I would not kill myself now, but I
understood. —Slowly I turned back from the pond and just as I was
coming into the lighter, brighter part of the park I heard a voice
behind me.

'Well, well, Grace.'

I turned quickly. My heart jumped and clattered.

'It is you, ain't it? Are you going to kill yerself?'

'Hello, Poppy.'

Poppy regarded me. 'Still got yer same old basket then? You never became a famous Painter after all then!'

And I stared at her – she was well-dressed and looked prosperous, she was wearing an elegant gown and a cloak and there were dark spots painted onto her face (to hide the pox it was always said: those dark, fashionable patches), something, a kind of strength about her, and at last I found my voice. 'What happened to you, Poppy? I came back, but you were gone.'

'Not so easy on your own, is it?'

The cold sun shone down on to the green grass. 'I have never forgot your kindness to me, Poppy, I looked for you but – oh, truly, I've often thought of you; why are you walking here, in the Park?'

'Why are you? It's a free country.'

'Of course, I only meant –'

'Sometimes I need fresh air.'

'Tell me what happened to you, Poppy. I am so glad to see you, I've wondered and wondered about you, truly.'

Poppy laughed, the same old laugh, but out of a different, older face.

'Why do you talk funny?' she said.

I shrugged. It was too hard to explain.

'Me, I run me own business,' she said. 'I got lucky, I met a man – it's what you should've done, look at you, all dowdy still, we could've set ourselves up, you and me, we had a bit of Class, Ah – but you weren't really one of us, was yer? I seen you a few times but I always made sure you didn't see me, you were always with the gentry.'

'*Where?*'

'Oh – at the Theatre. I got to go to the Theatre and the Opera too, you know! In the end.'

'I'm glad then.'

She peered right into my face. 'You're pale ain't yer?' She was silent for a moment, looking at me, and then she said, 'You know what, Grace? Don't mind me sayin' but we've both got older, we can say things. You've had a funny life too, haven't you, pretending you're someone you ain't, always worrying about your Pictures – and in the end I've probably been as happy as you have, or more even. You don't exactly look radiant to me.'

And suddenly I laughed, she had made me laugh, a real laugh, like I used to long ago. 'You probably have been happier, Poppy, it's true what you say! But – I could never stop wanting to be a Painter – and – I am a Painter now.'

'Well, when you're Rich and Famous as well, I live by the church in Hanover Square. That's where I run me Classy Business from, right next door to the Church.' I must have looked startled: she laughed again, the Poppy laugh. 'You still don't really know the world, do you Grace?' And with a slight wave of a gloved hand she turned and walked away from me towards Piccadilly, one of the elegant Ladies in the Park.

I tried at first to ignore it but I began to dream faces – the faces of my Family that had become so dim came back to me as they had in Bedlam, and then I began to wonder again: do people ever actually paint Dreams? do people ever paint Pain? or Desire? or the wild throw of the dice? or Love? or Madness? —I pondered as I had when I was mad whether it would be possible to paint these things. —But I had nothing to paint with, to paint upon – so, silently, *I began yet once again*: I accrued small sums of the housekeeping money as I used to, to buy paint and brushes, and silently in the night I began the stealing again, the old things, the discarded things, bits of broken board, bits of torn canvas; sometimes I found wonderful things that my brother had no use for or had forgotten: an old beautiful jug with no handle to place my brushes, a large piece of board.

But this time it was quite different. The difference this time was: I *knew* I could do it.

The first, small, Portrait I painted very slowly, just a little part every day: that painting was of Poppy – she had an odd and interesting face, aged, but still energetic somehow and alive, and this time, this time she looked mostly like Poppy and I did not scrape this small painting off, to re-use the board, but placed it on the wall, I would give it to her one day.

Then I began painting again in earnest, the shadows and the light and the truth and my understanding – and at last, *at last* I painted our Family, all the rackety Wiltshire Marshalls at last, all the faces that had come back to me so clearly: first I painted Tobias, who looked like Claudio (I hoped that Tobias was still sailing the seas and I painted a red Pirate's scarf holding back his hair and a gay smile and I suddenly smiled too – I clearly saw Tobias sitting at the dining-table in Pall Mall, relieving Sir Joshua Reynolds of his watch); I painted my Father, looking at his cards; and I painted Philip as he had looked long ago when I had loved him, all the charm and the warmth; surreptitiously I observed him over the dinner table, found what was there still of the good things and I *longed* to show him what I had done, to share our days that had gone.

Finally I tried to paint the black man. —Mr Hogarth had painted black men: often small, knowing figures, who commented it seemed on the foolishness of the world; Sir Joshua Reynolds and Mr Gainsborough had both painted black men as Gentlemen: noble, dignified, in clothes of London fashion; I remembered again the ridicule of the black men in white wigs in Bristol. Sir Joshua had even painted a noble savage from the South Sea Islands, a hero dressed in white. I painted the old man at Bedlam differently, I painted him because I wanted him to be known, and because I had learned something. —I painted very slowly, remembering his desolated face, I did not paint tears, that seemed wrong, too easy. I painted pain.

And I was there, back at the dinner-table of my brother, the food purchased as usual, making sure all was well as usual, pulling the curtains, sometimes closing the shutters if the afternoon was raw, and Roberto fixing me with his beady eye. I understood that my brother had told his guests that I had been ill: if they knew further of my illness never for one moment did anyone ask inquisitive questions or make me feel uncomfortable. —All over again I listened to the Artists talk at the table, it was as if nothing had changed – but everything had changed in me; I saw that kind, wise Miss Ffoulks was so glad that I was there again and although I was just living from day to day (for that was enough, just now), I knew that one day, somehow, I would give Miss Ffoulks that Painting of the black man in Bedlam I had just finished, and tell her what I had learned from her; and Angelica was especially loving to me; all was well again, and the talk was of Line and Colour and, in particular, the exciting new premises that were being designed inside Somerset House, for the Royal Academy of Arts.

There was very much talk now of the new America, John

Palmer told us what he had heard of Artists lives there painting pictures on the floors – on the *floors!* – of the new houses, for there were few carpets; going round the new settlements on horseback with their tools of trade in their saddle bags, painting portraits and signs and wardrobes and fire-screens, earning their livings like gypsies.

'I should like to go to America and try my luck', said John Palmer, 'now that they have won the War to be themselves,' and his eyes were old and wistful. —John Palmer treated me with special, unobtrusive kindness, once he bought me some unexpected flowers, and sometimes I wondered again about his home in Spitalfields: he would go off in his cloak, so threadbare now as darkness fell on these cold, wintry nights, with just a small lantern to guide him, and would simply disappear from our lives until next time. —How I would have liked to speak to him and Miss Ffoulks truthfully at last, and show them my own work, I wanted to have friends to whom I could speak openly, because I had learned, at last, what it was to share and Mary-Ann was only me, after all (it was of course James Burke that I longed for. But I had cut him out in little stars, for I could do no other.)

But in the night I painted with a new, quite different confidence.

Mr Thomas Gainsborough was the Portraitist everybody spoke of these days; he and Sir Joshua Reynolds were the fashionable Painters now, their names on people's lips now; Mr Hartley Pond however disparaged Mr Gainsborough's work, and his odd habit of dressing people in modern-day clothes.

'His paintings will be out of Fashion in a year, mark my words!' said Mr Hartley Pond. 'He seems to know nothing at all of the History of Art: in Portraits clothes should be above fashion, timeless. Reynolds has the sense to often put his subjects in the eternal clothing of the Ancient Greeks – those Paintings will never age.'

But Mr Thomas Gainsborough, we knew, had moved to a house in Pall Mall: how could he not become one of our dinner guests? — He did not come often (it was said he was not much interested in his fellow Artists) but when he did come he added great gaiety to the table – amusing and full of life and full of drink – and I noticed that Mr Hartley Pond continued to attend, charmed as we all were.

'Do you hear my ducks and my hens?' Mr Gainsborough

enquired of the di Vecellio family, his neighbours. 'Do they disturb you?'

'You keep such animals in your garden, Mr Gainsborough?' Angelica asked him in surprise (she obviously had not acquainted herself with the crowing of the rooster).

'In my garden, *Signora*, and indeed in my house when my Wife can be persuaded, for I prefer to draw them rather than people, that is the Truth of it!' and we did not believe him, and we laughed. 'I do also have pigs on occasion, but not regularly: my Wife will not abide pigs. It is only unfortunate that Nature does not sell,' he added, 'but I must of course make the pot boil!' and dock leaves and nettles that he had picked by Millbank fell from his jacket, and I saw that Philip could not help liking him despite being jealous of his success, for it soon became abundantly clear that Mr Gainsborough (although he too of course was a Member of the Royal Academy) cared not a fig for the Art World, made his success in his own way.

And then one day I heard them speak of the two Woman Academicians that James Burke had told me of.

'Tell me, how did women become Academicians?' I asked the table in general. 'And might there not soon be, therefore, Women students at the Royal Academy School?' and if my brother looked at me I did not look at him.

Mr Gainsborough was there again that day, I remember, and he answered my questions in his usual gay manner. 'One of the Woman Academicians is married to a Painter, *Signorina*. And the other has covered herself twice: she is the daughter of a Painter and she is –' and he suddenly laughed, 'let us say she is given very much attention by Sir Joshua Reynolds – and how else, for a Woman, after all?' and he leaned back in his chair with a glass of rum and turned it so that it caught the late afternoon light coming through the window, for I had not yet lit the candles. He was still smiling. 'It does not show us well, I suppose, but no Woman could survive without a male Painter either in the Family, or in love, to plead her Cause.'

'Then I should have been a Painter too,' said Angelica, laughing too. 'For Filipo would have assisted me!' For a split second then I was aware of my brother: I stared at him: I suddenly felt as if old, old anger would choke me and I wondered: if my brother had supported me and encouraged me, would there be three Women Academicians now? I saw Philip look away from my fierce eyes (presumably he thought I might again throw something) and I quickly moved to light the candles.

'As we always say, Women must paint Countryside views if they *must* paint, for it is not becoming for Women to paint Portraits,' and Mr Hartley Pond took a pinch of snuff as I went about the table with my taper. 'It is simply not seemly that a Woman should stare so openly at another person in that way – mind, they stare at *themselves*, I believe!' and he laughed his thin laugh. 'Their Self-Portraits, incidentally, are execrable!' and Roberto the parrot laughed too from Angelica's shoulder, copying Mr Hartley Pond and ruffling up his feathers.

'And Signorina Francesca,' continued Mr Gainsborough, 'the Royal Academy classes are only open to Male Students of course!' and I thought he spoke mockingly, for he was not (I had already heard from Miss Ffoulks) a friend of Sir Joshua Reynolds (I believe they were jealous of each other) who was the President and presumably made the rules (as well as encouraging suitable Lady Painters). 'And even the Male Students may not attend the modelling classes when a Female is modelling, unless – and I assure you I quote from the Prospectus exactly: *unless they are over twenty; or Married; or a member of the Royal Family* – who presumably are Unshockable, unlike mere Mortals.' And the assembled gentlemen round the table laughed, for there were many very young royal children, and then they began to create with the pencils they always carried wild (somewhat intoxicated) pictures among themselves, passing a paper to each other, of royal Progeny running about a nude Female model, and throwing balls.

And then Mr Gainsborough, a good deal inebriated I should say by now, said simply, 'I never had Formal Training. I never went on the Grand Tour. Joshua Reynolds may pontificate and palaver forever, but I just look at the World about me.'

I was lighting the candles on the sideboard now, and I actually dropped one, I picked it up quickly and only smiled, I went on making sure the glasses were full around our hospitable table and everybody was comfortable and I was silent as usual but I wanted to sing loudly! —I had worried *so much* that I never had Formal Training, that I had never gone on the Grand Tour, and suddenly

Mr Thomas Gainsborough, revered and admired and successful Portraitist, told the world *he had not had any Formal Training either.*

Never again was there ever the slightest sign of the *travail* that had afflicted me.

I had acquired at last, from everything that had happened, the thing which I had admired so long ago in Miss Ffoulks.

It was not from books, but I had acquired Learning.

PART FOUR
1780

FOURTEEN

The bustling carriages and carts fought their way through the rest of the traffic on the Strand to deliver their valuable (or worthless, depending on your point of view) cargo at the magnificent Italianate portals of the new entrance: they were delivering Art to the illustrious, British, ROYAL ACADEMY OF ARTS, for its grand opening in its new, glorious premises in Somerset House on the Strand. There was shouting and laughing and yelling and much slipping on piles of soft, steaming manure as carriage after cart dropped its parcels of paintings at the gates.

America may have been lost; business-men may have panicked; Mr Garrick the famous actor may have died; that claimer of continents for Britain, Captain Cook, may have been murdered in the South Pacific but all was back to normal, business was booming, and the Painters with their wares were salesmen like everyone else beneath all their talk of Art: they had to share the Strand with spice-sellers and gown-sellers and book-sellers and milliners and wine-sellers and print-shops and street-criers and gun-suppliers and hostelries and star-gazers and purveyors of fine cloths and boot-makers. The Strand was over-flowing with carriages and people and bustled skirts and big boots and small link-boys; the smell of food permeated the air and also the smell of horses, and outside the church opposite a band was playing valiantly, the trumpet sadly somewhat off the note.

Footmen and servants ran and carried (it was raining slightly, April showers); some painters carried their big canvases, carefully wrapped, under their own arms, not trusting any carrier. Hundreds of paintings were being received to be judged by the Royal Academicians for their worthiness: worthiness for inclusion in the first Royal Academy Exhibition in the beautiful new premises in this magnificent building, once a ruin of a palace, now completely rebuilt. No matter that the Navy was near and Admirals passed importantly in their hats and their bright blue jackets and muttered of the French. The new Royal Academy premises, with the support of King George III, at last were completed for all to see, just inside the porticos. To the right of the entrance pillars, just as important as the Navy, stood this new beacon for English painting: Michelangelo might be sculpted over the door but there were real, valued *British* painters now to follow in the footsteps of the Old Masters. Most of the Academicians had of course been to Europe and seen the Old Masters but here was proof at last: Art no longer began at Calais. O the excitement! There was very much to-ing and fro-ing and fevered conversations and the sound of boots ringing on the stone cobbles as the canvases were rushed in to be observed, and judged, by the Royal Academicians.

And such decisions to be made! And not only which paintings to be shown: this Official Opening was to be one of the most important days in the London social calendar. The King and Queen of England would arrive along the Strand in their golden carriage; they would face their own recently-painted portraits by the President of the Academy, Sir Joshua Reynolds, as they climbed the new, high, terrifying winding staircase. Past the sculptures on the ground floor; past the library and the Antique Academy on the first floor (with more sculptures); further and further up to the proudly-named Great Room – the gallery at the top of the new building with its large glass cupola enabling light to come in from the sky to shine upon the new and illustrious glories of British Art.

There was much discussion as to whether Queen Charlotte would be able to advance to the very top, up the steep winding staircase. Did she, God forbid, suffer from vertigo? Gold thrones were finally placed on the landings, to allow her to rest from her exertions.

Gossip and tittle-tattle swirled: in the newspapers, in the coffee houses. It was rumoured that their Majesties had not taken to Sir Joshua and did not wish to be painted by him again. It was rumoured that Mr Thomas Gainsborough and Sir Joshua, the Kings of the Portrait Painters, would not speak to each other. It was rumoured that nude models ran up the new spiralling staircase.

And the Academicians had themselves been painted: a group portrait of the famous artists, surrounded by paintings and sculptures from abroad: from Europe: that is, from the Classical Tradition. The Academicians looked calm: no hint in the painting of the fights and the back-stabbings, of artists betrayed and excluded and friendships ruined that lay behind the forming of this Academy. The gentlemen stared out at the world serenely. However, the nude sculptures shown in the painting posed a problem for the artist: there were two Lady members of the Academy, they could *not possibly* be seen with nude men, albeit in marble. The problem was solved by making the two women *into paintings themselves*: their likenesses hung upon the wall in the group male portrait – there but not there – and thus protected from nakedness.

All the excitement in the newspapers meant that the next five weeks would see the new rooms thronging with people talking at last (it was hoped) about the Art of England instead of the Art of Rome or Venice or the Netherlands. There was continual discussion of the newly-painted ceilings of gossamer-draped goddesses (very flimsy gossamer) representing such esoteric subjects as the Theory of Painting, and Design, and Colouring, and it was scurrilously hinted at in the newspapers that at some time in the past Sir Joshua Reynolds may well have tarried with one of the lady Academicians, gossamer-draped herself.

With such publicity crowds of visitors were inevitable (and crowds of visitors were much to be desired) but the usual problem reared its troublesome head: the *right* crowds were wanted. It was certainly unacceptable for unwashed people to attend. But how could a British Institution, paid for by public funds, set up with the gracious acquiescence of the King of England, be closed to some of his subjects because there was an entrance fee that some may not afford? It was obviously out of the question that there would be an entrance fee. They had tried to deal with this problem at past, less illustrious, exhibitions by charging for a programme but people merely bought one and shared it with their acquaintances. But now it was accepted that either catalogues or constables were required, to keep out undesirables. Catalogues were therefore deemed compulsory, price one shilling, and the following Public Announcement appeared:

As the present Exhibition is Part of the Institution
Of an Academy presented by Royal Munificence, the
Public may naturally expect the liberty of being
Admitted *without Expense*.
The Academicians therefore think it necessary to
Declare that this was very much their desire but that
They have not been able to suggest any other Means,
Than that of *receiving money* for Admittance, to
Prevent the rooms from being filled by *Improper Persons* to the entire exclusion of those for whom the
Exhibition is intended.

Filipo di Vecellio was in a towering rage. He could not, of course, withdraw from this momentous exhibition, he must be seen to publicise his Art (for what was the Exhibition after all but a marketplace, for all the talk of an 'English School'. Art was trade, despite the President of the Royal Academy's talk of 'Intellectual Dignity' and 'Beauty').

'And why does he champion History Painting when he is so bad at it!' shouted Filipo di Vecellio. 'As far as I can see the only recommendation for History Painting is that the canvases are Large, not that the canvases are Eloquent!' He shouted all this at his wife, at his returned children, at his sister, at his servants, at his dealer. He had a new dealer. It still rankled in the artist's heart that his old friend and dealer James Burke had gone abroad so suddenly and for so long: when he had returned, he had not even had the courtesy to renew the acquaintanceship. The new dealer was a short, fat, very rich man called Mr Minnow. Filipo di Vecellio shouted most loudly of all at Mr Minnow. 'Have you *seen* one of Joshua Reynolds' Epics? They are an embarrassment as he must know! At least I do not put my hand to something that is beyond me, at least I have Grace! Four hundred and eighty-nine works exhibited and I am insulted!' Mr Minnow was summarily dismissed. Signore di Vecellio did not care, was heard to shout again. 'Well, at least if we sell from the Royal Academy we will not have to share our fees with *Dealers!*' The family of Signore di Vecellio had not seen him so angry, ever, and sent an urgent missive to Mr Minnow begging him to ignore such insulting and impassioned talk and to return immediately. It was all very distressing, for Signore Filipo di Vecellio was on the whole – everybody knew it – an amiable and charming man.

'Such an insult to a Founding Member of the Royal Academy!' he kept shouting in the huge dining-room of his opulent house in Pall Mall as his sister poured soothing Indian tea and the returned Mr Minnow murmured in his ear.

Finally, the root of the trouble was made clear. Filipo di Vecellio had been to the new Royal Academy to see the paintings before the Exhibition opened on the morrow. The President, Sir Joshua Reynolds, had many paintings hung favourably (not to mention his portraits of their Majesties); Mr Thomas Gainsborough had many paintings hung in auspicious places. Of Filipo di Vecellio's offered eight portraits, only *two* had been chosen to be hung in the Great Room at the top of the new building and the other six were to be shown, most inadequately, in the smaller gallery next door. When he had first started work, portrait painting was perhaps about the sitter: now it was definitely about the artist, and the respect due, and the *signore* felt respect was not being paid. 'One of my Portraits is hung next to a historical water-colour by an insane Academy *student*: a William Blake, who does not wash, apart from being quite incapable of the Epic Style. *The Death of Earl Goodwin* indeed!'

Worse, one of Filipo di Vecellio's two portraits in the Great Room had been hung 'below the line'. He had been ranting about 'the line' for days. The 'line' was a thin pelmet about eight feet from the ground in the Great Room and the best place for pictures to be hung was just above the line – not too high, but with their bottom frames touching the pelmet. Then, when the room was full of people, spectators could look up very slightly and see the best pictures. It was clear that if people had to look higher to see the paintings further up, the neck would become strained; it was also clear that if pictures were hung 'below the line' they would not be seen at all through the crowds.

'Sir Joshua's *Portrait of a Gentleman* and Mr Gainsborough's *Portrait of a Gentleman* and even paintings by that American Mr West and paintings by that foreigner Mr Zoffany', (Filipo di Vecellio forgot for a moment that he too was a foreigner) 'have all been hung in more prominent positions than even my best Portrait of Lord Alderly. Even the Portraits of that deceased cartoon himself, Mr Hogarth, find favour these days, everybody knows he went down to the prisons and painted the faces of murderers' – the only piece of information that really caught the imagination of his son, Claudio, whose mind was really elsewhere – 'yet here he is exhibiting next to Royalty! And Sir Joshua's portraits of their Majesties are poor, very poor, I account my portrait of Queen Charlotte infinitely more like.' (He forgot also that he painted that picture over ten years ago.) Signore di Vecellio was particularly incandescent about the paintings of Mr Thomas Gainsborough, his neighbour in Pall Mall. 'Gainsborough paints people in the fashionable clothes of today' – his daughter Isabella's pretty, sulky face came to attention at the word 'fashion' – 'and as I always say, as Mr Hartley Pond always says, such compositions will last less than a wink of an eye, for Fashions change and Mr Gainsborough's Portraits will soon be out of fashion and dowdy, and yet there they are – on the line, *on the line!*'

Only his sister Francesca understood how much more there was to his rage than he could express. He had defied them all, misled the whole of London and become one of its most successful portrait painters. To do that he had denied his origins. Yet here, towering over him now was Thomas Gainsborough, son of an English *miller*; Joshua Reynolds, son of an English *vicar*; the despicable, immoral George Romney, son of a *joiner*. All of them had come up through some sort of apprenticeship, not glorious like her brother who had literally burst on to the artistic scene from nowhere, like a firework. It was a bitter, bitter pill for him to swallow that his flame had flickered and almost died; that after all his magnificent subterfuge his English contemporaries had left him behind, after all. (And indeed Signore Filipo di Vecellio perhaps should have considered himself lucky that foreign artists were acceptable to the British Royal Academy: French Academicians would not have dreamed of it.)

His wife, the beautiful Signora Angelica di Vecellio – who had begun, so unusually, to keep to her room – called him to her, soothed him, said she would attend on the morrow and they would take their place where they belonged in London Society: he stared at the loved, changed face and seemed for a moment as if he might weep.

The great day dawned, streets wet with rain: the Glorious Day for the Art of the Great British Nation.

The Strand soon became cluttered, and then totally blocked: impassable as noble carriages attempted to disgorge their noble passengers – their Majesties were delayed by the turmoil. Peddlers rushed about with lemonade and milk and pies and apples, adding to the fearful, exciting commotion. A fishmonger had somehow got his cart among the crowds outside Somerset House and was shouting of live haddock for sale, as if people might take one and place it, still wriggling, in a pocket as they entered the illustrious portals.

Finally – the Royal Monarchs safe – the new Royal Academy was unveiled to the waiting world. With an entrance fee disguised as a catalogue as a deterrent, the crowds could not have been expected to be so large, so wild, so unwieldy; people clutching catalogues rushed up the exciting, narrow – dangerous, even – winding staircase; gowns and hats and ribbons were caught, entangled. Shoes fell off, several ladies fainted and one inebriated gentleman fell from a great height and was only saved from certain death by the density of the crowd.

It was, truly, glorious, despite the passing Naval gentlemen, busy with their wars, snorting in derision at some of the people fighting to be admitted. The gorgeous ceilings were gaped at and the various naked statues gasped at; up the staircase, in the Antique Academy, the Medici Venus stood modestly (a plaster copy from the Uffizi Gallery in Florence) and naked Roman gladiators in marble sprawled immodestly as they faced their destiny (young ladies were hurried away before they swooned).

Finally, approaching the last landing and the Great Room, exhausted spectators were treated to a panel that showed *Minerva Visiting the Muses on Mount Parnassus*. The Academicians had meant that the students at the Royal Academy must look ever upward: the perspiring visitors felt exhorted onwards also but almost collapsed with exhaustion and exertion in the heat. At last, reaching the very top, they pushed and shoved into the Great Room under portals bedecked with words, in Greek, that translated as: *Let no-one uninspired by the Muses enter here* (luckily hardly anybody pushing and shoving understood that the words meant that most of them were actually too ignorant to enter).

Inside the Great Room were a huge number of paintings of all shapes and sizes, hung *hugger-mugger* as one of the newspapers reported afterwards. The paintings hung, crowded very close together, above the line, below the line, on the line: gentlemen's portraits, epic paintings of scenes from history, portraits of courtesans near to portraits of nobility, frames touching, faces near. Although both un-named, Mrs Sarah Siddons the actress and Our Lord were displayed not far apart.

Sir Joshua bowed, Mr Gainsborough bowed, Signore Filipo di Vecellio with his beautiful veiled wife bowed; heads craned, people pushed, voices raised, ladies emitted faint shrieks, perspiration poured: a bright, glorious, noisy, democratic, thrilling, hot, sweating *British* Art Gallery. There was so much noise and such a smell of humanity that ladies fainted and had to be treated with *sal volatile* and people were squashed against each other and suddenly a young lady cried, 'How dare you sir!' to a deeply shocked and serious young man, who turned quite pale in the embarrassment of such a public misunderstanding: she most surely could not think that he had *meant* to brush a hand against her bosom? Surely she understood that he had been pushed by the crowds? And as the spinster Signorina Francesca di Vecellio, who had been studying with great interest the portraits by Sir Joshua and Mr Gainsborough nearby, tried to move away she turned slightly and found herself almost in the arms of the art dealer James Burke, who must have been standing very closely behind her, unobserved. She stumbled slightly: an older woman in a grey gown. He caught her arm and also her waist; in the general *mêlée this* scandalous behaviour was not noticed (and, besides, what would have been scandalous behaviour towards a young lady was surely only chivalry towards an older one).

Francesca di Vecellio was a woman of great calm and control but she could not stop the blush that spread quickly to her cheeks; she immediately stepped back, away from the arms that had once held her in more intimate ways than this. They were surrounded by raised voices as the enormity of what had just happened was realised, there were shocked squeals and conflicting accounts; James Burke easily spoke beneath the noise.

He did not say, *Are you well?* He did not say, *Why does Angelica cover her face?* He did not say, *I think of you still.* His face did not suffuse with lost love.

He simply said, 'Are you still painting?'

She saw the once beloved face that she had not seen for so long. She had painted it dozens of times: in joy, in agony – not just on canvas or board but in her head and in her thoughts and in her day-to-day living – never was he entirely absent, this man who had finally made her an artist. She saw him still, always saw him, that first moment in her sewing-room as he stood, amazed: one hand arrested at his cuff, his body absolutely unmoving, his face unbelieving: that was his gift to her.

Signorina Francesca di Vecellio therefore looked down for one moment at her gloved hand to contain herself. The voices around them had begun to subside, it became clear there had been a terrible mis-understanding, the bosom not being knowingly brushed, everybody bowed and apologised and a general hum of goodwill rose again.

James Burke spoke to the woman beside him very quietly, his head near to hers. 'I want to sell one of your Paintings. For a great deal of money.'

She did not understand. He saw that she did not understand. He still spoke low. 'I do not mean like before. Something has happened, Grace.' And if he saw her flinch at the use of her name he did not show it. 'I have – found a Market where you will sell. I believe I have found a way to make you an extremely rich woman.' Still she looked at him blankly.

'It is my profession, you remember,' he said, not intimately, but professionally, and Signorina Francesca di Vecellio saw hooded grey eyes, those eyes that had always been so open and direct. 'I am, after all, a Dealer in Arts.'

Because of the noise, because of her confusion, because they had not spoken together ever since he left her room that terrible night, because of all these things perhaps she misheard him; it seemed to him that she misheard him. But perhaps she spoke deliberately.

'A Dealer in Hearts,' she said. 'Indeed.' And she turned away to her young niece, Isabella, who was conversing with rather alarming vivacity to a young gentleman with his own hair elaborately coiffured, the latest style, but as she turned Mr Burke laid his hand, just for a moment more, upon her arm. 'I will find a way to come to the house.'

And in the pulsating, perspiring crowds in the Great Room Filipo di Vecellio still smiled and nodded gracefully; people bowed to see him. And his wife, the veiled Signora Angelica di Vecellio, once known as the most beautiful woman in London, would never, after that illustrious day, be seen in public again.

After such an unforgettable artistic opening there were, immediately, reactions in the newspapers: critics and commentators and members of the public.

'Please remove the casts, which are the terror of every decent Woman who enters the Antique Room ... Apollos, Gladiators, Jupiters and Hercules, all as naked, and as natural as if they were alive!!!!'

*

'Has decency finally left the discretion of the Institution? Sir Joshua Reynolds, President, though neither a father nor a husband yourself, please remove the casts which are the terror of every decent woman who enters the Antiques Room ...'

*

'The concourse of people of fashion who attended the opening of the Royal Academy Exhibition yesterday was incredible, it is computed that the door-keepers did not take less than 500 pounds from the Admission of numerous visitants of all ranks.'

*

'The happy arrangement of the Pictures and the Magnificence of the Apartments render it a very grand spectacle and not to be equalled in any part of Europe.'

In short: a wild success. More and more people attended, the newspapers thundered disapprovingly: ARE THE STANDARDS OF ART FINALLY TO BE SET BY THE MAN IN THE STREET? But the Exhibition was adjudged the most successful showing of British Art ever held: comparisons were made with the *Salon Carré* in the

Louvre Palace in Paris, over six hundred thousand people entered the new porticos on the Strand.

And a letter was delivered next day to Signorina Francesca di Vecellio in the house in Pall Mall. She glanced at the handwriting, placed it in her pocket and went on about her business. Late that night, finally, in her sewing-room, she slowly undid the seal.

> *Grace,*
>
> *As I said, I will find a way to come to Pall Mall and speak to you further about selling your Paintings. The Market has changed, I believe I can make for you a good deal of money; much, much more than we discussed previously. I believe it is possible that I could make you a rich Woman in your own right.*
> *James Burke, Esq.*

FIFTEEN

The art dealer James Burke visited the house in Pall Mall some time after the opening at Somerset House. He enquired after the Signora Angelica: she was not able to see anybody. He asked to see Signore Filipo di Vecellio. They spoke in the artist's studio where James Burke had once been the most frequent visitor, there where the small Rembrandt portrait hung and the other old paintings that the *signore* had acquired.

There was a great coldness between the portraitist and the art dealer: who would have thought they had once been such friends? Filipo di Vecellio held hard feelings: the fat Mr Minnow was in no way as energetic, or powerful, as James Burke. But business was, after all, business: Filipo di Vecellio was known to be a collector. On his long tour of Europe the Art Dealer had seen many collections of old art, many Old Masters, a few for sale, and had quickly understood that the prices were rising every month: there was now very much money to be made buying and selling, and James Burke had news for the Italian. James Burke had heard that an old and well-known Dutch collector was very ill in Amsterdam; it was said only King George had a better collection of Old Masters in the whole of Europe. The family were flocking round like vultures: there would be a sale, an auction to be sure, when the Dutchman died. The two heads did not bend close together as once they had, the friendship could not re-ignite, but they had shared so much of the past that there were things to speak of as is the way with broken friendships; finally Filipo confided that his wife was ill, that he longed for, hoped for, her to be well again.

Then rather stiffly Filipo di Vecellio invited James Burke, as he once had so often, to stay for dinner. John Palmer and Miss Ffoulks were greatly delighted to see the banished old friend but the presence of the beautiful Angelica was much missed, like a bright light gone. There were other visitors: Dr Charles Burney was there, whose daughter Fanny had published a daring *novel*, almost unheard of in a woman; and Mr Thomas Towers, a writer of biographies of famous men, a rotund gentleman wearing, oddly, more than one waistcoat. The painter's sister was there as always: her dark gown and her quiet presence, her hair almost hidden under her neat white cap, and the *chatelaine* dangling at her waist; as always she supervised the servants, made sure the food and drink was plentiful; did not seem to particularly engage, or not engage, in the various conversations with any of the guests, including Mr James Burke, art dealer.

Later front doors banged: the gentlemen were gone no doubt for a stroll through St James's Park in the last of the evening sun, and a visit to a club or one of the coffee houses.

Or not.

There was a tap on the door of the sewing-room of the sister. James Burke, art dealer, stood in the dark hallway at the top of the house.

'You had paint on your right hand all through dinner,' he said, and for a split second he smiled oddly at her, and then the smile was gone and the grey eyes stared in the piercing manner.

She did not speak.

'May I see what you have been doing?'

He believed implicitly that she would allow him, no matter what had happened between them, for he was the only person who knew her secret. Secrets.

But.

There was too much now that was not shared also: there were other secrets. He had been to Europe with his wife and she had been to Bedlam: the heaviness of the past stood between them like an impenetrable forest.

At last, almost reluctantly, she stood aside and he went into the sewing-room.

On the easel was a finished painting of a woman standing by a window. There was a mirror behind her on the wall. The woman was reading a letter; you could not see her whole face, but by the fall of her neck and shoulders and something else – the atmosphere evoked by the light and dark painting – it was clear that the letter had broken her heart. Never for a moment did Grace take her eyes off his face: something like real shock, something like pain, or regret, then he was in control. He saw the way the light was caught in the mirror, fell past it then on to the woman's gown, shadowy yet rich with reds and yellows and browns. He stared at the shadows and the bright, dark figure.

When he spoke his voice was expressionless. 'You still paint yourself, Grace.'

She flared at him. 'I do not! That is a young woman. I am no longer young.'

He answered her calmly. 'Perhaps other people would not see it, but I would always know that face is your face.' He put up his hand, not allowing her to speak. 'I will pay you eight – no, ten – guineas for this if you will allow me to purchase it now.'

She felt a blush of surprise on her face: looked at him in disbelief: it was almost as if he had struck her. This was what many real painters earned for a small portrait; it was much more than John Palmer ever earned. There was silence in the room that smelled of paint and oil and fumes from the cigars and port which had wafted up from downstairs.

James Burke looked again at the painting on the easel: the shadowy beauty and the sadness. 'Listen, Grace.' The only person in the world, except Poppy, who called her by her real name. 'I want you to be guided by me.'

She looked away quickly. 'Guided by you,' she said woodenly but there was something dangerous in her low, low voice.

'Let me see your other Paintings.'

She pointed to the picture of the woman in the Park where it hung on the wall.

'That is Poppy.' He threw a quick glance at her – he remembered very well who Poppy was – and then studied the picture but this picture was not of a girl but of an older woman: *Did she still see Poppy?* While he was looking upwards she turned the painting of the black man to the wall and left it there: that was not for him to see. Instead, she turned, one by one, the Portraits of her family to face the light. 'That is my Father. That is my sister, Venus.' She saw how he struggled to retain his blank face, for he knew something of these persons. 'That is Tobias, I think of him as a Pirate.'

'The red rose.'

'I know. It is soft-hearted and wrong, it perhaps spoils the Portrait, but you will see that I have shadowed the rose almost to darkness, so that it does not take the attention if you do not know the story. Rembrandt himself did paint a flower, in Philip's paint-ing. I meant not to put it in but – I could not help it.'

In an extraordinary gesture he put his face into his hands as if he needed to contain himself. And then he turned from the paintings to face her and said quickly, 'Grace, what difference would one hundred guineas mean to you?'

'*One hundred guineas?*'

'More – for a painting if, as I say, you will allow yourself to be guided by me.'

She looked at him in disbelief. Was he insane? Again a silence. Then she said, 'Even Sir Joshua cannot earn that for a Portrait; a full-body perhaps but not for a Portrait. Philip has never earned anything like that much for a Painting, you know that.'

'You are a far, far better Painter than your brother. You know that. But you must take your own face entirely out of your Painting.' She could not speak.

He pointed to the small sofa where once they had sat so often.

'Sit down,' he said.

'Grace,' he said.

Listen.

—and it took enormous control not to hit James Burke: *sit down*, he said to me politely in my own room, it was almost unimagin-able, after what this room had seen.

But he had shocked me into frozen silence: he knew very well what a hundred guineas would mean to me.

We had not been alone together since he walked away from my

room on the autumn night and thrust twenty pounds into the hands of a woman in the basement in Meard-street, off Covent Garden, beside where the street-girls plied their trade. Unspoken, immovable, that pain lay between us like a mist.

'Grace.' And I saw the enormous effort he was making to clear the unspoken away so that we could proceed with business. 'Grace. We must forget the past, if we are to proceed with the future.'

Something dangerous in my face must have made him pause but only for a moment. 'I am sorry about the past, but the past is gone, nobody can go on and on living in the past. I know you became ill, you cannot think that I did not hear of that. But it is done – neither you nor I can change what happened.' I said nothing. Again he made a tremendous effort. 'Grace, I want to talk to you about something completely different. Please – sit down.' Finally, silently, I sat.

He took a deep breath. 'Listen to me,' he said. 'Much has changed in the Art World since you and I – spoke of these things. Many matters are different. There is more money in London than ever. I believe that I can, now, make your Fortune.'

'And how would that be arranged?' Even I could hear my dry, wry tone.

'You must trust me.'

I did not even speak to that.

'You are now so – so at the height of your Powers you could do anything,' and again he looked at the Paintings: at my Family, at Poppy, at the young woman reading the letter. 'Your paintings are dazzling, Grace, truly,' and I understood he was not trying to flatter me, he spoke his thoughts and I felt my own hope and my own belief fluttering there, breathing in his words, there where my heart was – though I was at pains to let him know nothing of my thoughts or feelings. 'I wished so much you could have seen what I saw in Europe,' – he was on dangerous ground but he went on, 'You are a much better Painter than many of the Artists I know have ever been. I do not think you know how good you have become.'

'I do know,' I said quietly. He looked at me then and saw that I spoke my own truth. And then I laughed slightly. 'And so, James, I would like to be appreciated and recognised before I die of Old Age! If I am as good a Painter now as you say I am' – I heard that

I spoke even more in that dry, droll manner – 'I wish to become a Member of the Royal Academy, like my brother.'

He was taken very much by surprise I think, but he laughed also. 'Grace, never mind Recognition and Appreciation just at this moment. I can obtain for you money, and that can give you the Freedom you have so craved.'

'You wish to continue to sell for me, under the name of a man?' He did not know I would not accept that now: I had travelled too far, I wanted my paintings to be signed GRACE MARSHALL.

'I do wish you to sell under the name of a man,' he said – and he put up his hand before I could speak. 'But another name, not the one we used before. That is why you must take care not to paint your own face that you know so well. I want' – I saw he hurried on before I could interrupt him in any way whatsoever – 'I want to sell one under the name of . . .' He leaned towards me, candlelight caught the face I had once so loved, his grey eyes gleamed. 'I want to sell one – just *one* – under the name of Rembrandt van Rijn.'

He took no notice of the stunned look on my face. He went on quickly. 'I know men who could so work upon a finished modern painting that its origins become unrecognisable.'

'*Rembrandt van Rijn?*' I could hardly say it.

Suddenly he sat on the sofa beside me, so near that I could have put out my hand and touched that face; I moved slightly. 'Grace, there has always been Fraudulence in Art, always. We know as a certainty that Peter Paul Rubens had a workshop where he had many pupils and assistants, and we know that in some cases it is not possible to discern between what he actually painted and what he signed that had been more or less painted by others. Our own plan is not at all outside the realm of possibility – indeed William Hogarth himself was once involved in a fraudulent Rembrandt etching – we are just more ambitious! It is thought now that Rembrandt collaborated with other Painters, that he too very likely finished and signed works begun by his pupils – not to defraud perhaps, but simply to keep up with his orders when his Fame was at its height. You yourself began by assisting your Brother, you know very well his assistants now do a large part of his work. We take it further, that is all. Should we not succeed at our highest Goal we will at least imply the Painting is from the *time* of Rembrandt, from the *school* of Rembrandt.' I stared at

James as he spoke on and on, his voice and his face were tense and heightened and audacious.

'In France I know of a Painter who worked as if in a factory: he employed badly paid workers to do the skies, more badly-paid workers to do not only the sleeves but the cheeks, the clothes, the hair – his Art passed through an army of workers before it was signed! A Painting is often *nearly* a Fraud!' He hardly stopped for breath and then he went on; he spoke of paints, boards, oils, colours: all these things I could have unstintingly. And I thought of Philip, and John Palmer, and the painters who painted yards of sky.

I listened to James Burke talk on and on without speaking myself; he was so near to me as he outlined his plan that I could feel his breath on my cheek; I looked down at my hands so as not to have to be so close to the grey, grey eyes.

'Rembrandt is of the greatest importance in the development of Art,' he said, 'and he has suddenly become very, very much more collectable. They all copy him at times, all of them, including Joshua Reynolds for all he may say that Rembrandt does not follow the Classical Style. Rembrandt paints in a Style all his own, and by some miracle you fell upon the same uses of light and shade even before you saw a Rembrandt painting. You have had the great good luck of living for years with a Rembrandt Portrait, and you have been a quite miraculous student; you may not even know how you take his Style – his Style of etching and his Style of painting has been copied a hundred times – many Artists just call their paintings, especially their self-portraits *after Rembrandt.* I believe that you are so talented, and so at the height of your powers, that you can do what I suggest.'

At last he stopped speaking.

'Well, Grace?' He waited in silence at last, not looking at me now, looking at the painting on the easel, but I heard his uneven breathing.

I understood that in some twisted way I had been given the greatest compliment any modern Artist could possibly be given. *And he believed it.* Still I did not speak. It was not what I dreamed of. But perhaps it would *allow* me to do what I had dreamed of. He got up from where he had become so dangerously close; I saw that he was still staring at the Painting on the easel, the girl with the letter, and something, a shadow, passed across his face. Finally he turned to me again. 'I have made it my business to suggest to your Brother that he travel to Amsterdam in the near future: there would be much of Rembrandt's work for you to see there, so you must, somehow, arrange to travel there also.'

I stared at him.

'Time is of the essence,' he added brusquely, 'if you will agree. Other people would have to be involved, the people who would be working on the Painting, to age it. We are awaiting your reply.'

I realised then that he did not understand. I was imagining *one day* and he was imagining *this day*.

'You do not mean now? You do not know?'

He stared at me blankly.

'Filipo did not tell you?'

'What do you mean?'

'Angelica is not just ill. She is dying and I am with her a great deal. We have had all the doctors, but it is no use. She has only a few months to live.'

I liked him for a moment then, his shock, and then his true, sad regret. He sat down again beside me. 'But – he said he hoped she would recover.'

'He dreams she will recover. She will not recover.'

He sat beside me with his head bowed for some time, so that I did not know if he was thinking of Angelica or his plans for Mr Rembrandt.

And then I said, 'Did Philip tell you why she is dying?'

He looked up. 'Some disease – that only Women contract, he said to me.'

So I nodded in silence. That was true, I suppose.

At last James stood and I could feel the regret, perhaps regret for the glory days that were gone when Angelica presided over the dinner-table of the new young Artists with Roberto on her shoulder, the most beautiful woman in London. 'We will speak of other matters another time then.' Then he looked back at the easel. 'But – I want to take that Painting now. Will you sell it to me?'

I stared at the girl with the letter. 'Very well.'

From his waistcoat he drew a pouch, and in front of me, in my sewing-room, he counted out ten guineas pieces. —Then he stood for just a moment looking at the room he had once known so well. —And then without saying anything else, James Burke picked up the Painting and left my room.

I looked at the money on the small table, picked it up so that it spilled through my hand.

I never held that amount of money in my life, not even the night I stole so recklessly, that last night I worked on the *piazza*.

SIXTEEN

It was a fine time to be an Englishman.

Foreigners were suddenly less welcome. Often now there were riots against them in London: NO FRENCH ACROBATS one poster read, and the Sardinian Chapel that Filipo di Vecellio and his sister Francesca had once visited was pelted with rocks. People spoke of the *British* Royal Academy and the King advised that he preferred British Artists who had not damaged themselves by making the Grand Tour all over Europe.

An old song from the Seven Years' War came back into fashion and groups of foolish lads with bottles of English gin roamed the streets carousing, some said the words had been written years ago by Mr Garrick himself.

> *With lantern jaws and croaking gut*
> *See how the half-starv'd Frenchman strut*
> *   And call us English dogs!*
> *But soon we'll teach these bragging foes*
> *That beef and beer give heavier blows*
> *   Than soup and roasted frogs.*

A few months later a mad Scotsman (it was put about that he was mad), Lord Gordon, took it upon himself to lead a riot of anti-Catholics rampaging through the streets of London shouting about the Parliament. For a few terrifying days, London was like a wild place: foreigners and Englishmen were killed, both; the Sardinian Chapel was attacked again; Fleet Street was set afire; the foreign walls of the house in Pall Mall of Signore di Vecellio, the well-known Italian portrait painter, had been daubed with red paint – the word PAPIST was writ across the wall and the Signorina Francesca di Vecellio looked down from one of the attic windows on to the fashionable street as crowds pushed by and the King ordered his troops to fire. Four hundred and fifty people were killed in London before dinner was held again in the house in Pall Mall.

The rioters were imprisoned, or hung in groups at Tyburn or Newgate; London became itself again, more or less, and the next sensation in Pall Mall was caused not by violent protestants, but by the arrival of the Celestial Bed.

This Celestial Bed was, indeed, a Sensation; in fact when it arrived in triumph in Pall Mall it was advertised (very discreetly) as one of The Wonders of the World.

The Celestial Bed stood in an Emporium called the Temple of Health which had just been opened in one of the large houses in Pall Mall. The Temple of Health advertised many health cures, including mud baths and massage, but its central jewel and great drawing card was The Celestial Bed which was described as standing on Forty Pillars of Brilliant Glass of great strength, encrusted with jewels, decorated with nymphs, and with mirrors above.

'What are mirrors for, in a bed?' asked Isabella of her aunt, as the residents of Pall Mall observed their new neighbours.

The Proprietor, Dr James Graham, gave long and learned lectures about Health and The Flowing of Life's Forces and Juices (certain forces and juices in particular). He informed the populace that on The Celestial Bed about fifteen hundred pounds' weight of artificial compound magnets were so disposed and arranged so as to pour forth powerful tides of *magnetic effluvia* to give a *sweet, undulating, tittulating, vibratory, soul-dissolving, marrow-melting motion* (that is, in simple language, to shake the bed gently up and down as illustrious couples lay upon it). At the end of his lectures, and at the end of his pamphlets in small lettering, there were instructions as to the manner in which couples (honourable married couples *of course*) could hire the bed for the evening: the party need only send a line, intimating the evening they proposed to visit the Temple of Health (including a fifty-pound bank note) and a Ticket of Admission would be sent forthwith by the bearer, sealed up:

> Neither myself, nor any of my servants, need ever
> know who the parties are who repose in this chamber
> which I call the SANCTUM SANCTORUM.

And he added, finally, that a Vestal Nymph would be in attendance if required.

The other inhabitants of Pall Mall (for it was a most fashionable and busy and excellent street) were confounded at the sudden further increase in traffic, the anonymous carriages and the huge crowds of interested bystanders who often would not go home. When half-naked nymphs began to be painted on outside columns of the big house, some Pall Mall residents began to complain loudly, especially at night when there was now a continual throng of gaping viewers all hoping for excitement; some residents commented that these sight-seers were no better behaved than the Gordon Rioters (although in this case lives were not lost, so perhaps the comparison was a little exaggerated). But Mr Thomas Gainsborough found the whole proceedings particularly amusing: he lived next door to this Temple and gained much entertainment from the accompanying procedures of The Celestial Bed and the cloaked couples who came and went from these premises in closed carriages. The crowds of interested spectators, who found the salacious comings and goings all very entertaining also, called and laughed along Pall Mall, their voices reached into the nearby large houses of the gentry.

One particular room, in one particular large house in Pall Mall where the voices of the interested spectators could be heard, was a room with no mirrors; only shadows.

The candle-lamps were turned down low. They flickered uneasily sometimes, as if they might suddenly whisper out altogether and leave only darkness. Huge shadows fell across the walls and over the twirled and cherub-covered ceiling: smiling, chubby faces and luscious pink bottoms drifted; ghostly; trailing clouds. Shapes of heavy furniture stretched up the walls, dark and distorted. Sometimes, if the woman in the bed moved, the shadows moved: the woman was surrounded by shadows. When the servants came in, or the husband, or the husband's sister, bringing their own lamps, the woman always turned away from the light.

But it was the other shadows that made the room so dark: the shadows of youth and beauty and the music and the laughter and the cherubic pink bottoms. These shadows haunted: lost, eaten away.

The two children, Claudio and Isabella, had both been summoned, stood now outside the dark room. The boy – but of course he was a man now, almost seventeen years old – did not want to enter the room again, could not bear the air, the stale smell of decay; most of all could not bear the huge bed and the small figure. He shouted at the servants in other parts of the house, quiet only when his father appeared, or his calm aunt in her white cap. The girl, almost seventeen years old also, waited silently, her face quite blank.

Tonight they had suddenly been instructed to wait outside the room for their father. The girl was motionless, but her breathing was nervous; beside her the boy breathed with something that might have been fear.

Sometimes still, when they passed that first, wondrous portrait of their mother where it hung on the staircase in their house in Pall Mall by St James's Park, the son and the daughter thought they caught the warm scent: musk, or jasmine – they could not name it, only that it lay there, potent, part of memory.

Clocks ticked in the large hallway, several chimed the quarter. Then they heard their father's footsteps.

'Come,' said their father.

Inside the room there were no clocks, for clocks, like light and mirrors, were feared; time, in the darkness, was gone: gone golden days of fashion and beauty and laughter. Their aunt was beside the bed; the candle-lamp held by their father shone away from there; the children moved like ghostly figures, reluctant, towards the shadows, that is, towards their mother.

'Claudio. Claudio.' And then after a small silence, 'Isabella.' A damp, thin hand held theirs briefly.

'Claudio,' said the whispered voice in the shadows. And from the shadows too, they saw old Roberto the parrot, perched on one of the bedposts, silent as death.

The girl, Isabella, suddenly took up one of the candles, held it up the better to see the most beautiful woman in the world. For a brief moment, before her aunt like lightning, and yet so gently, moved, the girl saw her mother.

Her mother had no hair. Her mother's face had holes in it, as if something had eaten her.

It was the lime.

The lime in the beauty potions. The lime in the famous Venetian Ceruse that had made her skin so white had eaten away the face of beauty.

—Angelica had come to find me the day she finally understood what was happening to her. —She had thought it was only a terrible dream; even now she told herself it would go away; she thought her Beauty – the one thing she had that she valued, the only thing she truly owned (it seemed to her) – would come back.

'I will wear less,' she said to me that day she came to find me. 'It will go away,' and she looked to me for confirmation that this was so. (By then you could clearly see where the flesh was eaten away below her eye; she had covered it carefully that day – with Venetian Ceruse.) Such was her terror when she came into my room so unexpectedly that she did not see even what was in front of her – except the quilt: the quilt of many colours where I had sewn my own pain – through the small door to the sewing-room there was an easel, but she did not see it; there were Paints but she did not see them, nor my Paintings; she saw me as she knew me: her sister whom she had not been able to marry off to a rich noble friend – the housekeeper. —The only reason she noticed the quilt was that she tripped on it in her hurry to reach me, and just for a moment the colours caught her, I saw them catch her attention – the brightness – and then lose it again as she clung to me and begged me again, *It will go away, won't it Francesca?* but already it had been rumoured about town: the dangers of the Venetian Ceruse, the white paste that made white skin whiter, that fashionable whiteness that was considered then so beautiful; when I bathed her I saw the terrible skin, once so white and shining, finally scarred and black with holes eaten into the sad flesh right down to the bosom where she had applied the deadly lime – to make herself *more* beautiful: yet she was named the most beautiful woman in London already.

Later she asked me for the quilt, some part of her remembered the brightness perhaps, and in the last months I comforted her as lovingly as I could with the coloured quilt which held the bright colours of pain.

When I had made Angelica that gaily-ribboned hat she liked it at once, insisted on wearing it to Vauxhall one summer afternoon long ago, and when they had gone, her ribbons and her perfume flowing behind her, I had painted her in that hat, such happiness and gaiety and delight.

That painting is burned now, like all the paintings then.

But the more ill Angelica became the more she had wanted me to sit with her, until she slept; the small light burned always beside her, for although she hated the light she was scared of the dark, and one night when I saw that she had fallen asleep I brought my charcoal and my paper back into her room and I drew the sleeping face of Angelica – I could not stop myself. —Although her hair had long gone and the marks of the Poison were everywhere, for some reason her eyelashes still grew dark and they lay upon her poor face as a last remnant of her Beauty, covering the dark eyes. —I turned the lamp slightly and she stirred in her sleep but did not wake – with the light that way I could draw her Beauty still: even as her face was eaten away, the lovely structure of the bones was there – I drew more shadow than light so that the marks on her face blended into shadow. —And over her, in my last Portrait, the quilt that she had asked for, all the colours, bright colours, drifting into the shadows. —For weeks I worked on this picture in my Studio for I wanted to capture her in oils but still something was wrong, I could not get it right, and then a few nights before her death, as I sat with her, embroidering, she suddenly asked for Isabella, when the girl came I made to leave them but Angelica said quickly, *No, stay Francesca, talk with us too*, as if she was – it seemed perhaps – afraid to be alone with her daughter – the lamps had been moved away from the bed, it was upon Isabella that the light shone, her dark hair and her pretty (pretty is quite different from beautiful) but rather sulky face; Isabella wanted to talk of Fashion and Florence and Paris, did not see how painful this was to her Mother – finally I managed to change the subject by telling them I had passed the new Temple of Health in Pall Mall the previous day, and I had seen that old quack we all knew in our youth, with the Silver painted on his hair, Doctor James Graham, who was promoting his Celestial Bed and had advertised for a Nymph to assist him in his miracles.

'I remember Dr Graham,' said Angelica suddenly. 'Long before he went to America and became famous we knew him, Francesca, remember? He asked me, not altogether in jest, if *I* would be his Vestal Nymph and dress in white robes and sing and play the harpsichord while he extolled his very expensive – Emollients,' and she smiled slightly.

'What exactly is a Celestial Bed that interests everybody so?' Isabella asked, and although I believe there is much entertainment to be gained from Doctor Graham's lectures on bodily fluids, I felt that this was probably not the time to acquaint Isabella with these facts.

'I expect it is something to do with Angels,' I told her, and once more the shadow of a smile crossed Angelica's face, named after all for an Angel, and there suddenly was the last of her beauty, there in her dark eyes, deep black pools of distress, almost the only thing I could see of her face that evening, because of the way the light fell, and sorrow on her face like a whole river of unshed tears, and the bright quilt in shadow – in desperation I made some excuse and literally ran to my Studio, and I worked to show those dark, deep eyes and then the Painting was finished, less than one week before she died.

SEVENTEEN

The most beautiful woman in London had all but been forgot as she wasted away in the room without mirrors. All the fashion and the gossip and the *soirees* and the *convesatziones* and the promenades and the balls, all the beautiful gowns and the gorgeous potions: all these blossomed elsewhere now, and new young adventurers were now named the most beautiful women in London as the black corsage with its elegant horses made its way to St James's Church at Piccadilly.

But Sir Joshua Reynolds and Mr Thomas Gainsborough and many other Academicians had attended the funeral of the beautiful woman: a sign of respect for a fellow Academician. They had all, all of them, gone out of their way to be cordial to Signore di Vecellio since his house had been daubed with the word PAPIST: they stood by their colleague in shame at their countrymen. Now they were all at St James's Church with solemn visage. Mr John Palmer came to the funeral in his shabby clothes and Miss Ann Ffoulks was there of course in a black bonnet with flowing ribbons, and Mr Hartley Pond (who carried a black snuff-box) and James Burke.

After the sad goodbye some of the Academicians and some of the close friends came once more to the house in Pall Mall that many of them knew so well and had such happy memories of; they drank tea with Filipo di Vecellio (and then whisky when Miss Ffoulks had departed, Mr Burke escorting her) and when the condolences had been repeated the artists all spoke of the forthcoming Summer Exhibition, the second one to be held at the Royal Academy's new premises at Somerset House. They hoped for the same public excitement, and the same financial success.

'You will exhibit again of course, Filipo,' said the Academicians kindly (for all knew the Italian's portraits were not now given the respect they once had). Then, as they repaired upstairs to the comfort of the drawing-room, Sir Joshua Reynolds saw the old painting of Angelica, where it hung on the stairs: the extraordinary portrait when, through love, the painter had transcended his skill. The President of the Royal Academy stared at the painting for a long, long time, pausing there on the bend in the staircase, his face expressionless.

And then he turned to Filipo di Vecellio. 'I remember seeing this many years ago. But you have never exhibited it.'

'No,' said Filipo di Vecellio, and they saw he could not look at the painting, just then.

'This one, Filipo,' said Sir Joshua Reynolds. 'No matter its age. It would be a fitting Memorial, and a Tribute to your Skills. It must hang on the line in the Great Room.' It was a gracious gesture, that night of the funeral, and Filipo di Vecellio bowed graciously in return, his great pain still not letting him look at his masterpiece.

The artists drank more whisky, became more expansive, all shouting into Sir Joshua's ear trumpet as the host's sister lit the lamps and shadows fell across the polished wooden floors. John Palmer, not an Academician, stared into his whisky and was silent. Filipo di Vecellio spoke of taking his son, Claudio, to the now-advertised auction of Old Masters in Amsterdam that James Burke had alerted him to.

'For the moment we will begin with Amsterdam,' he explained, 'and then one day when he is a little older he and I shall make the Grand Tour and he shall see our Italian Heritage.' And John Palmer nodded expressionlessly into his whisky, and for a moment the assembled artists nodded and sighed and remembered their own Grand Tours, and Time – so present that sad day – gently brushed the air.

'Absolutely essential Training for every young Artist,' said Sir

Joshua. 'To see the frescoes of Michelangelo is to have seen the greatest Art the World has ever known.'

'I would like my Studies to be over,' said Claudio importantly, 'so that I can commence my work as a Painter in earnest.' (He did not see how the older men smiled into their glasses at his ignorance and his pomposity.)

'Young man,' said Sir Joshua dryly, 'our Studies will be for ever, in a very great degree, under the direction of Chance: like travellers we must take what we can get, and when we can get it, whether it is, or is not, administered to us in the most commodious manner, in the proper place, or at the exact minute when we would wish to have it.' And the Signorina Francesca di Vecellio smiled to herself slightly, and Claudio bowed his head, gently rebuked. (All in black, all of them in black, Sir Joshua with his ear trumpet, the daughter Isabella's dark head, the stricken face of the bereaved husband, as the evening fell dark outside and the sister of the artist drew the curtains and the shutters, and the yellow flame of the candlelight flickered and the famous artists of the day became shadows in the sad room.)

'You will buy to sell?' asked Sir Joshua, himself a collector.

'I will buy,' said Filipo di Vecellio, his drawn face lightening a little at the thought. 'And sell,' – knowing it would keep the others interested: those who made money from painting portraits elevated themselves by investing in Old Art. He knew very well Sir Joshua had recently spent a great deal of money in Europe. The conversation turned to assuring themselves *they* would not be cheated by fakes that abounded in foreigners' markets. They remarked on the sale of Rembrandt's *Adoration of the Kings* for the extraordinary sum of three hundred and ninety guineas – and that was at least three years ago! To what heights might these Old Masters go? John Palmer who painted poor people in Spitalfields drank more whisky, did not speak.

'And then one day my son shall have a Grand Tour,' said Filipo di Vecellio again, 'before he becomes a Painter, like his Father.'

—and quite suddenly there in the room as I collected the teacups I saw Philip's ship pulling away from the Bristol quay, and me on the shore aged ten, as the morning lightened and Philip gone from me on his Artistic Education, and I left to mine.

Later that bleak night of the Funeral I sat in my room with my last painting of Angelica. —Her workroom with all its bright fragrance and colour had long been empty and tonight Roberto sat with me, mourning, his head down; sometimes in his unhappiness he pecked at his own feathers, pulled them. They fell about the room like white drifting tears.

Angelica.

She had given me Freedom, by putting me in charge of the household money, and she had imprisoned me by giving me the children. —From my window I could see down over the King's Garden into St James's Park; there were no shining stars at all that night, how dark London could be when the day had gone, just the odd faint moving light as someone was guided, by one of the link-boys perhaps, along the dark paths. I had stayed with Isabella till she fell asleep that night, tears still on her cheeks, she was not so much older than I was when I first came to London.

I stroked her arm, for comfort, over and over as she wept. 'You and I shall travel to Amsterdam also,' I said to Isabella. 'I have a plan.'

EIGHTEEN

The second Exhibition at the Royal Academy in Somerset House opened with almost as much excitement as the first: fig leaves, however, had been judiciously applied upon any appurtenances or protuberances deemed offensive.

The spiral staircase was again full of pushing, perspiring people as entrance to the Grand Room (via the naked sculptures on the first floor) was attained for, and it was well-known now that a view of a nicely turned ankle (and perhaps more) could be obtained while loitering by the plaster copy of the famous Apollo Belvedere in the vestibule and looking, directly, upwards.

People gossiped loudly. Sir Joshua Reynolds, the President of the Academy, again had the most portraits exhibited in the Grand Gallery – fifteen. But of as much interest were the two large History paintings, also in the Grand Gallery, *both* entitled *The Death of Dido*, *both*! One was by Sir Joshua Reynolds himself and the other by a *foreigner*, a new younger artist named Henry Fuseli who (it was whispered) had begged to see Sir Joshua's work in progress – and then had had the impertinence to go home and paint the same subject. Some said the foreigner's painting was better, and malicious laughter drifted. It was also noted that this year the royal portraits were by Mr Thomas

Gainsborough whom (the whispers continued) their Majesties preferred.

Sir Joshua Reynolds, President, moved in state through the crowds, and if he did not always hold his trumpet to his ear who could blame him?

Signore Filipo di Vecellio attended the Exhibition with his two children and his sister; they were all dressed in mourning black and made a fetching picture as they stood in the Grand Room for some moments beneath the painting of the beautiful, deceased Signora Angelica di Vecellio, which was hung, most exquisitely, 'on the line'. It was titled, simply, *Portrait of a Lady*. Angelica smiled gently down, like an angel.

Later Isabella di Vecellio was seen in animated conversation with the exquisitely coiffeured young gentleman she had paid so much attention to at last year's Exhibition and she blushed prettily as they spoke together.

There was another *scandale* in the pushing crowds of this exhibition, only this year it was of a sodomitic nature (duels and the law and hurried flights to France), and the newspapers thundered about the unsuitable Proximity of Bodies in the Royal Academy.

In short: another grand success.

Soon after, the di Vecellio family left for Amsterdam.

The Signorina Isabella di Vecellio had, to everybody's surprise, absolutely *insisted* on coming on the journey to Amsterdam with her father and her brother: she would not be dissuaded, cried and wept and sulked when told it was a journey more for gentlemen.

The older *signorina*, that is Signorina Francesca, busied herself about the house, did not offer an opinion. Finally Filipo di Vecellio sighed.

'Well well, very well, Isabella. You will have to come also, Francesca. Isabella cannot possibly travel abroad without a Chaperone.' And his daughter kissed him lovingly, and he went off to his studio, half-mollified; he did not see the gleam in his sister's eye as she instructed the servants about the day's requirements.

In fact all the reasons for this journey were perhaps more complicated than first understood. Filipo di Vecellio fervently wanted to buy Old Masters for his growing collection, certainly, but he had also discovered that his son Claudio had got himself caught up in bad company and was following the illegal cock-fighting, and gambling all over London, and was badly into debt. Claudio di Vecellio owed more money to the cock-fighting men than his father understood: thought only to get away from London. Isabella di Vecellio had been led to believe by her aunt that a short trip abroad would make her a most interesting young lady and Isabella required to be interesting to one young gentleman in particular.

Just as they were leaving the house in Pall Mall, a letter arrived for the older *signorina* but such was the activity involved in all the piling of luggage into the carriage, such was the last minute seagull-like swooping and diving into the house by Isabella as she thought of another necklet or shoe, that nobody observed Francesca di Vecellio put the letter unopened in the pocket of her cloak.

Perhaps the hearts – even the unconscious hearts – of those aging siblings, Philip and Grace Marshall, might have recognised something they were familiar with when they arrived at last in Amsterdam: something like the city of their youth, Bristol. Trade bustled along the canals; rich, important merchants bargained and called; the trading ships travelled perhaps to the West Indies not to the East Indies but the business was the same: spices and silks and sugar and slavery and steel. Tall narrow houses belonging to merchants rose from the canal sides. Ropes coiled and rats scurried alongside ships and barges and there was talk of black tulips and gold and the air of merchanting kicked and shuffled at their memories as they walked beside the canals and through flowers and crowds to the Dam Square. Isabella observed in dismay that the women of Amsterdam looked lumpy and respectable; Claudio looked hopefully round thin corners of cobbled alleys for young men and fights and excitement.

The sun shone brightly, the canal waters sparkled and all the bridges were full of bustling life and bright, bright flowers. They had settled into a fine *stadspaleis* on the *Herengracht*; huge windows looked out over shining water, boats sailed past, people called and hurried and there was the smell of bread, and sausage. Filipo di Vecellio was in his element: he had met some of the art merchants and rich collectors in London. He had an invitation for his family to view, in the fine Town Hall, a famous Rembrandt painting of some of the burghers of Amsterdam who in the olden days had served part-time as the city's military guards: a painting vulgarly known as *The Night Watch* but known, by those who knew these things and understood painting, to be painted through rays of sunlight. Then they were to go at two o'clock – here Filipo di Vecellio could hardly contain himself – to the Auction of Old Masters: the sale at last of the paintings of the recently deceased merchant, which were rumoured to include a Rubens, a Titian and several by Rembrandt van Rijn.

First they were ushered up staircases and into the Town Hall of Amsterdam.

The small family stood, dutifully in some cases, before the famous painting styled *The Night Watch*. Isabella yawned politely behind her hand: a scene of soldiers. Claudio ignored the faces: nevertheless found much interest in the swords and the lances and the muskets, and a drum being played in a corner. Their aunt stared at a small girl, caught in light among the men in strange shadows, who was carrying a chicken. She observed the way the painter had used the light, how it fell across the dark painting, lighting the leader of the Militia, and the beautiful heavy shining embroidery on the clothes of some of the men. The face of Filipo di Vecellio was full of longing: perhaps to own this painting, perhaps to paint like this – who could know? Perhaps he thought suddenly of his wife Angelica. The family moved about the large painting, their footfalls were soft on rich, heavy, embroidered Eastern carpet, voices were quiet around them but shouts came in through the windows from the square below.

Then Filipo rushed off to view the paintings before the Auction; he insisted Claudio attend him and his sister was walking almost ahead of him, so anxious was she to view the paintings, but then Isabella cried quite loudly, 'I am so *bored.*'

'Stay together with her, Francesca,' instructed Filipo, 'you can wander about and look at pretty things.' And no-one saw the impatience and almost a look of rage in the aunt's eyes.

'We will of course join you for the actual Auction,' she said firmly as the men hurried off.

Because it was such a soft, warm Amsterdam day the two women sat on a bench beside one of the canals in the sunshine, their straw hats keeping the sun from their faces. Francesca thought of *The Night Watch*; Isabella sighed loudly and sulked. The Finishing School had made her petulant, and the aunt, hearing a particularly theatrical sigh beside her, was reminded suddenly of her sisters in Bristol, and how they frowned. Finally Isabella could stand the silence no longer.

'It is all your fault, Aunt Fran! You *made* me come on this tedious Journey! You did not tell me it would take *months* to reach Amsterdam and that we would have to stop and visit *every* dreary church along the way! And you promised me there would be beautiful Jewels here, diamonds from the Indies you said, that my Father might purchase for me, and interesting Gentlemen – and instead we have had to travel in smelly coaches over terrible roads and every time we stopped we had to go into yet another old Church in case it held Art – I am sure we have entered every Church between London and Amsterdam, no matter the Religion! And even I know Protestant churches do not hold real Art. Let him take me to Florence if he wants Art, and we can find our Relations!' (All her life Isabella had imagined elegant, mysterious foreign women in beautiful gowns in beautiful houses in Florence, with whom she might dwell.)

She threw her head back dramatically. 'When are we returning to London?' This was about the tenth time she had asked her aunt the question since they had set sail from Dover and Isabella had experienced her first sea-sickness; she had then been jumbled and tumbled and suffocated in rattling coaches for many days and overcome by the smell of all manner of foreigners all speaking in foreign tongues to each other, ignoring English people. It had been too much to bear. And in a final cry now she added, 'I miss Roberto!'

'But *Isabellabella*,' (the aunt used the name from their childhood) 'we have only just arrived! Look how beautiful it is, the water sparkling in the sunshine. And *The Night Watch* is a very famous and well-known painting, many people will be most interested and indeed impressed to hear you have seen it. And this afternoon you shall attend an important Art Auction.'

'Oh yes,' the girl answered hurriedly, 'it is all most Educational, of course. But look, all the Dutch women are ugly, with funny hats, there is nothing fashionable here. And where are the Jewels?'

'Dear girl, I promise you we will look for Jewels. Your Father is much taken with the Auction today, but after that we will find you Jewels.' And as Isabella had only just turned seventeen and her mother had recently died, and as she had – indeed she had – let herself be persuaded that she must come on this journey by her aunt making much mention of Jewels and Gentlemen, Francesca moved slightly and put her arm about the girl as she occasionally had when the children were young. Isabella looked surprised, for her aunt seldom made such gestures. But she stayed there in the bend of the arm and there was the scent of flowers and the water did sparkle and Isabella gave a little sigh, not unhappily, and after some time she said to her aunt in a little, enquiring voice,

'I will be, won't I, as you told me, such an *interesting* young Lady when we get back to London?'

'You will be, Isabella! You will be much sought after – as long as, if I might just say this, you do not sulk.'

The girl did not seem to hear, suddenly spoke breathlessly, 'Did you notice Mr Georgie Bounds at the Royal Academy Exhibition again this year? The man who paid me much gratifying Attention?'

'Is that the Gentleman with the – modern – hair?'

'Yes! I am sure I love him, Aunt Francesca.'

Francesca had not understood her niece's thoughts on the subject to be so dramatic. 'And what makes you so sure, Isabella? That you love Mr – Mr Bounds?'

'I told him we were to travel to Amsterdam and he was so very impressed, and told me he had never met a young Lady who had made that Journey and that I was to tell him all about it upon my return – and he is seriously interested in what I might have to say, really, for he is the son of a Picture Framer who frames many of the Paintings for the Royal Academy Exhibitions. Did you notice how very handsome his Features were?' The aunt's heart sank: Philip would never consent to an entanglement with the son of a *Picture Framer*. 'Do you think he will love me?' asked Isabella. 'For I will be so Knowledgeable.' And Francesca hugged her niece to her without answering and sent up a little prayer of gratitude to Mr Bounds the Frame-maker's son, who had, unbeknown, assisted her to travel to Amsterdam to see the pictures of Rembrandt van Rijn.

Before two o'clock, hungry – they had consumed only hot chocolate since morning in this foreign place – the whole family were nevertheless to be seen in the very crowded room of the auctioneer.

Filipo di Vecellio frowned – there were many foreign buyers besides himself, people were pushing rudely for a better look, consulting their catalogues and whispering to one another: were the paintings real or fake, were they worth a hundred guilders, or only one?

And there were more works by Rembrandt van Rijn than Signore di Vecellio, or his sister, had ever seen. There were a number of drawings: they seemed to be done with a quill, with ink, and sometimes brushwork added, the faces full of life: young women, old men and women, a beggar. The sister thought: *he shows beauty in the faces of old people: something inside their eyes*. There was a painting of a young woman in a hat. There was a large religious painting: a dark, disturbing Judas. And there were several self-portraits: Francesca closed her eyes suddenly, almost dizzy, opened them again, stared for a long time at the man from whom she had learned so much, and might gain so much, she felt her heart beating fast in her chest. His face, half-shadowed, looked travailed and worn in one of the paintings, as if to say *it is not easy: it is not supposed to be easy*. Just as the Auctioneer was gathering his papers and his gavel, Francesca caught sight of another smaller painting of a young woman: *I know her*. The young woman stood with the light from a window catching that face, the gown shadowy, yet rich with reds and yellows and browns, beautifully embroidered. Francesca pushed through other people until she came close. The woman in the painting was not doing anything at all. Just being. And thinking.

A Frenchman in the crowd (a *Marquis* had she but known, might indeed have guessed from the gold on his lace) observed the woman standing in front of the painting; something in her face took his attention: it was as if her eyes bored into the picture as she stood there. She turned her attention to him most reluctantly as he spoke.

'*Cette un Rembrandt*. That is, of course, a Rembrandt Portrait,' he said.

'I know,' she answered, hardly looking at him.

'We are led to believe the subject is Hendrickje Stoffels, the last Mistress. Perhaps you know of her.'

She had not known this was Rembrandt's mistress: but it was the face in Sir Joshua Reynolds' painting of the woman bathing. Perhaps she should have guessed. 'She is beautiful.'

'She is loved,' said the *marquis*, 'that is perhaps different.' And the woman standing before the painting turned to him at last, surprised.

'Yes,' she said.

At that moment the Auctioneer called loudly and as the Frenchman disappeared she was not sure if he had said to her, *I shall have it*. Her brother was beside her.

'The same woman, surely, the woman bathing, in the painting that Joshua Reynolds owns!' he said in excitement. 'This is a real find.'

His sister could not find the words as she stared: the woman, how the light caught her gentle eyes and the shaded curve of her cheek, and her hair.

'It could be a Fake of course,' said Filipo.

Francesca stared up at the woman. 'I believe it is not,' she said.

'A clever Copy perhaps?'

'I believe it is not.'

He glanced at her. It was she who had persuaded him to buy the other small Rembrandt, years ago: it was now one of his most valuable possessions. He looked at the painting again. It was stunning: he wanted to own it: *I shall have it*: he would pay whatever was required.

The brother turned to find a good seat. The spinster sister breathed in suddenly, an observer might think she was breathing the painting into herself.

It was the first painting to be auctioned. Because there were so many foreigners present it was agreed finally that the bidding should be in guineas. A Dutchman caused a gasp of surprise when he started off the offers: two hundred guineas (there were immediate angry murmurs that he was probably in league with the Auctioneer, trying to make the price artificially high). When the frantic bidding reached *three hundred guineas* the crowded auction room which had been noisy and excited was suddenly so quiet as to seem to be empty. At last there were only two bidders left: Filipo di Vecellio and the French *Marquis*.

'Three hundred and twenty-five guineas.'

'Three hundred and forty.'

'Three hundred and forty-five.'

Somebody in the room coughed, tried to muffle the sound.

The woman stood there, waiting; a pale hand, a beautiful rich red embroidered sleeve. Francesca actually heard her brother beside her swallow.

'Three hundred and fifty,' he called.

There was an excited silence.

And then, extraordinarily, the Frenchman said in a quiet, bored voice, as if he wanted this tedious business over, 'I bid four hundred.'

Four hundred? Did he actually say four hundred – fifty guineas more with one throw? Was this what a small Rembrandt had come to be valued at?

Filipo di Vecellio bowed his head. It was over.

His sister bowed her head also: *this* is what James Burke had meant.

And then the thrilled crowd moved, and voices rose excitedly, and laughter, and then the next painting was brought forward.

Signore Filipo di Vecellio bought several paintings, but his heart was not in it.

He made several more appointments over the next few days to meet sellers and merchants but somehow Amsterdam was disappointing, after the Auction. They saw many tulips and met many art collectors. On the last evening Filipo had an appointment to meet one more dealer. Isabella drooped, no suitable jewel had been found. Filipo di Vecellio insisted that his sister and his daughter not go out alone: Claudio would escort them if they wished to venture. Before the sun set they looked for Claudio for one last hunt for a beautiful diamond perhaps, but Claudio had disappeared.

'He will have found some Netherlandish gambling friends,' said Isabella crossly. 'He can smell them.'

Francesca could not bear her niece's disappointed face: Amsterdam was such a safe place, surely they could go out on an Adventure on their own. They wrapped their cloaks about them, the streets were deserted – until they turned into some alleys behind the Dam Square. It seemed to be a night-market of some kind, people everywhere, they were jostled but unmolested in the crowds; at last they found several stalls of jewellery with their mysterious flickering candle-lamps and both women caught sight of the most beautiful gold pendant, sparkling in the night and the lamplight, and a small red ruby shining in the middle.

Isabella was transfixed, speechless. 'It is from the Indies,' said the trader.

'Please, *Zia Francesca*!' Isabella turned at last to her aunt. '*Please* make Father buy this for me. I do not want diamonds, I want this Pendant – everything will be worthwhile, this whole tedious journey, if I can wear such a piece as this in London, and' (looking at her aunt) 'I heard you, really: I will not sulk!'

They found Filipo returning from his bargain-searching: he was very disapproving of their night-walk, asked his sister how she could be so foolhardy – but Isabella tugged and pulled at his waistcoat in her prettiest manner and finally he called a carriage and returned with them to Dam Square and the crowds and the Jewellery stalls, and Isabella did acquire her pendant and hugged and kissed her Father and told him she would love him for ever.

When they got back to the *Herengracht*, a crowd of youths were shouting in the distance; they were about to enter their own *stadspaleis* when Isabella suddenly cried out, 'It is Claudio!'

They peered along the canal as the youths got nearer. It was Claudio and he was being followed and harassed as he tried to return to the big house: the youths shouted at him in another language and Filipo di Vecellio had to brandish his sword-stick in a very dramatic manner before they finally turned away, still swaggering. Their foreign voices argued in the darkness and then one of them called in English, 'Cheat! You are a Cheat, English boy!' as they disappeared into one of the side alleys. Claudio's face was cut and he was finding it hard to catch his breath.

'They attacked me – I did not know them,' he said nervously to his Father, but they had all heard the word *Cheat* and Filipo sent his sister and his daughter away to their room. But they heard his raised voice.

When her niece fell asleep, still clutching her precious pendant, Francesca di Vecellio, on the last night in Amsterdam, finally opened the letter from James Burke. The beautiful canal lay below her, a boat passed trailing lights, a tree leaned over the water. Candle-lamps flickered in the tall houses on the other side of the canal. Her first small taste of what they all talked of: the Grand Tour. She looked at last at the paper there in her hands and wondered what she would feel if it said now, as he had so often said those days, *Amazing Grace*.

Grace,
I am glad you are to travel to Amsterdam.
I hope you will see much work of your mentor Rembrandt van Rijn: I
think it will give you much pleasure.
When you return I will contact you immediately about the matter of
which we spoke. As I said to you, I believe I can assist you, much
more than previously.
James Burke, Esq.

And Grace Marshall smiled a wry smile, for the letter did call her Amazing Grace, in a way. And she thought of the small Rembrandt painting at the Auction, and the shock on all the faces when it was sold for four hundred guineas.

They left Amsterdam next morning, Claudio very pale and quiet and Isabella insisting on wearing her gold and ruby pendant at all times, and in not much more than three weeks they were back in London.

NINETEEN

It was noticed that, soon after the *signore* had returned from abroad, there was a new regular face at the dinner-table in Pall Mall: a lady about town and noble. Lady Dorothea Bray was a pretty woman, not quite in the first flush of youth but attractive and charming. And she was the younger sister of a somewhat dissolute Duke, and she was unmarried: Signore Filipo di Vecellio had painted her before his wife died. No-one in the world would have accused the *signore* of impropriety while his wife lay ill but Lady Dorothea's tinkling laugh was now heard more and more often at the dinner-table in the house in Pall Mall, and occasionally she gave charming orders to the sister, the housekeeper, Signorina Francesca di Vecellio. The dinners were boisterous (if truth be told they had indeed become somewhat rackety and wild now; so much wine was consumed that Francesca di Vecellio dryly suggested they grow their own grapes, like the old lady on St Martin's Lane).

One afternoon not long after the travellers' return, James Burke was again a guest at the dinner-table – business was business, after all – James Burke wished to know what all London Art Dealers wanted to know: having bought, did Filipo want to sell? Filipo had acquired paintings in Amsterdam and would be selling to the highest bidder, and James Burke would act as his dealer if required. Art was a business, just like any other. Miss Ffoulks and John Palmer again showed their pleasure to see their old friend and Lady Dorothea smiled and laughed in his direction, for indeed with his piercing grey eyes and his own hair tied behind, which was now so fashionable (even though he had been wearing it that way for many years), he was a most handsome man. Dr Charles Burney of the famous daughter was again present, and two rather rakish actresses. Roberto, who had been in the care of Euphemia the maid, was still thin and battered: he was old now of course, and he had never recovered from the death of his beloved mistress and looked on balefully, all Isabella's pretty cajoling could not cheer him, although sometimes he perched near to her. The bright, late-summer light shone on to the table from the big windows, across the beef and the fish and the oranges, and slanting into the crimson-coloured wine. There was much talk of Rembrandt and Amsterdam, interspersed with somewhat salacious gossip of the machinations of Royalty and the wildly handsome and naughty Prince of Wales, and London society, and the theatre. The atmosphere was delightful, the guests thought. Even the two children seemed to enjoy their first European journey, now that it was over; Isabella blushed prettily as she felt admiration for her new-found erudition, understood that as her aunt had foretold she had indeed become more *interesting*: she mentioned *The Night Watch* rather proudly and twirled her pendant from the Indies round her fingers.

Lady Dorothea looked at Isabella, her head on one side as she regarded the daughter of her dear friend Filipo. 'Such a pretty child,' she said. 'I must take her in hand.' Roberto cocked his head to one side also, seemed to listen at length and silently, just as Mr James Burke the art dealer did, but he also disgraced himself (the parrot that is, not the art dealer) by trying to bite Lady Dorothea's be-jewelled finger.

Claudio, to everyone's surprise and his father's pride, seemed to have learned from his journey: he had begun painting in earnest, talked of *The Night Watch* several times, described the long lances and the drum, talked of having a studio of his own.

'He shall be a Painter like his Father,' said Filipo proudly. 'I shall see to it. He shall have everything he needs; another di Vecellio in the annals of the Art of this country!' (The guests did not know what Isabella and her aunt had witnessed on the boat from Ostend to Margate: Claudio seeing England so near, had finally broken down and confessed his large gambling debts to his father and at last a bargain had been agreed, there upon the English Channel. The father would pay the debts: the son, much chastened, would give up the cock-fighting, complete his studies in London, and become a Painter.)

In the dining-room the painter's sister sat between John Palmer and Miss Ffoulks and spoke to them quietly as others shouted about Royalty; she made them laugh at her descriptions of the bone-shaking coaches and the terrible roads; she held their attention when she spoke of the Rembrandt paintings; Miss Ffoulks listened with great interest to hear she had seen another painting of Hendrickje Stoffels, Rembrandt's mistress.

'What is her story?' asked the housekeeper at once.

'I could find nothing,' said Miss Ffoulks. 'But – I believe they had a daughter.' Grace Marshall looked down at her plate.

Dr Burney was finally persuaded to speak about the success of *his* daughter Fanny's novel, *Evelina*. 'At first I did not know', he said proudly, 'that it was penned by my own daughter!'

'I do not think Private Thoughts should be made Public!' said Lady Dorothea, 'I should not tell mine for all the World,' and her white bosom quivered as she leant across to their host, and smiled most charmingly.

'I think a Novel is not private thoughts, but a Fictional tale,' said Dr Burney.

'Art is a Public Matter,' murmured John Palmer, 'and one must take care, for imagine if we Painters painted what we really thought!' And Lady Dorothea's bosom leant forward again, and the arm of John Palmer was tapped playfully with a fan.

Mr James Burke said that he must, most regretfully, leave to attend to some urgent business; the housekeeper, as always, showed the guest out: it would have been noticed, and rude, if she had not.

Laughter echoed from the dining-room as he turned to her at the front door. 'What did you learn?' he asked quietly, and she knew what he meant although they had all been speaking about such things at the dinner-table: *the galleries and auction rooms, the cobbled streets, the churches and the canals and the flowers, the foreign nights,*

The Night Watch. *And, of course, Rembrandt van Rijn.* All, all these things she had talked of so often, with him.

'Everything,' she said simply.

He reached into his waistcoat and withdrew a piece of paper. 'It is of immense importance that you meet me tomorrow, there is someone I want to introduce you to if you feel now able to agree to my . . . proposal?'

She did not exactly answer, but she said, 'I saw another painting of Hendrickje Stoffels.' She spoke expressionlessly, her face blank again.

'The mistress of Rembrandt?'

She nodded. 'It sold for – four hundred guineas.'

'Your brother told me. He was very disappointed to have lost it,' and he handed her the piece of paper. 'It is perhaps best for me to introduce you to my – Colleague – in a public place, for I cannot of course bring him here.' Another gust of laughter flew out from the dining-room. 'This paper is a ticket to the Eidophusikon in Lisle Street for its Evening Presentation tomorrow.'

She looked at him blankly.

'It is the newest sensation!' he said to her with a small smile. 'It provides Moving Pictures!' And then he bent to her and said so quietly she could hardly hear above the noise of the guests, 'We are to re-sell the Painting I purchased from you before you went away, your painting of the girl with the letter. We will speak of this tomorrow.'

The door closed behind him and the housekeeper went back to the noisy dining-room.

TWENTY

The Eidophusikon was, indeed, a sensation.

The Eidophusikon advertised itself as *Various Imitations of Natural Phenomena represented by* – something never seen before – *Moving Pictures*.

A French painter had worked at Drury Lane Theatre as a scenic and lighting designer, bringing thrilling new mechanical devices on to the stage. People thronged to Drury Lane to see his moving ships (which were felt to be much more interesting than the actors now that Mr Garrick was dead). Now the Frenchman had decided to remove himself from the theatre and have an exciting new mechanical device all of his own in his house in Lisle Street. It was rapturously successful.

Many were kept out by the prohibitive cost of five shillings. But, for five shillings, spectators could see five Imitations of Natural Phenomena all of which moved (with musical accompaniment). Dawn, storms, moonlight – these things could be seen shining, fading, *moving*; there was the sound of rain, there were rumbles of thunder, sea crashed upon rocks as the light darkened. A moon would rise over London accompanied by the harpsichord, a sun would set on foreign parts, a ship was to be wrecked *in front of their eyes* by a terrible storm. It was absolutely, astoundingly, thrilling!

The house in Lisle Street crowded with people with five shillings to spend on this wondrous new marvel.

Among this crowd James Burke stood, waiting, with a companion. His alert eyes travelled to the door each time it opened. When she came he could not believe that she had brought her niece, Isabella.

'Good evening, Isabella.'

'Good evening, Mr Burke.'

'Good evening, Signorina Francesca.'

'Good evening, Mr Burke.'

There was a slight uncomfortable silence, then James Burke turned to introduce his companion.

'This is Monsieur Laberge, a visitor from France.'

The Frenchman bowed, both women bowed, but both women saw at once there was something, something not quite correct about the man: his hair or his clothes it was hard to say, something. Isabella, uninterested, turned away looking for Mr Georgie Bounds, the frame-maker's son, to whom she had sent a message that she would be attending this new attraction. Mr Bounds bowed and grinned from across the room.

'Excuse me for a moment, Aunt Francesca,' said Isabella breathlessly and disappeared. The crowds swirled about, anticipating the Natural Phenomena they were about to observe. 'There is to be specially composed Music!' someone called, 'and moving Clouds. And the crashing Sea!' Grace Marshall waited.

Thomas Gainsborough suddenly bounded through the door. 'Good evening, *Signorina*!' he said to Grace. 'Good evening James, have you seen this yet? It is remarkable, remarkable. I help, you know! I sometimes do the thunder!' and he disappeared.

Chords suddenly sounded from a harpsichord, and then there was the plaintive sound of a flute. The Frenchman said in a low voice, 'I had heard of your extraordinary talent, *Signorina*. I have also now seen your painting of the girl with the letter. I congratulate you. I would deem it an Honour to work with you.'

James Burke said, his voice also low, 'Well? Monsieur Laberge wishes to hear your answer also. Will you do it?'

She had prepared herself. She looked firmly into the grey eyes, and then at the Frenchman. 'Yes,' she said. 'I will do it: if you show me the people who will – change it.' She was not prepared now to be just an unknown lady in an attic.

'*D'accord*,' said Monsieur Laberge, surprised, but nodding his assent.

'Ladies and gentlemen!' called a foreign voice. 'Ladies and Gentlemen, please enter the Theatre.' And everybody shuffled and crowded towards the large beautiful room full of flowers, and gold and elegant crimson chairs, trying to get the best view of the small stage. The harpsichord and the flute played thrillingly. Grace beckoned to her niece and bowed warmly to the gentleman with the curled hair beside whom she was standing, inviting him to sit with them: this then was Mr Bounds, the frame-maker's son to whom she owed much. They sat in the third row as the lights were dowsed and the first phenomenon began: *Aurora*. They stared transfixed as the effects of dawn suddenly filled the room: there were sounds, as if of a breeze, and, in a house in Lisle Street in the night, the morning summer sun, it seemed, rose into the sky, golden, higher and higher, moving in front of their eyes; it rose over Greenwich Park where cattle were grazing as clouds drifted across the sky and birdsong commenced. Following these delights (they had been told) there would be noon in Tangiers, sunset in Naples, and a storm with real thunder.

And all the time, as people sighed and gasped in admiration and delight, the *signorina* sat with her niece and Mr Bounds, both of whom looked to be in a seventh heaven – because of the spectacle or because of each other – and no-one would know that the older *signorina* thought: *it is beginning*.

There was nobody to notice that several days later the *signorina*, with her housekeeper's basket, made a visit, with a gentleman, to a house behind a maze of alleys off Covent Garden, in the less salubrious part of London. They turned deeper into the network of dark corners, past open sewers and stinking gutters, and memories. The narrow, dilapidated house she was led to was full of small, busy businesses: a penny newspaper with its small press; a tailor in a back room, children crying everywhere and his wife bent to the window to catch any light as she sewed; clerks bent over wooden desks in offices. The *signorina* followed the art dealer. Skirts were not as wide as once they had been but she still had to hold up her petticoats to climb the narrow, uneven steps, the petticoats caught on splintered wood. At the top James Burke knocked and called out his name, they heard footsteps and then the sound of a bolt being drawn. Three men were waiting for her in a small high attic where from a row of windows the light shone. In a far corner two other men painted at easels – she saw that they were copying something – they never looked up once or seemed to notice or hear. Canvases and boards and paints and paintings lay everywhere and there was the smell of paint and size and varnish mixed with sour milk and old meat and chamberpots and candles: the only new thing in the room seemed to be the big shiny bolt on the door. The dubious Frenchman from the night of the Eidophusikon, Monsieur Laberge, was there, and two Jews, she saw: short men in shirt-sleeves and waistcoats. Something was burning. To her astonishment she saw it was the frame that had been put on the painting of the girl reading the letter for which she had received ten guineas: hers but not hers: darker, older, and now in a blistered gilded frame.

'You will never come here again,' said James Burke with no preamble, 'but this is what you required to see: this is where the boards and canvases are prepared. A great deal of work must go into obtaining the Materials you are to use for of course they must be authenticated as from the time of the Painter, and these men are infinitely skilled in the knowledge of different Schools of Painting, from different times.' She saw that the other men looked at her curiously, presumably their – she thought of a word – *accomplices* were not usually women. She looked again at her own painting in amazement. If she had seen it in an art auction would she have stopped and stared?

She turned to James Burke in confusion. 'What are you doing with this?' she said in a low voice. The girl still held the letter as if her heart broke, yet it was a different painting.

'We will try to sell it at an auction next week as a painting over a hundred years old, by a minor painter of the French school.' He ignored her small gasp. 'We cannot hope for more – you used one of your brother's modern boards to paint on, and that could be ascertained easily enough if we were selling at a high price. And there was still something of you in the face: you see we have shaded it very, very slightly. But we will try to sell it – as a minor work, but an old one nevertheless. If we are successful, and I believe we will be, for these gentlemen have made a good job of what we had, we will go ahead with the plan I have outlined to you.'

She looked at him, back at her painting.

'You must not Varnish the next Picture, lady,' said one of the Jew-men, suddenly, harshly. 'The Varnishing is the skill. We will do the Varnishing when you have finished. We shall send you board, for we understand that is what you are most used to, we have old boards that are very suitable, Rembrandt often used board for Portraits. The Painting you are to do now will be an early Rembrandt, we cannot hope for more than that even', the Jew-man bowed perhaps ironically, perhaps not, '– with your skill, and particularly your skill with light and shadow, we feel an early Rembrandt is our best chance of success. And' – he added – 'we ourselves will lay the ground before we deliver the board to you. Rembrandt's grounds were carefully prepared, and even his ground was warm and –' he searched a moment for a word, 'humane.'

The three men were surprised when the Italian woman suddenly smiled. 'I am glad of our partnership, *Signores*,' she said boldly in her odd Italian accent, 'I will await the materials – and I must have the best brushes.' And then, as she turned to the door, she saw the face of one of the men in the corner who had suddenly heard her voice. It was her brother's old assistant who had found her painting in her brother's studio, all those years ago. He was older and dirtier, but it was him.

'Well, well *Signorina*,' was all he said. Shocked, she did not acknowledge him, moved swiftly to the door, made her way down the narrow staircase.

James Burke came quickly after her. At the bottom doorway they passed a group of sulky young girls being herded into the basement, their high voices complained and a man's voice told them to be silent as the two visitors emerged into the grey alley.

'I will walk back with you, you should not walk alone here,' said James Burke.

—'You should not walk alone here,' he said to me in the dark alleys of Covent Garden, as if he had forgot my story. And as if he had not let me walk to, and from, Meard-street that day, walking alone here.

TWENTY-ONE

Outside, in the privacy of the alley, she turned to him at once.

'But one of those men was once Philip's assistant! He knew me – I have told you of him!'

'It does not matter,' he answered brusquely. 'He could never betray you without betraying himself, we have very much information on him if he were to cause trouble. He and his companion do impressions of Old Masters that would never pass here, but do well enough in the Provinces. He is a Frauder now.' They turned down towards the Strand. 'But Monsieur Laberge and the Jew-men are Experts. They find old wood in old buildings, and that is the best of all: the inside of a cupboard of an old, old house and such like. They will paint several grounds on to the board before you use it, so that it will be seen that the board has been used again and again, as was Rembrandt's habit. The paint cannot look modern, or be a modern colour that was not available a hundred and fifty years ago, so you must not begin painting until we bring you the correct paints – they have many secrets and Recipes for the preparation of the colours in the old way, things I do not know, just as your brother has his secret Recipes, and Sir Joshua Reynolds, and Thomas Gainsborough. You know enough of Painters' secrets, I hope, not to ask too many questions. And when your Painting is finished, Monsieur Laberge and his men will darken the actual paint with smoke, as you saw today, and use resin and their special method of varnishing to age it. To dirty it, frankly, as you see they have done with the girl with the letter.'

'You did not tell me that this is what you wanted it for.'

'You had not agreed, then, to go along with our plan – your Painting was worked on very carefully while you were away as you can see, as an Experiment. For your next Painting, they have acquired some very simple old frames which they have removed from some genuine old Paintings of little worth. One of the Jew-men has also perfected an early Signature, which will be, just, discernible. Then, finally, your next Picture must be Authenticated by Experts and Dealers.'

'By you?'

'Of course, but not only me.'

'I would rather paint on canvas. I like the feel of the canvas.'

'You have not painted enough on canvas because of your – circumstances,' and they both thought of wood and the stretchers that were needed to prepare canvas, things she had so little of in the small sewing-room. 'Many of his Portraits and Self-Portraits were on board. And as I say we can get the real old panels and so it is safer that way.'

'You have said that you would pay me one hundred guineas. Do you hope to sell it for much more than that?'

'The interest in Rembrandt in England at the moment is extraordinary. If your brother had had the courage to go on bidding in Amsterdam he could probably have doubled his money in a few years.' He regarded her carefully for a moment. 'However if the auction of the small Painting goes well I have decided to pay you up to two hundred and fifty for the Fake Rembrandt.' He spoke casually, as they walked, but his companion stopped in the street, a glove dropped.

'*Two hundred and fifty*?' He bent politely for the glove. 'You will pay me *two hundred and fifty guineas*?' She stared at him, tried to take in his words. Her life would be changed *completely*, with one painting; she found that she could hardly breathe. He tried to make her keep walking but she could not move: stood stock-still on the Strand as people hurried past, buying and selling and thinking of money. She could not help herself: she repeated it a third time,

'*Two hundred and fifty guineas*? Are you telling me that you are really hoping to sell a Painting *by me* for double that amount?' For had she not heard, all her life at her brother's dining-table, about the greed of dealers, how they always had so much of the sale price in the commission, how rich they were.

He forced her to walk on, by taking her arm briefly, but she almost shook him off as she tried to comprehend.

'We hope, Grace. We do not know. This will be an intimate Painting of course, not a big epic like *The Adoration of the Kings*. But I am a supreme Optimist in my field: this is London, not Amsterdam, and Rembrandt is the rage here – Royalty themselves look for Rembrandts now – King George owns several of the Paintings and a number of Etchings and Mezzotints.' He looked at her carefully. 'But your Fee is fixed at no higher than that, whatever happens. Half of what we sell it for – up to two hundred and fifty guineas if it sells for five hundred or more. I am an Art Dealer. And you understand there will be other people to pay.'

She tried to pull herself together and then she looked at him very openly for a moment, her curiosity got the better of her; she may have known the answer now but she wanted to hear what he would say. 'James, I have never made money. You know very well two hundred and fifty guineas would change my Life for ever. But you have always made plenty of money and now you are involved in a Scheme that is fraudulent, however you look on it. My Reputation cannot be sullied, after all, because I do not have one. But yours could be ruined for ever if we fail. Why do you need to do this, what is your reason?'

His hooded eyes. For a moment she thought he would not answer and then for a split second the mask slipped: she saw his face, his real face, the face she had once known so well. 'I suddenly find I need more Finance than I at present can obtain,' he said bitterly, and she understood it was so: his wife Lydia was still gambling. And then just as suddenly he pulled himself together, his face was bland. 'I would be a Fool not to try this,' he said, 'knowing your Talent. Rembrandt van Rijn is at last the rage of the Art Market, and there is simply not enough of his work available. You once persuaded your brother to buy a small Rembrandt – he was alarmed because it cost thirty-five guineas. Now it could, possibly, sell for ten times that amount in London. He told me how he lost the painting in Amsterdam to a

Frenchman who added fifty guineas more to the price without even bargaining! Mind my words well, Grace, half the Nobility of Britain yearn for a Rembrandt now: the Duke of Bedford has one, the Earl of Porteus, the Duke of Argyll, the Duke of Bridgewater – and as I said his Majesty has several in Buckingham House. At this moment Rembrandt's prices are now higher than anybody else's. We could make a Fortune with half a dozen paintings, if we wished.'

Her voice was loud in the street as she stopped again.

'One!' she said. 'You said one! I will only do one! I want to do my own work!' Somebody stared at the loud-voiced lady and James Burke touched her arm very slightly; she caught herself, they walked on. They came to the Charing Cross and turned towards Pall Mall. And then he asked a last little question, like a knife.

'Will you really change your Life at last, Grace? Will you really leave your Brother? You have not left before.'

'*I could not leave before!*' and he flinched at the intensity of her answer. '*I could not leave Angelica then. I could not leave the children then,*' and if a shadow passed over the man's face she did not see it. Again she stopped in the street and again she was oblivious of the people. 'You of all people know what I have always wanted and how much it has cost me!' And they both stopped, appalled. They had crossed a forbidden boundary. She recovered first, took a deep, deep breath. 'I want to work as an Artist in my own Studio, with my own Life, before I die.' And she did not look at him now: she looked past him, into the future.

Still she had her basket over her arm as if it was an ordinary day. Into that basket he placed a small pouch of money from his cloak.

'Buy the brushes you would like best,' he said. 'Nothing else. The rest will be delivered to you, even the oil.'

'When will I be paid the full Sum, the – ' still she could hardly say it, and her voice was very low, ' – the two hundred and fifty guineas for my work?'

'When we have sold it.'

'You will *pay me*, if you sell it well,' she still found it hard to visualise this, which is why she repeated it over and over, 'two hundred and fifty guineas.' She put it as a statement, yet it was still a question.

'Yes.'

'Very well.' They began walking again along Pall Mall. 'I am going to paint Hendrickje Stoffels,' she said, 'his Mistress.' And this time it was James Burke who stopped in the street in alarm.

'No! No, you must not do that. That is too dangerous.' A cart rattled past at that moment and spattered mud over them both: so intense was their conversation neither of them moved.

'Why?'

'That is too difficult. You must not paint her, nor his wife Saskia, the other woman he painted often, nor yourself. You must paint a new person, and we will find a name and an explanation for her later.'

'Why?'

And she saw James Burke almost shake himself in the summer morning, so anxious was he to explain. 'You have seen his paintings of Hendrickje. They are infused with light and love as well as shadow. And it is – you know I have studied many paintings for many years – it is his wonderful – his – his luminous Talent but also his *love* that informs the paintings of Hendrickje in particular: we feel it, we feel the – the universality of her face, even though she is one particular person.' He was standing stock-still trying to find his words. 'You always paint truthfully, Grace, and vanity means nothing to you, I know that. You have somehow, over all your years of work, found and grasped the meaning of *chiaroscuro*, the use of light and shade, as he did – we have talked of all this, you and I. You know how to use paint in a way that is grand and gorgeous and affecting and full of shadow and brightness, as he did. You have by some miracle the most wonderful Talent of painting *like* him but, forgive me, you are *not* him. I do not believe you should attempt to paint his Mistress.' And she felt herself blushing at the rebuke. 'His own love shows in the paintings of Hendrickje: that would be too difficult to copy – surely, Amazing Grace, you understand that?'

Amazing Grace: words of their intimacy. He had forgot himself. But it was as if he did not notice, he went on quickly, 'And most importantly after all, we have decided you shall paint an early Rembrandt when he did not yet know Hendrickje; when his particular skill was growing but perhaps not at its full Maturity. But it will work,' he said and she could see an underlying excitement in his face. 'You must paint with *your* love.' He suddenly understood the dangerous ground he was again traversing, quickly ended the conversation. 'You can do it, I know you can do it. I will not come to your house, I must leave you here.'

He turned away and then turned back. 'As long as we have success in selling at Auction the girl with the letter, we will begin. We will sell at Mr Valiant's in Poland-street. He is' – and he searched for the right word – 'he is understanding. And Grace, whatever we sell the girl with the letter for, I will not pay you more at this time, for it took a great deal of expense to age it. It is an Experiment we might say.'

'Very well,' she said. 'But I should like to be there when it is to happen.'

'Very well,' he said, echoing her.

TWENTY-TWO

Art Auctions in London, always popular, had become big social occasions. Dukes had always required Old Masters, now there were other bidders: successful painters themselves, well-known members of the theatre and the opera, rich tradesmen – they out-bid each other, the prices went up. There were advertisements in the newspapers, and a notice in the window of the auction house.

> COLLECTION of Fine PICTURES
> brought from abroad by Mr Thomas Evans
> will be sold by AUCTION from Mr Valiant's
> New-Auction-Room in Poland-street, the corner
> Broad-street, near Golden Square on Saturday the
> 29th of this inst. The pictures may be viewed on
> Wednesday the 26th, and every day after
> till the hour of the SALE which will begin at 11 o'clock
> in the forenoon precisely.

Mr Thomas Evans, a well-known and rich and knowledgeable collector, had acquired over three hundred pictures from his recent travels in Europe: some were of lesser merit, but some were excellent examples from the Dutch and French schools. The jewel in the collection was a Titian which Mr Evans had bought some years ago in Venice and was now selling to finance further collecting activities. The auctioneer, Mr Valiant, knew there were wonders here – but that there would no doubt be an imitation or two among the paintings. Indeed he was never averse to adding one or two doubtful acquisitions of his own; he exhibited miniatures and drawings and bronzes with the paintings: as in all auctions there was treasure and there was dross. Mr James Burke came to see him as the paintings were being prepared along the walls, spoke to him about a recent French acquisition he was anxious to sell quickly, by the little-known French painter Henri Maraux. Mr Valiant admired it.

'I like this. *La Lettre*. Yes . . . I have not heard of the Painter but I like it, I believe I have seen something like it, yes.' Mr Valiant pondered the painting, looked at the dealer. 'Hmmm. I will certainly auction it with the big Collection, most certainly. Hmmm. Unusual. Its worth, I wonder, Mr Burke?'

'Maraux,' said Mr Burke thoughtfully. 'Not a well-known Artist but a friend I believe of the Le Nairn brothers and painting at that time. A pretty thing, I think, I have sold several of his Paintings. Lovely old patina.' And Mr Burke placed his fingers very gently at the bottom of the painting where the gold frame was blistered, so as not to touch the old painting itself. 'Thirty guineas perhaps?' And Mr Valiant nodded sagely, thinking of his percentage. Many of Mr Thomas Evans' paintings from abroad were more in the ten- to fifteen-guinea line, except the French and Dutch examples – and of course the Titian, the pride of the collection: Mr Valiant expected the well-known collectors of London to be bidding for that one, he expected he might make a fortune from the Titian. Who knows what else he might sell?

The auction started at eleven in the morning, sharp. Over a hundred people crammed into the auction rooms. Some – ladies mostly in large hats and high hair – sat on the benches provided, the rest crowded against walls and windows. Nobody in particular noted Signorina Francesco di Vecellio, who stared for some time at the old French painting *La Lettre* on the wall with all the other paintings: the painting that she had worked on in loneliness, and confidence, in her sewing-room in the house in Pall Mall, when she came back from Bedlam. A girl stared out the window, you could not quite see her face but you understood her thoughts in the half-light: it was not a portrait in the true sense of that word but something caught, some sad, private pain – something, that caught the attention.

Mr Valiant started his familiar patter, started with the less valuable paintings which were sold in lots.

'And what am I bid for six Flemish masterpieces of last century? Signed and authenticated as a genuine painting of the Flemish school.'

Paintings went for ten guineas, fifteen: up to twenty.

Several paintings from the Spanish school caused excitement, one reached forty-one guineas: a painting of soldiers playing cards. The auctioning, finally, of the Titian caused an immense wave of excitement in the by now hot and stuffy room. The masterpiece was brought forward, goddesses glowed and shimmered, and people sighed at the beauty. Mr Valiant had been hoping for perhaps four hundred and eighty guineas; the Duchess of Seldon (one of the ladies in the highest wigs of all) took it up to almost six hundred, and the smell of the excitement, and the odour of tightly packed bodies, rose on the air. One of the other ladies fainted and had to be carried out to recover in Golden Square. Her shoe fell off and was lost in the *mêlée* and was last seen somewhere down Broad-street being kicked in the mud and the muck by wild street-children.

The selling of the small French painting *La Lettre* by the artist Henri Maraux for the sum of thirty-one guineas was then something of an anticlimax, naturally – although it was the Duchess of Seldon who made the bid, almost as a small afterthought, after her Titian triumph.

Grace Marshall watched in amazement as the lady with the high hair took both the rather large Titian painting and the small painting of the girl with the letter to her bosom as her own, as if she would trust no other. When she made to enter her coach, which stood waiting, the Duchess had to bend her head completely sideways to get her flower- and fruit-bedecked wig inside. Grace Marshall's last view of her benefactor was of her clutching the paintings to her while her head poked forward at an extremely odd angle inside the coach, because her wig was too tall to allow any other stance. She looked like a mad, exotic bird.

'The first test is over. I will find a way to bring the prepared board,' said James Burke quietly as she passed him on her way out into the grey light in Poland-street. 'Then the paints.'

She nodded. Said nothing. *Thirty-one guineas for a Painting by me, Grace Marshall*.

On her way home, if she had not (still, unbelieving, seeing in her head her own painting and that of Mr Titian clutched together) taken the short route through Broad-street she would not have seen the noisy, illegal cock-fight down the dark alley where she had once long ago in her distress come herself and placed the bets on her life; would not have seen her nephew Claudio, jacketless and sweating in the chilly air, his hair tousled as he shouted in vain for his bird to win. The faces of the crowd of men were wild and concentrated and cruel; hot, dangerous violence in the air, feathers and blood and screams of the fighting cocks, and perhaps in the shadows she would not have seen the other face, if the man had not, at that moment, turned to look towards Broad-street.

For a split second she was certain it was her brother, Tobias.

She was so stunned that she said his name: not as a question but as a statement, *Tobias*. She moved forward instinctively into the *mêlée* but the man disappeared into the shadows; had she been mistaken? She stood stock-still in the noise but nothing happened: nobody came, nobody called *Gracie!* Only the shouting and the birds screeching and the slap of the bets going down.

When Claudio suddenly turned and saw his aunt, a dark blush spread over his face, he looked about him for some sort of escape although even then his eye was drawn back to the ring, but as the shrieks and shouts and feathers filled the air in the alley where blood ran, and guts of birds fell, his aunt turned away quickly and was gone.

She burst into her brother's studio without knocking; a client bowed, just leaving.

'*I saw Tobias*.' She could hardly breathe.

He was handing brushes and paints to an assistant, washing the paint on his hands with a rag. He waved the assistant away. He kept washing methodically.

'It was him. I am sure it was him. But he disappeared.'

'Why do you tell me?'

She looked at him in astonishment. 'It was *Tobias*. Our Brother.'

'And so?'

'But – we are all the Family he has. *He is our Brother!*'

'Tell me, Francesca, what does that actually mean? What is a 'Brother' if you have not seen him for over twenty-five years? What have you in common now?'

And she knew the answer of course: it was the past that was shared. But Philip had changed their past, and created them again.

'I am surprised he is not in Newgate Prison. And I told you long ago you would have to choose, and you have chosen. Do not mention him again.'

At the dinner that afternoon (skies darkening earlier as if to warn that winter was approaching: the painter's sister lit the candles earlier than usual), Claudio and Isabella were present as usual, and Lady Dorothea Bray of course. Claudio looked evasively at his aunt, her face was blank; her nephew excused himself abruptly when dinner was over. There were several painters present and they talked of the Titian, some bitterly.

'Still we wait for our own Acknowledgement,' said one of them angrily. 'When will an English Painter fetch six hundred guineas? Not even Sir Joshua Reynolds himself can sell for a quarter that, nor Thomas Gainsborough neither!'

'Give it time, give it time,' the others murmured filling their glasses, for they could hardly say 'Down with all Foreign artists' when they were drinking the fine wine of their Italian host.

Filipo had finally, requiring to be paid the sum of four hundred guineas for his kindness, taken on a young apprentice as well as his usual assistants: a young painter named Saul Swallow who would learn from the great Master and finally prosper by his association. Already Mr Swallow was painting whole storms and mountains in the background of portraits (such was the fashion just at the moment) and he ate with the family most days as part of his apprenticeship bargain. This particular day the young Mr Saul Swallow leant across the table to the old sister, to Signorina Francesca di Vecellio. 'Have you heard, *Signorina*, that I am keen to write a Biography of your Illustrious Brother? I am taking notes already – a Boswell, you might indeed call me.'

'That will be a very interesting Enterprise, Mr Swallow,' murmured the *signorina*, passing fruit across the table as the meal came towards its end.

'I hope', said Saul Swallow, 'that you will speak to me freely.'

She looked at him, startled. 'About what exactly?'

'About your Childhood. About your Family. About Florence. About – all sorts of things. Your memories. Perhaps the day when you realised your Brother's great Talent.'

Francesca looked across the table at her brother. 'I do remember the day,' she said. 'I remember it very well, today especially,' *for today I sold a Painting by me for thirty-one guineas.*

'You remember the Actual Day,' cried Mr Swallow.

Suddenly, and most unusually, the whole table turned to the quiet sister in her grey gown, including her brother Filipo with an infinitesimal warning look in his eyes. And then there was a tiny silence at the dining-table in the house in Pall Mall. And then the sister spoke. 'He used my Chalks,' said Francesca di Vecellio.

'*Your* Chalks, *Signorina*?' The apprentice's voice was puzzled. She was, after all, only the housekeeper.

And into the silence the sister spoke. 'My brother will tell you that I was a great failure at Drawing, although I did try!' she said, smiling. 'Our brother Tobias' (she saw his look but took no notice) 'would find Colours for me around the city. And indeed the Chalks were given to me also, for my Ninth Birthday, but our Parents were exasperated with my efforts, it was not I who had the Talent!' *and what would you all say if I told you that today I sold a Painting for thirty-one guineas?* And she smiled again and said, 'And so, Mr Swallow – that very day of my Ninth Birthday as I laboured so unsuccessfully, my brother simply took up the Chalks and drew the faces of our Family as if he was born to it!' And the guests around the table cheered the story, and Lady Dorothea Bray's laugh tinkled, and everybody turned to Filipo di Vecellio in admiration and the two thoughts hammered over and over in his sister's head, *I have sold a painting for thirty-one guineas. But was that Tobias?*

'But – I did not know you had a Brother, *Signore*,' said Mr Swallow from his end of the table, puzzled, holding his notebook.

'She speaks of long ago,' said Filipo di Vecellio, pouring more wine. 'The rest of our Family are dead.'

TWENTY-THREE

And now the type of guests at the afternoon dinner-table changed, for Lady Dorothea Bray had more hand in the invitations: other ladies about town, and men of more noble birth than their host, who were pleased to while away the afternoon with his food and his fine wine, pleased too to associate with what they thought of as the rather raffish company of artists and writers.

The conversations became more spiced: louder; different kinds of stories; royalty, dubious exploits; one young man could be heard saying it was common knowledge that Queen Charlotte had a pet zebra, and wondered to what use it was exactly put, he swore he had seen it that very afternoon as he had been making his way to his host's house. Mr Hartley Pond, revelling in this new sophisticated company, now often joined in even if the stories were not about Art at all, took great delight in reciting one afternoon a story his father had told him: of noble young blades, who had had a good dinner, roving about the *piazza* in Covent Garden until they came upon a particularly unattractive older woman whom they proceeded to bundle into an empty wooden barrel which they then, singing noisily, rolled along the streets – this activity becoming one of their favourite modes of entertainment. One of Lady Dorothea's friends hooted with laughter and suggested they all go and try such sport. The afternoons became very much louder and lasted very much longer, and perhaps Miss Ann Ffoulks was not seen quite so much as previously.

Euphemia the maid observed these changes with a blank face. Euphemia missed the old days, was sorry that Mr Burke came now so seldom to the house in Pall Mall: she had always had an eye for the handsome art dealer, and was not entirely certain that her mistress Signorina Francesca had not also enjoyed his company in earlier years. (Just once Euphemia had been most surprised to see him leave the *signorina*'s room, as dawn broke over London.) But Euphemia kept her thoughts about this event, and other things, to herself.

One morning Mr Burke did call: Euphemia opened the big front door welcomingly but Mr Burke only smiled at her and asked that she be sure that Signorina Francesca di Vecellio received a parcel. Euphemia (who knew very well how the *signorina* had painted alone in her room over many, many years) thought Mr Burke's parcel looked very like a board, for painting, but as usual Euphemia said nothing as she smiled, made a small curtsey, and discreetly took the parcel upstairs.

The Artist's sister left the house every day with her basket over her arm as she had always done: she visited the fishmongers and the costermongers and the butcher-man and chose the day's food, and if she was seen at a Colourman's premises it was of course assumed that she was buying materials for her brother. Under the bread she hid camel-hair brushes and, best of all, hog-hair brushes. She bought charcoal and pencils, and paper to sketch her ideas on. Each day these things were secreted calmly in her sewing-room and then she went about her business of preparing for guests, planning with the cook, going to the Strand with Isabella for another gown.

One wet grey morning she received a message to go at once to a certain part of St James's Park, by Rosamund's Pond. Respectable ladies did not walk by the pond; sometimes despairing bodies were found in the pond (and she remembered that was where she had last seen Poppy). But who would notice a respectable older lady with her cloak and her basket?

Who stopped there for a moment and seemed to meet briefly with a Jew in a cloak, or perhaps not, it was raining and hard to see.

They took shelter under a tree; rain dripped through branches but neither of them seemed to notice. He had brought her a transparent glaze and many small pudding-like parcels of paint, quite different from the ones in the colour shops. 'Begin all with dull, warm Colours, even though the prepared board itself is dark, as you will have seen. Rembrandt's greatness – part of his greatness – was his understanding of the effects of different Colours upon another.' He showed her pouches of greys and blacks, and light and dark browns, hard to see clearly in the dim light as rain fell. 'That was often how they began at that time. Then you can apply other Colour, but the dark will keep the basic tone as we need it to be. The glaze will allow you to find deeper and lighter shadows if you wish.'

'Where have you obtained these?' She held the pouches in her hand, felt the strange rubbery encasing.

He looked at her unwillingly. 'We obtain them direct from the Colour-makers across the river in Southwark, the Dye-men. They make them for us, from our own Recipes.' He looked at the rain: he was obviously not going to say more.

'I do beg your pardon,' she said demurely.

'I am sure your Brother has his own secret Recipes too, *Signorina*.'

He handed her a glass bottle. 'This Oil is especially prepared to mix with the Paint, it is something very like that which was used in earlier times. And I have given you old copper green and vegetable pigments, not the new, brighter yellows. Time is not kind to many Colours.' She understood then how much she still did not know: understood this was a lesson from a Master, there in the rain near the pond, in St James's Park.

'Thank you,' she said humbly, carefully placing the paints and the glaze and the oil in her basket under bread and oranges. He still stood there as the rain fell, seemed not to mind getting so wet.

'Do you know what the late and most admirable Mr Hogarth said of Time?' he asked her suddenly. 'He called Time a Vandal – *a Vandal that disunites, untunes, blackens, and by degrees destroys.*'

The woman in the park seemed startled. 'Was he speaking of Paint?' she said. 'Or Life?'

The Jew looked at her sharply and did not answer. She saw his face was full of many things, and pain, and wondered what his life had been. *I would like to paint that face*, she thought.

'Thank you,' she said again. She made to turn away, turned back. 'I am sorry – I do not know your name.'

'No harm there,' he said briefly, and was gone across the grey park without further communication of any kind.

She walked quickly towards Pall Mall in the rain with her cloak about her, and her covered basket: she was carrying such precious things in her basket, they must not get wet, they must be safe in her sewing-room: she did not see him.

'Hello, Gracie,' he said.

He was a dark, middle-aged man and he looked ill and he was wet with rain.

'Come under a tree, Tobias,' she said, her Italian accent quite gone, in shock, from her.

At first they did not speak: Tobias kept smiling nervously, his sister stared at the man she had seen at the cock-fighting. He was still thin and dark, he had his hair tied back like the sailors, but he looked ragged and unkempt and although he was dark, as she was, he looked somehow pale and (as he kept smiling) she saw that he had lost some of his front teeth.

There was a bench beneath the big tree, it was wet with the rain but half-sheltered: in some sort of silent consent they sat down.

'Did you become a Pirate?' she said at last. And he laughed, still nervous.

'Sort of,' he answered and his eyes flicked away. And then he said, 'Do you still paint pictures, Gracie?'

And she could not help but half-laugh also: indicated the paint and the oil under the bread and oranges in her basket that lay between them now on the bench. 'Yes,' she said. 'Philip is the Famous Painter, but I still paint my Pictures.'

'Philip? Oh.' He sounded almost disappointed. 'You were the Painter, Gracie!' And her heart seemed to contract with this acknowledgment of the past.

From some pocket about him he felt for something: finally drew out a small, battered blue stone. 'I got this for you a long time ago,' he said almost shyly, 'in case I ever saw you. I've been carrying it about for years. I got it in Arabia, they said it could be ground to make the most famous Blue Colour of all. Well, that's what they said,' he added uncertainly as she held the blue stone in her hands. 'It was a long time ago.'

She rubbed hard at the old, rough stone for a moment, scratched it with her nail, and finally a thin blue mark appeared on her fingers. It was *lapis lazuli*, the most beautiful, the most expensive blue in all the world. She sat staring at the blueness where she had rubbed it, and the beauty.

'And where is the Gold? You said you would bring me Gold!' She said it lightly, meaning to make a joke: he had promised her colours and gold as he sailed away. But it did not come out right, there in the rain under the tree, for her voice broke and she suddenly rubbed quickly at her face.

'I don't have any Gold, Gracie. I haven't got anything now.' And she at once remembered Philip's old words, *You would have to choose. Between me and Tobias.*

Rain dropped through the trees, on to their hair.

She did not know if she wanted to know the answer to her next question. 'How did you find me?'

'I got your Letter once, I went to where they said you worked in Bristol – funny old lady she was, Gracie – but that was years ago. I got robbed once and your Letter was gone. But I always looked for you, when I came to London, but I was always away soon again and I never saw you.' He paused. 'Now I've just come back to London again. This is strange, Gracie, isn't it? Talking, I mean, after all the years.' And it seemed to her that perhaps he rubbed his own face also. 'When I saw you pass at the cock-fighting I followed you of course, I've been watching the house.' She felt odd, uneasy, past and present colliding: Tobias hiding under the long tablecloth, appearing in dim corners; she worried about her precious parcels of paint and the oils, which should be safely in her sewing-room not under a tree in the rain in St James's Park. 'I've seen Philip.' He flicked her his odd, shifty look. 'He's a rich man, Philip, I can tell. He's done well for himself then, if he's a Painter.'

'He will not – help you, Tobias. You must not expect it. He pretends he has no other Family, he has made himself into – someone else.' Still the blue on her hand, wet with rain now, staining her fingers. 'Are you still a Sailor?'

He made a shuffling, embarrassed movement, knocked her basket with its precious paints and oils – she gasped, he moved very quickly to pick everything up, put the paints back carefully, covered them carefully, a rolling orange retrieved: she held her blue stone. 'Not much sailing now,' he said, in answer to her question, 'unless they're desperate. The ships go without me now Gracie, they like young men.' And she wondered if also they liked honest men, and the rain fell upon them.

'I'm on the run,' he said finally.

'Who from?'

'A lot of people. I've only just got to London. It's bigger here, and safer.' She tried to take it in: *on the run*, what did that mean?

'Do you know Claudio?' He looked blank. 'The boy in the cockpit.'

'Oh,' and his face quite lit up, 'the boy who looks like me? I'd just come there for the first time. I saw him see you, it felt – strange, to see his face. He looks like me, doesn't he, Gracie – and he has plenty of money, I see. Is he your son or Philip's son?'

'He is Philip's son – and you must not encourage him to gamble, Tobias, for Pity's sake, he has lost a lot of my brother's money.'

'I see him most days now. Now that I know him. But I haven't let him see me, till I found – how things are.' He stared at Grace and swallowed. 'He looks like me.' He said it again wonderingly, almost wistfully. She could not bear it. This was her brother but he was from another world, a world that was gone, *Time is a Vandal* Mr Hogarth had said. She stood quickly from the bench; he stood reluctantly.

'Wouldn't the boy like – a Relation? We didn't have Relations did we? But – I got tales to tell, Gracie,' and in her head she saw Claudio, listening in fascination to his Uncle Tobias and running away to sea.

'Oh God, you must keep away from him, Tobias. Claudio thinks – he does not know our past, he knows nothing at all about us.' She saw again the wistful face, something twisted in her heart. 'Where do you live?' She could not bear this, she could not bear what she might hear.

'Here and there,' he said, jauntily, as if it did not matter. 'I'll see you around then, Gracie, you can find me round the cock-fighting,' and she saw that he cast a quick look at the bread. She knew she had let him down; she knew he had hoped for help. Still she held the blue stone.

'Oh Tobias!' She suddenly grabbed both his arms. 'Tobias, I am so sorry but I cannot – I cannot help you, not yet – I do not have anything of my own, not yet – everything is too difficult and too complicated, maybe one day I'll be able to help you but – not yet. I am – I am – so sorry.' And she thrust the bread into his arms, and the oranges, and she was gone across the Park in the rain with her precious basket, she was almost running, *I did not even thank him, he kept the stone for me all the years*, she clutched it in her hand; and worse thoughts battered at her: *you could have given him the guineas from the sale of your Picture, he is your brother*, rain on her face.

When she had unpacked her basket in her room, the old colours from the Jew-man and the old oils safe at last in the bottom of the mahogany wardrobe, she found that the pouch of money, of Philip's money that she carried with her to buy the food, was gone.

'I was robbed in the *piazza*,' she told her brother and if Mr Minnow, his dealer, had not been there Philip would have been even more angry at her carelessness but they both saw her white, shocked face.

The old blue stone lay beside her easel.

I cannot think of Tobias now.

But she half-laughed. At least he had one pound, fourteen shillings and ninepence, the exact amount in Philip's purse.

Nevertheless that night a woman almost hidden in a dark cloak might have been seen on the peripheries of a noisy cock-fight in Broad-street, shadowed and still, watching as the feathers and the blood flew and the men shouted: in the recesses of her cloak a pouch held five guineas, half her money, looking for a dark man, a sailor; she waited for a long time inside the savage shouting, her cloak about her face, but he was not there, he did not come.

TWENTY-FOUR

She began the painting.

Every single night she worked. Candles surrounded her easel, the lights flickered, shadows danced across the blank, dark, warm board so carefully prepared for her by experts in attic rooms down dark alleys; dark, glowing, velvet and dancing dreams haunted her night and day, *I can see it, almost, the light and the dark, I can feel it*. She did not, yet, touch the prepared board, she was trying to find the picture first on paper, then on other boards. But at last, at last: she picked up her charcoal to begin properly, to at least sketch in the picture she saw in her mind. She would start, and then rub out with her fingers and start again. There was a figure of a girl. She wore a beautiful gown. There was a chair and a window. After many days she at last picked up her new, prized hog-hair brush to begin actual painting. She would start, her head full of ideas, and she would stop. She kept in mind that at first she must paint in the darker, warmer colours though she longed to begin more brightly: to begin with life. When at last she felt brighter colour could be used in parts of the painting, she many times mixed her colours and her oils and then, dissatisfied with the exact colour she had made, mixed again.

And sometimes as she painted she would allow her dream

again, *I will, I will before I die become a real, true Painter, like the other Painters.* The dream sustained her, night after night after night: she saw again that bright light room and an easel and a palette, and paintings on the walls.

And sometimes a thin, hurrying ghost in the night flitted down the staircase. A small light, a creaking door: she was in her brother's studio, staring at the Rembrandt painting: the girl, the light, the way the sleeve fell, breathing it into her before she began her own work. One night the old sad parrot Roberto, living out his lonely nights in his cage in the old workroom of Angelica, shrieked out and the ghost stood stock-still, seemed to disappear into the shadows.

A girl appeared on the board. Almost she looked out at the world – not quite.

Lady Dorothea Bray, Filipo di Vecellio's new friend, knew nothing of Mr Bounds, the frame-maker's son. She made many airy promises to Isabella, spoke of Royalty, said that Isabella should be seen in more illustrious society. Her father agreed, but decreed that her aunt was also required, as chaperone. Isabella became swept up in new gowns and hair; her aunt wondered if Mr Bounds was quite forgot. Sometimes it was midnight, sometimes it was two in the morning, before the chaperone was free: it was like torture to her to sit through *soirees* and salons and opera and theatre that she had sat through twenty years before and Isabella giggling behind her fan at other young people across the theatre and the knowing face of Lady Dorothea Bray and no Mr Garrick crying to the heavens with his beautiful voice.

One night she was more tired, and more reckless: she took the small Rembrandt painting from the wall of her brother's studio. With the painting in one hand and a small candle in the other she disappeared up the staircases and into shadows. *Paint with love*, James Burke had said and it seemed she could not. Perhaps she should try to paint one of Rembrandt's actual faces after all: she was not to paint herself, which meant she was not to paint the imaginary Mary-Ann whom she had known since she was a milliner's apprentice. She stared at Rembrandt's woman: whoever she might be, this was not Hendrickje. She could *not* paint the right face: the night was almost morning and she had not found what she wanted. She fell briefly asleep, a candle singed part of her gown: it was the smell of burning material that woke her before she burned herself, the Rembrandt portrait, and the house in Pall Mall to the ground. She got such a fright that night that, as the first dawn light rose over St James's Park, she crept down the creaking stairs, returned the portrait, and then told the servants that she was ill: all day she lay in her bed-room, the door of the sewing-room tightly closed and colours and shadows raced about her head unchecked, wild and mad and nothing like Rembrandt at all.

But then, like all the other times, she hauled herself up somehow, told herself again: *just let me do this: just this, this one chance, this one Magnificence* . . . She saw again the easel in the big, light room, a hat-stand in the corner.

Weeks passed. Winter set in, cold and hard, and her studio was freezing and she had to wrap herself in many shawls, and then had to throw them off as they restricted her movement with her brushes. Mr James Burke sent a message, asking how she was progressing. She did not reply. More and more she mixed the pigments and the special oil and then used her own thumb and fingers to find the texture she wanted, rubbing and rubbing afterwards to get the paint off her hands so that they became red and raw. Parts of a painting came together. The girl was there, sitting in a small chair, beside a table. She wore a beautiful intricate embroidered gown, the sleeve fell so gracefully where the arm reached out towards a book. The book was discarded on the table. Light from the window caught the side of the girl's face in a way that Grace knew was right. It was right, but it was not finished. She filled with paint the shadows, the rich sumptuous gown, the particular way the head bent towards the book, the way light and shade caught the body and the head. But she could not paint the expression.

She had never had a real model, except for herself. She needed a real face in front of her. She had never sat at the easel and looked up and painted another person: she had never had another person there right in front of her and the old words from the dinner-table taunted her, *Women must do Countryside views if they must paint, for it is not becoming for Women to paint Portraits, it is not seemly that a Woman should stare so openly at a person in that way*.

Rembrandt had painted with love, James had told her. And the old *marquis* in Amsterdam had said it also. *'But who do I love?'* she said to herself over and over.

And understood again what she had lost, to gain what she had gained.

Night after night she battled with paint and with oil and with an image in her head, and with weariness: the more tired she got the more bizarre the mind-pictures became and the colours bright and wrong as the days declined and winter snapped angrily at the heels of the devious, bustling city.

Even her brother was concerned. 'Francesca, *cara*, you look so tired, are you unwell?' Unusually, he spoke across a crowded dinner-table, everybody drinking and eating. 'Should we get more servants? You need only say,' and he smiled at her, his charming smile.

'Surely you know your Sister never sleeps,' said Thomas Gainsborough, sprawled, his chair balanced backwards and a glass in his hand.

'What do you mean?' said Filipo startled, his glass halfway to his mouth.

'I see her light burning.'

If Francesca di Vecellio could have turned paler she would have done so. 'Are you often up late, Mr Gainsborough?' she said quickly.

'I like to paint by candlelight, Signorina Francesca,' he said. 'Our Portraits are so often viewed in artificial light on the walls of the houses of our Sitters – so it seems to me I must paint for them to be viewed that way.'

Francesca was so amazed that she said at once, eagerly, too quickly, 'Yes, yes of course, you are right, yes, do you always paint by candlelight? – Is that part of your – that is – your Style?'

He laughed. 'I have to confess that sometimes I close my shutters and draw my curtains even during the day! Not always – not my Landscapes – the painting that I enjoy most, not them. But Portraits, yes, I feel they should be painted in artificial light.' And the conversation among the painters turned to colour, and oil, and the *signorina*'s night lights were forgotten.

Perhaps.

Mr Gainsborough lingered as the others began their walk down Pall Mall to a new gambling club in St James's.

'Signorina Francesca?' She turned back to the doorway. 'Signorina Francesca, do you yourself paint by any chance?'

She looked at him. 'Why do you ask that?'

'Because, *Signorina*, I have observed that your hands and your gown more and more these days often have paint upon them.'

For a moment they stood in the dark hallway in silence, *if only I could talk to him*, then she moved to open the front door for him and answered at last. 'I am just an *amateur* of course, Mr Gainsborough. Flowers.' Voices called along Pall Mall and even just inside the open door their breath was frosty in the night as he regarded her. Francesca knew how heavily he had been drinking, how heavily he always drank: his eyes twinkled and he swayed slightly. She had no idea what he was thinking. And then he said casually, 'At Mr Newman's in Gerrard Street there is a new Remover. I find it very satisfactory. Thank you, Signorina Francesca, as always, for your Hospitality. I must leave you now, for tonight I again provide Thunder for the Eidophusikon.' In the dusk he looked up at the sky: a storm was obviously brewing, and he laughed. 'Our Thunder, in my opinion, is much better than the real thing!' And Thomas Gainsborough, now the most sought-after Portrait Painter in London, bowed and smiled and wove off down Pall Mall at dusk as the coaches with their flickering lights noisily rattled and twinkled and threw filthy mud and overflowing effluent into the air, and just then a warning streak of lightning flashed across the sky.

Francesca di Vecellio went slowly back to the empty dining-room. For the first time in her life she picked up the unfinished decanter of wine and drank straight from it, gulped the liquid down as Artists, they say, have always done, as if it would help.

Next morning she looked away from a pale face in the mirror in despair. She went to Mr Newman in Gerrard Street to obtain the new paint remover, she walked with her basket to the fishmonger by the Strand, through huge puddles of muddy, mushy rain left by the storm. Her shoulders, should anyone have noticed, were hunched under her winter cloak in cold and weariness and defeat: she could not do it: it was *ridiculous*, a ridiculous dream: she would live forever in Pall Mall – housekeeper to the Artist. Up in the *piazza* at Covent Garden sellers called their wares: CABBAGES!

CAULIFLOWERS! DRINK MY FRESH MILK! But the milk was weakened with bad water, all the regular shoppers knew.

As she was buying cheese, trying not to slip in the mud, she heard a girl's voice.

'May I have milk, Father?'

She turned and saw a rotund gentleman who looked slightly familiar to her, there with his daughter: they had stopped at the milkmaid, the father was searching his waistcoat for coins and the girl stared at the milkmaid, fascinated by the way she carried her pitchers of milk upon her head. Without thinking Francesca di Vecellio called out quickly in her Italian accent, 'A moment *Signore*!' and the rotund gentleman turned to her, startled. She was startled too, for he was a writer who had been a guest once at dinner, at the house in Pall Mall.

'Signorina di Vecellio! Good morning.'

'*Scusi, Signore*. The milk. It is not safe to drink the milk here.'

The milkmaid let out such a torrent of abuse that a crowd immediately gathered. She screamed at Francesca di Vecellio, spat at her, tried to attack her as she held her milk on her head; the gentleman and his daughter hurried the older woman away, slipping through the muddy snow and the shit and the slurry.

'I am so sorry,' said Francesca several times, trying to catch her breath. 'We know not to buy her milk in the *piazza*, for it is dangerous to drink. It is mixed with bad water, it will make you ill.'

'Why was the Milkmaid screaming?' asked the young girl, more puzzled than scared.

'I am taking away her living,' said Francesca. And without thinking she added, 'I would scream too if someone did that to me,' and like a flash of lightning, just then, she saw herself screaming in the private room in Bedlam and she looked about her quite wildly in the London winter street and saw the face of the daughter.

'*God!*' she said.

The gentleman and his daughter looked shocked. The housekeeper's basket was heavy on her arm, fish and mutton and a huge cauliflower and eggs and big loaves of bread with the paint remover right at the bottom. The rotund gentleman (she could not remember his name) took charge of the situation.

'Shall we sit for a moment in the Church of St Paul?' he said kindly, taking the basket, indicating the church at the side of Covent Garden.

'Thank you,' said Francesca. 'Thank you.'

They sat at the back of the high-windowed church as black-gowned clerics glided by and Francesca tried to re-collect herself. She was so exhausted from lack of sleep that all had an air of unreality, yet she stared at the girl nevertheless. The gentleman reminded her they had met before, introduced himself in a quiet voice fit for a place of worship: Thomas Towers, writer. She nodded, remembering now, a jovial visitor who had worn a number of rather flamboyant waistcoats all at once in an odd manner, and arrived with Dr Burney. Now he introduced his daughter: Eliza Towers. She lived in Surrey but was visiting her father in London. Francesca could not stop looking at Eliza's face. It was not exactly beautiful, but it was absolutely right. She felt wild and torn and out of control, *I have to use this face*. She could not be open but she was too tired to be closed. She made a gigantic effort to pull her sanity about her.

'Mr Towers,' she said, and she smiled at Eliza, 'it is my brother as you know who is the Painter. But I – that is – sometimes, quietly, I – I try my hand – as an *amateur* you understand, I would not bother my brother with my fancies for all the world – I would never tell him of it,' she added helplessly, she felt herself moving into deeper and deeper water, 'what I am trying to say is' – she took a deep breath – 'is that if you and Eliza would allow me, I would be so grateful to draw her but I would not tell my brother what I was doing.' It made – she knew – both of them seem so small, her brother and herself. At the front of the church the black-clad men lit candles.

Thomas Towers looked at her shrewdly, and then at his daughter. 'Would you like to be drawn, Eliza?' They saw that she was pleased, she nodded her head; she was perhaps fifteen.

'If you are to draw her you must do it soon,' said Thomas Towers, 'for Eliza is to return to Surrey at the end of the week. I have rooms in Frith Street, number six, perhaps – if your Brother would allow it' – he saw her face – 'no, no I mean –'

'– I walk these streets every morning, Mr Towers.'

'Of course. I mean to say perhaps you could – join us there for coffee this time tomorrow – if you like coffee, *Signorina*, I know it is not to everyone's taste.'

Francesca laughed: he saw how the laughter lit up her tired, drawn face, saw her dark, dark eyes. 'I grew up in Bristol,' she said, 'where the trade ships came sailing home with—' and then she realised what she had said and clamped her hand over her mouth in horror. 'That is – *scusi* – we were briefly in Bristol once when I was a girl and I – because of the ships and the trade, you understand – I got a taste for coffee very early in my life,' and she got up quickly, nearly colliding with a candle-snuffer.

To Thomas Towers' credit he said nothing more.

'Tomorrow then,' said Francesca quickly. 'I will do the preparatory Drawings tomorrow,' and she was gone from the church and Thomas Towers stared after her.

'I should like to be a Picture, Father,' said Eliza Towers.

Again she was awake most of the night, staring at the unfinished painting, rubbing colours in, scraping them off, perhaps, if she could paint that grave young face . . . *but I am so tired* . . . she was so tired she hardly knew what she was saying to people any more – never before had she betrayed their Bristol origins by mistake, *if I can just get the face*, the thought went round and round in her head all night: she saw what she wanted to do, the face looking away from the book, with the shadows, and light coming from the small window.

In the morning, in the mirror, huge eyes stared at her out of a drawn face. She prepared herself to go to Frith Street, charcoal and paper in her basket; then she heard an unfamiliar sound outside her door and then an urgent knock. Swiftly she picked up her basket and closed tight the inner door to her sewing-room. When she opened the door out into the passageway her nephew Claudio stood there, dishevelled and wild, obviously he had not been to bed.

'Claudio. Whatever has happened?' Claudio had never come to her room since he was a small child, never.

'I have to talk to you.'

'Let us go downstairs.'

'No, I have to talk to you privately – now!'

Reluctantly she nodded. 'Very well. Come in.' He almost pushed past her. 'Whatever is the matter, Claudio?'

'I have to have money.'

'You know I have no money. You must ask your Father.'

'I cannot.' He threw himself upon her small sofa. Across the sofa was her quilt of many colours that his mother had found comfort in; the painting of Angelica flashed into her mind as she looked down at the boy. 'I promised Father I would leave the cock-fighting, you were there, you heard me say it. When we were returning to England. He thinks I am painting. Everyday he thinks I am painting.'

'I thought you were painting.'

'I *hate* painting!' The words spat out with extraordinary vehemence, startling her. She thought of him, playing a part then, at the dinner-table, telling his father's colleagues about Michelangelo.

'Where does he think you are painting?'

A shamed voice emerged from the couch. 'He rented me a Studio of my own.'

She put down the basket. '*A Studio of your own*? Where?'

'In St Martin's Lane. Like he used to do, he wants me to somehow re-live his time – I had money to buy my Supplies by myself, like he used to do. But *Zia Francesca*, I do not want to be a Painter! I do not have the skills.' She stared at him. Claudio had not called her *Zia Francesca* for years; she saw his thin dark young face, she saw her brother Tobias who had lost the teeth.

'You have some skills, Claudio – you have lived with Painting all your life, you know things, you know people.'

'I thought that would be enough, but it is not. I am a man! I am seventeen years old! I want another Life entirely!'

'What other Life?'

'Away from London.' He looked at her miserably, looking nothing at all like a man, only a boy. 'They say they will kill me if I do not find the money.'

'Who says that?'

'The street-men. The cock-fighting men I owe the money to.'

She looked at him in horror. 'Of course they will not kill you.'

'Who will stop them?'

Still she stared at him. 'What men?' *No, this could not be Tobias.* 'You are speaking foolishly, Claudio.'

'Who will stop them?' he said again and his voice was louder and more frightened. 'The King's army? The old drunk watchmen in their boxes? People are killed in London every night, you know that. They *say* they will kill me. You must talk to Father for me.'

Her head ached and she felt dizzy with tiredness. She must go downstairs to the servants, she must go to Frith Street, she must paint the girl who would be leaving.

'You will have to talk to your Father yourself, Claudio.'

'But I promised him before. He will only say that I promised him, if he cleared my former debts, to work only at my Studies and my Painting. But I do not want to be a Painter. Please, you have to help me.' He was crying: her seventeen-year-old nephew crying.

'What do you want to do if you do not want to be a Painter?'

'At the School they sent me to there was a farm nearby. When I could not come home because Mamma and father were so busy I went to the farm and helped the Farmer. I want to go back there but he does not hear me when I try to tell him. Please, please *Zia Francesca*, you must help me.' And to her consternation he leapt up from the sofa and threw both his arms around her, just as he used to when he was a child. And because she was so tired, and because he was now bigger than she, she fell, and he with her, to the floor.

To her nephew's immense surprise his aunt pulled herself up from almost underneath him, and from where she sat on the floor she began to laugh helplessly.

'Why are you laughing? You cannot laugh! Why are you laughing!' Still the tears started in his eyes.

'Claudio, I am an old lady! You cannot throw me hither and thither!' Slowly she got up from the floor, dusting at her gown. 'I am laughing at the irony of you wanting to be a Farmer when your father has tried so hard to give you the opportunities to do something so completely different and you gamble his help away. You remind me of some people I used to know.'

'What people?'

'Oh – some people – they were called the Wiltshire Marshalls – no,' as he seemed about to question her further, 'it is nothing. I will lend you two guineas to pay your Debts, you will then talk to your Father, tell him what you have told me, and require the money from him to re-pay me – but do not say it was I who lent it to you. Now I must go downstairs, the servants will be waiting for their instructions for the day.'

'No!' He was shouting at her as she fumbled for the money James Burke had given her for the girl with the letter at the back of the mahogany drawer, not wishing him to see. 'It is not a matter of two guineas. I owe them nearly five hundred.'

She closed the drawer quickly, turned; he heard her shocked voice. 'Five hundred guineas? But Claudio, you *cannot possibly* owe that much – he paid your debts not long ago. People, families –' She stared at her nephew. 'People in London live for years and years on that amount of money,' she said slowly.

'Father does not.'

She had to go to Frith Street, she could not wait any longer. 'Claudio, I cannot talk to your Father now, and anyway you know how early he begins in his Studio and he does not like to be interrupted. I will talk to him later.'

'He will be drinking later! There will be crowds of people here later as there always are! Then he will go to his Club later, as he always does. It will be too late later. What am I to do till then – they will kill me!'

'They will not kill you.' But how did she know if what she said was true. 'It will be best if you stay indoors today, and' – looking at him – 'sleep.'

'I will kill myself!'

But she saw his weak, shifty face, and she knew he would not. *I must, I must go to Frith Street.* 'I will see you at dinner, at three o'clock, and then before your Father goes out I will tell him you need to speak to him.' And his aunt hurriedly, distractedly, picked up her cloak and her basket and literally pushed Claudio out of the door of her room and closed it firmly. 'We will talk to him this afternoon,' and then she almost ran, down and down the long winding staircase, past the beautiful picture of his mother.

TWENTY-FIVE

At the address in Frith Street, Mr Thomas Towers and his daughter were already seated at coffee beside a fire. The large room was covered, every wall space, every table, even the floor, with books, books of all shapes and sizes. Mr Towers wore a cap instead of his wig, the cap brightly-coloured like his waistcoat and several shawls about his shoulders. He looked rather like a wonderful padded bear, a genial face looking out from many layers. Francesca di Vecellio apologised for her late arrival, she had been running, she was dishevelled in a way ladies of her age never were and she thought of her nephew. But Mr Towers seemed not to mind that she had been running, and Eliza was grave and contained and excited all at once, dressed in her best gown in readiness.

'Take off your cloak, put down your basket, drink coffee first,' said Thomas Towers. Reluctantly the visitor sat down, accepted coffee, smiled nervously, looked about the room, all the books, hundreds of books, the clock, several family portraits, more shawls on the chair by the large writing-desk. In the biggest bookcase she saw several titles bearing the name, THOMAS TOWERS. But after a few moments she took out charcoal and paper. She put her weeping nephew out of her mind: *I must*.

'Let me start, Eliza,' she begged.

Eliza sat where she was directed, grave and important. And then the woman with the charcoal gave a tiny sigh, but how were they to know that this was her first real model?

The light was not good in the drawing-room in Frith Street, there were similar tall houses on the other side of the road. Thomas Towers quietly moved several candlesticks nearer to the girl, lit extra candles. Eliza sat gravely, staring at Francesca di Vecellio. 'I have never been a Picture before,' were the only words she said. The fire spat.

Finally the older woman held out a paper to the girl. 'It is not exactly right yet,' she said. 'I must do more.' And she immediately took out more paper.

'Look Papa!' cried the girl. 'It is only black, but – is that me?'

'It is very you,' answered her father, and he felt uneasy suddenly. This was not an *amateur*. He watched Signorina Francesca di Vecellio carefully as she drew again, saw how her eyes went from the girl to her paper, from her paper to the girl. Drays and coaches rattled past outside, horses' hooves on the cobblestones; they heard another milkmaid, BUY MY FRESH MILK; dogs fought just below the window. Inside the room all that could be heard was the breathing and the crackling of the fire and the ticking of the clock and the scratching of the charcoal and then the sound of the paper as the Artist reached for yet another sheet.

'Now please, Eliza, could I ask you to take down a book.'

'A book – what for?'

'I – I would like to draw you holding – but not reading – a book, as if, as if you were thinking of something else.'

Eliza obediently fetched a book – chose one by her father and smiled at him. The large clock ticked loudly, then chimed the hour.

'What books do you write, Mr Towers?' She spoke as she drew, half-listening only.

'I often write books about people's lives. I have studied King Charles II, and I have written something on Mr Handel.'

Francesca di Vecellio nodded, concentrating on her drawing. After a while she said, 'Are you like Mr Boswell, who followed old Dr Johnson round with a notebook?'

He smiled. 'There are various ways of writing of someone,' he said. 'And sometimes one must use one's imagination also. Perhaps it is easier to get a more honest view when people have died – I certainly await Mr Boswell's life of the great Dr Johnson with much interest.'

She bent over her paper. The clock ticked. After a very long time Eliza said very politely, 'Might I move my arm?'

The lady with the charcoal looked up, surprised. 'Of course.' And it was as if she shook herself slightly. She stared for a moment at the last picture she had done. 'Thank you,' she said quietly. And then she straightened up, looked about the room in Frith Street as if she had to remind herself where she was. Thomas Towers, asking her permission first, came and stood behind her: she felt something, a kind of tenseness, emanating from him, from his waistcoat and his cap and his shawls.

It was some time before he spoke. 'But that is extraordinary,' he said.

'Thank you.'

'I do not profess to know your Brother well, having only spent that one dinner at his table, but I imagine he would be very proud.'

'My brother must not know!' There was no way to wrap up the words.

'Let me see!' cried the patient Eliza, moving quickly to stand beside her father. There were six drawings. Two of Eliza facing the painter. One of her reading. Three of her looking away, past her father's book, her hand just touching it.

Eliza did not speak either, for a moment. At last she picked up one of the drawings of herself looking away, and one looking out at the Artist. 'They seem . . .'

'Yes?' The painter's large eyes were watchful.

Eliza struggled to find the words. 'The one of me looking at you, I think it is something that I see in the mirror. I do not stare often,' she added hurriedly, not wanting to seem vain. 'But the one of me almost reading, but looking away instead . . .'

The Artist was still looking up at her. 'Yes?'

'It is – it feels like it is more about what I – that is, because the face is not quite clear it seems to be a picture of the way I am feeling.' She looked at the adults to see if they would think her foolish but the painter was looking at her intently, and then suddenly stood. She did something odd then: kissed the girl's cheek briefly. 'Painting is – it is another Language, that is all. What you have said in words: that is what I drew. That is all.' Quickly she slipped the precious papers into her basket, underneath bread. 'It may be some time before I finish my Picture of you, Eliza, but on my oath I will finish it, and you shall see it one day.'

And she was gone.

There were the usual guests at dinner that day and also several of Lady Dorothea's young men-about-town with a pretty little actress who was a friend of one of them. Saul Swallow the apprentice who was recording Filipo di Vecellio's life cast admiring looks at Isabella (who tossed her head, for she was to embark upon a much more interesting experience than Mr Saul Swallow in a very few hours).

'Where is Claudio?' Signore Filipo di Vecellio always insisted his two children be present at dinner: he saw the conversation around the table as part of their education.

'Isabella,' said her aunt quickly, 'will you please go to Claudio's room and tell him that we are eating.' Isabella left the room rather sulkily, then remembered she had promised her aunt *not* to sulk and caught her eye across the table as she disappeared.

'You could have sent the maid, my dear,' said Lady Dorothea, smiling.

'I know Claudio was particularly anxious to speak with his Father,' she answered, smiling also.

Isabella was soon back. 'He is not there,' she said.

'Perhaps he has got caught up in his painting,' said her father, but he frowned as he passed the wine decanter.

Miss Ffoulks said something, as she often did, about her late relation, Captain James Cook: a memorial was to be erected in his home town of Whitby. 'I do hope it does the dear Captain justice,' said Miss Ffoulks. 'We miss him horribly. Such a terrible end for such a great and brave Adventurer.'

Lady Dorothea Bray suddenly leaned across the table. 'What was your exact relationship to the dear Captain, Miss Ffoulks?' she enquired sharply.

Miss Ffoulks looked taken aback. 'There was – there was some intercourse between his family and mine when we were much younger,' she said. 'I met him several times when I was a young girl; a cousin of mine married a cousin of his Wife, we are therefore – distantly, of course – related.'

'My dear Miss Ffoulks I believe you are getting old and fanciful.' Lady Dorothea laughed her special, tinkling laugh. 'I myself spoke this very week to Captain Cook's own cousin, and I mentioned your connection and do you know, he looked quite blank for he had never heard your name!'

Miss Ffoulks gave a small sound of distress. There was an embarrassing silence at the table. The Signorina Francesca said, 'I am sure Miss Ffoulks knows her own Family stories, Lady Dorothea,' and she looked to her brother to add his support to his old friend. Perhaps Filipo di Vecellio was worried about his son, perhaps he was entranced with the Lady Dorothea: he shrugged and said nothing. In the silence the young actress at the table began to speak of the time she met the late Mr Garrick and how he had praised her; Mr John Palmer leaned and put his hand briefly on Miss Ffoulks' arm.

In a moment or two Miss Ffoulks stood and excused herself from the table; half-heartedly Filipo demurred but Lady Dorothea put her hand upon his and left it there and laughed her tinkling laugh as the actress recounted her story. Signorina Francesca di Vecellio rose from the table and hurried into the hall and as she left Mr Hartley Pond murmured, 'Let us roll her in a barrel down Notting Hill.' Meaning perhaps Miss Ffoulks or perhaps the house-keeper, who could say?

The sound of the door closing on to Pall Mall echoed back into the dining-room.

All through that particularly distressing dinner, as her head spun and her legs ached from weariness, the housekeeper promised her-self she would soon be alone: she needed so much to be alone to think about the face she had drawn. The guests enjoyed the fish and the rabbit and the roast beef and the fruit pies and the many bottles of wine: the unpleasant moment with Miss Ffoulks was for-gotten, they all knew she would be back of course, Miss Ffoulks was always there. Today the conversation went on and on, regard-ing the amorous activities of the naughty Prince of Wales. Francesca listened with only part of her mind: she must begin now, tonight, she must capture the grave face of the girl, the girl Eliza as she sat so still in Frith Street with her father's book: she was ready now: she must do it tonight while everything was clear in her memory. No matter that she was tired, there would be time to be tired when she had finished the painting. The afternoon drew down, she lit the candles, as usual, pulled the heavy curtains and drew the shutters, to keep the grey winter afternoon outside so that the dining-room was contained to itself. She again drank more wine than usual, but who would notice that? The conversation finally wended out into the large hallway as everybody considered the evening ahead: Lady Dorothea swept to her carriage to prepare for the opera; the young actress who once met the dead Mr Garrick was already at the door, escorted by two of the young men, vying for her attention as they left.

Isabella was to be with society tonight; she was to go to the opera in a special box with Lady Dorothea Bray and perhaps even a member of the Royal family. Lady Dorothea and her sister would come for Isabella in their carriage, all was arranged, and Isabella almost bounced out of the room as she called the maid and ran upstairs to put on her best gown, asking imperiously for her aunt to follow also.

'You are going to the Opera, Francesca?' asked her brother, as he too stood from the table.

'No, Filipo, that is not necessary.'

'But who is to chaperone Isabella? You must go surely?'

'Lady Dorothea Bray is Chaperone enough I believe,' and she smiled, for who more suitable to chaperone his own daughter than his own new friend? But she saw he was in some way uneasy.

'I would prefer that you went also. Isabella is too young to be anywhere without a member of her Family.'

'Perhaps we should have arranged for you to go, Filipo.'

'I do not have the time,' he said, 'you know that. I am required at my Club.' She looked at his face – florid, still-handsome, and pleasant – some of the guests were still in the room.

Caution. Patience. Not long. The words floated at the front of her head.

'There is not a ticket for me this evening, Filipo,' she said. 'This is a very special Occasion. But of course if you would prefer Isabella not to go, I will advise her of your Decision.'

'I would prefer, for her future social Engagements, that you always attend.'

'Very well,' said Signorina di Vecellio, and then her brother had gone, all the guests had gone, the servants waited to clear.

Deliberately Francesca walked to the table and poured herself yet another large glass of wine and drank it quickly, then she hurried upstairs. In Isabella's room curling tongs, powder puffs, pomade, orange-flower water lay upon a chest of drawers and across the bed, as if Angelica had never died for beauty's sake – but no chloride of lime, at least. Her mother's elaborate and powdered hair and face-paint were no longer so in the fashion, especially for younger women: Isabella's dark hair curled prettily around her face with a little help from Euphemia. Flurried little tantrums ensued concerning the gown and the hair and whether a little rouge was appropriate; she wore the latest gown, gentle bustles at the back so that the material floated so flatteringly behind her small waist. To Isabella her aunt assured her that she looked so very beautiful that rouge was unnecessary. Her aunt also told Isabella that her simple hairstyle, with the flowers entwined, was very fine. Isabella wore the pendant from Amsterdam, of course. The carriage arrived and there was another little flurry of voices as the aunt saw her niece to the carriage of Lady Dorothea Bray, and no doubt Mr Bounds the frames-maker's son all but forgot.

Again the front door closed and Francesca actually lay her head upon it for a moment, and then jerked up, remembering: *but I did not tell him about Claudio.* She heard the sounds from Pall Mall, the voices and the carriage-wheels and the shouts of footmen and porters. *That face, I must paint the face, I will tell him tomorrow about Claudio.* Once more she drank deeply from the decanter, she must keep going *I must keep going.*

Finally, breathless almost with relief and exhaustion, carrying a candle-lamp, she reached her own room.

—it was as if I was ill, perhaps I was, or inebriated (perhaps I was) or mad again . . . as if in a fever I pinned the drawings of Eliza that I had done in Frith Street by my easel – the first real model I had had other than myself, in my life – there was something, something in her expression that I wanted to capture – it was not her mouth or her nose but, as she said herself, what she was thinking perhaps, or what I thought she was thinking as I had looked at her, some essence of what she felt – or was it what I felt? I could not be sure and it did not matter: I *knew*: at once now I understood that the bend in the neck in the painting was not right, not right

287

exactly for what I saw in my head; I scraped at the oils, I very gently used some Turpentine, a tiny drop on an old cloth.

I bent over the face trying to pull it out of my head and from the hasty sketches beside my easel – the rich, warm gown glowed, the beautiful sleeve, I could see that. But nothing was any use if I could not . . . if I could not . . .

. . . almost it was there, and yet not – fifteen-year-old Eliza, about whom I knew almost nothing, except that hers was the face for this painting: but there was something wrong, something missing . . . fifteen years old – when I was fifteen I was Grace Marshall and when I first arrived in London I looked with such delight at everything my brother showed me, such pleasure, I wanted to get that feeling in the girl: something bright, something . . . something warm . . . Rembrandt's paintings were warm . . . On and on now I worked and I worked and occasionally heard a clock.

I could not find it. I could not do it.

I stared at this painting.

Somewhere I heard a door bang, my brother, or one of the children but I could not think about them; the candles started to splutter and stutter, they had burned down and I had not noticed, perhaps that was why I could not do it, perhaps the light was wrong, I quickly replaced them; was Mr Gainsborough, too, working in candlelight along the street? the thought seemed companionable almost.

I stared at this painting.

Both doors were closed, my sewing-room and my main room, so the voice was almost upon me before I heard it:

'Zia Francesca! Zia Francesca!'

It was Isabella. *Why are the children choosing this time of all times to suddenly come to me and call the name of their childhood? what is the matter with them both suddenly?* I had time only to throw off my paint-coat – my hands were covered with paint, I had the sense to pull on some white gloves as I opened the door, if it looked bizarre in the middle of the night it could not be helped, the sight of my paint-covered hands would have been more bizarre still.

My niece was flushed and dishevelled and not in any way interested in the state of my hands.

'What has happened?' I ushered her quickly away to the stairs, we began walking downwards at once, towards her own room.

'I believe I am to be married!'

'Whatever do you mean?'

'I mean that I am going to be married!'

'To whom, Isabella? Is it Mr Bounds? Has he spoken to your Father?'

'To Lord Pawltry.'

'Lord *Pawltry?*' I stopped there upon the stairs to look at her. Lord Pawltry was three times her age and a rackety, raddled friend of the Prince of Wales, even I knew that. He had already had wives, several of them, although they were never to be seen.

'He loves me.'

Wherever had my niece been that she had received the attentions of Lord Pawltry? 'I thought you were to go to the Opera, Isabella. Did Lord Pawltry attend Lady Dorothea?'

'This was after the Opera. Lady Dorothea and her sister took me to a *soiree.*'

My mind, so full of the face of Eliza, looked at the flushed face of my niece, *I have to get back, I have to get back to my Picture.* 'They had no business to take you anywhere but the Opera, that was the arrangement.'

'I wanted to go. I had thought Mr Bounds would be there. He has been avoiding me since – since Lady Dorothea has been very kindly organising my new Social Activities.'

I heard my own sigh. 'Isabella you must go to bed, it is very late. We will talk of this in the morning.'

'If a Gentleman kisses a Lady, it means they are to be married, does it not?'

I looked at my niece and my heart sank.

'What do you mean?' I asked. 'Do you mean Lord Pawltry – kissed you?'

She nodded. 'In the carriage. He called me his lovely girl, and said he would introduce me to the Prince of Wales.'

'You were *alone* with him in the carriage?' Filipo would be furious, and say that I should have been there and indeed I should have been perhaps, for that was the role of unmarried aunts: to deflect the attentions of such as Lord Pawltry, and indeed the Prince of Wales. And then Isabella gave me a strange look from under her eyes.

'It was my first Kiss. Does it – does it mean I will have a child?'

Any moment I would scream or I would laugh. 'Isabella, we will talk of this in the morning. But – when people kiss it does not necessarily mean they are to be married and it certainly does not mean they are to have a child. Go now.' And I almost pushed her into her room and as I did so I caught sight of the gloves upon my hands, they looked exceeding odd.

Then quickly I made my way back up the staircase to my room. The Painting had not, in the interim, changed itself but as I stared at it, as I peeled off the absurd gloves and picked up my brush, I felt as if I did not know it. And suddenly, standing there with gloves in one hand and a hog-hair brush in the other, I understood the *ludicrousness* of the Charade: Grace Marshall trying to be the Great Master, Rembrandt von Rijn of Amsterdam, in between cock-fighting and the raddled Lord Pawltry!

I threw down the gloves and the brush to the floor – not I think in despair, truly, but in some other, wilder humour: *I am ridiculous!* – I was an aging spinster who was trying to copy the work of an Old Master and in my head suddenly I saw Rembrandt's own travailed face, and I was hingeing everything – *the rest of my life* – on one unlikely throw of the dice as my Father had so often done before me, my dear old hapless, gambling Father, and Claudio gambled and Tobias gambled – and Grace Marshall gambled too – and suddenly, extraordinarily, I began – not to weep as you might have expected at such exhaustion and frustration – but to *laugh*: at my rackety family, at my ludicrous Dreams and Pretensions, at Isabella and her first kiss with a raffish old Lord, and Claudio with the cock-fighting men, and it might seem that I was laughing cynically but I swear I was not. I was laughing in the old way because I understood: by agreeing to such a Charade I had made myself *utterly preposterous!*

I snatched up my palette knife and with no care any more for all my hours and days and months of painstaking work, I scrawled **GRACE** across the luxurious, gorgeous skirt of the beautiful gown in the fake, unsatisfactory Rembrandt painting – I heard James Burke's voice in my head, not this James Burke the fraudster but James who I had loved, who had quoted Mr Hogarth, *It seems to be universally admitted that there is such a thing as Beauty, and that the highest degree of it is Grace*, and as I scratched the name **GRACE** I saw her clearly: Grace Marshall of the hooped skirts running through Bristol like some kind of zany, ungainly bird – Grace Marshall who made paint from flowers and from butter and from earth from our Bristol garden where the fake Greek statue stood in a heroic pose and not one of us knew what a Greek statue was! and Tobias, not Tobias in the Park in the rain, the boy Tobias who had brought me a rose that day – and somehow in among all the mess of our childhood I was somehow *joyous* – and here she was now, that Grace Marshall: dour, old, and inebriated, *pretending to be an Old Master myself? pretending to be Rembrandt?* how could I *not* laugh as I scratched with the knife and I saw Tobias our brother picking up my fallen basket and taking Philip's money, *good for him!*, and I pictured again Tobias sitting at the dining-table in Pall Mall speaking of Bristol, perhaps the exquisite enamelled snuff box of Mr Hartley Pond would be the next thing to disappear, and I was still laughing as I tossed the palette knife right out of the window into the King's Garden and there was a pitcher of water and I threw water on my face and I picked up a cloth to dry my face and I looked up and I saw my eyes in the mirror and they were eyes remembering and they were bright.

I dropped the cloth as if it scalded me.

I went quickly back to my easel, drying my hands on my gown, and picked up a brush; Eliza's grave face stared back at me and I leaned towards it. *And I changed the eyes.* I put my eyes into her eyes: I painted eyes remembering something: in the painting the eyes that looked up from the discarded book now remembered something and in that remembrance there was a flash – of pleasure, of humour, wry even, something *warm* and the eyes were alive *the eyes were alive.*

Quickly, quickly, I picked up another brush; in long strokes I painted completely over the scrawl, the name at the bottom of the painting on the beautiful gown, I filled the scratch marks so completely, I painted over it so completely that it disappeared entirely, I remembered the gowns I had seen in several of Rembrandt's paintings and my gown, slowly, carefully, emerged again, became again the beautiful, beautiful thing that I had laboured over so long: the rich brown and the gold and the deep warm red – my thumb gave the paint just the texture I wanted where the gown met the floor, the shadowed folds fell exactly, almost I could feel them; the girl so like Eliza touched the book still but looked away, the light from the window caught the light from her eyes, the sleeve moved almost as she put the book aside and she glanced up, remembering something that amused her and it made me smile to look at it.

I could not stop now, I mixed colour with my fingers, I worked on the turn of the neck, the hands on the book – almost they were right now, almost now everything flowed and fitted together – suddenly I saw to make the book even brighter, light reflected off the pale cover of the book so that the look began from the book, from something in the book . . . something, something in the book had set off the train of thought, some knowledge, some recognition that gave the brightness to the eyes of the girl, I was almost shaking when I put the last strokes there, I had to pull my hands and my brushes away so that I could not touch it again and spoil it.

I turned away, and I closed my eyes, and then I turned back.

The chair was partly in shadow, one side of the girl's head was partly in shadow but the girl's face and her book on the table caught the light and the warm gown shone. And the eyes. The eyes glowed with life.

As I stepped away from the painting I looked up at the window and saw that the first grey morning light was just touching the room, and very faintly I thought I heard the crowing of Mr Gainsborough's rooster.

The painting was finished.

TWENTY-SIX

The next morning Filipo di Vecellio and his sister were the only members of the family who appeared for breakfast. He did not notice her drawn, exhausted face, or her scrubbed red hands, nor saw her gleaming, shining eyes, for his son had not come home, had sent no message, was not (it was quickly ascertained by sending the carriage) at his new studio in St Martin's Lane.

'And where is Isabella?'

'Isabella is still asleep,' answered his sister.

'Did she return late?'

'A little late.'

'You must go with her in future. That is your role.' He attacked several lamb's kidneys.

'About Claudio.'

'The boy is painting somewhere. He is seventeen years old. He is a man. He will be back.' She suddenly saw those far-off days when Philip was seventeen years old himself and thought he was a fashionable French *flâneur* as he strolled the streets of Bristol.

'Filipo,' she said. Something in her voice caught him, and he looked again at her: her thin face was haggard. He and his sister were seldom alone; he found comfort in the motherly figure of Euphemia suddenly appearing now, bringing in hot water for the tea from the basement so that they were not alone, the brother and the sister, but almost at once Euphemia was gone again.

'Well?'

'I told you that Tobias is in London.'

'And I told you not to speak of this matter.' A lamb's kidney was attacked further.

'I think – perhaps he is in some sort of trouble.'

'Of course he is in some sort of trouble. When was he not?'

'He no longer goes to sea.'

'What is that to me?'

'Would it – would it not be possible to help him in some way? Even for – for old times? He seems – he looks ill, could you not help him?'

'*Could I not help him?*' Philip exploded. 'Isn't it enough I saved one from the gutter?' There was a tiny, disbelieving gasp in the room: she lowered her head quickly so that he would not see her eyes. 'What do you suggest I do – invite him home with his thieving Bristolian ways? "My brother," I will say, "from Florence."'

'Filipo.' *I am so nearly gone from here, not long, not long, hold on . . .* 'Filipo.' She took a deep breath, looked up at him again. 'Filipo, there is something else. Claudio spoke to me yesterday.'

He stared at his sister. She knew something then. Kidney juice, wiped with bread. Then, 'Well?'

'He told me that he owed five hundred guineas to the cock-fighting men.'

'*Five hundred guineas?*' The bread dropped to the plate. 'But he has given up gambling. He promised me he had given it up. We agreed that he would paint, and the name di Vecellio would rise again!' He pushed the food away impatiently. 'He promised on the memory of his dead Mother.'

'You should not have made him do that. He is a child still.'

'He is seventeen years old!'

She shrugged. 'And he is the grandson of a man who gambled away a Fortune.' Silence. 'You gave him a Studio in St Martin's Lane, I understand. I did not know that.' Her brother still did not speak, it was not her business. 'Claudio came to me and asked me to tell you that he owed five hundred guineas. He was frightened. He said they had threatened to kill him.'

'What rubbish is this?'

'I said the same. But he was very frightened.'

Suddenly her brother was very, very angry. He jabbed the table suddenly with a knife. '*Five hundred guineas*? It is not possible. The boy promised me. He promised me! And if he told you this story yesterday why are you only telling me now?'

'You were already in your Studio, then there were guests, then you went out.' She slowly poured tea, he could not but see that her red, wrinkled hand was shaking. *She is old*, he thought. Her eyes were lowered. She pushed his cup towards him. 'I told him we would speak after dinner, but as you know he did not come.'

'You should have told me at once.'

'Yes,' she said. 'But you were gone.'

In their silence the clock ticked and the fire spat as the grey, freezing February morning tightened its grip and a dog howled somewhere along Pall Mall.

'*Five hundred guineas*?' he repeated.

'So he said.' She saw his fallen shoulders.

'His Mother should be here,' he said, and she saw that the words were wrenched out of somewhere deep inside.

'I wish she was.' And she saw that her brother (perhaps it was the way the light fell) looked old suddenly. *Well – we are both old. But I have painted something . . . and soon I can help Tobias even if he will not.*

'Did he tell you where he has been following the cock-fighting?'

'I have seen him in an alley off Broad-street, I happened to pass there one day.' She took another deep breath. 'Tobias was there also.'

Now he did look shocked. All sorts of realisations crossed his face, ran after each other: *Tobias and Claudio?*

'Does Claudio know him?'

'I do not know. But he knows Claudio.'

'Is he one of the people who is threatening him for money?'

'I do not know. But – I think he would like to know him, not to harm him.'

One of the kidneys was stabbed viciously. 'I swear I will *kill* him if I find he has made himself known in any way to my son.'

'Perhaps you should ask Claudio if he has met his Uncle. They look *so alike* Filipo.'

She suddenly thought he was going to hit her but the door burst open rather quickly and Euphemia came bustling in with lamb chops. From under her eye-lashes as she put them on the sideboard she looked at her master and then at her mistress. The *signore* got up suddenly and left the room.

Francesca di Vecellio declined chops, gave some instructions to Euphemia, then she made her way up the stairs again. In her hands now she carried a cup of hot chocolate. She paused for a moment at the painting of Angelica, caught in youth and beauty forever as she hung in her golden frame at the bend in the staircase. And she thought, *it is so simple but it is not enough said: art is a matter of truth.*

She went into the room of Isabella. Almost she laughed. She was *so unsuited* to the task before her (for was she not working in the alleys off the Covent Garden *piazza* when she was younger than Isabella now?) and so exhausted, and the room of Isabella was so tumultuous, and the figure under the quilt so small. But Grace Marshall was smiling. She had looked and looked at her own painting and she knew she had painted something beautiful. It was done. So that Isabella woke to find her serious aunt smiling at her and holding hot chocolate.

'Drink this, *cara mia*,' said the aunt. Isabella's dark curls fell untidily round her face. With an almost superhuman effort her aunt picked up a hairbrush and began to brush her niece's hair. And although Isabella made small, childish sounds of pain as the hair caught, she was secretly pleased, for her aunt had not brushed her hair for many years.

'Now you must listen to me, *Isabellabella*, for I cannot speak of all this again. You are seventeen years old and you are very pretty and it is not the – the fashion for seventeen-year-old young ladies to travel in coaches alone with old rogues like Lord Pawltry, who will certainly not marry you, and whom you must never, never allow to kiss you again.'

'It was more than a kiss,' said Isabella uncertainly, and there was a little tremor in her voice. The brush stopped, and then started again. After a moment the aunt spoke.

'What do you mean?'

Isabella was silent.

'What happened, Isabella?'

'Lord Pawltry – touched me.'

Now there was a slight tremor in the aunt's voice. 'Touched you – where?'

Isabella slowly put her own hand upon her own breast. 'It was horrible,' she said in a small voice.

The aunt brushed very rigorously. 'Where else?'

The niece looked very shocked. 'What do you mean, *Where else*? Nowhere else. What will happen?'

There was a somewhat long and charged silence in the room.

'Are you sure that was all?'

'Yes! I am sure! What will happen?'

'Nothing will happen, and Lord Pawltry is a Rake and a very, very dishonourable man. If it were known that he had taken such a liberty your Father would be very, very angry.' Her niece was silent. The aunt brushed and brushed as she took a deep breath and went on speaking. 'It is so very sad that your Mother is not here to instruct you in all the Social Knowledge of which she was, indeed, such an example.' (Quickly the aunt banished from her mind what she knew of Angelica's activities with worse than Lord Pawltry when she was Isabella's age, before she married Filipo di Vecellio.) 'You do not have a child if you allow a Gentleman to kiss you but, in the Society you are so anxious to be part of, you lose your Reputation as a person of consequence if you allow a Gentleman to kiss you – or in any way lay his hands upon you – before you have had a very, very long Acquaintanceship with him.' (Quickly the aunt banished from her mind the stunned face of James Burke, who turned from her paintings to enclose her in his arms without a single word.) 'On the matter of Marriage, it would be for a Gentleman – and certainly not Lord Pawltry, ever, who is *not* a Gentleman – to approach your Father if his Intentions were serious. If any Gentleman's Attentions are not serious they can only do you harm and you must request most urgently that they desist,' (and a picture flashed into her mind of another old raddled Duke in a box in Westminster Abbey on Coronation Day all those years ago, fumbling with her petticoat). The aunt sighed, for she was not finished, and her arms were exhausted, but it seemed to her that she must keep brushing Isabella's hair until she had said what had to be said. 'On the matter of Children . . .' And here she stopped for a moment, surprised by the unexpected, sharp stab of pain; she made a tiny involuntary sound, and then began again. 'On the matter of Children you must guard your body until you are married. Try to – try to remember that it belongs to nobody but you' *but how can I tell her of the wild fire?* 'One day you will love some-body, and only then, when he is your Husband, will you share your body.' (She felt the girl stir uneasily.) 'But never until then, and only because you marry a man who will love you and make you happy.'

A small voice. 'Like Mr Bounds?'

Her aunt sighed. Mr Bounds of the overly-coiffeured hair, Mr Bounds the frame-maker's son, whom Philip would find so unsuit-able. 'Perhaps like Mr Bounds. He seemed – fond.'

The small voice answered. 'But he says I have changed.'

'Then perhaps it is not to be Mr Bounds. But it must be someone who loves you and respects you. It may be somebody that you have never met yet.'

'Oh.' A small, disappointed sound.

Just the swish, swish of the brush.

And the aunt said, 'It is a strange word, *love*.' And still brushing the hair of her niece she suddenly, as if she had not meant to quite, spoke the words she had learned from the red-veined vicar in Bristol so many years ago:

> *Come, gentle night, come, loving black-brow'd night,*
> *Give me my Romeo; and, when he shall die,*
> *Take him and cut him out in little stars,*
> *And he will make the face of heaven so fine*
> *That all the world will be in love with night.*

'I should not *cut up* someone I loved,' said Isabella most sensibly, 'and I would want the person I love to be alive, not dead!' And her aunt laughed and then Isabella laughed somewhat grumpily and said, 'If dead people become stars, then I shall prefer *misty* stars from now on, I do not want anybody else to die like Mamma,' and for a moment the aunt held the girl and rocked her like a child: *misty stars, we prefer misty stars* they chanted together, half-laughing, perhaps half-crying *misty stars, misty stars* like children with a rhyme and finally the aunt kissed her niece on the forehead, and left her.

In her sewing-room she stared and stared at the painting on the easel. The girl's eyes seemed to sparkle.

She opened the mahogany drawer to take some money.

Five of the ten guineas that James Burke had paid her were gone: she gasped, and then she immediately saw Claudio – *left outside her closed door as she hurried away to Frith Street.* It seemed a lifetime ago but it was only yesterday morning.

Isabella was at the dinner-table as the gloomy afternoon drew down, but most unusually her father had turned all guests away for he could not find his son. He had been back to St Martin's Lane, he had even been to Broad-street where the cock-fighting men arranged matches in alleys.

'Has he spoken to you, Isabella?'

'No, Father.'

'Do you know anything at all about his – troubles?'

Isabella was determined not to be caught in this. Everybody knew: if her father had eyes he would have seen long ago. 'No, Father.' She kept her eyes lowered.

Filipo di Vecellio stared at his sister. 'You should have told me earlier.'

And his sister stared back at him. 'London is a dangerous city. It is a great deal of money that he owes and I surmise they would rather have him alive than dead and I imagine he will have kept well away from them. It is my belief that Claudio knows how to look after himself – in most ways. If I were you Filipo, I believe I would go to Sussex.'

'To *Sussex*?' His surprised face.

'It seems possible to me that he has gone back to a farm near his School. He told me he worked there when it was – inconvenient – for him to come home.'

'That is ridiculous. Why would he go back there?'

'Because I believe he wishes to become a Farmer not a Painter.'

'A *Farmer*?' Now he looked horrified, unbelieving.

'He comes from farming stock,' she murmured as she got up to light the candles. And out of the corner of her eye she watched her brother.

Next morning, early, Signore Filipo di Vecellio left in his carriage, with his daughter the Signorina Isabella who had no choice in the matter and was sulking, to travel to Sussex.

As soon as the carriage had left, Signorina Francesca di Vecellio quickly sent a message to Mr James Burke, Art Dealer.

James Burke was uneasy; you might almost say (although such

a thing was unimaginable) that James Burke was anxious. He won-dered if he had been foolish, too ambitious. He urgently needed money but they could have sold many of her paintings for more reasonable sums and all made money. She was good, certainly (he made himself think of her as *she* and blanked out the soul of Grace, the essence of Grace, that is Grace herself, from his calculations) at what she did, better than good, she was outstanding. But Rembrandt van Rijn? They had been greedy perhaps. The message they were all waiting for, that the painting was finished, had taken so long in coming; the men in the attic in the alley off the *piazza* had become impatient, ugly even, as he insisted they must wait until she was ready. All the interminable grey days of waiting pressed upon him as his carriage finally took him to the house in Pall Mall whence he had been summoned. As he alighted he saw the horses' breath in the dank air, told the driver to wait.

They spoke briefly, politely, in the drawing-room, the art dealer and the sister of the painter; he commiserated with her, as Euphemia brought tea, on the worry regarding her nephew. And then she took him further upstairs, as if perhaps to her brother's studio. Further then: she heard his breathing. She opened her door.

The painting still stood on the easel in the sewing-room. The grey dull day gave a little light but she had lit candles, ready; their flames flickered slightly as the room was entered.

Francesca did not look at the painting now: she looked at the face of James Burke, Art Dealer. He tried to hide his reaction but he could not for his face went very red, almost as if he was to be taken with an apoplexy. For just a moment his guard – his ability now never to speak to her in a personal manner – dropped.

'*Grace.*' He stared and stared at the painting, rooted to one spot; she thought he might weep. It was all he said, just her name. But she knew from his face that she had succeeded.

It took some time for him to compose himself.

He kept staring at the picture, almost in fascination, went up close, moved away. When, at last, he spoke to her he spoke in a business-like manner about the transportation of the picture. When had she finished it? Was the paint dry enough for him to carry it by coach to Covent Garden?

'It is not yet completely dry,' she said. He peered at the paint.

'I am very used to this.' He had brought with him a parcel of thin board; he covered the picture carefully so that the board did not touch the paint; carefully he carried it downstairs, holding it upright from the bottom, past the drawing-room, past Euphemia polishing, past the picture of Angelica on the wall and the Canaletto painting of Venice, down to the street where the carriage was waiting. At the door of the carriage he stopped for just a moment, glanced at her with an unfathomable look on his face. 'Amazing Grace,' he said softly, and climbed in with his parcel.

She reached up to the window. 'I think it would be – fitting, James,' she said quietly, 'if my brother acquired the Painting.' And then she stepped back as the horses trotted away.

Almost with a pang, she saw the painting disappear. And then she shook herself slightly. For she understood that her new life had been set in motion, unstoppable.

And then she went back to the mahogany drawer and took three of the five guineas that were left. Once again she wrapped her cloak about her. She went to the alley: she heard the sounds before she got there, she entered the dark circle with her cloak about her face, insinuating herself into the shadows where men yelled and sweated with wild eyes, banging coins on to a rail while birds attacked each other. The smell of blood and sweat was so strong that day that she retched; blood and feathers and terrible cries, the birds or the men, it was all one and her eyes looked away from the fight, looked at the faces of the men, the gambling men, looked for Tobias: he was there: he had already seen her. She was shocked at his appearance: he looked dirty and drawn. He looked old, *but we are all old now*. She indicated to him to follow her, she walked away. He followed her along Broad-street, they merged with the crowds near Leicester Fields. Her cloak still hid her face; the day was cold and she saw his own threadbare jacket.

'I saw Philip yesterday,' he said. 'He came to the cock-fighting.'

'Did he see you?'

'I made sure that he did not, you say he would not make me welcome,' and he gave one of his nervous laughs.

'He is looking for Claudio, who is greatly in debt. He seems to have run away.'

'I have heard them talking of the boy. They think he is rich and they are angry, Gracie. You don't want to anger those men, they are dangerous. You must tell him. You must give him my message. He must keep away from there.'

'I think he is too scared to come anywhere near!'

'He is right to be scared, Gracie.'

'Where are you living?'

The same answer. 'Here and there.'

She grabbed both his arms. 'Tobias,' she said urgently, 'I am trying – I am hoping to receive a large sum of money.' *I cannot tell him it is a painting . . . I do not know if I can trust him . . .* 'It may take some months, but if I am successful I will help you, I will find a room for you – do not', she half-laughed but she remembered Poppy's stories, 'get taken to Newgate where they press people to death I have heard. I will help you, I promise Tobias, but I cannot do more till – till all is arranged.' And then she thrust the three guineas into his hands. She did not say *use it wisely*. She could hardly look at his face.

'You're a good girl, Gracie,' and she did, finally, look up and smile.

'I am not a good girl, Tobias. But I have a dream, and perhaps I can be good again, if my dream comes true.' And she did what she knew she should have done long ago: she reached up and kissed the man who she hardly knew but who used to be her wild brother, who had brought her colours.

TWENTY-SEVEN

Claudio was returned to London with his father and his sister.

It was clear to everyone, including all of the servants, that he was absolutely terrified: that he did not wish to take one step outside the door of the house in Pall Mall by himself for fear the cock-fighting men would be waiting for him.

'Nonsense,' said his father. 'They would have no knowledge of how to find you, they are thieves and street-men, all of them,' he flicked a glance at his sister, 'they know only shadows. You will accompany me to my Club where you will meet other Artists and make valuable Connections.' In truth Filipo di Vecellio seized this chance to have his son by him at all times: he insisted that Claudio must work at home, in the Studio, making himself useful by paint-ing clouds and arms on the bigger portraits – an insult to the boy of course who was long past clouds and arms. After dinner they would sally forth and Claudio had to become – unwilling, ner-vous – party to at least part of his father's business and social life, having failed so dismally at his own.

The boy's hang-dog appearance at the dining-table did not exactly add to the gaiety of dining occasions and he sent many un-cypherable looks to his aunt. She tried to ignore him, knew that he felt she had betrayed him by guessing his whereabouts, she felt her own betrayal: the five, precious guineas. The actual five hundred guineas that Claudio owed was not going to be paid: Filipo refused to accept there was any danger. Claudio was too scared to go outside the door.

'You do not understand what they are capable of,' he shouted wildly.

'I paid your Debts once, I told you I would not pay again!'

'I think – I think it – Broad-street is an unsafe place for Claudio,' said the aunt.

'Indeed!' said his father. 'I hope he knows it!' The boy became paler and kept a great deal to his room. A stalemate sat about the house like a depressing fog which reminded Grace somehow of the gloom that eventually fell upon the house in Bristol as Marmaduke gambled away everything they owned. If her brother made the connection he did not share it with her; Grace waited only for her own wild gamble: a message from James Burke.

Lady Dorothea had now assumed, as if by right, Angelica's place at the dinner-table: her assured laughter echoed. Sometimes now she asked the housekeeper to show her what money she had spent on food and wine. Sometimes Roberto the parrot appeared from nowhere and squawked loudly. Miss Ffoulks no longer attended and John Palmer looked bleakly into his glass. Putting on his shabby, worn cloak one day to walk back to Spitalfields he spoke darkly to Francesca di Vecellio at the front door.

'She has designs on your Brother, she will try to raise him higher.' And the sister whispered back to him, smiling at him, 'The days are much changed, I know, but you must not leave me alone to dine with these perverse people, John Palmer! You must keep coming here!' But she saw his morose face in the light by the door. It was almost dark – nobody walked alone in the dark – yet John Palmer, without a link-boy to guide him, lit the oil of his old lantern from the candle she was holding and disappeared into the gloom. She thought, as he left, she saw a shadow. She stood on the step, waited there. Nobody came.

A rumour took hold of the art world and of the world of noble collectors, even – it was said – coming to the attention of His Majesty who had a large collection of Old Masters that he kept to himself.

There was a Rembrandt, they said, an early Rembrandt that had been privately owned; Mr James Burke, one of the foremost art dealers had been approached they said; it was possibly to be put on the market. But nobody saw it, and Mr Burke himself was vague: 'I have heard tell of it,' he said, 'but I have not yet been granted a view.'

More weeks passed. There were crocuses dotting the green of the park as the days became longer, and at last the air warmer, and the candles no longer had to be lit long before dinner was over. Mr Gainsborough's pigs had piglets in the back garden in Pall Mall and it was said that Mrs Gainsborough was furious, and would not speak to her husband, instead sent him notes tied to the collar of her pet dog. Many of the Nobility left Town, for London stank in the summer.

In the mornings Francesca di Vecellio could be seen shopping round Covent Garden as usual, *where is he? when will I hear?* And (if anybody had been interested) perusing several rooms with big windows in Greek-street or Compton-street, or Leicester-lane. One of the rooms available was in Meard-street where James Burke had sent her so long ago: she turned away quickly.

While her brother and Lady Dorothea and Isabella and an extremely reluctant Claudio suddenly began appearing all together at the theatre, or a ball, or a visit across the river to Vauxhall Gardens, Francesca di Vecellio painted a small portrait of Eliza Towers, *Where is James? When will I hear?* One morning she took from the wall of her sewing-room the painting she had done of Poppy after she had met her in St James's Park – the older Poppy who still had the memory in her face of the days when they were young and in the shadows of the *piazza*. She put Poppy and Eliza in her basket. She saw the Portraits of her family turned to the wall: Juno, Ezekiel, their mother, *when I find a room for Tobias, he shall have some of these, he shall have himself as a Pirate on his wall if he would like it, and I shall have some on mine* and it felt cosy, and made her smile.

In Frith Street the writer Mr Thomas Towers looked very pleased to see her, sitting at his desk in his shawls and his woollen hat and his waistcoat, looking more like an amiable bear than ever (if bears could be amiable, which she did not know).

'I hoped you would come again, Signorina di Vecellio,' he said, as a maid poured coffee. 'I hope you will not be cold – I know it is summer, or they say it is summer, but still I build up the fire, for a Writer's life is such a sedentary one. I sit for many, many hours with my Books and my Papers and – as I am sure you have observed – I need several layers of clothes!' And he stoked the fire again so that the room, to Francesca di Vecellio, was stifling hot.

She reached quickly underneath the bread, took out one of the portraits. Again there flashed across the face of Mr Towers that look of slight perplexity as he gazed at the small picture of a grave girl looking at the painter. 'This is so very like her,' he said oddly. 'I – forgive me, I presume you know how very good a Painter you are?' She said nothing. 'I would like to buy it for her.'

'Oh, not under any circumstances will you pay me anything, Mr Towers. I was paid many times over by Eliza's patience. I would like her to have it as a Gift.'

He looked at her and smiled. 'Thank you, *Signorina*.' And the clock ticked and in the noisy street below horses clattered by, the knife grinder called, and then a milkmaid passed calling BUY MY FRESH MILK. Francesca looked about the room: there were many papers strewn.

'How is your Work progressing, Mr Towers?'

He sighed as he picked up his cup. 'I am writing more to add to my History of Mr Handel. More facts of his life have come to light.' He sighed suddenly. 'Writing is hard, lonely work, Signorina Francesca,' he said.

'Like painting,' she said, before she could stop herself. And then she coloured and sipped her coffee and was silent. He regarded her carefully.

'Do you have a Studio of your own, *Signorina*?'

'I – I paint at the top of the house in Pall Mall. Nobody comes there. Nobody knows.'

'Would your Brother not be pleased – and proud – to have another Painter in the family? Surely?'

'My brother would like his Son to be a famous Painter like himself.'

'But not his Sister?' She was silent, looked down at her cup, but her very silence seemed disloyal and she stood embarrassed.

'I must attend the fishmonger,' she said. And because of all that had passed, spoken and unspoken, between them, her words seemed perhaps incongruous and, to the surprise of both of them, they both laughed, and she said to him in a burst of words, 'One day before I die I *will* have a proper Studio, Mr Towers, like a real Artist,' and then, embarrassed again, she at once busied herself with her shopping basket.

Thomas Towers said, 'I will send this painting to Eliza, and I know she will be pleased. And Signorina Francesca, please do not be discomforted by my words: if there is anything at all that I could assist you with, I would be pleased, and proud.' She understood that he knew her secret, or part of her secret. She understood he knew she was a painter.

She walked out into the busy bustling street, avoiding the carts and the carriages and the drains and the peddlers with nails and tin and pies, and the street-children kicking an old cabbage; she turned her footsteps towards Hanover Square: *a house by the Church*, Poppy had said. She found it almost at once: a respectable unobtrusive house next door to the house of the Vicar; from it a particular young woman emerging who did not, quite, match the house, or the area.

'Excuse me,' she said to the young woman.

'Yes?' She was not interested. They never, ever spoke to strangers, not in Hanover Street.

'I am looking for – Poppy.'

'Don't know her. I'm Iris.'

But she put her hand briefly on the girl's arm. 'Your Mistress?'

'Oh, you mean Mrs Marigold?'

Almost, Grace laughed. 'Yes,' she said. 'Mrs Marigold, that will be her.'

'She died.'

'*What*?'

'She died.' The girl would have turned away.

'No, that cannot be right. I saw her – wait!' The girl turned back reluctantly. 'I knew her,' said Grace. She swallowed and said, 'I am Daisy.' At last the girl looked at the respectable woman carefully, but still she said nothing more.

'Is she really dead?'

'She died this winter. She had the Pox.'

Grace was stunned, stared at the girl in silence. *I wanted to see her again.* And something else, something important. *I wanted her to know that I was, after all, what I always told her. That I was a Painter.* She fumbled in her basket, brought out the picture. Without any words she handed it to the girl.

Iris stared. And then she said, almost in wonder, 'That's her laugh, I seen it!' Her manner changed completely, she looked with interest at the older woman.

'Who done that?'

'I did.'

'Did you? Ain't you clever! She was still pretty.'

'She was, always. And she was brave too.'

'I liked her,' said Iris, matter-of-fact. 'She looked out for us. I never miss people, ain't worth it, but I miss her a bit, and that's the truth.' She kept looking down at the painting and to Grace's astonishment a tear dropped on to the paint; she felt something like tears at the back of her own eyes.

'Would you – would you like to have this Picture?'

The girl looked at her disbelievingly. 'I can't buy this!'

'No, no! I came here to give it to her. Perhaps you would have it instead?'

And Iris smiled, Iris the street-girl. 'I'll show the others,' she said, 'we'll put it up for a bit of Decoration,' and she turned hurriedly back to the house, carrying the picture of Poppy under her arm. 'Lily,' she called, 'Lily! Look at this!' as she disappeared into the house.

Signorina Francesca di Vecellio looked shaken as she made her way back towards the Strand where no doubt halibut lay waiting for her, with their glassy eyes no longer caring of their fate, but the words of Mr Shakespeare ran round and round in her head, *When I do count the clock that tells the Time* . . .

—and I could wait no longer: I saw nothing of James Burke, I heard nothing from him, I began to dream that my Painting had been spirited away, that James and the Frenchman and the Jewmen and my brother's old assistant had taken it away, that they had tricked me, and Mr Thomas Towers sent me a short note telling me of an attic room in Compton-street that had good light from large windows and I went to view it: a light, bright room, *I wanted it so much*, and – I had to think of Tobias now, I would make sure Tobias was safe – I could not wait any longer – finally I was so desperate to begin to make my plans that I sent a note to his home.

Dear Mr Burke,
I would be glad to speak to you urgently
of a Matter concerning an
Auction of Paintings.
Francesca di Vecellio.

He was furious of course; he contrived to come to the house of
my brother on some matter of artistic business, I heard their stiff
voices and I waited in the dining-room.

'Ah, Signorina Francesca, good morning.' Euphemia smiled and
curtsied and reluctantly left with the coal scuttle, at once he spoke
very coldly to me and very quietly. 'Do not ever write to me of
this matter and do not ever write to me at my Home. It is too dangerous.'

I answered in an even more icy manner, except that I spoke even
lower. 'You have my Painting. I have nothing, and no news, and no
Payment from you.' I saw he was surprised: he had not expected
me, I think, to talk of money so openly.

'Why are you so urgent?' he said but I would tell nothing to
him.

'When will you auction it?'

'We are not ready,' said James Burke. 'It has only been a few
months! This is not some fol-de-rol, Grace. There are a great many
things to attend to, as you well know, as you have seen previously
but this is a much, much more complicated affair. They have been
smoking and dirtying the Picture, for age and wear – it is a long,
difficult process – and there must be layers of Varnish in case
anyone tries to remove a little, to verify the Painting. And there
is,' his voice was very low now, our heads were very close together
beside the fireplace, our words left us and disappeared up the chimney, 'there is the matter of the correct Frame, you know all that,
you have seen some of that. But then we must have Tax Returns and
Customs Certification – things about which you have no idea and
which take very many months to arrange, and which I do not think
we should be speaking of.' And I saw our secrets, rushing up out of
the chimney and flying across St James's Park,

'Do you think I will impart such Information?'

'You are the Painter. But everything else is technical and it needs
a long, painstaking time. The Painting must be as dry as dust

before it can be put on show. It has been varnished twice, first with a very slow-drying Varnish then with a quicker one; this allows the Varnish to crack slightly which gives excellent effect, they then rub dirt into the cracks. We must not exhibit until all is ready. You must trust me.'

This time the words were out of my mouth before I had even thought them, or so it seemed to me, 'What has happened between us that I should suddenly trust you?' and I took no notice of something on his face, something, some shock or pain. 'I simply require to be paid,' I said.

And then the shock was gone, and he contained himself, that way he had. His hat had been on the dining-room table, he picked it up and quickly bowed.

'The end of summer,' he said. 'People will come back to Town at the end of the summer.' And he was gone at once from Pall Mall, and Euphemia brought more coal.

For that side of the house in Pall Mall was always cold, like Frith Street, no matter how hard the sun tried to shine through the grey clouds.

I went to the cock-pit that night, to at least tell Tobias, but he was not there.

At last whispers of real information about the Rembrandt painting found their way round London. Definitely an early one, the whispers said. It was said to be called *Girl Reading*, a painting that nobody had even heard of. Mr Hartley Pond pooh-poohed the whisper. 'We would have heard of it if it was anything Genuine,' he said, 'if it was anywhere in Europe.'

The Art Dealer James Burke had seen it. 'I believe', he said to Mr Hartley Pond when they met at Mr Christie's auction rooms, 'that it is Genuine. I believe it is to be auctioned by Mr Valiant in Poland-street well before the end of the year, but I may be wrong, it may only be a Rumour.' And the rumour grew, was embellished, as it made its way around the drawing-rooms and dining-rooms of art lovers and art chancers and art collectors and art dealers and art auctioneers and the nobility of England and possibly Buckingham House. A *Rembrandt*. He was, at that moment, the most collectable Old Master in Europe.

Mr Hartley Pond, who had recently been touring the continent, relayed all this information over halibut in parsley sauce at Pall Mall.

'We would have heard of such a Painting if it was anything Genuine,' he re-iterated. 'If it was anywhere in Europe, I would know about it,' and he spoke knowledgeably of early Rembrandt paintings. Signore Filipo di Vecellio re-told his story of the auction in Amsterdam and the Rembrandt painting he had lost to a Frenchman, and the wine flowed and Claudio glowered and Isabella preened palely at the attention of one of her father's new guests. Lady Dorothea's laugh tinkled and the voices raised, as they so often did as dinner wore on; Francesca di Vecellio missed very much the brisk presence of Miss Ffoulks. Mr Swallow at the end of the table proudly mentioned again his biography.

'At least he does not take note of your Conversations,' shouted John Palmer, present for once, who was more inebriated even than usual, 'as Mr Boswell used of Dr Johnson. Then what stories we would hear!' And Francesca saw that her brother looked coldly at John Palmer and then he turned that same look upon Mr Swallow.

'Take care that you write my Biography while I live, young man, for I am the final Arbiter of the Truth of my Life, and I shall not have people scratching around my Coffin after I am dead.' And there was something almost menacing in the way he spoke so that a *frisson* of something, some warning, drifted about the table and Grace Marshall stared at the candle-flame.

TWENTY-EIGHT

It was late September when the notice of the auction suddenly appeared.

Another collection of European paintings was to be presented by Mr Valiant in Poland-street, the centrepiece of which was the new discovery of a painting by the Netherlands artist, which was advertised separately.

INCLUDING:
SPECTACULAR OLD MASTER
REMBRANDT van Rijn
GIRL READING
Viewing this TUESDAY inst.
AUCTION FOR ALL PAINTINGS
11am Saturday 2 October SHARP.

'I wonder they do not auction such a painting at Mr Christie's rooms here in Pall Mall,' said Isabella, wishing to be part of the conversation around the dinner-table.

'Mr Valiant is long established,' explained her father. He turned to the others as the mutton appeared and the wine flowed. 'But you cannot always be certain of Authenticity at his rooms – or Christie's rooms for that matter, or any other.'

'In the end we must judge for ourselves,' said Mr Hartley Pond (meaning of course that he himself would judge) 'for what does James Burke know after all? He is only a Dealer.'

But there was obvious excitement around the table as there always was when an important Auction was to take place. 'I and my dealer Mr Minnow will be present of course,' said Filipo. 'And I absolutely insist you must come with me, my boy,' he said to the sullen figure of Claudio, and nobody took notice of the inscrutable face of the Signorina Francesca, as she observed her brother across the dining-table.

When the Catalogue of Items was perused it was seen that, once again, despite the new Patriotism, there was not a single British Painting being auctioned.

The weather, those days before the auction, was appalling: wind and rain. But it made no difference. Big crowds viewed the collection of paintings, and the Rembrandt painting in particular, for as long as Mr Valiant would keep his doors in Poland-street open; he was too much of a businessman to close when there was such public interest, even though there was so much mud and rain and rubbish trampled into his rooms that he was almost in despair, hurrying and harrying his boy to sweep up after everybody, as the smell of dubious mud became more and more unbearable. Sir Joshua Reynolds came, and Signore Filipo di Vecellio, and the author Miss Fanny Burney with her father, and indeed the Dukes of Bedford and Bridgewater who were always looking to add to their collections. Day and night people came with magnifying glasses and opinions on the genuineness or otherwise of the unknown picture; 'This is a *Rembrandt* picture,' said the crowds of people to each other, most never having had the chance to see one before in their lives. They looked intently at the face of the girl. Gloved fingers had curiously rubbed at the old frame, Mr Valiant had to be quite severe; however one well-known, very rich, connoisseur was given permission to scratch very very slightly at the varnish, which he observed minutely upon his fingernail and then declared himself satisfied. The day before the auction a gold coach stopped briefly in the narrow street, blocked the traffic completely, and the Prince of Wales was seen to enter the auction-room also, his magnifying glass in hand. Mr Valiant, astonished, thrilled, and anxious that his rooms smelled of sewers, bowed very low. But some more lowly person in the street had recognised the figure of the heir to the throne who was always asking Parliament for money, to spend – so said scurrilous newspapers and cartoonists and patter-men – on ladies and clothes and perfumes and curling tongs. One stone was thrown at the gold coach, and then another. A small mut-tering crowd gathered outside the auction-rooms, it might have become ugly and Mr Valiant feared for his windows, his reputation, his paintings: luckily one of the Prince's escorting gentlemen per-suaded the Royal personage away from the Rembrandt painting before real violence was done. Mr Valiant found that he was per-spiring so profusely at the honour, and the terror, and the smell that His Royal Highness might have noticed, and the disaster averted, that he had to send home for a dry shirt.

People praised the beautiful colours of the girl's gown; the lux-urious rich dark reds, so beloved of the Dutch artist; the recognisable use of light and shade, so profound and so telling; and the wonderful, bright-eyed face: admiration for the painting *Girl Reading* danced about London.

TWENTY-NINE

Mr Valiant prayed it would not rain again on the day of the auction but alas his prayers were not answered: the heavens opened again and remained open, mud and filth lay in Poland-street and sewers overflowed and he saw turds floating down towards Broad-street, accompanied by cabbage leaves and oranges and chop bones and, of all unpleasant things, a dead dog. Nevertheless at eleven a.m. sharp, as Mr Valiant himself had insisted, he was ready at his box: his auction-rooms by now could not have fitted a single other person inside and by now rivulets of mud and water ran freely along the floor. Paintings to be auctioned, big and small, hung together closely on every wall; the crowds pressed by the Rembrandt painting where it hung in the place of honour; they stared at the girl, at the way her face was raised away from her book, a private, off-guard moment of remembering something, something that amused her, made her eyes so bright. Almost, the girl regarded the spectators with some interest, but not quite. They all spoke of the warmth and grace of the Portrait, the way the sleeve seemed almost to move. By all it was agreed a thing of beauty; everybody seemed to ignore the smell of hot, wet bodies and congealed mud; and nobody gave a moment's thought to the footmen shivering wetly outside the auction-room doors beside the lines of carriages: Poland-street was now completely blocked.

Signorina Francesca di Vecellio attended with her brother and her niece and nephew. Claudio's father had absolutely insisted that the Old Master must be viewed by his son. The boy was almost physically man-handled into the family carriage and then from the carriage into the auction rooms (Poland-street being far too near to Broad-street and the cock-fighting alleys for his liking), he was almost forcibly led by his father towards the Rembrandt painting. And there the boy Claudio seemed, quite suddenly, absolutely dumbstruck. He turned a strange shade of red: his father, believing him to be suffering from a surfeit of cowardice, admonished him through clenched lips to be a man. They had obtained seats upon wooden benches in the third row: Filipo di Vecellio and his son, Thomas Gainsborough, John Palmer. The Italian painter's sister was separated from her brother by the presence of the Lady Dorothea Bray in a large, flower-strewn hat, to the detriment of the view of the people who sat behind. Everybody kept shifting uncomfortably, trying to observe proceedings over other hats and high wigs and ornamental head-pieces, trying to work out which nobles were there on their own account, which had sent a representative, who would be bidding for Royalty.

At first Mr Valiant auctioned minor works: another Spanish card player; a *Portrait of a Lady* by an unknown painter but likely from the Flemish school; an odd, large Roman bust lately from Malta. Bidding was brisk but the sums offered small; the attention of everybody wandered; it became clear that some of the nobility whose carriages caused such confusion in the mud outside were not wanting to have their time wasted by Maltese monuments. Boots themselves seemed to steam; rain rumbled at windows: it was all most unfortunate.

Mr Valiant was an old hand, his dais was tall, his voice was loud, his hammer was precise and his eyes were sharp. He knew he could not hold off the moment, called now for the Rembrandt painting to be brought to the easel beside his lectern. The room came at once to attention. Although the painting was not large it was carried forward very carefully, almost religiously, by two of the assistants and placed where it could be seen by everybody in the room.

The door blew open over and over; finally it was locked against any late-comers, although no other single person could have fitted now into the auction-rooms anyhow. Filipo di Vecellio, glancing across at the recalcitrant door, saw his old dealer leaning against a wall; they caught each other's eye, each bowed slightly. It was known that it was Mr James Burke who had finally arranged this painting for auction: he would indeed make a pretty penny. Filipo di Vecellio remembered the shocked silence in Amsterdam when the Rembrandt painting had fetched four hundred guineas. Here in Poland-street his heart beat fast: he had examined this painting very carefully as had other painters, he thought it superior to the one in Amsterdam. Thomas Gainsborough and John Palmer did not collect paintings in the same way but enjoyed these mêlées immensely. Claudio di Vecellio continued to sit next to his father with the same peculiar red face.

The dealer James Burke looked at Signorina Francesca di Vecellio: she had been engaged in conversation by Lady Dorothea earlier but now she stared at the painting that was on show; such intensity was almost naked as she stared upwards. He was embarrassed in some way, looked away.

'Ladies and Gentlemen!' The auction of the painting by Rembrandt van Rijn began.

Mr Valiant explained the antecedents of the painting: it was clear from its customs certificates that it had come from the Netherlands to France in the last fifty years. The stamps of authentication on the back, the seals of several collectors over the last hundred years gave its history better than Mr Valiant could. The seller was an anonymous member of the French aristocracy who (it was merely hinted) was in some financial disarray (a small snigger in Poland-street at the foolish French); a French dealer had been delegated to sell it in Amsterdam but the family had been persuaded to move the sale to England where Rembrandt was held now in as least as high – if not higher – esteem as he was by his own countrymen. There was, however, a reserve price on the painting, for a Dutch buyer would acquire it if the reserve was not bettered.

'The Reserve! The Reserve!' The crowd required the relevant information.

'The Reserve is known to me and to the Dealer, Mr Burke. But I will give you a clue. It is a little more than three hundred and ninety-nine guineas!'

There were outraged shouts, followed by indignant murmurs: it was known that Rembrandt's *Adoration of the Kings*, a much bigger painting, had been sold in London less than five years ago for three hundred and ninety guineas. The Duke of Luxmore was heard to say most heatedly that twenty years ago he had acquired a better Rembrandt painting than this – in fact a self-portrait of the artist – for nineteen pounds, nineteen shillings and sixpence. But he looked most longingly at the painting. And most knew that four hundred guineas was exorbitant, yet not that exorbitant, not now, for a painting by the Old Master.

When the muttering died down the bidding began: one of the be-hatted ladies in the very front row quickly raised her gloved hand and offered four hundred and five guineas. It rose quickly to four hundred and thirty.

The Duke of Bridgewater offered four hundred and forty.

After a little tense lull, a spokesman for the Duke of Portland suddenly offered five hundred guineas. There was a gasp in the auction room.

The Lady Dorothea Bray was too involved in the sport to notice that the Signorina Francesca was literally quivering beside her, gloved hands clasped tightly together. On the Lady Dorothea's other side her dear friend Filipo was showing signs of stress that she did notice. The bidding had reached five hundred and fifty guineas very quickly and then he, for the first time, put up his hand.

'Five hundred and seventy,' said Filipo di Vecellio.

His sister gasped aloud, looked across at her brother, then looked across the room to the dealer Mr James Burke where he stood by the far wall. The dealer caught her eye for a split second, looked away with an impassive face, stared at Mr Valiant.

'Five hundred and seventy guineas,' repeated Mr Valiant. 'Am I offered anything further than five hundred and seventy guineas?' and in the Dukely silence they assumed he would bring his hammer down, but the be-hatted woman in the front row again raised her gloved hand.

'Six hundred guineas,' she said clearly. The whole room gasped louder. This was outrageous. Lady Dorothea Bray was seen to be looking at the Italian artist Filipo di Vecellio in great anticipation, and something else – *Of course, she is his mistress*, the unspoken thought went quickly around the room – but Filipo di Vecellio did not notice, he only had eyes for his adversaries: the envoy from the Duke of Portland and the woman in the front row whom he did not know.

'Six hundred and ten,' said Filipo di Vecellio.

The silence in the room was like a roar, people hardly dared breathe. Mr Valiant looked at the other two bidders left in the game. The Duke's envoy shook his head. The woman in the front row put up her gloved hand very, very slowly.

'Six hundred and fifty,' she said but her voice was less sure than it had been.

Filipo knew it was his. 'Six hundred and fifty-five,' he called joyously.

Just as the hammer was to fall the woman in the front row raised her hand one more time.

'Six hundred and seventy,' she said and Mr Valiant had to lean forward and ask her to repeat the figure, so quiet now was her voice.

'I am bid six hundred and seventy guineas,' he said, his hammer raised.

And perhaps it was the Wiltshire Marshalls' gambling blood, something reckless anyway, that dealt the last throw.

'I bid seven hundred guineas!' cried the dashing Signore Filipo di Vecellio.

The muddy, perspiring rooms exploded; Mr Valiant's hammer was still held in the air; history was being made in Poland-street. Mr Valiant's loud, loud voice called for silence and then all eyes turned to the woman in the hat. She turned slightly and gave a mock bow in Filipo di Vecellio's direction.

The hammer fell.

The Rembrandt painting *Girl Reading* had been sold to the well-known (although slightly unfashionable) portrait painter from Italy, Signore Filipo di Vecellio, for seven hundred guineas.

His sister, the Signorina Francesca di Vecellio, fainted, straight into the arms of her nephew, the red-faced Claudio di Vecellio who, in the uproar after his father's victory, had violently pushed past his father, towards his aunt.

With some difficulty the sister of the triumphant buyer of *Girl Reading* was half-carried, half-pulled through the crowds of people to a small room down two steps at the back of the auction-rooms.

It was clear that Signore Filipo di Vecellio was exasperated at his sister's turn, and his son's disappearance, just as the moment of his triumph was sealed by the fall of the hammer. But the ever-present Lady Dorothea Bray tapped his arm with her fan in a manner that conveyed that she would take charge of this little matter, and so the *signore* turned back to all the people who were congratulating him, slapping him upon the back and shouting general huzzahs – especially after the rumour flew about that the lady in the front row (who had disappeared) was most likely bidding for the Prince of Wales. This auction would be reported in the newspapers, that was a certain thing, and the Italian Portraitist's name would again be upon people's lips. He could not contain his triumph, called for champagne. The envoy for the Duke of Portland looked once more upon the Painting in a longing manner, visibly moved to have lost it for his gracious employer. The mud and the rain did not matter, in fact the rain had suddenly stopped as if it too could not believe what had happened; there was a general air of great celebration inside the auction-rooms and nobody thought of leaving.

In the small back room, Lady Dorothea Bray wafted *sal volatile* under the nose of the poor woman; the poor woman was, in any case, completely conscious and brushed the smelling salts away (although politely of course). She understood it was her red-faced, breathless nephew who had brought her hence, and thanked him as she sat up; the kindly wife of Mr Valiant brought brandy in a small green glass, the Duke of Portland's disappointed envoy nevertheless sent good wishes, Mr John Palmer looked in to make sure all was well. As he left he passed Mr James Burke the dealer, come to ascertain the same. As his Aunt Francesca stood palely, it was to Mr James Burke that Claudio di Vecellio directed his attention. His agitation was so great that although his face had lost some of its alarming puce colour he had difficulty breathing and speaking. But he literally put both his arms round James Burke in a most peculiar manner and almost it seemed that he pushed the dealer against the wall. This action would have caused much more attention had not the auction-rooms been still in such an uproar.

James Burke had known Claudio since he was a child, so was surprised, but not unduly alarmed, at finding himself pressed flat. At that very moment, luckily for all, Lady Dorothea, laughing gaily, tripped down the little steps and took Claudio firmly by the arm.

'Your Father wishes you to share this Triumphant Moment, dear boy,' she cried, and Claudio was unceremoniously pulled back up into the auction-rooms and the celebrations, so that the odd little moment was over almost as it began, and for a brief moment Francesca and James Burke were almost alone. There was the smell of brandy and *sal volatile* and perspiration and mud as their eyes met.

'Congratulations,' he murmured, and the kindly Mrs Valiant who was hovering in the background thought he was congratulating the family on their acquisition.

'*Dio mio*, never, never again!' she answered him, and the kindly Mrs Valiant thought she was commenting on the large amount of family money spent. Then Signorina Francesca di Vecellio moved past Mr Burke the art dealer, her skirt brushing him as she moved up the little steps, and she was back among the crowds, pale but contained. James Burke moved back also into the swirling mass of people. Neither of them saw Claudio di Vecellio, his requirement by Lady Dorothea and his father concluded, standing alone, staring at the painting that his father had acquired with his mouth still opening and closing, rather as a fish's mouth opens and closes, when it is trying to survive.

THIRTY

Such delight, such a crowd, at Pall Mall for dinner later that afternoon. The Rembrandt portrait had at once, after various financial activities between the auctioneer and the dealer and the purchaser, been brought home in the carriage to Pall Mall and was already hanging in the large hallway; the old battered parrot squawked loudly at such intrusion but nobody cared; the informal guests crowded round to stare and admire, returned to the dinner-table and poured more celebratory wine, went back to the painting and the voices rose—

—holding inside me a wild feeling of mounting hysteria I had had to hurry to the *piazza* after the Auction, after my ridiculous fainting, to buy more food, hurrying in the pouring rain back to the house, bustling about before guests arrived, telling the cook to expect many people for dinner that afternoon, arranging for wine and I hurried into the dining-room and then I – the housekeeper – suddenly stopped quite still in the middle of the room.

My brother had paid seven hundred guineas for a painting by his sister.

And at last that long thin slither of steel that had entered my heart laughed aloud: for this was my extraordinary revenge over

Philip Marshall of Bristol, who had torn my precious Pictures into pieces so long ago. And I stood then so still in the empty dining-room – I heard the carriages passing along outside, and the voices of the servants urgently calling to each other downstairs, and the crackle of the fire in the grate – and I had the most peculiar feeling as I stood there that I was possessed of great wings that lifted me, that held me aloft, even as I stood there.

This is enough.

And – if I can describe it – all the stones of anger that had sat for so long upon my shoulders and inside my head were gone. There was no doubt in the world any more: *I am a Painter* – I had come so naively from Bristol clutching my Drawings and my Drawings had been destroyed, but I was one of the lucky ones, I had been helped over and over: I could not have progressed in my sewing-room without living in my brother's house and being so much in the company of Artists, and James Burke had sustained me, had – I allowed the word to float there – *loved* me and I had grown into an Artist.

This is enough.

I did not want to paint as Rembrandt van Rijn ever again – I did not think I *could* do something like that again: in my heart I felt it had been a momentary miracle that had taken hold of me and caught the eyes and finished the painting. —Now I would paint my own way, I could be Grace Marshall again at last, I would have money, and the knowledge of my success, to sustain me.

Euphemia brought in great high jugs of red, red wine.

There were so many people at our table that afternoon of the acquiring of **Girl Reading**, there was so much eating and in particular drinking as Philip celebrated his Purchase; I do not think I ever saw such drinking in that dining-room as that day, and Lady Dorothea sat opposite Philip with very bright eyes and she laughed, and teased guests a very great deal, and Isabella also sparkled and chattered because the highly-coiffeured Mr Georgie Bounds was somehow present, swept along that day with the crowd of well-wishers and hangers-on, and I saw how Isabella looked at him, and he seemed to look fondly back and I smiled, and she smiled back at me, my niece Isabella, and the news of the Auction raced like wildfire across London, the knocker sounded again and again on the door and I wished Miss Ffoulks might appear once more and it was said that Filipo di Vecellio could have sold Rembrandt's *Girl Reading* that very afternoon and added a further fifty guineas to the price, and my Picture hanging there on the wall for all to see – the voices got louder and louder as the afternoon wore on, the room was hot and smelled of wet clothes and beef and fish and smoke and wine – and Claudio seemed to me to have slightly gone out of his mind; his odd behaviour with Mr James Burke was not repeated with anybody else but he still looked almost apoplectic: his dark face kept changing colour, from red to pale and back again – had he been threatened once more? and then suddenly Claudio pushed back his chair and staggered out of the room and I heard the bang of the big front door (the boy who would not leave the house) but his Father was too busy with other matters that day, and indeed so was I, his Aunt.

I *revelled* in the conversation, which came back all the time to *Girl Reading* – *The Exquisite Painting*, I heard someone call it – they kept getting up to look at it again; they talked about its light and its shadows, the way the light fell across the girl and her red-brown gown, and her eyes, the light in her eyes as she looked up from the book; they compared the rich, luxuriant sleeve that I had spent so much time on to the sleeve in one of the paintings by Rembrandt that the Duke of Portland already owned; they talked about the *look* in the eyes of my girl: *Memory*, someone said, the painting should have been called *Memory* and they asked Philip where it might permanently be displayed and he answered that he had not decided whether it should be in his Studio, beside the other Rembrandt, or on the stairs somewhere near to the Portrait of Angelica, and the wine flowed. —I watched old John Palmer, he studied the Painting for a long, long time, smiling slightly, and finally late-afternoon sun appeared and tried to shine and dry the filth and the mud of the morning, as the wine flowed in the celebrating house. —But at last although this might sound strange, the more they praised Mr Rembrandt the more it made me want desperately to start out at last on my own as my *own* person as an Artist – I kept thinking *I must not die now – before I have been myself*: as if I had just been prescribed a deadly disease rather than just defrauded the art world of London – something about the waste of years and years locked in my sewing-room: suddenly everything was very urgent to me: I was one of them now, one of the Artists that sat around our table (Mr Gainsborough was there that afternoon, leaning back in his chair the way he did when he had drunk a great deal and the chair balanced, but only just). —I felt as the afternoon wore on a kind of real panic: I did not want to have to pretend for another day longer: I must leave Pall Mall *now*; I must take the room in Compton-street *now*; most of all, I must acquire my money from James Burke *now* – I would talk to Philip about my decision to live alone: I knew now I would not say it in anger, I would not speak of Tobias; Philip would make of it what he would: I was not angry, only urgent.

So somehow, as the dinner crowd broke up at last, many leaving for *soirees* or clubs or cards or a walk in the Park in the late afternoon sunshine, I managed to send two notes: the first was to Mr Thomas Towers in Frith Street, I asked Mr Towers to immediately ascertain for me, if he would be so kind, that the lease on the room in Compton-street was still available: I would take it: I would have the means at my disposal to pay for it in twenty-four hours.

The second note was to James Burke, despite his admonitions that I should not contact him at his home: my note to him simply said, *Immediate Payment Required*, and was unsigned.

I had been, publicly, acclaimed as an Artist: what I had thought of so naively as a girl had come to pass after all: my Destiny.

THIRTY-ONE

When Claudio di Vecellio left the house in Pall Mall he looked neither to the left nor to the right nor behind himself, as he had been doing most anxiously for days. He simply called for a carriage and required to be taken to the house of Mr James Burke, in Mayfair. It was clear to the driver of the carriage that the young man was extremely inebriated.

When Mr James Burke came later to the house in Pall Mall, to give his further congratulations and good wishes to Filipo di Vecellio, people were taking their summer evening strolls in St James's Park, for the sun shone bright now, the rain was quite gone, and if mud caught at boots and shoes and at the hems of ladies' gowns it was no matter for there was always mud and dirt in the streets and the parks but there was not always evening sunshine. When he heard that Filipo di Vecellio had gone he asked to see the Signorina Francesca. He waited for her in the formal first floor drawing-room.

Her dark face was pale when she entered but her eyes, her whole body, seemed alive and full of energy. She entered swiftly, smiled at him as she formally held out her hand, and her hand was warm and glowing.

Euphemia hovered, wishing to give them tea, or a small cake.

'Signorina Francesca, you expressed a wish to see the Eidophusikon once more,' said James Burke. 'I thought this day of your brother's Celebration might perhaps be a suitable time.' And almost at once they had left the house – and Euphemia thought wryly, *Do they think I am idiotic? They want to be alone these two* – and they walked, not to Lisle Street where the Eidophusikon might be found, but along towards the edges of St James's Park. A beautiful pair of high-stepping horses trotted past in Pall Mall, white and elegant, pulling a small landau, and as it passed they heard laughter and voices on the air. It was warm now after the ravages of the morning; the evening sky was pale red through the London mist, and streaked with gold. He guided her to the side of the Park where fewer people promenaded so that they could walk, in company but alone.

She spoke unguardedly, as soon as she was sure they could not be overheard. And such was her freedom of mind she did not notice his face. 'James, I have heard them, all afternoon, speak of my work with Great Reverence,' and she laughed the way he remembered her laughing long ago in her room with him, in their private world, and her black eyes danced. 'James, if I had not seen it all and heard it all with my own eyes and ears I would never have believed it possible! Imagine it selling for such a sum – it is extraordinary!'

'Some extraordinary events need a little Assistance,' he said dryly. She looked puzzled and he walked in silence for a moment casting little sideways glances at her, as if wondering what, and what not, to say. 'The Woman in the front row who kept up the bidding was a Friend of mine.'

'She was bidding for the Prince of Wales!'

'So I have heard it suggested. But I do assure you she is, actually, merely an Acquaintance of mine. It was a Risk, but it was worth it.'

She was astonished, stopped walking, stared at him. 'You put that about as a Rumour, about the Prince?'

He walked on. 'My dear Grace, it is easy to start a Rumour. You merely whisper something loudly at a Social Gathering. The rest takes care of itself.'

'But – we might have lost everything!'

'There would have been enormous Publicity once it reached nearly six hundred guineas, which it did unaided because the Duke of Portland was so keen to acquire it also. That is unheard of for any such Painting and – if my Accomplice had unfortunately acquired it – we would have been able to auction it again. There had not been a whisper that it might not be as it seemed – for which you must take great credit.'

And because her heart was high and her defences down she still went on. 'And I can lead my own Life at last, James. Thank you.' And then she added, 'I would have the money at once, my Plans are all made.' And she looked up at him, still smiling.

He did not smile back. He stared at her in silence and for once she could not read his face. She stopped walking again abruptly: she stood there in the evening light, very, very still: alert now. He was looking at her yet, and she could not read his face. 'What is the matter?' she said.

'What Plans?' said James Burke.

'I am leaving Pall Mall. You knew that. You've always known that.'

'Now?'

'Yes, now.'

'But where are you going?'

'That is nothing to you. It is not your business.' Something – pain – flashed in his eyes.

'Grace—' but she interrupted him.

'I wish to get away from that house now as soon as possible. I have seen and heard the great and the worthy praise my Work – even Mr Gainsborough, James – it is wonderful, and it makes me proud, but it also makes me . . . I cannot stay another moment longer in my brother's house.'

He began walking again so that she must walk also. Then he spoke and this time his voice was grim.

'Your Nephew believes the Painting to be by you.'

She was so taken by surprise that she tripped: quickly he caught her arm although they had been walking separately until now. Somebody turned to stare. 'You must keep walking naturally,' he said lightly, and the couple walked, her arm on his to support herself, so great was her shock, with all the other couples and crowds who promenaded there, flirting behind fans, and laughing: a summer evening in London as if the morning storm was only a dream. And down a path, looking delighted with one another, came Mr Bounds and Isabella. The aunt stood stock-still, her hand still upon the arm of Mr James Burke.

'Whatever are you doing here alone, Isabella?' she said, and then, collecting herself, she stood apart from the art dealer (as if the young people would have noticed old people). Isabella blushed but Mr Bounds the frame-maker's son stepped forward manfully.

'*Signorina*, I have asked Isabella to become my wife and she has made me the happiest man in England by agreeing.'

'But – ' Her mind whirled, so far away were her thoughts from this matter. 'Mr – Mr Bounds you must know, surely, that you must speak to her Father, not to Isabella. This is not how such things are done!'

'*My* Father said I must first ascertain the feelings of Signorina Isabella. I have tried for weeks to find her,' he smiled at his beloved, 'but she has had – other Interests.'

'No!' cried Isabella, 'I did not!'

'I have now however ascertained her Feelings and I shall now at once return to Pall Mall and ask permission of Signore di Vecellio.'

Grace could hardly stand; she saw her niece's shining face. Somehow she made herself smile. 'Go quickly then to the house,' she said and the two young people, thus blessed, hurried away. At once she turned back to James Burke. 'It is absolutely impossible that Claudio should know that,' she said. 'It is *impossible*!'

'He said he was speaking to you in your room.'

'He never, ever comes to my—' but already she saw him, throwing himself upon her small sofa, talking of the cock-fighting men, crying, actually knocking his aunt to the floor, and she saw herself, so anxious to get to Frith Street to paint the girl: she closed the door, yes, but she ran down the stairs *before Claudio*: quickly the movement replayed itself in her mind: she saw herself pick up her basket, close the door and then hurry past him and down the stairs. Later she had believed only that he had gone back into her room because he saw she had some money, saw where she kept it. 'I thought he had only stolen my money,' she said.

'Indeed? He is, then, truly a Gentleman, your Nephew.' James Burke forced her to keep walking. 'He told me that he went back into your room – he did not tell me about the money, of course – and then he opened the door to your sewing-room where he used to play as a child and saw how it was, with many canvases and boards facing the wall.'

'But he knows I am an *amateur* in my little room. They all know that and laugh of it.'

'Claudio is not entirely a fool. He is used to looking at paintings. He knows what an *amateur* is.'

'But the Picture was not finished then! He did not see the face!'

'The Painting of the girl reading was on your easel. I told him he must be mistaken, I told him it would be impossible for you to have done such a thing, but he insists it is the same Painting.' Now it was James Burke who stopped walking, and now his eyes burned with suppressed rage. 'He said he had been greatly surprised by the Painting sitting there in your sewing-room, and also that he had studied the gown you had painted carefully – he thought it beautiful, he said, like one he had seen in Amsterdam. And as soon as he saw the Painting at the Auction-rooms, he realised that, somehow, whatever had been done to it, it was the Painting he had seen in your room. Claudio is a foolish, weak, immature, unstable and . . . cunning boy, and is a great danger to us. He came to my house in an inebriated fashion and was seen and heard not just by me but by my Wife and by my servants. I took him into my Study but great damage has been already done. He was wild with his plans and his schemes.'

She could hardly make any sound. 'What are they?'

'That we give him money, of course. He will otherwise, anonymously, inform – I told you he was cunning, he has thought it through – *not* your brother, but Sir Joshua Reynolds and Mr Hartley Pond that the Painting is a Fake. You know we cannot risk that.'

It was at that moment that she realised just how much she had depended on her world changing at last: her heart began to beat violently, she could feel it pumping and pounding. 'Where is he?'

'I have no idea. I told him his plan was preposterous, that I had collected the Painting in France. I told him I did not believe him, that I would inform his Father if he repeated such nonsense. But I also had to say that I would speak to you when I could. Of course we will have to tie him to us in some way.'

'What do you mean by that?'

A pieman wandered by in the dusk, carrying his wares on a tray on his head. There was a smell of onions, and of bacon. James turned away impatiently, led her away from anyone, even a pieman, who might overhear.

'I have made a decision.' He spoke briskly. 'We may have been found out, but we must under no circumstances be caught. We do not want him racing about London imparting this Information – indeed I would wish quite frankly to throw him into the Thames!' He breathed angrily. 'There will have to be certain Guarantees from him, but I know enough of young Claudio to handle him. His Debts will have to be paid.'

She watched his face. She knew him so well. There was more.

'We will have to use your Brother's money to do all this. You will begin another Painting at once—'

'No!'

'—you will begin another Painting and we will pay you for the second one.'

She heard the words. *The second one.*

'It is extraordinary what we have achieved and we can achieve it again – not in London, that would be too dangerous – but in Paris or Rome or I will take it to Russia where the Empress Catherine is known to be an extremely avid Collector. I have done business with her agents before, when the Walpole collection was sold. It can all be done in a year.'

She tried very hard to speak normally, to breathe normally, to speak very quietly. 'James, I cannot wait another year. You must do as you wish but I will not paint another. I *cannot* paint another.' And then she suddenly grabbed his arms, as a child in Bristol used to do so long ago, so great now was her sudden, chilling fear that everything was lost. '*Where is the money now?*'

He disentangled himself carefully, walked on so that once again she must follow if they were to converse. 'The money has been arranged by your Brother. The money has been paid.'

'Then give me my share, I do not care about anything else.'

'He is your Nephew, Grace. Not mine. We were undone by your carelessness, not mine. His Debts will be paid and part of that money will have to be that which would otherwise have been paid to his Aunt.' His voice was hard now and whatever the expression was earlier when he looked at her, it was gone.

She was unable to speak. For in the end it came back once more to the same thing. *Money, money, money.* The sky had darkened as they had been walking, the link-boys' lights and the promenaders' lamps could be seen winking around them. James Burke's face was partly in shadow.

'But, after all, Grace, Grace – there is much to cheer you! You have triumphed over your Brother at last, have you not? You have a greater Revenge than you could have dreamed of all those years ago.' And he did smile at her, his old smile for just a moment, knowing his girl, her dreams and desires. 'I must deal with Claudio somehow, it cannot be helped. You must begin a further Painting at once, one more, and I will sell it on the wider European market for even more money. It will be our Glory, even more than this extraordinary day.'

Again she stopped, held his arms, both of his arms. 'James, I cannot live in Pall Mall any longer. I must have my own life before it is too late. Nobody will believe Claudio, he could never announce that his Father's prized Painting is a Fake!' He said nothing. 'James, that Painting took many, many months of my life – twenty-five years of my life you might say for that is how long it took me to learn what I have learned. I am glad to have succeeded but I do not want to succeed as a Fraud, I want to succeed as an Artist – you *know* that, James, you of all people. I must do my own work now.'

'One more, Grace. You cannot make this kind of money without me. You possibly cannot make any money at all. I will buy you your Freedom. After one more Painting. One more and I will pay half of everything we make.'

'*No!*'

The pieman called PIES, but there were not many people at that end of the park and his cry was half-hearted and dreams crumbled, there in the park.

She put her hand to her face, almost (it might have seemed) to stop herself screaming out, as if she was stopping her own mouth. Then she waited for a moment, breathed deeply. 'No, James. You will not *buy* me my Freedom. I have earned my own Freedom at last and you know very well that I have. I have worked and worked night after night after week after month after year and I have earned my own Freedom and I must have it at last,' and to her alarm she suddenly felt tears in her eyes, she who did not weep, and her voice choked in her throat. 'Please, James,' she said then, understanding how near she was to failing and falling, *'please* let me have the money, you will not be bothered by me again, I have planned everything.'

'Have you?' And he asked the question again. 'What have you planned?' She did not answer him and he stepped nearer to her and then, in the falling darkness in St James's Park, he put his hand to her face and very gently wiped at the tears. She was so surprised, so thrown by that old familiar touch that the tears in her eyes suddenly froze. She felt the remembered hand, there on her cheek. Nobody had touched her face since he had touched it last.

A crowd of people suddenly caught them up from behind: people laughing and talking and running in the fading light and several little poodles yapped and ran with them and the pieman seeing custom called loudly now PIES! PIES! and several young men stopped and obtained these edibles. And then from nowhere it seemed some women suddenly stood beside the young men with the pies and one spoke brazenly, 'Bit of fun, lovey?', twirling a sheepskin bladder tied with red ribbon between her fingers, 'Two shillins in the Park, lovey?' And she laughed and then the young men laughed very loudly but one of them, stuffing his pie into his mouth as he went, followed deeper into the Park the one with the red-ribboned *accoutrement*. Grace Marshall followed them with her eyes, her face expressionless. And then she turned from James Burke and made herself walk in the other direction, across the Park. Perhaps he was thrown: involuntarily he called out 'Grace?' to the *signorina* as she went away from him.

The wings she had felt on her shoulders had turned to stone. She walked away from him in the cruel London night and in her head red ribbons danced and drifted and she heard the laugh of the street-girl. She walked almost to the end of the Park in the darkness, almost to Rosamund's Pond, saw that the stars had come out, bright bright stars, not misty stars as Isabella had decided to prefer rather than to cut up love.

Grace Marshall stared up at the bright stars and then – because she had no other plan left, did not know what else to do – she turned back towards Pall Mall.

In the darkness on the step leading up to the big house there was an even darker shadow. She saw his eyes in the light of a coach as it rumbled past and the blood everywhere, coming from the thin jacket.

'I did not tell them, Gracie, where he lived.'

She knelt down quickly. 'What? What are you saying? What has happened?'

'The boy . . . Claudio . . . he came back to the cock-fighting this evening and I was there, he . . . he was boasting to them – you do not boast to those men, Gracie – I came right up to him quickly and listened, for I saw he was in Trouble . . . I stood right beside him . . . he told them he would be getting very much money immediately, that it was all arranged but—' Tobias suddenly seemed to choke blood or cough blood as he tried to speak further.

'Never mind that now, Tobias, it does not matter, just rest, just be still.'

'. . . the boy saw by their faces that he had to have the actual money in his hands to pacify them, he disappeared pretty quick – but they'd seen that I looked so like him, they said that I must know him . . . said I would know where he lived . . . they wanted the money from him now . . .' the shallow harsh breathing, 'he shouldn't have returned . . . but I did not tell them, Gracie.' She put out her hand to him, the blood through the jacket still ran, there was blood everywhere on her hand and on her gown and on the doorstep.

'What did you . . . how did you get here?'

'They . . . thought they had – done me . . . *cut off their tails with a carving knife*, wasn't it, Gracie? . . . they left me and when they were quite gone away I walked to here.' She could hardly hear him, bent right down close to his face. 'Tell him . . . he must not go back there . . . they'll kill him true . . . he does look like me, doesn't he?'

'Yes, he does – from the moment he was born – just like you.'

'I didn't have any children, so I'm glad.' A whisper. 'You'll remember me then, Gracie?'

'*O God* I have always, always remembered you, dear Tobias,' and she held him, and as she felt him flickering away from her, terrible harsh sobs came out of her body as she knelt there: *grief; guilt; the Vandal that is Time*, and she saw a thin shadow of the blue of the beautiful *lapis lazuli* against the stars, not misty but shining so bright: *cut him out in little stars*.

And Grace Marshall understood all that her Destiny had cost.

*

She knelt beside the body for a long time. The manservant, and then Euphemia, had come to the door and they had to look away for they saw her face, they saw tears fall on to the dead tramp and all the blood and they had never seen her cry before. When she had contained herself she said to Euphemia, 'Fetch Filipo,' and when the *signore* came they saw his shocked face also before he turned away, made brisk arrangements.

THIRTY-TWO

Perhaps one of the reputed, drifting ghosts in the dark danger of one of the alleys heard it first? Where the fog that hung over London lay always: grey, and dank, and secretive.

It started as a whisper in the dark: there down the alleys somewhere in Covent Garden perhaps, somewhere close to one of the dingy passageways of tailors and ale houses and bordellos and dubious prints of Old Masters; or in a Mayfair drawing-room perhaps; or down by the docks perhaps where the big ships sailed back and forth to the West Indies with their special trade; whatever: the whisper traversed London, passed the Royal palaces, crossed the *piazza*, sped up St Martin's Lane and down again to Leicester Fields and the Strand.

So that even as Signore Filipo di Vecellio luxuriated still in his new fame as art collector *extraordinaire* – accepting as his due the many compliments that came his way, as the *Morning Advertiser* wrote of THE GREAT ART AUCTION, mentioning the Italian portraitist several times; ignoring the occasional scurrilous new Pamphlet (obviously penned by the Evangelists) admonishing of Waste and Shame and Greed in the big city – even then the ghosts had drifted. Nobody understood how the rumour began, but it was repeated at dining-table after dining-table like wild-fire, there with the meat-bones and the wine and the beer and the fish and the cabbage.

The newly-acquired Rembrandt painting *Girl Reading*, which had been bought for seven hundred guineas and quickly become the toast of London, was a Fake.

Filipo di Vecellio heard the rumour in horror: he immediately sent a message to his banker.

James Burke heard the rumour in horror: he sent an immediate note to Signorina Francesca di Vecellio. No answer was forthcoming. He then went at once to Covent Garden to divulge the news to the Frenchman and the Jew-men in the attic; on his way there, quite by accident, he found Claudio di Vecellio on the *piazza* and imparted the news, holding on to the boy's collar angrily, not caring who might see: *Was it you, Claudio?* But Claudio heard the rumour from the Art Dealer in such unbelieving horror that James Burke understood it could not be so: Claudio realised at once that all his plans would be ruined. He had talked so boastingly to the vicious cock-fighting men (not knowing that he had an uncle watching close by who would later pay to save him); telling the men jauntily that all was arranged, that the money owing was forthcoming and more with it – in fact so great had been his excitement and his confidence that although he quickly realised he was not yet welcome at Broad-street, he had borrowed from a money-lender to bet on an illegal boxing match near the *piazza* and had later lost another five guineas. When he heard Mr Burke's words he looked back across the *piazza* in utter terror, clung almost to the older man. James Burke shook him off: Claudio ran home to Pall Mall as fast as his thin legs would carry him, not daring to look behind.

Isabella di Vecellio cared not one jot about any rumour, all she wanted was to marry Mr Bounds, but her Father had most rudely ejected Mr Bounds from the house; she kept to her room, would not speak to her father, and seemed never to find her aunt available for consolatory purposes. Isabella decided to starve herself to death, and then everybody would be sorry; she also contrived to still meet with Mr Bounds, who insisted he would come back and speak to her father again and again until his permission was obtained.

The rumour grew and grew and ran through the city like a fever. Finally the gentlemen of the press heard the rumour: this delicious twist to the story of the painting was also published, causing even bigger headlines. Several hacks appeared at the house in Pall Mall, causing great distress to the owner. Signore di Vecellio was informed by his banker that his bank draft had been cashed: however, Mr James Burke did not seem to be part of the scandal for he appeared through the evening light at the house in Pall Mall, banging angrily on the door, large as life, furious, and ready to refute all rumours.

In the big hallway the Dealer and the Italian stood beneath the object in question; the girl reading looked, just slightly, amused as she looked up, past the book she was reading: she looked past the two gentlemen below her as if she remembered something.

'I presume you think I am both an ignorant Dealer, and an ignorant Businessman, Filipo,' said Mr Burke icily to the man who used to be his friend. 'I understand perfectly well what is occurring here. An old Trick indeed! Perhaps you are already in cahoots with the original Seller? One of you has started this Rumour: I know that. Either *you* think the Painting is worth less than you paid for it, and wish to return it, or the original Seller thinks it worth *more* than he got for it, and wishes to re-sell it. So you start a Rumour, one of you. I myself refuse to be a Pawn in either Strategy, and I particularly resent my Honesty and fine Judgement about a work of Art of Genius being questioned in this way.'

Filipo di Vecellio was outraged. 'That is a gratuitous Slur!' he was heard to shout at his erstwhile close companion. 'How *dare* you accuse me of such Subterfuge! I have no idea how such a story, so damaging to me and my Reputation, has suddenly erupted! I insist that you remove yourself from my house at once and return my money until this matter is settled!' and Roberto the parrot screeched from the drawing-room.

The reading girl looked past them.

'The money has of course already been dispatched to my Client in France. Let him return it if he is not part of this Subterfuge!'

'I will take you to the Courts, you may count upon it!'

Mr James Burke bowed wrathfully and, just as he turned away, his eye was caught by a movement above him; he looked upwards, looked past the painting of the reading girl which hung there, so beautiful, in the big hallway. The sister of the painter stood on the stairs above him; she looked down upon the two men in silence.

He gave a formal bow. 'Signorina Francesca.'

She bowed back from the staircase. 'Good evening, Mr Burke.'

And it almost seemed to him (he could not be sure: the light was not good) that, very faintly, she smiled.

'Take this Painting down immediately!' thundered the *signore* to his servants. 'I will not be made a poltroon by Tricksters!'

THIRTY-THREE

> DO ARTISTS KNOW ART?
> WITH THEIR HAND ON THEIR HEART?
> OR IS ALL JUST A FART
> IN THE STORY OF ART?

sang the street balladeers barging past the milkmaids in the *piazza*; along the Strand the penny patterers declaimed poems about foolish daubers who were really nothing but drunken debauchers. The balladeers sang all along Pall Mall, past the Temple of Health and The Celestial Bed; they sang again up into Covent Garden where the inns overflowed and the bawds plied their trade; and along St Martin's Lane so that Sir Joshua Reynolds could hear them as he sat in Leicester Fields with his eagle and his ear trumpet. And a ghost – Mr William Hogarth's ghost – laughed in derision from the other side of the Square where he had once pleaded so passionately for British Art.

The balladeers were enjoying themselves as they always did come a scandal:

> DO ARTISTS KNOW ART?
> WITH THEIR HAND ON THEIR HEART?

WHO BUYS A FAKE?
A FOREIGN OLD RAKE?

And some wag had thought to add as a little chorus:

HERE WE GO ROUND THE MULBERRY BUSH!

which had deliciously obscene connotations so that the ballad sounded extremely saucy and all the beggars and gin-drinkers and pickpockets and scoundrels and ladies of the town who had heard in amazement of seven hundred guineas being paid for a *picture*, took enormous delight: 'IS IT ALL JUST A FART, IN THE STORY OF ART?' they sang all over London to the tune of Th*ree Blind Mice*. There was a cartoon in the *Morning Advertiser* depicting Signore Filipo di Vecellio with dark greasy foreign hair, painting money.

And Claudio di Vecellio cowered once more in Pall Mall and dramatic thoughts disturbed his mind, *This painting must not be considered a Fake by anyone but me, else I am doomed*. His aunt had been so odd, so pale: she had spoken to him only once, 'I have been advised that it is even more dangerous for you to go anywhere near' (as if he did not know it himself) 'Broad-street,' but she had said it to him as if he was not really there. She arranged the dinners as usual, he tried to catch her eye but she never looked at him now, never, nor addressed him: it was as if he was not present. Had Mr James Burke told her of blackmail? Had he been overheard speaking so wildly to the dealer and so the rumour started? Claudio's heart kept lurching in his chest: only he must know it is a Fake. What had he done? *What have I done? Who heard me say it? They will surely kill me!*

The picture in question had been removed from where it had hung in the hall, so when Mr Gainsborough whistled in, in his usual cheery manner, escorting, to everyone's surprise, Miss Ffoulks whom he had met at the door, the whistle stopped in the middle of a bar and he stared at the blank wall in disappointment.

'Lud, my friend!' he called to Filipo, 'You have not, I presume, let the fools persuade you? I loved that Painting.'

'Then you pay the seven hundred guineas,' growled Filipo; he had decided to hold dinner, as usual, to show that he was not intimidated by rumours, but he was more surly than his guests had ever seen him.

Miss Ffoulks could hardly hide her disappointment. 'I hoped I might be welcome, I so longed to see what I have heard so much about,' she said. John Palmer took her hand with pleasure and said how glad he was to see her returned. Miss Ffoulks and the Signorina Francesca did not speak privately to each other, not a word, but a very, very careful observer might have noted that they caught one another's eye once, and they both smiled. It seemed the dinner might restore everybody's spirits but Filipo di Vecellio sat morosely at the head of the table. He felt this to be a terrible turning point in his life, and here was everyone cheerfully drinking his wine and eating his food. The dastardly James Burke had cheated him: very well, he would be revenged, he would ruin *him*. He had heard that Sir Joshua Reynolds was specialising in full-length portraits, could now command for them almost two hundred guineas: Filipo did not paint full-lengths, only portraits, was lucky now to command much less than one quarter that sum, he had to work like the very devil to keep up his opulent life-style. And now: was his reputation as a collector to be laughed at also? Lady Dorothea could do nothing with their host, finally turned to Mr Gainsborough for respite.

'You speak to him, Mr Gainsborough,' she said and her manner was quite sulky.

'Come, come my friend, Filipo, it is some Jape!' said Thomas Gainsborough, 'Set about by some jealous Collector. The Painting is beautiful, and will surely be the more worthy after!'

Filipo said, 'D'you think so, Sir?' and Miss Ffoulks (who could have lived for ten years on what her old friend, whom she had not seen for so long, had paid for the picture) nevertheless smiled at him, and nodded encouragingly. The Italian's face brightened for a moment, that perhaps this was true, and the wine flowed and as always the painter's calm sister was there in the background, to be sure that all was comfortable.

'Where is Isabella?' the host suddenly enquired furiously to his sister. 'I require her at the table, not sulking in her room over a frame-maker!'

'She is unwell, Filipo.' The housekeeper said nothing more, did not say that she had promised Isabella a little tray and sympathy when the guests had gone; she had advised her niece this very morning to wait until the matter of the painting was decided before either she or Mr Bounds further pursued their suit.

The apprentice Mr Swallow, with his grandiose plans for biography, made himself as small as possible at the far end of the dinner table, for here was a story indeed, and here he was, part of it, but his Master was so volatile and so Italian that if Mr Swallow drew attention to himself in the slightest manner he might be dismissed from the company. On the whole it was a tense afternoon and conversation was stilted. However, the wine flowed.

'After all,' said John Palmer at last, 'it was at this very table that Sir Joshua made the comment that there can be no Plagiarism in Art. It is indeed a beautiful Picture, that has already given us much pleasure. So what does it matter?'

'Of course it matters!' said Filipo, angry again at once.

'But why? We all liked it so very much last week. Are we to dislike it today?' Filipo glanced at John Palmer in open displeasure.

'I will only pay seven hundred guineas if the painting is by Rembrandt himself. Anything else is worthless to me, as is your foolish opinion.'

'But you were so fond, only yesterday.'

Signore di Vecellio suddenly smashed his fist on the table and shouted, 'I am sick of you at my table, John Palmer!' His sister stared at him in horror. 'You have been coming here, day in day out, like a leech, for a hundred years, so do not try my Patience further!' There was a terrible silence in the shadowy flickering light of the candles in the dining-room, and then the sound of a chair scraping against the boards of the floor. John Palmer's old face was pale as he made for the door, holding his wig in his hand; of course everybody thought Filipo would finally call him back, but he did not, and Lady Dorothea Bray's hand lay approvingly upon his.

As he reached the door, John Palmer turned. 'I thank you, old friend, for your great hospitality over the years.'

Francesca di Vecellio made to stand.

'Leave him!' shouted her brother wildly.

And then John Palmer was gone, they heard his heavy footsteps, and then the big heavy front door opening, and then closing again.

'That damned scoundrel Burke! I am sure he was party to this

Scandal,' was all Filipo di Vecellio would say to break the embarrassed silence, and he drank more wine and did not apologise to the ladies for his language: seven hundred guineas, and his reputation, were at stake.

Throughout the art world powerful people discussed this matter urgently (including Sir Joshua Reynolds, the President of the Royal Academy, who was in France but who quickly sent a letter, making his thoughts known): it was decided the present state of affairs, where artists could be laughed at in such a way, and openly mocked in the newspapers and the streets, must not be allowed to continue a moment longer: it would indeed affect reputations (and sales and prices). It was clear there would be a court case if Signore Filipo di Vecellio thought he had been cheated, but the rumour had come from nowhere and was likely malicious; surely it would be proper to first have the picture examined, in private, by experts and artists and critics. Sir Joshua's message said the matter must be dealt with hurriedly and conclusively.

'We are private Men,' boomed one of the Academicians. 'We should deal with such a matter in a private Manner,' (as if the gentlemen of the press would not be waiting outside the Royal Academy with poised notebook if they were not allowed inside). For indeed the Academicians, relying on the Academy and its Exhibitions for their reputation and their sales, were only private men when it suited them.

And what better place for this inspection to take place than at the Royal Academy of Arts in Somerset House? Such elegant premises and sober judges would surely give the affair more dignity. Art experts with the knowledge of old methods would be called. And the eminent critic Mr Hartley Pond, of course. As luck would have it an eminent French critic was already in the country on other business (an affair of the heart the rumours said – but as he was a Frenchman it may only have been a racist slur): he sent word he would speed to London at once.

THIRTY-FOUR

It was early morning, when the natural light would be at its best.

The press-men, some of them shady-looking fellows, were there first, taking notes. A large group of Royal Academicians, all artists in their own right and proud, arrived under the porticos of Somerset House. Then the Art Experts, five of them, arrived. Then the carriage of the eminent French critic happened to arrive at the same moment as the carriage of Mr Hartley Pond: unfortunately these two eminent gentlemen had fallen out in the past. Each was jealous of his reputation: they had agreed to work together on this matter because of its importance but each was determined to out-shine the other. They alighted on to the cobbles, bowed stiffly while yawning behind their hands at the perhaps unreasonable earliness of the hour. Interested spectators and passing drapers and bakers and vintners stared at the group of men; some of the press-men stamped their feet in the morning chill and horse dung steamed on the Strand.

The press-men were made to wait downstairs with the Porter. It was well-known that some of the newspapers would like to give the Royal Academy – and what was seen by many as their ludi-crous pretensions – a bloody nose. It was imperative therefore that all was seen to be done methodically and with decorum: the Porter, a large red-faced bluff person, was to make sure the press-men stayed where they should be; however a spokesman would come to the press-men immediately at the end of deliberations and a statement would be given. All the newspaper men would then be invited upstairs to see the painting for themselves.

Finally the Academicians and the Experts and the Critics, many respected and respectable men, were led up the infamous, steep, narrow staircase to the first floor and into the big-windowed Council Room of the Royal Academy. King George and Queen Charlotte stared sternly down; portraits of the Academicians themselves also hung all along the walls there (several glanced up to observe their own likenesses as they entered) and fires had been lit in the fireplaces at each end of the room. On one of the tables used for meetings, quills and paper and ink were set, with which the Experts might take notes if required. Candles flickered in the darker corners but the best light, the main light, came in from the large windows.

An easel had been set up by the windows: there sat *Girl Reading*.

It was extremely odd to the Academicians as they entered the Council Room to see a pale figure, a woman in a grey gown and small lace cap, already standing there alone in the long room, staring at the picture. The reason for her unlikely presence was quickly ascertained (for no women should be here unless they were one of the two female Academicians and even they knew better than to attend uninvited): this woman was the sister of Signore Filipo di Vecellio, the now-owner of the Rembrandt in question. The woman was standing absolutely motionless, staring at the painting: just the one painting on an easel in the Royal Academy in Somerset House, and all the experts in London present, and daylight slanting through the long windows. The woman seemed in the morning light so fragile that several of the assembled gentlemen felt she may faint at any moment (indeed several artists present remembered her fainting at the auction of the painting); they looked impatient, did not want to be worried with womanly vapours just because her brother may have been cheated. However, the pale old *signorina*, the artist's sister, could hardly now be ordered from the premises, although it was felt it should be a matter for men only and the Porter should have kept her out. In fact, it was odd that she had gained admission in the first place (none of them knew, except her brother who had forgotten, how Grace Marshall of Bristol could always, all her life, find a way to gain entrance to a place she wished to be). Finally it seemed (although there was much muttering) that there was nothing to be done but to begin the examination. The Italian himself was seen to be irritated by the presence of his sister, took more comfort from the fact that his son was by his side. The dealer James Burke who had been responsible for the sale of the painting suddenly appeared at the doorway, insisted on being present also at the proceedings in the illustrious room, and he could hardly be turned away either: he was representing the anonymous French seller, of course, but he was also a very well-known dealer in Art and he made it clear he felt his honourable reputation impugned by these proceedings and he would stay.

There were perhaps twenty-five men present in total.

Mr Burke and Signore di Vecellio did not speak to each other; Signorina Francesca di Vecellio did not even look in Mr Burke's direction; he was most extremely surprised when he realised she was in the room, cast several quick – furtive almost – glances at her, at the pale dark face and the dark expressionless eyes.

At first all the be-wigged and un-wigged heads pored over the painting, pushing a little to get a better view: they stared at the thickness of the paint in certain areas, at the colours, at the light and shade, at the luxuriance of the gown. At the girl. Large magnifying glasses were brought forth from many embroidered waistcoats.

Then it was agreed that the Artists themselves should properly examine the painting.

It looked small, and rather lonely; that is until they stood there, each man, examining with great interest this thing that had called such commotion. Then it caught them, something: the beauty of the painting moved people in ways that surprised them. A silence.

Nobody wanted to speak first, in case they were wrong, until Mr Thomas Gainsborough, Royal Academician, who came seldom to the premises, said simply at last, 'It is a fine, fine Painting.' And then others nodded and murmured, 'It is beautiful, certainly.' Finally the Artists, who were there of course to give an opinion but were not experts in fakery, stood back, lit cigars; some walked up and down the long room talking quietly together.

Now the five Experts came forward: now small palette knives were brought forth. Out of deference to the Experts the Academicians brushed the cigar smoke away from the easel by the windows. Out of deference to the woman they used the chamber-pot in the Antiques Academy next door (where students were sent to draw life from statues), but resented it rather. Slants of sunshine suddenly shone in for a few moments, making the room even lighter; soon clouds gathered again and the brief sunlight was gone.

Again heads pored over the painting. All the Experts held up to their eyes their own special magnifying glasses of different shapes and sizes: everything must be noted most carefully. The frame was examined, the varnish, the paint, the board itself: the picture was turned over and over, the old certificates of customs on the back examined again and again. The experts murmured together, some took notes on the provided paper, with the quills and the ink.

Very fine, infinitely careful, gentle scrapings of varnish and paint were acquired from a small corner of the painting and studied under the magnifying glasses. The huge clock in the library ticked and tocked, the pendulum swung calmly.

An Old Master under their hands:
tiny mark
tiny scrape
careful
careful.

The huge clock struck another hour.
The old, cracked gilding on the frame was observed minutely.
Much time passed.

Finally perhaps it was felt that the painting *itself* was not being examined properly by the Experts, for at last the conclave of expert gentlemen stood together in front of the picture and stared at it for a very long time. Murmurs arose: *Fine, very fine*, said the voices over and over, *Very much of his early period*. The colours were authentic, the frame was authentic, the work was very similar to other paintings by Rembrandt at that time: these men knew very much of these things, and were satisfied.

And also: the painting was beautiful.

At last the two Critics, Mr Hartley Pond and his French coun-terpart, came forward portentously: they studied the painting in silence for some time and then conferred briefly. Most unusually the eminent French critic and the eminent English critic agreed in this case (and it was, at last, the dinner hour also). Mr Hartley Pond finally (annoying his French colleague immensely) chose this moment to address the Academicians as if he was the only real Critic whose opinion was worth listening to.

'Gentlemen.' He looked at them almost in disdain. 'The Experts are about to speak of technical matters, but I would like to contribute a word first. After all the tests are completed, after Science is assured, there is still the 'Soul' of the Painting to be considered. A real Artist does not just paint a face: there is something else, something mere Mortals can only aspire to. A real Old Master paints a *Soul*, and this painting by Rembrandt van Rijn has such a *Soul*. I am only a humble Critic' (a small powerful smile upon his lips) 'but I will stake my Reputation here. This painting is by Rembrandt. It is genuine.' And he bowed his head. The French Critic did not wish to be outdone, stepped forward, clearing his throat.

But the Experts had already elected a spokesman and he now, ignoring the Frenchman, began to address the Academicians. Signore Filipo di Vecellio felt his heart beating.

'Gentlemen,' said the Expert. 'My eminent Colleagues, and the finest Critics of the day', (he bowed at the Englishman and the Frenchman with equal respect) 'concur. We have examined this Painting for many hours as you have seen; we are agreed that this is an authentic Painting by Rembrandt van Rijn. We feel that Signore di Vecellio might rest assured. We are willing to put our valuable Reputations at risk and to advise the gentlemen of the press who are waiting below that we are certain of the authenticity of *Girl Reading*. We hope thereby that the matter will be closed.'

A great shout of triumph went up that could very likely have been heard downstairs where the press-men waited. Everywhere huge sighs of relief and words of congratulation; Claudio di Vecellio kept saying delightedly to his father, 'See! See Father!' so nobody heard the almost inaudible sigh from the pale woman. But suddenly the voice was loud and clear.

'*No!*'

It was because it was a woman's voice in this male company that her voice was heard. What an extraordinary surprise it was that the woman should speak at all. They turned to her in amazement.

James Burke in particular looked shaken, he stepped towards her but she put up her hand and the room went silent, more in shock than in obedience to her oddly forceful small gesture.

'I painted this Picture,' she said simply. The explosion in the room was not amazement or anger: it was simply laughter, loud raucous laughter and, clearly heard, the supercilious neigh of Mr Hartley Pond. And then general hurrumphs of embarrassment for poor Filipo di Vecellio: first the authenticity of his painting was called into question and now his sister had run mad.

People had even begun leaving the Council Room and the Antiques Room, for it was a family matter and would be no doubt dealt with, and it was time for dinner; the door to the anteroom to the staircase was actually opened. But the woman spoke again and her voice was firm.

'I painted this Picture.' There were now exasperated sighs as well as laughter and somebody was heard hoiking into the spittoon in disgust: it was realised that nobody could leave for their awaited dinner just at this moment because they knew that the journalists from the *Morning Chronicle* and the *St James's Press* waited below for the result of the deliberations, and to be shown the picture – they could not have a madwoman running amok from the Royal Academy premises. The door of the anteroom was quickly closed again; the gentlemen gathered back in the room with the painting and the madwoman. Claudio di Vecellio stared at his aunt in disbelief and anguish. *What is she thinking of?* He would lose everything *again*.

Signore Filipo di Vecellio took command at once. 'I do beg your pardon, Gentlemen. This has of course been a great strain upon our Family. My Sister has been unwell before, and we will see to it. I would wish to thank you for your meticulous attention to the Rembrandt Painting, and if you will allow us to leave I will detain my Sister in another room until the Journalists have admired the Painting. Then perhaps we can all meet at the Turks Head for a dinner that I will be very happy to invite all present to share with me as my Guests.'

'I painted this Picture,' said the woman for the third time, and this time she looked straight at her brother. There was great embarrassment in the room, again mainly for Signore di Vecellio who should be so unfortunate as to have a mad sister. Now the spokesman for the Experts himself came towards her kindly, clearly used to dealing with unfortunates.

'My dear,' he said, 'this has no doubt been a most worrying time for your Family and we understand you will all have been under a great deal of strain. Why not wait with your Brother until it is easier for you to leave the Academy? This is a story, after all, with a happy ending.'

'Not yet,' said the woman clearly. It was not clear whether she meant she should not leave yet, or whether the happy ending was not yet. She walked towards the painting in a perfectly dignified manner, and nobody stopped her which was most peculiarly odd for she could have damaged it of course: it was as if they were bewitched by her madness. She stood beside the painting and stared at it. She pointed to the rich gown with all its glowing colours, 'I painted that gown.' And then she pointed to the girl with the wonderful eyes. 'I painted that Girl,' she said. 'Much has been done to the Painting to age it – but it was painted by me.' She looked as if she would say more but Signore di Vecellio interrupted.

'She is not a Painter,' he said, 'of course she is not a Painter. She is my housekeeper!' He was so incensed, so embarrassed, so angry that he took his sister very harshly by the arm but she shook him free; he then perhaps used more violence than he intended, but he was angry beyond words to be humiliated and shamed in his hour of triumph. She was then half-dragged, half-carried away from the painting by several of the gentlemen including her brother. She began to scream as she was hustled and carried. It was absolutely imperative the screams were not heard downstairs for this was to be a day of celebration of Art and Art's Reputation, and was not to be sullied, so a hand was put across her mouth, which she bit; someone then hit her across the face. James Burke stood as if nailed to the ground: the look on his face might have revealed many things, but nobody was looking at James Burke. The door of the anteroom to the staircase was shut firmly so that sound was muffled.

In the Council Room, while a hand still was held over the mouth of his sister, Filipo di Vecellio explained to several of the Experts that his sister had spent some time in Bedlam, so that this behaviour was not altogether new. 'Then the Porter will fetch her away to the Asylum,' said one of the Academicians, and already someone quickly opened and closed the door of the anteroom and hurried downstairs, 'for he knows what to do, for occasionally a Person has gone mad at an Exhibition. I request your patience for just a little moment longer, Gentlemen,' he said then to the gathering. 'Everything is being dealt with and we shall descend to the pressmen with our Statement, as arranged. They will be invited to see this Rembrandt for themselves, and we shall repair to the Turks Head in a very short time.' And the gentlemen hurrumphed again and spat and longed for a drink, and the somewhat farcical situation might have continued had not the strangest thing happened.

The woman who was being held had heard the word: *Bedlam*.

With an almost superhuman strength she pulled free for a moment from her tormentors. She stood before them, dishevelled now and breathing in great gulps, with her hair undone and her lace cap awry. For a moment nobody approached her, although they were ready for the slightest sign of danger. And in that moment she looked at James Burke, and then she turned her head to look once more at the painting as it sat there, beautiful and Rembrandt-like in the early afternoon light. Nothing in the world seemed more unlikely than that this hysterical, aging woman had painted such a beautiful thing.

And then she turned back to the assembled gentlemen.

'I will speak to the Journalists downstairs if you do not allow me to speak to you,' she said. 'I will shout to them as you bundle me past, or I will send a message to them if you choose to lock me away.' She saw the disbelieving, disapproving, angry faces, felt the stillness of James Burke, Art Dealer. 'Surely you Gentlemen must know that there are anonymous, knowledgeable men in dark alleys all over the world who have the skills to authenticate paintings as Old Masters. It was', she did not look at James Burke, 'my own idea. I took my Painting to some such as I have described and' – she gave an odd little smile, and those near heard an odd little sigh – 'I asked them to authenticate me.'

Then she took a deep breath.

'I can prove it,' she said.

—for I was from Gambling Stock, after all. I was not certain, but I was *almost* certain, that I could prove it.

Of course I had not intended any Violence in the Royal

Academy, I regretted the screaming, I regretted my brother's harshness towards me, I would rather have done it with Dignity but they had grabbed me and pulled me and silenced me and spoken of me as some mad thing and the reason in particular why I bit the hand that was held over my mouth was not because I was insane but because of the stink of it: the smell of meat and shit and cigars covering my mouth and my nose.

Now they all stared at me; the faces are burned in my memory forever, all the Academicians that I had wanted to be part of: anger, dis-belief, red faces, embarrassment, one or two amused faces for this would make such a fine story to relate over dinner-tables; my brother's steely rage; and Claudio's shocked, thin face, like Tobias.

'Do not let her touch the Painting!' someone called in alarm, and they moved again as if to take me away.

And then the strangest thing happened. It was James Burke who saved me. 'Let her prove it,' he said. 'For if I, as the Dealer, have been duped I wish to know of it,' as if to say to me, *go ahead, go on, you have already cleared me, let me see you prove it*.

There was a loud chorus of disagreement and disapproval: why were they even listening to a madwoman? 'Take her away,' was the general cry. 'Hide her in one of the other rooms upstairs, lock her in the Grand Room, until the press-men have gone!' but Thomas Gainsborough forcibly held several Academicians back. 'Let her at least speak!' said Thomas Gainsborough who was observing everything, I was dimly aware, with intense interest.

'Let her prove it,' said James again. 'It is my Reputation as an honest Dealer at stake here,' and his grey eyes said to me again, *Prove it*, and the eyes were wild and glittering; he looked almost mad himself.

'But I tell you she is not even a Painter!' shouted my brother, almost uncontrollably but now people were holding his arms, as if he might kill me else. 'Why are you listening to her for even a moment!' he cried. 'Have you all taken leave of your senses?'

I had placed my basket in one of the dim corners of the room. —I walked to it, shielded the contents with my body and removed a cloth and a small bottle, and walked back towards the Painting, there was a small gasp of silence and then Philip shouted again, although some still held him, 'I beg you gentlemen to stop this Farce immediately!' and someone else called in anger, 'Do not let that Madwoman touch the Painting!' and I knew I would be dragged away again any moment if there was further delay.

'I shall touch a small part of the gown,' I said calmly. 'Or perhaps if you would rather, one of the Experts might follow my Instructions.' Intakes of breath: the *effrontery* of the Madwoman. Then: not Mr Hartley Pond, not an Expert, but the French critic moved towards me quietly. I think he had been insulted enough by Mr Hartley Pond and the Experts ignoring him, to do it.

'What have you in the bottle, *Madame?*' he said, bowing slightly as he approached me.

'It is Turpentine, *Monsieur.*' And as I removed the cork from the bottle the sharp fumes caught me, and a flash of memory – Turpentine dripping through my hair so long ago when Philip had so violently thrown me to the ground of his Studio and torn up my Drawings. 'I shall remove a small part of the Varnish, and a little paint from the gown.'

'This is a very, very valuable Painting, *Madame.* You will damage it if you touch it with Turpentine.'

I could not help it, I laughed (another sign that I was mad of course, but it really was not madness, except that everything about this occurrence was madness: just a small pleasant laugh). 'I think you yourself will be grateful, *Monsieur,* if you allow me to damage it in small measure.'

I saw him catch my meaning: he understood I spoke of his Reputation, it was not he who had spoken so portentously of the Soul of Rembrandt. I saw him measure me – I may have looked dishevelled but now that I was not being pulled about the premises I am sure I looked and sounded perfectly calm: I *felt* perfectly calm for it was All or Nothing now. I saw his look: either I was mad. Or I was sure.

Philip's loud, hoarse voice. 'I forbid you to touch my Painting! It is mine! I forbid you!' The French Critic turned very, very Frenchly, and very slowly, towards my brother. '*Monsieur,* I have been asked to verify this Painting and—'

Mr Hartley Pond broke in, his voice shaking with anger, 'I know this Woman well! This Woman is a *housekeeper!*' and I saw Thomas Gainsborough looking at me intently.

The French critic repeated his words, 'I have been asked to verify this Painting and—'

'—you have already verified it!'

'—and if I wish to further verify before I *sign my name* to anything, I must do so.'

A tiny whisper in the room, 'Damnable Frenchies!'

And after a moment or two the Frenchman turned back to me and bowed again. There were angry intakes of breath in the long room. 'Very well, *Madame.* 'Instruct me exactly.' I moved to him, and whispered something into his ear that the others could not hear. He looked at me, startled.

But one of the Experts then came forward. 'Allow me, *Monsieur.* I, after all, am the Expert.' And, with the look of one of Leonardo da Vinci's martyrs upon his face, he put a small dab of Turpentine upon the cloth and rubbed gently at the bottom of the Picture where I showed him. It was a meticulous hand he laid to my Painting: careful, slow, methodical. But before he went further, the French Critic went to him and whispered something into his ear that the others could not hear. The Expert looked at me startled also: I knew he thought I was insane, but after a brief look of confusion he went ahead. The paint of the skirt under the Varnish, began to come away. 'Be careful now, at this moment,' I said. 'There will be a mark' and in my head I said, *God in heaven I hope there will be a mark: the palette knife, did I scratch lightly or deeply? lightly or deeply? I tried to see myself doing it that mad night, but I could not.* I heard the breathing of the French Critic beside me, he smelled slightly of roses, *I cannot be sure, I cannot be sure,* I hoped the thickness of my paint on the red-brown gown had not obliterated the mark for ever, my heart was pounding in my chest: Everything in one, last, throw of the Dice.

Now the room was completely silent: no coughing, no hoiking, just the breathing of the watchful gentlemen.

And then – and then the beginning of the scratch of the palette knife appeared imperceptibly and I think no-one but my own heart heard my infinitesimal sigh. 'Rub carefully and gently,' I said so quietly, 'towards the left.' He understood at once now: he had to remove part of the rich red of the skirt. The reading girl looked away, amused; his breathing became faster as he worked and what I wanted him to see appeared. More colour was gone: there was enough information now for him to stop but I said, 'Further.'

The Expert turned to the mesmerised gentlemen in the room. 'She says she has written her Real Name,' he said.

And finally there it was. From underneath the luxurious, beautiful red-warm gown of the girl, emerged the name I had scrawled with the palette knife so wildly when I had laughed because the face in the painting had still eluded me.

GRACE.

There was a wild, wild cry from my brother. He stared at me in both disbelief and a terrible kind of anguished recognition and then he seized the thing nearest to him: the bottle of ink on the table, and he hurled it frenziedly at the painting so that black liquid fell down the painting and covered the laughing eyes of the reading girl.

THIRTY-FIVE

It was dark when Euphemia the maid opened the door of the house in Pall Mall that evening. Mr James Burke stood there. He looked extremely strange – and rather beautiful (she thought to herself): his hair was wild, and his eyes. He carried a large, and obviously very heavy, parcel.

'Where is Signorina Francesca?'

Euphemia's voice was, unusually, subdued. Euphemia could seldom be described as subdued. 'The Signorina Francesca is not here, Mr Burke.'

'No, I suppose not.'

He stood with his parcel, people were passing; carriages rattled past along Pall Mall, their lights flashed and a dog rushed by, barking at the horses.

The maid's voice dropped to almost a whisper. 'If you will step inside a moment, Mr Burke?' He did as requested, the big door into Pall Mall echoed as it closed. James Burke put his large parcel on to a table, there in the hall, next to a candle-lamp. The painting of Angelica still hung there: ageless, beautiful, at the turn of the staircase.

From somewhere above another door opened. Signore di Vecellio's voice from the drawing room: *'Is that her?'*

'No, *Signore*.' The drawing-room door banged shut.

Silence in the house. Then James Burke thought he heard the voice of Lady Dorothea Bray, but could not be sure. And then Roberto the parrot gave a loud shriek from somewhere, and then was quiet again.

The big clock in the hall ticked and tocked.

'We are all at sea here, Sir,' said Euphemia.

He looked down at her, spoke very quietly also. 'Do you know where she is?'

'No, Mr Burke.' And then in a rush of words. 'Oh Sir, we all knew she painted of course.' She looked apologetic. 'I knew *you* knew, Sir.'

'What do you mean?'

'That she painted, Sir.' Euphemia decided this was no time for niceties. 'I seen you, years ago. You knew she was good didn't you, Sir?'

'I did, yes.'

'I did too, Sir.'

He was taken aback. 'You saw her work properly?'

'Years ago I thought to dust her room, Sir, she was always so busy, I meant to help,' and then the words came tumbling out, 'then I seen the Paintings. After that I used to go and look at them sometimes while she was buying the food, I liked them so much. She so often destroyed them after. I thought it was a shame, Sir.' And then she stopped and looked up to the first floor before she went on. 'She did not come back today, for the first time ever in my life. And she has not returned now. I made so bold as to go into her room. It is empty of some of her clothes, Mr Burke, and all the Painting things are gone.'

He tried to hide his shock, then endeavoured to make light of the matter. 'She could not, surely Euphemia, have left here for ever with all her Worldly Goods without being noticed!'

'I seen her go out with her basket as usual yesterday to buy the food and I would swear she had two Paintings under her arm and when she came back she did not have them. And last week there was a fire, Sir.'

'A *fire*?'

'Nothing unusual in that of course, for we often burn things at the back. But there was a big fire one evening, I thought it must have been started by the Master for I noticed there was Frames and Paints, but perhaps it was her own things burned. You know as well as me how often she has destroyed her work and now I think she might have burned some of her clothes as well for she took nothing but her basket when she left this morning as usual.' She took a deep breath and spoke almost now in a whisper, 'And a tramp died on the doorstep and she cried and cried.'

'What do you mean? What tramp? Why was she crying?'

But Euphemia was suddenly aware that she may have said too much, even to Mr Burke. Euphemia had seen the face of the tramp. 'Mr Burke, the *signore* has been shouting about the Picture since he returned, I am afraid Lady Dorothea cannot calm him, and the Signorina Francesca has returned not at all, and Master Claudio is running about the house so wild I fear he may do himself damage and the Signorina Isabella is weeping and sulking in her room and I cannot think what to do with her. Shall I tell the *signore* you are here, Sir?'

Extraordinarily Mr Burke laughed. 'I think I might be the final straw, Euphemia!' But his face darkened almost immediately. 'Please give that Parcel to Signore di Vecellio, give it to him at once.' And in a very low voice, 'I will try to find her.'

Euphemia stared at him. She knew what she knew. 'God Bless you, Sir,' she said awkwardly. And, unspoken conspirators, the door was opened quietly by the maid, all the candles flickered for a moment in the draught of the night air, and James Burke was gone.

He walked quickly back down Pall Mall towards the Strand.

The maid picked up the very heavy parcel. She walked slowly, breathing very heavily, up the stairs to the drawing-room. The Master had said she must never speak of the tramp but Euphemia had seen what she had seen: she had seen the face of the tramp. She puffed and climbed: the parcel was so heavy. Euphemia did not know that she was carrying seven hundred guineas as she climbed upwards; she would no doubt have fainted if this piece of information had been brought to her attention. She tapped nervously and clumsily upon the door for the parcel restricted her movement, and entered without waiting.

Signore Filipo di Vecellio was a handsome confident man, always aware of his appearance. The maid saw a grey, huddled figure at the fireplace and Lady Dorothea sitting on a sofa, her face tight and angry; her dressed hair shook as she spoke and small birds thereon fluttered. Lady Dorothea flicked her eyes to the maid, flicked them away again and went on talking.

'Why do I have to say it over and over, Filipo? I do not know why you give any Credence to her story at all! Rembrandt himself could have written *Grace*! Grace has many meanings! Grace is not her name! What does it mean to her – *Grace*?'

There was no reply.

Lady Dorothea unconsciously pulled at her corset in an angry manner, her breasts wobbled slightly, and the small birds.

'That Painting could never have been painted by a Woman, and in particular it could never in one hundred years have been painted by your dreary sister. That is absolutely impossible and you know that perfectly well – you *live* with her, after all – do you imagine she forged a Rembrandt painting in the attic after Dinner?'

He did not answer. He half-turned to the servant who still stood in the doorway with the heavy parcel. 'What is it?'

'Please Sir, Mr James Burke left this for you. He said you were to have it immediately, *Signore*.'

'That Blackguard! That Cheat! That false Friend! He became rich because of me!' His voice rose and rose. 'And he had the Impertinence to accuse *me* of cheating!' The parcel was so heavy that the maid, uninvited, moved and placed it on a table beside him. He looked at it, and then suddenly scrabbled to open it, motioned to the maid to help him. She gasped first. Lady Dorothea, watching, gave a tiny, noble scream.

The money lay there. Seven hundred guineas. Not even a draft from a bank, but actual money. Like a grey ghost the *signore* put his hand just once into the sea of coins, to ascertain if they were real perhaps. It would have to be counted but all was clearly here: seven hundred guinea pieces.

'There, Filipo!' Lady Dorothea's face was at once suffused in smiles. 'There! You are no worse off after all! Mr Burke must have been taken in also and is doing the honourable thing.' Euphemia could not believe what she had, so briefly, held in her arms: stared at the money in disbelief and fascination.

But the grey face of Filipo di Vecellio did not suddenly brighten as Lady Dorothea might have expected. 'Now it does not matter,' she repeated and she laughed her tinkling laugh, 'for you have lost nothing at all!'

For how could Lady Dorothea Bray know what Filipo di Vecellio had lost when he saw the name on his beautiful Rembrandt painting: GRACE. At every moment pictures flashed into his head over and over at terrible, terrifying speed: the spinning small girl the house in Bristol his mother with her petulance and her adoration of her older son the father's debts he saw the younger boys fighting over a small cart he saw the drawings of their family that he had done with her chalks that sunny day. And of course: he saw the drawings of their family that *she* had done. And that he had torn to pieces in St Martin's Lane over twenty-five years ago.

Philip Marshall had thought that he had obliterated the past.

But his own past had lived with him, in his house, for twenty-five years.

Suddenly poor, mangy Roberto with his battered white feathers appeared in the doorway, squawking and complaining, as he had done every day since Angelica had died.

The maid and the noble-woman stared in alarm as the grey-faced man suddenly rushed from the drawing-room; they heard footsteps running further upwards; they heard the door of his studio bang shut. Roberto perched, beady-eyed and biting at his feathers, near the mantelpiece.

The two women then stared at all the shining coins – and if the truth be known neither of them wished to leave such a valuable sum with the other. Filipo had a safe but it was in his study and only he knew how to open it, of course. The coins glittered in the candlelight from the chandeliers: two dragons, as it were, stood guard, not to mention a mad parrot.

At this moment Claudio burst into the room, then stopped, as if he had been punched, when he saw the money.

'Claudio,' said Euphemia the maid at once, 'go and ask your Father what he needs doing with the Money from Mr Burke.'

'Go away!' shouted Claudio immediately. 'Go away both of you! I will manage the Money!' And he approached the huge pile of coins as if bewitched. 'Go away,' he said again.

At this point Euphemia, who had known Claudio since he was a baby, actually forgot herself so far as to laugh. 'You'd only gamble it away on them birds, Master Claudio! Go and get your Father!'

Lady Dorothea looked shocked at such behaviour from a servant, nevertheless waved Claudio away to do as he was bid. The boy stared again at the money, the shining, golden money; he suddenly lunged forward, pushed at the maid who screeched in surprise. And then Claudio fell across the table, covering the coins with his body; the coins rattled and clanked as they were pressed between flesh and wood, some fell on to the polished floor just as the clock sonorously struck eight o'clock.

Mr Georgie Bounds, the frame-maker's son, passed Mr James Burke in Pall Mall and bowed, but so intent was Mr Burke on his own thoughts that he did not see.

When Mr Bounds was shown into the noise-emanating drawing-room by one of the servants, he came upon a most extraordinary scene. Lady Dorothea Bray, the young Claudio di Vecellio and Euphemia the maid seemed to be partaking of some kind of mad dance, knee-deep in guinea pieces and speaking in very loud voices; Claudio kept shouting, 'It is Mine! It is My Money!' and flaying the air with his fists while the women screeched at him to stop and the battered parrot squawked.

Mr Bounds, his hair especially coiffeured for the occasion, had come to see Signore Filipo di Vecellio to ask, again, for his daughter's hand in marriage. He was wearing his very best embroidered waistcoat. He found the scene almost shocking (the money, the women, the anger, the old parrot adding to the general air of pandemonium) but he was a sensible and masterful young man and he understood that Claudio di Vecellio had completely lost control of himself and was alarming both Lady Dorothea and the maid, and possibly the parrot. Claudio, as well as shouting, was shovelling coins into his clothes with both hands; Euphemia was trying to restrain him; and Lady Dorothea had now resorted simply to screaming.

Into this *mêlée* Mr Bounds stepped, despite his fine hair and his waistcoat. He restrained Claudio manfully, pulled him away from the coins and the ladies. Lady Dorothea did not pause to thank him but, wildly adjusting her hair and her gown, hurried to the door calling 'Filipo! Filipo!' They heard her footsteps clattering upwards.

Euphemia bobbed a curtsey. 'Thank you, Mr Bounds,' she said, trying to catch her breath. 'I am not as young as once I was.' Claudio struggled on wildly for some moments and then, defeated by the much stronger Mr Bounds, at last was still, breathing heavily.

In the next moment Signore di Vecellio (followed by a panting Lady Dorothea) arrived back in the drawing-room, almost apoplectic now with rage and Mr Bounds, feeling he may have exceeded the rules of propriety, released Claudio immediately. Claudio swung his fist at his captor, missed, and then just stood red-faced and panting: several coins dropped from his clothes. They heard each coin make a sound, *plink*, on hitting the wooden floor.

There was a silence of sorts as people tried to control themselves: although Mr Bounds had no idea why this extraordinary financial debacle was taking place he had the sense to not, at this point, raise the subject of marriage.

'Euphemia,' said the *signore* at last in a strange voice, 'there is an empty portmanteau in the corner of my Studio. Please fetch it immediately.' And the portly maid bobbed and was gone, running up the staircase.

Claudio was then addressed. 'Empty your pockets, sir.'

'It is mine,' said Claudio again, but with much less conviction.

'No, sir, it is not yours,' answered his father heavily. 'I repeat: empty your pockets.'

Most reluctantly Claudio discharged further coins from about his person. *Plink*, they fell. *Plunk*.

Squawk! cried the parrot.

'Lady Dorothea,' said the *signore*, 'forgive me. I must ask you to leave.'

'But – dearest Filipo –'

'I must insist.' He gave no explanation. But there was something very cold and very final about his words. Lady Dorothea was almost dumbstruck but he repeated, 'I must insist.' At last, with what hauteur she could at this stage manage, Lady Dorothea, adjusting her gown still, walked towards the door, but with several backward glances at the Painter. *This could not, surely, be the end? What fault was it of hers? This could not be the end?* She had banked on marriage: she was no longer young, she badly needed marriage. (It had been whispered among her more unkind friends that he may be a Foreigner, but that this was her last chance.) For Lady

Dorothea Bray had made a fatal mistake in her life: she had used herself too much, before she had secured a husband. She looked back one more time: Roberto dived upon her upswept bird-decorated hair and Lady Dorothea screamed as she ran from the drawing-room, pursued by the parrot, down the wide staircase past the beautiful painting of Angelica.

Euphemia arrived with the portmanteau.

'Young man,' said the *signore* to Mr Bounds – whom he may have recognised, or whom he may have taken to be some passing servant, so disturbed was he – 'please assist Euphemia to collect together the Guineas. There must be seven hundred, else they are no doubt about the person of my son.'

Claudio stood, mute; Euphemia and Mr Bounds bent to their unusual task.

It was at this moment that Isabella, who had received a message from Mr Bounds regarding his intentions, now breathlessly entered the drawing-room in her best gown and wearing her beautiful gold and ruby pendant, hoping to be clasped to her father's bosom in acquiescence and love. Instead she saw her beloved scrabbling about the floor with the maid, and her father and Claudio embroiled in some sort of silent tragic scene from Mr Shakespeare. Isabella, like Mr Bounds, had the sense not to mention marriage at this moment, nor to move from the doorway. Some instinct made her blow out the candle she was carrying: she stood there like some pretty, inquiring ghost in the silence; only the sound of the coins falling one by one into the portmanteau as they were collected. The *signore* looked at his shameful son. He then transferred his gaze to the shameful money.

It could be said that all of Signore Filipo di Vecellio's dreams, that is the dreams of Philip Marshall of Bristol, died on this one, long day.

THIRTY-SIX

But she has nowhere to go. She has no friends. The wild grey eyes of Mr James Burke flashed as he walked; suddenly, very quickly, he turned north towards Brook Street. He walked up and down, he had never visited: found the house by asking; the knocker banged. Miss Ann Ffoulks came to the door herself, he heard her slowly walking along the hall.

Afterwards he thought that she had not looked very surprised to see him as she had ushered him in most politely. In her tiny drawing-room another, younger lady sat; like Miss Ffoulks she was dressed in a dark gown and white cap. There were books and pamphlets and teacups on the table with the candle-holder, and a port bottle. And immediately his eye was caught by a painting on the wall: the most extraordinary painting of the shadowed face of a black man. It was – he stared at it – a painting of pain. It was like nothing he had ever seen yet he knew: *that is one of Grace's Paintings*, and he could not, for several moments, tear his eyes away.

'This is my friend, Miss Constantia Proud, Mr Burke,' and he forced his attention from the painting and bowed to the woman at the table. 'This is Mr James Burke the Art Dealer, Constantia. I believe I have mentioned him to you. Shall you partake of tea with us, Mr Burke? Miss Proud has written these most interesting Pamphlets about her travels in the Mediterranean, for her Brother moves in Diplomatic Circles and Miss Proud attends him often as his Hostess.'

'Another time I would enjoy such a Discussion, and such Information,' said James Burke swiftly, 'but I am on a most urgent quest to find Signorina Francesca di Vecellio.'

Miss Ffoulks regarded him impassively. 'I am no longer a regular visitor to the house in Pall Mall,' she said.

This did surprise him. Miss Ffoulks and old John Palmer were always there, always with interesting matters of the world to discuss. 'But they will surely have suffered from your absence, Miss Ffoulks, for you added much to that dining-table, as I well remember from the time when I was also welcome.'

She nodded at his compliment but said, 'Not all the present Guests to the house found me so entertaining, Mr Burke. I was there, just once, several weeks ago, with Mr Gainsborough, hoping to see the famous Painting that Filipo had acquired but the – Rumours – had started and the Picture had unfortunately already been taken from the wall. Otherwise I have not been there for many months.' She gave a small wry smile. 'And that very day I returned, Filipo fell out with old John Palmer. I should think that that Friendship will not be repaired either.'

And Miss Ffoulks sighed, perhaps for the days that were gone. 'I grow old, Mr Burke, I expect.' James Burke, so involved in his own affairs suddenly noticed: Miss Ffoulks did indeed look pale, and perhaps old too. *It must be more than twenty years*, he thought, *that we began to dine together so regularly and I suppose I thought her old then*, and something, some thought, shuddered through him as if someone walked upon his grave, which made his quest even more urgent.

Nevertheless he addressed the old lady politely. 'Are you well, Miss Ffoulks?'

'As I say, I am an old woman, Mr Burke. I will not bore you with the complaints of Age!'

And then he could not wait. 'You will have heard the news nevertheless, Miss Ffoulks?'

It was Miss Constantia Proud who answered him and she was

smiling. 'If you mean have we heard of the beautiful and fraudulent Picture to which an Italian housekeeper has laid claim,' she said, 'let me tell you we have been celebrating all evening! We have even consumed port! Perhaps that would be more to your taste at this time?'

'And you were the Dealer I believe, Mr Burke,' said Miss Ffoulks expressionlessly.

'And as such, I must find the Artist,' was all he answered, *I do not know how much they know*, and again his eyes were drawn to the painting on the wall. 'Miss Ffoulks, it is a matter of urgency! Can you assist me?'

'Do you wish her well or ill, Mr Burke?'

The two women watched him carefully. He had not settled and the small room was filled with his presence and his agitation and they saw turbulence in the grey eyes. And then, extraordinarily, he laughed. 'Upon my life I do not know whether I wish her well or ill,' he said. 'She has cost me many things in my Life, including very likely my Reputation as an honest Dealer. But, Miss Ffoulks, Miss Proud – if you had seen her at the Royal Academy with all the Gentlemen Painters of England you would have been proud of your Sex. In my life I never saw such a rewarding scene – nor one, incidentally, as my Banker this afternoon has made abundantly clear to me – that has cost me so much money!'

It was Miss Proud who spoke. 'My dear Mr Burke, I have travelled the World, as you have heard, but seldom in my most interesting life have I experienced such pleasure as I did upon hearing about this Painting.'

And Miss Ffoulks smiled. 'I have not seen Francesca since yesterday when to my – Mr Burke, I must say this – to my extraordinary surprise she appeared at my door and *gave* me – ' did Miss Ffoulks' voice break slightly? '– this wonderful Painting which she said – she said she could not have painted if she had not known me.' Just for a moment the old lady could not speak. And he looked up again at the extraordinary Painting that he had never seen, knew nothing of, the Painting of the black man, and back at Miss Ffoulks. *She must know then*. Then Miss Ffoulks straightened her back and continued. 'If you would spend a few moments describing the scene at the Royal Academy to Miss Proud and to me, dear

Mr Burke, I will tell you where I believe the Painter is.' And she indicated the empty chair.

Laughter echoed out presently from the house in Brook Street: it left a smiling, drifting trail, in the darkness.

THIRTY-SEVEN

'And you *knew*?' said Grace Marshall, in the small room in Spitalfields.

Finally, as darkness fell, she had found him. She had walked from the Royal Academy, leaving quickly with her basket during the wild, artistic disorder and ink-throwing, and she had walked until she found him: she and Miss Ffoulks had agreed yesterday that Spitalfields would very likely be a better place just at the moment, than the middle of London. 'You knew *always*?'

'I knew always,' said John Palmer. 'When Philip was trying out his new persona in Rome he tried it first on me. It was myself who suggested he play with the real name of Titian – only true connoisseurs would have known that *Tiziano Vecelli* was Titian's real name – we thought di Vecellio was near but not exact, in case of any questioning, and we decided Philip should be born in Florence, not Venice as Titian was. It seemed – well, almost a Jape, at the beginning. We were young and poor and struggled to paint street portraits for a few lira so that we might eat. And Philip suddenly had this wild idea to become an Italian. Of course I knew.'

'But never by so much as a look . . .'

'A fast Friend never betrays,' he said. 'Never.' And she remembered the look on his face as heavily and slowly, that afternoon in

Pall Mall, John Palmer had left the dining-table of his old friend: the embarrassed silence; her brother's cruelty.

'He will ask you to return.'

'I will never return,' said John Palmer simply. 'They are gone, those old days.' She saw his lined, tired face.

'You must have felt many things when he suddenly became so very fashionable?'

'I felt many things. I knew quite well that he and I were equally as good as each other at what we did. It would have been impossible not to feel envious when he rose like a Comet. But –' John Palmer sighed '– but mostly I admired him. He had Ambition and Determination and Energy. I had some Talent also, but there are many other qualities that an Artist requires to survive. London is littered with failed Painters like myself: I am lucky perhaps to still be alive. Philip succeeded, against all the odds, and I admired him – and was always grateful for his hospitality.' And she remembered that she too had admired her brother Philip when she came to London: the hard work, the long, long hours, the dedication. John Palmer was smoking a pipe, something he did not do in Pall Mall. And then suddenly he laughed.

'But *you*, my clever, clever Painter! – he was secretive about his Family altogether, even to me, but *surely* my dear he must have known from the beginning that you were also talented? I wonder that he was not proud of you!'

'He knew,' said Grace Marshall. 'But he chose not to know. I expect over the years he forgot.'

'It was staggeringly beautiful, what you did. It does not matter that it was not Rembrandt, it was beautiful – I myself would have liked to own such a Painting.'

'Thank you.' And she smiled and her dark eyes lit up her troubled face. 'I began drawing in Bristol – it is true that he used my Chalks, that day of my Ninth birthday. And I have painted ever since I came to London.'

'But, I do not understand – do you mean – in your own room upstairs?'

'In my own room upstairs. At St Martin's Lane first. And then in Pall Mall.'

He shook his head ruefully. 'Of course we thought you were a Lady *amateur*. We even joked of it – oh, in a fond way my dear – if we saw paint on your hands.' He looked down at his own: old and dirty and paint-besmattered, the paint was embedded deep in the skin and the nails, as so often with painters. And then he looked back at her. 'He could have helped you. He should have helped you. We have spoken of that, have we not? That a Woman cannot succeed in the Art World unless she has a Father or a Husband – or a Brother – to assist her.'

'Indeed.'

'You *sat* there, while we had those conversations?'

'Yes.'

'I am – ashamed,' he said. He puffed at his pipe, the smell of tobacco wafted. 'And your Brother chose not to assist you.' He puffed and puffed on his pipe. 'Well, well. He was – jealous, I presume.' She was silent. 'I know my dear that he is a jealous man. I have always known that. He did not want Rivals.' He sighed heavily once more, shook his head in disbelief. 'We could *never* have guessed, and you so quiet at the table. God's Breath! One does not, really – forgive me – expect a Woman to have such an extraordinary talent as you have proved: it is not in the scheme of things!' He saw the strong, bitter perhaps, dark-eyed woman before him. 'What shall you do now Francesca? —Ah forgive me, it would feel so odd to call you Grace after so many years. I heard the story of what happened this morning at the Royal Academy because Thom Gainsborough sent me a note, he thought I would be extremely interested! Many people will know by now no matter how they cover it up, as of course they will. I presume it would be almost impossible for you to return to Pall Mall in the circumstances?

'Of course it would be impossible. I knew that, when I went to Somerset House this morning.'

She did not say what other realisation had haunted her since she had arrived at Spitalfields and asked for John Palmer, and found him here and thrown herself upon his kindness. *This is how I must live now.* His room smelled; it was sparse and dirty, old canvases lay in corners, and there were empty paint bladders, and used brushes. This was how someone who *really* had little money lived. In other rooms in the house there was the sound of raised voices, mainly French.

'Is this a house of silk-weavers?'

'All the houses here are full of silk-weavers, they all work in big rooms at the top. They are Huguenots: Protestants escaped from France.'

'But – why have you chosen to live so far from the centre, from other Artists?'

'One must live where one's life is, Francesca.' There was a child crying and the sound of terrible coughing and in the street a drunken woman singing of *l'amour*. Whatever else this was, it was also the home of a failed artist, and Pall Mall was the home of a successful artist. The stove was lit but she saw that his supply of coal was low. Already she had seen a rat.

She wondered that he had been able to present himself so respectably day after day in Pall Mall: as if he could read her thoughts he said, 'I would always, in any Weather, go down to the River, before I came to you. I thought of it as my Tidying-room! There are many who live much, much worse than me, Francesca. This room is not unbearable to me, I have lived here for a very long time, and I have – Friends here.'

'And you walked home here, *every evening you came*, after dinner? It took me a very long time, this day.'

'I was grateful for dinner, as you must have known Francesca. The walk was nothing, I was used to it.'

On the wall were pinned many charcoal drawings, some paintings – good drawings and paintings, it seemed to her – of people, of places; several of the same woman; one of Philip painting energetically. It caught Philip as he had been when he was younger, it caught him exactly, but the edges of the paper curled and held dust.

It was a room. It was a life.

'Of course you must stay here, Francesca, if you can bear it, until you decide. Philip never bothered to come here once in his life. You are welcome to stay here. There are other places in the house I can sleep.'

'Of course I could not do that!'

'There are other places in the house I can sleep, Francesca,' he said quietly, 'I do assure you.' And she suddenly thought: *perhaps he has another whole life here, here in Spitalfields*. Did he have a wife? a family? a life anyway they did not even dream of, cocooned in Pall Mall, with money. And she remembered the day she had seen him, the slice of bread secreted inside his jacket, and was ashamed.

'I have food,' she said quickly. In her basket she had bread and cheese and apples, and some small articles of clothing. And two guineas: all the money she had left – after Claudio had taken most of it, and some shared with Tobias – from the payment for her painting 'from the French school' that the lady with the high wig had clutched to her bosom in the coach. All the money she had, in fact, in the world.

John Palmer hesitated, looking at the food, and then declined; she had not the heart to eat in front of him, although she had not eaten since she left the house in Pall Mall early in the morning, with her basket and her Life, to attend the Experts in the Royal Academy.

He saw that she was exhausted; soon afterwards he left her, to make herself as comfortable as she might, saying they would speak again in the morning. The cesspit at the back of the houses in the street was so disgusting that she had to stop herself from retching as she squatted. She did not wash, for there seemed to be no water. She did not remove her clothes. She bolted the door as he had instructed and lay upon the bed in a kind of energetic exhaustion, thinking of everything that had happened on this extraordinary day. She was drifting and cold, thoughts jumbled: *Mr Hartley Pond's face, her brother's face, the name appearing under the skirt, walking on and on and on with her basket*: half-awake half-asleep she was suddenly aware of John Palmer's voice calling her. She got up and unbolted the door, tousled and dis-oriented. French singing drifted in through the window, *l'amour, l'amour . . .*

'I beg your pardon, Francesca.' She understood at once that he had been drinking. 'There is someone looking for you.' At once her heart gave an unpleasant leap. 'I did not know whether you wished to be found.'

Someone from Newgate Prison? Her brother come to murder her? 'Who is it?'

'James Burke.'

'James Burke?'

'Aye.'

'Does he carry a cleaver?' She half-laughed, and John Palmer smiled.

'He does not.' He lowered his voice slightly. 'I would say, however, that he is in some disarray, which is an interesting thing in itself for I never saw James Burke in disarray in my life, even in all his Troubles!'

'What do you mean? His "Troubles"?'

'You do not know about his wife?'

She answered quickly. 'A little only.'

John Palmer shrugged. 'She gambles. He is always in need of money. He comes home here with me sometimes,' he laughed grimly, 'for a change.'

And she saw them: James Burke and John Palmer sometimes leaving Pall Mall together as night fell: the tall younger man and the squat older one, the shadow from their lanterns flickering and disappearing along Pall Mall.

'Do you wish to be found by Mr Burke, my dear?'

With an effort she pulled herself back to this room in Spitalfields. 'Would you stay?'

'If you wish.'

'Please.'

While John Palmer went to fetch him she wearily sat on the only chair. She caught her hair back from her face again, as if it mattered.

James Burke could not hide his surprise to see her sitting, so disordered and disarranged: John Palmer caught his look. 'Well there you are, James,' he said, 'that is how it is. Here is the Painter – the most famous Painter in London this evening I do believe, and I do agree she should, rather, be drinking Champagne!' And if James Burke was surprised at what he saw, the other two people in the room were surprised also, for it was odd indeed to see the dealer so disordered and dishevelled, and his hair so wild. He looked like an artist himself rather than the immaculate, calm, beautifully-groomed art dealer of note, and for a split second Grace's hands itched in the old familiar way to catch him, to catch indeed the faces of the two of them whom she had known for so long: the same faces and yet, now, so different.

'Excuse me for only one moment,' said John Palmer, 'I do not have champagne but I know where there is wine and I think wine will be useful. Do not damage her, James.'

'I will not damage her,' said James Burke, and Grace Marshall said nothing, and John Palmer disappeared into the darkness and a French woman's voice screamed outside the window.

'L'argent! Où est l'argent, Monsieur?' And the rat, or another rat, ran across the room to the safety of the skirting board.

'*L'argent!*' screamed the voice again.

'*L'argent*,' repeated James Burke. He sighed suddenly. 'Money: well, it is always, in the end, about money.' She did not speak. He stood beside the fire that had gone out. 'Grace, I have to ask you one question. Why did you do it?'

'I had nothing left to lose.' She answered him blankly, as if he was a stranger. 'It does not matter now.'

'Yes, it does matter – you need my help now more than ever! What can you do, Grace, by yourself, no matter what you have proved? You cannot even lease a Studio by yourself, you are a Woman.' And the mask that he had so carefully in place at all times, trembled. 'You do not understand what you have done, Grace, and not just to your Brother. You have made fools of the Academicians of the Royal Academy – that is one thing (and you were lucky that Sir Joshua Reynolds was out of Town). But you have made a life-long Enemy of Mr Hartley Pond, and Mr Hartley Pond is a dangerous man. He – the great and powerful Critic – was heard by every Royal Academician to praise the Soul of a painting done by a *housekeeper*. I do not think you can survive as an Artist in London at the moment. Although I know it is your Dream.' He sighed. 'One more Painting, that was all you needed to do.'

'I *told* you I would not paint another. My business with you was finished.'

'No,' he said.

'You do not understand,' he said.

'You have never understood,' he said.

But she looked at him in dread, as if she did, for she saw that the mask was gone: it was James Burke, the man she had loved: she knew the face before her now better than any face in the world and she could not bear it.

'Your business with me will never be finished, Grace, although we do not speak of it. Because of the child.'

She was so immediately angry that she stood up in the small dim room. He could tell by her face that these words had crossed some boundary in her heart but he could not hold back now: the grey eyes flashed. 'My wife could not – would not – have children. Until there was *our* child I did not know if the fault was with me. That was the only child I could ever have.'

She answered him like lightning. 'Do not say that! It was you who told me many months ago that the Past was over! You could have had children with a hundred women!'

'No.' His voice was low. 'I was wrong. The Past is never over. You know well that I loved you, Grace.'

'If you loved anything you loved my Talent!' But she knew it was not true.

'I loved you, Grace. I left England at once because' – and she saw that he struggled to make his words fair – 'because I saw that you would not allow yourself to – to be trapped to give me what I wanted so much. I could not bear it.'

Her control was gone, the words came out wildly. 'You left me by myself that day, to go to Meard-street alone and I not only lost the child – *I lost myself!* I *will not* be blamed for *your* loss also! you could have found plenty of women to please you! *I could not have done it!* I had already forfeited too many years – and then – now – when I had done the Painting, you would not pay me and I lost something else that day that you know nothing of – no! do not ask me – so I did it James because I had nothing left to lose and I was suddenly determined that if I was not to be paid money I would at least be paid *attention* by all the other Artists, I had to be recognised somehow – that I was one of them! You do not know everything about me now, James Burke – *fighting to be a Painter has cost so much* – *it had to be worth it somehow*!' Just at that moment John Palmer lurched back into the room with an armful of bottles. He was not too drunk to feel the atmosphere; her words *it had to be worth it somehow* seemed to echo in the stuffy, dirty air of the room with the torn canvases and the paint and the old brushes.

'Are you all right, my dear?'

Her heart was beating fast. Slowly she recovered herself, slowly she sat again on the chair. She did not speak. James Burke did not speak. John Palmer put the bottles on the table, stoked up the fire with the last of his coal, looked for containers to drink from. He filled them with the wine: one was a glass, one was a cup, one was a dish.

'I'll drink from the dish,' he said and he pushed the glass towards the woman and the cup towards the man. 'To Art,' he said, lifting the dish to his mouth and some of the red liquid trailed downwards on to the floor. 'To the Artist who fooled the lot of them!'

James Burke did not move. Grace seized the glass and drank gratefully: anything to remove the face of the man who still stood beside the fireplace. Then she rose and took the cheese and bread from her basket. She and John Palmer tore at the bread: James Burke at first touched nothing, then at last he came to the table and drank the cupful of wine in one long swallow. There was only the one chair: finally the gentlemen sat, their knees almost touching, on the small divan that served as John Palmer's bed. He kept their various drinking containers filled, as a good host would.

'So you're a Forger then, James Burke?' John Palmer's cheeks were red now.

James Burke looked down at his cup, filled it again from the bottle, and did not answer directly. Then he spoke for a moment as if she was not there. 'I have put it about that she fooled me too, that others were the Forgers. I may escape this time but' – and he smiled dryly at John Palmer – 'I imagine my Reputation will never be quite the same.' Again he drank the cup of wine quickly. 'My Wife has had a terrible shock, she believed I was a bottomless purse and it has now been made very clear to her this day by my Bankers that I am not.' He emptied yet another cup of wine down his throat, not looking at either of them; then he turned to her again at last. 'How did you start a Rumour that swelled so quickly?' he said dryly.

'That part was easy,' she said, speaking in the same dry tone as he, 'for it was you who taught me, James; you told me it was easy to start a Rumour. You told me you merely whisper something loudly at a Social Gathering. Some weeks ago, soon after the Auction, I went to the house in Brook Street. Miss Ffoulks was there and her friend Miss Proud who I trusted immediately.' He nodded. 'I told them the story –'

'Everything?'

'Not – everything. Many things. And I – almost – felt that Miss Ffoulks was not quite surprised – as if perhaps a puzzle was solved; she said she had often wondered about my Painting but had felt it impolite to ask – not like you, James,' and she cast a quick look at him. 'They had not, at that stage, seen anything of my work but they took my story on Trust, for which I shall be eternally grateful. The next day Miss Ffoulks and Miss Proud were to go to the Foundling Hospital where the great and the good, as you know, sometimes congregate. There they both murmured loudly in noble Ears.' And John Palmer threw back his head and laughed heartily.

'To really answer your question, John Palmer,' said James Burke. 'Whether I am a Forger or not, I was sure she was good enough – and I was proved right.' And he shrugged. 'But what shall you do now, *Signorina*?' And he bowed from where he sat on the bed, an ironic gesture, and she knew he had recovered himself.

'I cannot go back to Pall Mall, of course.'

'I have this evening repaid the seven hundred guineas to your Brother.'

She looked at him sharply. 'So you could have paid me, after all.' His face closed.

'I had already paid the other people involved. So I borrowed money this afternoon,' he said. 'At very high interest from my Bank, if you are so anxious to know of my affairs. I do not wish to be dragged through Law Courts.'

'Nevertheless I cannot go back to him, for he will never forgive me for what I have done.'

'Indeed. Euphemia said some of your clothes had gone.'

'I could not take much.'

'And your Paintings and your materials?'

'I burned much of my work.' She saw his face. 'I kept two. Miss Ffoulks has one. The other is being – attended by a Friend.'

'You do not have any Friends, Grace – present company and Miss Ffoulks excepted of course, and even these, after all, were friends of your Brother.' *And they both knew, Grace Marshall and James Burke, that they remembered (there in the room in Spitalfields) what she had told him, long ago in the golden days: that – apart from ghosts – he was her first and only friend: I cannot tell people the truth of myself she had said, I am a Fraud. But I do not need another friend ever in the world James, ever again, she had said, for I have you.*

A long silence in the room as they drank red wine: if John Palmer felt the tensions he did not comment.

'I do not, any longer – care for my brother,' said Grace at last, out of the silence. 'But I owe him very much of course, because he came back for me – the good things and the bad things, I know that. He came back to Bristol for me.'

'You know they came from Bristol?' John Palmer looked at the art dealer in surprise.

'I told him many years ago,' said Grace, 'but my brother never knew that I had done so.' And they gave no further explanation.

'Philip must have *known* you could paint,' said John Palmer again, shaking his head. 'Surely no-one can take so little notice for twenty-five years, even if you are – forgive me, my dear – a Woman.' He filled their containers with wine once again. There was only one candle and the wine shone red and now their faces flickered and danced as the candle grew low.

'You did not notice, John,' said James Burke.

'I thought she was a Lady *amateur*. I never saw her work. You were a Dealer so I suppose you had the right to ask her. I was only grateful to be at the dinner-table so often.' And they saw his face in the candlelight, the lines and the pain.

'What shall you do, Grace?' asked James Burke again. 'You cannot stay here obviously – with respect, John Palmer, with respect,' and the old man merely raised his drinking dish. 'You do not have any Friends, Grace,' he repeated.

She flashed at him. 'You do not know everything of my Life now, James Burke. I have a Friend who knows my whole story, and he will help me.' He looked at her as if she had hit him. She saw – but why should she care? He had broken his promise, he had not given her the money, and he had set this whole train of events in motion. 'Both Miss Ffoulks and Miss Proud offered me a room. But,' and for the first time they heard the wistful note in her voice, 'I feel I cannot stay in London now. Perhaps I would be taken to Newgate Prison and pressed. I am a Frauder, after all.'

'You would be safe here, and you can stay here as long as you can bear it!' said John Palmer. 'I do little painting these days, and there are other places as I told you, where I can sleep.'

James Burke stood abruptly from the small bed. He turned to John Palmer. 'I have something I need to say to her alone before I leave. Could I ask you, John, to let me speak privately, just for a moment . . .'

John Palmer ascertained from Grace's face that she was not afraid. 'My Friend lives only on the floor above,' he said. 'If you call loudly I will hear you,' and he staggered, now, out of the door.

They had all drunk a great deal. In the small room there was some wine left in one of the bottles, the candle was fluttering at its end. James Burke leaned down and filled his cup and Grace's glass.

In the dim candlelight as he leaned over she saw: the mask was in place, he was totally contained.

'Grace Marshall and her Mysterious Friend!' he said and he raised his cup and red wine spilled slightly on to the table, and the red of the wine was caught in the wavering light. 'If I had not loved you, Amazing Grace,' he said, but his tone was mocking, not gentle now, 'I would have loved you at the Royal Academy for it was magnificent! The Painting, as a Rembrandt, once my Colleagues had finished with it, was magnificent! And you, Grace, unmasking it, were magnificent also!'

'Mr Gainsborough helped, but if you had not insisted, they would likely have stopped me,' she said curiously.

'I did not think that you could do it! I could not believe that you could do it! And, once you had started there was no going back: I understood that you may ruin me, but you would not betray me personally, and for that at least,' again he made the mocking bow, 'I am grateful. I have insisted all day long, to all who ask, that the Fraudulence must have been dealt with by others, that I was given False Papers. As the money has been returned in full I think there is very little anyone will want to do – and I do not think you will be taken to Newgate, and certainly will not be pressed. I have not heard that they press women there!'

'Are you *sure*? I have heard that they have wheels and they press people.'

'I do not think so. It is not I think an Offence to make Fools of people – now that the money has been returned that is perhaps the only real Offence left. It is your brother and Mr Hartley Pond who will never forgive you and – well, I am not sure who is the more dangerous if you will allow me to say so: I know your brother very well. As for the others, the Academicians and the Experts – they will cover up the story, I am sure it will not become publicly known that they were duped by a Woman, although it will always be known by them. But what I wanted to say to you in private is this: the Painting. I will be sorry if the Painting is damaged beyond recall by the ink – we shall see. The heavy varnish will have helped us and I believe we can sell it again if you are willing, for now it is notorious as well as beautiful and I have had two offers of two hundred Guineas by Members of the Academy if I can restore it!'

She looked at him incredulously. 'Even though they *know*?'

'*Because* they know, Grace.'

'Half of that would belong to me then! Give me my share of the Money.'

He looked at her in the light that was left. He had leaned away from what was left of the candle, so that she could not see his face. 'So then it is, in the end, the Money?'

'Everything is, in the end, the Money,' she said to him fiercely. 'You taught me that. My brother taught me that. My life in London has taught me that. *I want to paint.* I want to be free to paint my way. It was for Money to buy my Freedom that I followed your ridiculous plan—'

'It was hardly ridiculous.'

'—and it is Money that I have now lost because you did not keep your word to me, and when you and John Palmer ask me what I shall do I cannot answer because, as everyone knows, as everyone has taught me, *Life itself is about Money! Money is the answer to everything!*'

He was very still then for a long moment. Then he emptied his glass, reached inside his coat. 'However,' he said coldly, 'you have advised us that you have a Friend of your own who will assist you in your new Life. Tell him it will be best if you leave London.' He pulled out a paper. 'I gave your Brother his money in guinea coins and that exhausted my capacity for carriage. I have here a draft for one hundred guineas which I believe I will recoup yet, with *Girl Reading*. If you present it at my Bank, here –' he showed her '– they will give you the money at once because I have already borrowed it and arranged it. I think anyone who did what you did at Somerset House deserves to be paid.' He leaned across the small table towards her: the man she had loved.

'And a part of me – the foolish part of me which you will not see again – is glad that it turned out this way for I shall treasure the faces of the Artists and the Experts and Mr Hartley Pond for as long as I live. I know very well of the Fashions and Frauds of the world I live in. I have had to praise them for years, and some of them I despise! You are a wonderful Painter – you are probably the most talented Painter living in London.' The candle spluttered then at his verdict and then went out, but he went on speaking in the darkness as if nothing had happened. 'You will never become a Royal Academician, Grace, but it does not matter because you are an

Artist. A real one, not one to be honoured in that public way – you know you have been honoured privately by them anyway, and they will never forget it, and nor should you: you have to know now how good you are.' And then, across the table in the darkness he put his hand upon her cheek, as he had done in the park when the pieman was calling his wares in the distance. The warm, strong hand lay there and because it was dark and therefore he could not see her she allowed herself to close her eyes, just for a moment, and in the dingy, cold room she let her cheek rest there, as if it belonged. For just that moment in the dark they sat there, the man and the woman.

Finally Mr James Burke took his hand away, stood up, accustomed his eyes to the darkness to find the door. 'I will not be in touch again, Grace, but advise your – Friend to contact me with your whereabouts. I will try and send people to you, for such is your Notoriety already that even though you are a Woman, you will build up some sort of living as a Painter, I am certain.'

'As a Freak? As a Fraud?'

'It is not, exactly, as you planned. I understand that. Good luck, Grace.'

And James Burke would have gone then, except for one thing. There was the sudden sound of horses, then there was immediately a great shouting and banging and then Signore Filipo di Vecellio, followed with dismay by his old friend John Palmer, burst into the dark room.

'*Where is she*? I have ascertained that she is not with Miss Ffoulks so she must be with you! She has no Friends of her own. *Where is she*?'

At first he did not see.

John Palmer was carrying a lighted candle; he moved forward reluctantly: the light and the shadows danced, and showed that James Burke stood by the door. Grace Marshall had stood also, at the sound of her brother's voice.

At the sight of her Philip Marshall lost control completely. He lunged at his sister in the dim light, set upon her like a man possessed (as indeed he was), threw her so hard against the wall that she fell downwards. It took both James Burke and John Palmer to pull him off. And then hold him back from lunging again. 'Judas!' he kept spitting at James Burke, trying to free himself. '*Judas!*'

He screamed at his sister as she lay there. 'I kept my promise! I came back for you! And you have destroyed my whole Life!'

From the floor Grace Marshall said faintly, 'You should then, perhaps, have taken more care with mine.'

And then for what seemed like an eternity nobody said anything at all, just the sound of harsh breathing and the shadowy figures in the room: the woman thrown to the ground, the two men holding back a third – like figures in one of the Epic Paintings so beloved by certain of the Artists. Then finally the rustling of Grace Marshall's petticoats as she at last slowly stood from where she had fallen. They all saw the blood upon her face and upon her gown. The men still held Philip tightly; he struggled wildly in their arms.

It was hard for the brother and the sister to see each other's eyes in the dim uncertain light from the one candle.

With some difficulty Grace slowly gathered up her basket that held her life. The bank draft for one hundred guineas lay there on the dirty table beside the empty bottles. Silently Grace Marshall picked it up and walked out of the door.

Somewhere in the Spitalfields street the same drunken Frenchwoman still sang of *l'amour* in the dark, dark night.

PART FIVE

Dear Friend, dear Thomas,

 Forgive me for taking so very very many months to write this Letter to you – your kind friends who were visiting Florence, they will have told you, assisted me to find a room when I first arrived, before they returned to London – I have a room that is perfectly sufficient for my needs and my Studio is light and bright and noisy along the Arno river and I can see the old bridge, the Ponte Vecchio from my window; they were most, most kind . . . I keep asking people how the name Firenze was turned by the English into Florence, but none can tell me.

 Where can I start, Thomas, after such a long time?

 I paint and paint and paint, when I first got here what I kept painting – I know this sounds ridiculous, it does, even to me – was the feeling of Freedom, of being Free (as if such a thing can be painted). —Colours filled my canvas but I hardly knew what I was doing, only that I must do it – sometimes still I forget to eat, often I forget to sleep for I am so used to painting in the night with candles burning around my easel that I still feel that the night-time is the best time to paint, you know that candles have always lit up my world. —I experiment all the time with colours now – those meticulous, shadowed true faces of Rembrandt van Rijn have become filled with colour and light: my own faces at last.

 Finally, I am returning your Chapters.

 Oh Thomas, it is so strange to see it all writ down – it seems to

make more sense when it is writ in your way, in the neat Chapters –
for in my Life it did not seem sensible or neat at all. —You will forgive
that sometimes in my Impatience, when I saw I had not explained it
to you quite as I meant in those last days in Frith Street, sometimes
I – I did not intend to Thomas but – I seized my own quill and put
down my own ill-written account for you to put in elegant writing.
—Lately because of reading your Writing I found myself trying to
paint it all, to paint what I had tried to describe to you in words but I
still do not know if it is possible to paint memory or pain or ambition
or love – some things come out in wonderfully strong and strange
colours: but Tobias is so blue, and gone. Miss Ffoulks was kind and
wise and yellow-orange, John Palmer in Spitalfields was brown and
dark green sometimes: the candlelight and the curling paper on the
walls and the torn canvases and paint in the corners. And Mr
Gainsborough of whom I was so fond and to whom I was so grateful,
dead of the cancer: how can I paint him? or you, dear Thomas in your
shawls and waistcoats! —Bristol emerged out of a grey-bright mist of
gold, and when I tried to paint Bedlam there was a group of figures
screaming, dark and white, I think I was trying to paint the **sound** –
that Painting frightened me so much that I did not even scrape at the
board, I burned it. —I do not exactly know what I am doing in my
work, much of it seems weird and not really painting at all for I think
I have tried to paint the unpaintable and there is none to tell me, so I
just keep on.

What I have painted that makes sense at last is a proper large
Painting of my whole Family – a 'Conversation Piece' as my mother
had so required long ago! I did it Thomas, after all – a strange, uneasy
group in a drawing-room: a picture of Tobias and Ezekiel and my
Father and Juno and Venus, all of us, Philip too, and me. Something
of our rackety life in Bristol in all the faces, in my Mother's face that I
have sometimes caught in mine – how could Philip think we could do
away with them?

I sometimes wonder what has happened to my brother, whether he
is still an Italian! but I do not long to see him or speak to him, not any
more; I think sometimes of foolish Claudio, who caused so much to
happen; and of Isabella: those only half-loved young people – I know I
did not do entirely well by them and it was not their fault – heavens,
Thomas, you see why I cannot write like you, upon my life everything
comes out so jumbled I think you will not make sense of it, I know I

could not really have made a life for Tobias but his death pains me still, perhaps I could have done differently, I hold the blue stone sometimes and see his last face.

Florence is – oh again I do not have the words – beautiful and rough and wild and gorgeous, stinking drains and Art and old voluptuousness and lemon groves – I am not unaware of the irony of my settling here, in my mythical Birthplace, and I speak Italian as if I always spoke it. Only – I miss London, Thomas. I had thought of it, I realise, as mine.

I do not yet have any financial problems but I am frugal of course, for the Future must be paid for somehow. —You will smile but when the Tourists came earlier in the year I plucked up all my Courage and followed the example of my brother and John Palmer and I set up my stool near the **Ponte Vecchio** and made Portraits for a few **lire**, I will never have my brother's facility with faces but I had some success for I think, sometimes, I catch the heart. —And I enjoyed being in the crowds, all the shouting and laughter and music and drama that is Italy, for otherwise I do not talk very much, and – oh Thomas – I hear nothing at all of Art and I do not know if what I seem to be trying to paint now makes sense – though I do go often to the Uffizi Gallery and I talk to the wonderful, wonderful Portraits there and ask them what they think. —Mostly I hear only my own thoughts. I still do not know how to paint that.

I would not change the silence though, Thomas, for the dining-room of Pall Mall, though it was my Academy and my Education. I have graduated now.

I send you my very warm wishes, and gratitude, dear friend Thomas. —I count those long days when I opened my heart to you as some of the most painful, and yet some of the most important. —I know you thought to make a book of my History, if I would agree when I saw it. You must write as you think, Thomas. Just as I paint – always painted – because I cannot help it.

Good wishes from your grateful friend,
Grace Marshall.

P.S. I enclose a paper for you to, if you will, take care of.

THIRTY-EIGHT

Mr Thomas Towers was bent over books in his room in Frith Street when a visitor was announced. Mr Towers hid a small sound of satisfaction when he understood the identity of the visitor: it was someone not entirely unexpected.

The visitor carried a large parcel of paper. His greying hair was tied back, in the fashion, his eyes were grey too, and sharp: but he had about him the look of a man who was fighting demons.

They bowed.

James Burke looked about the room, saw the rotund, oddly-dressed writer; the piles and piles of papers; and books, books: books of all sizes filling every space and cranny and shelf in the room. And on the walls another painting that he had never seen – his heart lurched in shock to see it here in this unknown room in Frith Street – for it was a Portrait of Angelica, so ill: it must have been painted just before she died. He stared for a long time at the beautiful, ravaged face, the bright, shadowed, coloured quilt. The fire burned and spat; carts and carriages rattled by continuously; a ray of cold April London sunshine tried to find a way in at the long windows as the two men waited in silence and it seemed as if a conversation might not begin at all. Finally James Burke spoke abruptly, almost rudely.

'So you are the Friend, Sir, of whom she spoke?'

Mr Towers, wrapped in his usual waistcoats and shawls agreed that he was.

'I thought—'

'Of course you did.' Mr Towers' gruff answer was to the point. 'But I have a Wife, Sir, of sorts, who nevertheless prefers to live elsewhere – and Grace Marshall only ever loved one person.' And the room was suddenly very still.

After some moments James Burke spoke reluctantly, indicating the parcel of paper in his hands. 'There is much – painful reading here,' and then, the words dragged out of him, 'I thought I knew her so well, but there was much that I did not know . . . the part about Bedlam was . . . for I know my own contribution,' and Mr Towers had to lean forward to hear, the voice was so low, '*unbearable to me.*'

Mr Towers had the sense not to speak. There was another long silence. Then the visitor made himself continue.

'And I did not know about her brother Tobias at all. I mean, that she had met him again.'

'No.'

'That is a – difficult part of the story.'

'Yes.' Mr Towers sighed then. After a moment he said, 'There are many momentous changes happening in our World, Mr Burke, and not just in France. We live now in what they are calling the Age of Enlightenment and begin to learn much about ourselves. We understand perhaps that the Child maketh the Man: the story of Tobias Marshall – and of Grace and of Philip Marshall – began long ago.' He sat pondering, among the papers and the books and the knowledge and then he added, 'Tobias had his heroic moment, nevertheless.' Carts rattled below, and dogs barked, chasing the wheels. 'I hope for Claudio's sake his own story will be different; perhaps the farm he has been sent to may – lead to other pathways. They attacked him quite viciously, I believe, the cock-fighting men, for they found him eventually and he was saved only by the intervention – and Money – of his Father.'

'God's blood! The boy Claudio caused very much trouble!' said James Burke. 'I cannot be sorry for him – I have to say I felt to attack him myself!'

Finally Mr Towers invited the visitor to sit, but the visitor did not sit, he instead fidgeted with his hat, ill at ease. 'It was your daughter, then – *Girl Reading*?'

'Yes.'

'You know that Painting now hangs in the home of the Duchess of Seldon, who followed the story with such interest and was very glad to buy it.'

'I heard so.'

Another long pause. At last James Burke put his hat upon a shelf on top of some books, placed the large parcel of paper he was carrying on the top of all the other piles of paper on the writer's desk, and walked to the window. He stood there looking out.

They heard the clock ticking, and the sounds and calls from the street below: BUY MY MILK! and the clip-clop of horses passing.

Mr Burke turned back into the room reluctantly. 'Why did you send this Manuscript to me, Mr Towers?'

Mr Towers sat back carefully in his chair. 'I insist that it shall be published, Mr Burke. Her History must be told one day. I am well aware that there are many who consider a Life should not be portrayed in this way, with so much Intimacy, but how else can this story be told?' The clock struck ten in the morning. 'I thought you should know of my Intention.'

'There are many things in those papers, Sir,' the visitor answered brusquely, 'that I would not care for the World to know.'

'There are many things in these papers that others than yourself would not care for the World to know, Mr Burke. However, as I say, we are told that we live in a new age where Knowledge, and the pursuit of Truth, is paramount.'

James Burke suddenly laughed abruptly. 'I wonder that you philosophise quite so calmly, Mr Towers. This is the real World we live in, Sir – most people's Lives would perhaps not stand so microscopic a looking-over!'

But Mr Towers did not smile. 'I am a student of other Lives, Mr Burke. That is my Employment.'

'Some might call you a Leech.'

'As some might call you a Fraud, Mr Burke, and a user of other people's Talent but –' he raised both his hands in a gesture of peace '– let us not quarrel. I am not talking of rushing to the printing press at once, I merely put it to you that such a life as Grace Marshall has lived should not be unknown, and it will be unknown if we do not take steps to rectify the matter.' He picked up the manuscript, ruffled absent-mindedly through some of the pages, put it down again. 'When I asked her to tell me her whole story she was at first much disquieted. But once she started I think she was glad to tell it all at last. I tried only to write as she told me – but you will have seen that she sometimes got exasperated that I did not perhaps properly grasp her meaning, and so she added her own words.'

'As I saw.' James Burke smiled slightly. And then again, almost to himself, 'As I saw.' He cleared his throat, turned back to the street.

'Shall I order coffee, Mr Burke?'

The visitor did not answer, perhaps he did not hear, but something about the fall of the shoulders at the window made Mr Towers think that coffee was advisable and he rang for the maid. Coffee was acquired, Mr Burke seemed to revive.

'I am very glad that she is painting so – ferociously, Mr Towers. From her Letter to you, Sir, which you kindly attached to the Manuscript, I would think, extraordinary as it may sound, that although she has at last found a style quite of her own with her new interest in Colour and in the way she is endeavouring to paint *feelings* – yet the thing is, Mr Towers, she appears to be – once again – in the vanguard of a new Movement. Fuseli moved things in that direction whether one likes his work or not; and there is a precocious young man – a boy almost – Turner, is his name, who the Academy has admitted to the School and his Genius is already understood in the development of a new, different kind of Art by the younger Academicians. I heard one say he paints *coloured light* – I think Grace would understand that meaning. Turner is painting in watercolours meanwhile, but I would gamble my Life that as he develops he will turn to oils. The art of Painting is changing. Sir Joshua Reynolds was important in his time but—'

'—is it true,' Mr Towers interrupted, 'that the last uttered word of Sir Joshua Reynolds, on his resignation from the Royal Academy, was *Michelangelo*?'

'So it is recounted,' answered James Burke, smiling very slightly. 'All I mean to say is that times have changed and the younger Artists may perhaps recognise what Grace is doing now, remarkable though this may seem.'

Mr Towers nodded. 'I too have heard of the work of young Mr Turner.' The carts and the carriages still rattled on outside. 'Grace is a quite extraordinary Painter and I do believe she will be recognised one day. But perhaps not in her Lifetime – unless I publish this Manuscript.' He glanced across at James Burke who stared out again at the street. 'Of course many people say that it is Posterity that counts, Mr Burke.' His fingers lay upon the papers, drumming slightly. 'And yet, knowing the difficulties of her Life, I am not so sure. Lucky indeed is he, surely, who – as well as being recognised by Posterity – *is affirmed in his own Lifetime*. Grace was affirmed by her Peers in private of course whether they knew it or not but . . .' He let the words hang in the room, unfinished.

The old clock told the time, on and on. Mr Towers now stood also and walked towards one of the long windows, looking out over the busy London street as his visitor did. But Mr Towers also observed the Art Dealer: conflicting thoughts flew across the handsome face and the grey eyes stared out, unseeing, troubled.

The clock chimed the half-hour; dogs barked, a pieman and a knife-sharpener began to call their wares, almost in unison: BUY MY PIES, KNIFES SHARPENED, BUY MY PIES.

Mr Towers pulled his numerous shawls about his shoulders and went back to his desk. An altercation suddenly arose from below, very likely between the competing pieman and knife-grinder; the voices rose, and fell, and then drifted away.

'Her Brother still makes a living,' observed Mr Burke finally. 'He closed up the house in Pall Mall when his son was sent to the country, but I hear that he still paints Portraits from St Martin's Lane to whence he returned, although I myself am not, you may understand, welcome there. But of course the Art World gossips, and I hear many things.' He shrugged. 'People like a bit of Notoriety – he does well enough.'

'How does he now sign his paintings?'

'I am told he still signs them *Filipo di Vecellio*.'

Mr Towers laughed. 'He did not want then, after all, to become himself?'

'He did not. He always maintained that the whole story was, rather, a figment of his Sister's deranged Imagination! That Grace Marshall did not exist.' And this time both men smiled together for the first time, for they knew that, indeed, she did.

'And the Signorina Isabella?' asked Mr Towers.

'The Signorina Isabella is now Mrs Georgie Bounds and seems to be a most contented young lady, and Euphemia the maid has gone to that small establishment.'

'Ah, Euphemia.' And Mr Towers nodded to himself. 'You may like to know, Mr Burke,' he said dryly, 'that after Grace had departed for Florence and before I began writing, I managed to speak to one other person, and that person was Euphemia. She was indeed a mine of perspicacious information, having joined the di Vecellio household almost at the same time as Grace. Euphemia did not miss much of what was going on. And it was she who told me about Claudio trying to acquire the seven hundred guinea coins!' And now both men laughed.

'Isabella's Father's fall, and the witness of Mr Bounds to part of it, was no doubt great good luck,' said James Burke shrewdly. 'Mr Bounds would never have been an acceptable son-in-law else, being only a frame-maker's son. Now I am sure – for he was a most generous Host, but always careful with his Finances – Filipo can get Frames for his Portraits at a good price! So Isabella will perhaps live happily ever after – although I hear from Miss Ffoulks that the girl nevertheless still asks for her Aunt. Miss Ffoulks also tells me that Mr Bounds is very fond, and even agreed that Roberto the parrot should live with them as well as Euphemia, which is love indeed for that parrot is particularly vindictive on occasion as you know!' and both men smiled slightly again.

Silence. And then Mr Towers said, 'So the story is over, Mr Burke, in a way. And yet – not quite.' Mr Towers opened a drawer in his writing-desk and drew out a single sheet of paper. 'I suppressed one paper that she sent to me last year, when I sent you the Manuscript. Here is her Will.'

James Burke, his face suddenly shocked, moved so abruptly that he knocked a nearby chair to the floor and he did not even notice. '*She is not dead? She is **not**!*'

'She is not dead, no.' Thomas Towers got up from his desk and offered the sheet of paper to the other man who stood there, shaken, beside an overturned chair in the room in Frith Street. James Burke took the paper almost reluctantly; he looked about him, saw the chair for the first time, picked it up and sat upon it. And then he began to read.

This is the Last Will and Testament of I, Grace Marshall, late of London and Bristol.

I write this Will in a lemon grove above Florence – lemons scent the air everywhere and I write looking down on the Ponte Vecchio, the old bridge, which James Burke first told me of, and which to me has always been the bridge of sighs.

For it is here that I think of my Love, James Burke, Art Dealer of London, and it is to him that I leave my Paintings and my Worldly Goods such as they are, for he was not just my Love, but my Teacher and my Friend and he made me know that I was a Painter. —It was by loving him, with all its paths taken and not taken that I learned, finally, how it is to be an Artist. Without love Art can be good, of course, but I do not believe it can be great. And so for his love, I thank him.

Grace Marshall,
Florence.

Men of course do not weep but for some time James Burke was unable to speak. He sat for a long time with his head bowed. But when he raised his head his voice suddenly burst out in anger. 'Perhaps you see yourself as a Puppet-Master, Mr Towers.' (And Mr Towers observed that there were tears upon his cheeks, after all.) 'You seem to believe you can change the end of the Story – that you are not just the Author, but that you can have some effect on the Outcome!'

This time Mr Towers did not answer. And so the two men sat on, in the room in Frith Street, with a great silence between them.

But when, at last, James Burke had contained himself and stood up from the chair by the window with the paper still in his hand, his face was different: some change: something decided. Slowly he walked from the window and placed Grace Marshall's will back on the writer's desk.

'I am more grateful than I had understood that this is not yet the time for Wills and Testaments,' he said. 'You are the Writer of other Lives, Sir, you will know if many are not conflicted by Obligations and Desires.' One more time James Burke looked about the room: the crowded books and papers and knowledge and history, and the manuscript there on the desk.

'However, you have made it clear to me, whether you intended to or not, that it is not only an Affirmation of Art that should come in a man's lifetime.' And he almost nodded to himself, as if the conversation was really with himself. 'The Affirmation of Love is necessary also.'

Mr Towers waited.

The visitor picked up his hat.

He moved towards the door.

'I am gone, Mr Towers,' said James Burke simply, 'to Florence.'

ACKNOWLEDGEMENTS

With grateful thanks for their information and advice to:
Tony Lane, Maureen Chadwick, Richard Dorment, Danielle Nelson,
Gillian Chaplin Ewing and Mic Cheetham.

I am indebted to the writers of the following books:

The Pleasures of the Imagination: English Culture in the Eighteenth Century by John Brewer; (Harper Collins, London, 1997)

Artists and Their Friends in England, 1700–1799 (2 vols) by William T Whitley; (Medici Society, 1928)

The Lives of the Most Eminent British Painters and Sculptors (6 vols) by Allen Cunningham; (John Murray, London, 1830–37)

English Female Artists (Vol 1) by Ellen C Clayton; (Tinsley Brothers, 1876)

Anecdote Lives by John Timbs; (originally published by Richard Bentley, London, 1872; reprinted: Bardon Enterprises, Portsmouth, 1997)

Art on the Line edited by David H Solkin; (published for the Paul Mellon Centre for Studies in British Art and the Courtauld Institute Gallery by Yale University Press, 2001)

Rembrandt in Eighteenth Century England edited by Christopher White; (Yale Centre for British Art, 1983)

London: a Social History by Roy Porter; (Hamish Hamilton, London, 1994)

Visits to Bedlam: Madness and Literature in the Eighteenth Century by Max Byrd; (University of South Carolina Press, 1974)

Selling Art in Georgian London: the Rise of Arthur Pond by Louise Lippincott; (published for the Paul Mellon Centre for Studies in British Art by Yale University Press, 1983)

Three Thousand Years of Deception by Frank Anau, translated by J. Maxwell Brownjohn; (Jonathan Cape, London, 1961)

A History of Make-up by Maggie Angeloglou; (Studio Vista, London, 1970)

Hogarth: a Life and a World by Jenny Uglow (Faber & Faber, London, 1997)

Joshua Reynolds: the Life and Times of the First President of the Royal Academy by Ian McIntyre; (Penguin Books, 2004)

Thomas Gainsborough by Isabelle Worman; (Lavenham: Dalton, 1976)

The Discourses of Sir Joshua Reynolds edited and annotated by Edmund Gosse; (Kegan, Paul & Co, London, 1884)

Medical Tracts: Dr James Graham's lecture on his Celestial Bed; (London, 1783)

ROSETTA

Barbara Ewing

'A delightful plum pudding of a historical novel' *Sunday Times*

As a child, Rose dreams of travelling to far-flung places, particularly to Rosetta, the mysterious town in Egypt after which she is named. Transfixed by this exotic world, she imagines that one day she will visit the land of the hieroglyphs and history. But instead Rose must marry the handsome and duplicitous Harry Fallon. With Harry, Rose discovers passion, but also a terrible secret – and so she sets out alone on a journey to Egypt, determined to learn the truth about her husband's past and to realise her long-held desire for adventure.

Set in London, Paris and Egypt, amidst the conflict and upheaval of the French revolution, *Rosetta* is an enthralling tale of adventure from the author of *The Mesmerist*.

'Engrossing . . . fascinating historical details' *Time Out*

Sphere
£6.99
978 0 7515 3761 1

THE MESMERIST

Barbara Ewing

'First-rate . . . A consistently entertaining, amusing and enlightening novel' *Sunday Telegraph*

London, 1838. The controversial practice of Mesmerism, with its genuine practitioners and its fraudulent chancers, has hypnotised the city. Miss Cordelia Preston, a beautiful, ageing, out-of-work actress terrified of returning to the poverty of her childhood, suddenly emerges as a Lady Phreno-Mesmerist. In her candle-lit Bloomsbury basement she learns to harness her talent – in completely unexpected ways.

But success is fragile when you have a past filled with secrets. On a wintry, moonlit night a body is found in Bloomsbury Square, and what began as an audacious subterfuge erupts into a scandal. Cordelia's past is revealed, bringing not only heartbreak but terror – and the mystery of a cloaked figure who waits for her in the shadowy London streets.

'Written with insight, intelligence and style, a highly engaging and entertaining read' *Sydney Morning Herald*

Sphere
£7.99
978 0 7515 3760 4

Now you can order superb titles directly from Sphere:

☐ Rosetta   Barbara Ewing   £6.99
☐ The Mesmerist   Barbara Ewing   £7.99

The prices shown above are correct at time of going to press. However, the publishers reserve the right to increase prices on covers from those previously advertised, without further notice.

―――――――――――――――――――――――― sphere ――――――――――――――――――――――――

Please allow for postage and packing: **Free UK delivery.**
Europe: add 25% of retail price; Rest of World: 45% of retail price.

To order any of the above or any other Sphere titles, please call our credit card orderline or fill in this coupon and send/fax it to:

Sphere, PO Box 121, Kettering, Northants NN14 4ZQ
Fax: 01832 733076   Tel: 01832 737526
Email: aspenhouse@FSBDial.co.uk

☐ I enclose a UK bank cheque made payable to Sphere for £ . . . .
☐ Please charge £ . . . . . . to my Visa/Delta/Maestro

Expiry Date ☐☐☐☐   Maestro Issue No. ☐☐

NAME (BLOCK LETTERS please) . . . .

ADDRESS . . . .

. . . .

. . . .

Postcode . . . . Telephone . . . .

Signature . . . .

Please allow 28 days for delivery within the UK. Offer subject to price and availability.